Gathering Peace

iUniverse LLC
Bloomington

Gathering Peace

Copyright © 2014 Peggy Warren

All rights reserved. No part of this book may be used or reproduced by
any means, graphic, electronic, or mechanical, including photocopying,
recording, taping or by any information storage retrieval system
without the written permission of the publisher except in the case
of brief quotations embodied in critical articles and reviews.

This is a work of fiction. All of the characters, names, incidents,
organizations, and dialogue in this novel are either the products
of the author's imagination or are used fictitiously.

iUniverse books may be ordered through booksellers or by contacting:

iUniverse LLC
1663 Liberty Drive
Bloomington, IN 47403
www.iuniverse.com
1-800-Authors (1-800-288-4677)

Because of the dynamic nature of the Internet, any Web addresses or
links contained in this book may have changed since publication and
may no longer be valid. The views expressed in this work are solely those
of the author and do not necessarily reflect the views of the publisher,
and the publisher hereby disclaims any responsibility for them.

Any people depicted in stock imagery provided by Thinkstock are models,
and such images are being used for illustrative purposes only.
Certain stock imagery © Thinkstock.

ISBN: 978-1-4759-6164-5 (sc)
ISBN: 978-1-4759-6165-2 (e)

Printed in the United States of America

iUniverse rev. date: 05/09/2014

Dedicated to the pursuit of dreams

My Disrupted Self

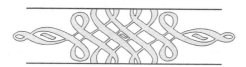

I'm only eleven so maybe that means I'm not old enough to vote in family affairs. Or that's what I figured when suddenly my perfect life in a four bedroom house turned into an anything but perfect life in a 31-foot trailer. This all happened super fast when Dad quit work and went nuts. His sister said it was a mid-life crisis, something about Dad needing to find himself. The stupid part about that is I didn't even know he was lost.

Anyway, he and Mom sold our house and our cars and bought the trailer, along with a station wagon to haul the beast. Maybe moving into a trailer and travelling all over the country to find a new thing for Dad to do would sound like fun to most people, but not to me.

The big shock came when I got home from school a couple of weeks after Dad quit, and there on our front lawn was a sign that said FOR SALE. I charged into the house, dropping my books on the floor and then tripping over them as I ran into Mom. She was on her way out.

"What's that sign doing? This is OUR house Mom. You can't sell it!"

"It was supposed to be a surprise, honey. The sales agent put the sign up while I was out and I was just going to get it." Her voice was calm enough, but her eyebrows squished together in a not nice frown.

Jacque and Jolie, our twin toy poodles were scratching my legs like crazy, wanting me to pick them up so they could lick my face and make me feel better. Normally that's what they did when I felt bad. I swept them up, but this time the kisses didn't work. I put them down and they wouldn't stop scratching my legs.

Mom whisked them up. "Let's go take the sign down before the boys come home." She headed out the door with the poodles in her arms.

I followed. "Why don't we just put it in the garbage, because you can't sell the house."

Mom handed me the poodles and pulled the sign out of the ground. She leaned it against the side of the house. "Why don't we get the dogs their dinner and put them in the yard. Then we can talk without upsetting them." They were definitely upset, their little bodies quivering in my arms.

Mom headed into the house and I wanted to grab her and shake her and scream bloody murder.

In the kitchen she got their dinner and took it outside the door to the fenced yard. The poodles wriggled out of my arms and scooted after her. Food always fixed bad feelings for Jacque and Jolie so it was fun to watch, but it sure didn't fix them for me.

Mom came in and closed the door. "Don't be mad, honey. Honestly, your dad has something exciting he's going to tell you about at dinner tonight. So please don't jump to conclusions until you've heard." She took my hand. "C'mon, we'll go sit in the living room and talk about it."

I pulled my hand back. "I don't want to sit anywhere Mom. Just tell me what's going on and what could ever be exciting enough to lose our house." I didn't wait for an answer. I ran up the stairs to my room, slammed the door and threw myself on my bed. Tears sprung out so fast that my pillow was soaked in seconds.

I heard a knock but I didn't answer. Then I felt what I knew was Mom's hand on my shoulder. Her body dented the bed behind me and I rolled over. When I saw her I grabbed the sheet to wipe my face. "Why, Mom? How could you do something like that without telling us." The tears stopped and I bundled the sheet and squeezed my fingers tight around it.

Mom's whole face scrunched up, not just her eyebrows this time. She got a Kleenex out of the box on the table beside my bed and handed it to me. I didn't take it.

"I wanted to tell you, but Dad insisted on making the news a surprise. Maybe that was thoughtless and I'm sorry."

"Sorry isn't going to change anything is it? Can you take the sign down forever?"

Mom put the Kleenex on the bed and untangled the sheet from my fingers. She squeezed both my hands in hers. "No, Zoey. There's more than just the sign, and Dad needs to be the one to tell you about it. Honestly, it'll be fine."

She let go of my hands and lay down beside me. She stretched her arm over my body with her hand holding my waist through the sheet. "Please," she said, "just trust that it'll be a good thing for all of us."

I couldn't think of anything good of my own to say because what I wanted was for Mom to get off my bed. I didn't want her holding me or being there at all.

Maybe my body stiffened and she felt it because she got up, bent over and kissed my forehead. She smiled and I could see her eyes were wet. She picked up the Kleenex and held it, but she didn't stick it in her eyes. She said, "Dad's over at Aunt Alyssa's, so I'm going to call and let him know you saw the sign and make sure he's ready for your reaction. Then I'm going to take the dogs for a walk. Do you want to come?"

"If it's okay I'd like to lie here right now. D'you mind?"

"Of course I don't mind."

I watched her leave. Her slumped body looked so heavy and I knew that weight was from me being so awful. I sure hated doing that to

Mom, but the sign had smacked me so hard I couldn't help bursting out. Part of me wanted to tell her I was sorry, but that would've been a lie, so I didn't. Sure I was sorry for hurting Mom, but I wasn't sorry for saying what I did.

I lay there looking up at the puffy clouds that my white organdy canopy over my four poster bed had always reminded me of. Suddenly they weren't looking dreamy anymore, they were looking like just what they were, material folded into puffs.

I'd lived my whole life in the same house on the same street and gone to the same school with the same kids since kindergarten. I'd had my best friend Amy practically glued to me from day one, and I didn't want any of that to change, ever.

So when Mom said "It'll be fine" I knew it wouldn't, because "fine" is a word Mom uses so she doesn't have to say what she really thinks. I used to see that a lot when she'd have Dad's work people over, ones she didn't even like, and she'd get all gushy polite. I hated that. I can't do anything about Mom being like she is, but at least I've got her figured out.

I should've known that everything would get different after Dad quit work, but honestly I never thought about it. I mean at home he still dressed up and went places and even wore business clothes when he worked in his den. Both he and Mom were sometimes in there when I'd get home from school, which should've been a signal that something was going on. But I sure never thought it'd be something that would destroy my perfect life.

Before Dad quit work he was a big shot at Proctor and Gamble, in charge of selling everything. For as long as I could remember, in the morning he'd drive to his office in Baltimore that was a long way from our house in the suburbs. After work he'd drive home and we'd all have dinner together in the dining room and talk about whatever was going on with any of us. Dad didn't talk much about himself. He did listen and sort of try to pay attention to what we were saying. But a lot of times it was obvious his head was still at the office, because as soon as he finished eating he'd light up a cigarette, grab his briefcase and go right to his den. He'd even work on lots of weekends. Sometimes Mom would have friends over for dinner, or they'd go places, but he sure worked a lot.

For all I knew that's the way all fathers were supposed to be, or at least the ones who worked hard and made lots of money. Mom has always been the boss of me, my brothers, and the house, and Dad, well he was the boss of people at work. Mom never complained about any of that, or at least not around me.

But a couple of weeks before he quit work I sure got to find out Mom wasn't exactly happy about Dad working so much. I heard her on the phone telling someone that Dad was a workaholic, and she sure didn't say it in a nice way.

After Dad quit work, Amy and I talked a lot about what he might do next, but we never talked about anything he might do that would ruin our entire lives.

Just like Mom said it would, the whole thing poured out at the dinner table that night. It all started off like any other dinner, except that my body itched waiting for Dad to say something. I mean Josh and Ty knew nothing, and I was too scared to blab it right out.

Mom put a platter of meatloaf, mashed potatoes and peas in front of Dad and he dished it out like normal, passing everyone a plate while my brother Josh, who's fifteen, went on about going to summer football camp. How Dad planned to go from football camp that wasn't going to happen, to the house sale that probably was, well I just plain couldn't wait for whatever he had planned.

I blurted, "Why's the house for sale Dad?"

Josh practically went airborne. "What? What're you talking about?"

"A For Sale sign was on the lawn when I got home from school. The real estate people put it up when Mom wasn't looking. It was too late to hide it from me, but she ran out and hid it from you guys."

"Hey I like it!" said my other brother Ty, who's thirteen. "Moving would be a great idea."

"That is about the stupidest thing I've ever heard," said Josh. "If there's some big secret reason for it, Dad, let's hear it. You already know I'm going to football camp. I don't get it!"

Dad's shoulders sagged. He dropped his knife and fork on his plate. Then he took a big breath before he looked at me and said, "I'm sorry you had to find out that way, Zo. Honestly, I've been waiting for just the right time to tell all of you and it's a little sooner than I wanted, but..." Then he took another breath and sat up super straight before he plastered a big grin across his face. "Are you all ready for the ride of your lives?"

"I'm ready," said Ty with just as big a grin.

"I'm not," said Josh, slamming his knife and fork down on the table, spewing food every which way. "I'm not moving anywhere!" He swept his napkin over the mess and scrunched it on his knee.

Dad's hand scrunched his napkin on the table. "You're awfully quiet, Meg. Can you give me a little help here?"

"You should've said something before now, Sam. I told you and you wouldn't listen, so all I can say is I'm sorry kids." Mom tried to smile but a real smile didn't work.

"I messed up," said Dad, "and I'm sorry about that. But honestly, like I said, it's going to be the ride of our lives, so can I tell you about it?"

Josh and I said nothing, but Ty said, "Hey, don't everybody make this a downer. Whatever it is would be better than hanging around here for the summer. C'mon guys. Brighten up!"

"Shut up!" said Josh.

"Tell us Dad," I said. "Why would selling the house ever be the ride of our lives? It sure doesn't feel like it so far."

"That's fair," said Dad with his big smile gone. He picked up a huge catalog that was on the floor beside his chair, put it in front of him and went on to describe how our normal family was about to explode into something like a circus act, all of us moving into an Airstream trailer while we traveled around the country looking for a new thing for him to do.

He patted the catalog. "The picture on the cover is the Airstream I'm going to buy, and inside are all the sights we're going to see." He passed the catalog to Josh who sat beside him.

Josh took a quick look at the cover, flipped through a few pages, shoved it over my way, scooted back his chair and left the room without a word. As if he hadn't noticed, Dad kept right on spouting off about the fun we'd have.

I looked at the catalog cover and all I could think was the Airstream looked more like a spaceship headed for the moon than a place where five people, who hardly ever spent time together, were supposed to not only spend time, but actually LIVE together, like ALL the time.

"What do you think, sweetheart?" asked Dad. "Looks like fun, right?"

"I don't know, Dad. It's different." I passed the catalog to Ty without opening it.

"What's that supposed to mean?" Dad asked.

I didn't get a chance to answer because with one look at the cover Ty took off like a rocket. "Wow! This looks great Dad, a real state of the art way to travel. When do we leave?"

Dad's grin came back. "That's more like it. Thanks, son. Now, why don't we get into this great dinner your mom's made."

"What about Josh? He needs to eat," I said.

"He needs to do more than eat," said Dad, gobbling up the meatloaf.

Everybody stopped talking to at least try to eat when Mom said, "Maybe apple pie would taste better than meat loaf at this point."

She got up and whipped the half full dishes off the table, practically unhinging the swinging door on her way into the kitchen. Ty followed her with the rest of the plates, but he came right back. You could tell he didn't want to miss a word because he was practically glowing.

"I'm going to help Mom," I said. My plan was to go in the kitchen, yell at Mom and break some dishes.

I got up just as Mom came through the swinging kitchen door carrying two plates of pie. "You can get the other ones on the counter, Zo, but before you do, tell me what *you* think of the surprise."

"I think you and Dad ought to go and let us stay here. Josh is old enough to take care of everything, and besides Aunt Alyssa lives down the street." I disappeared into the kitchen.

Aunt Alyssa is Dad's sister and has always been like a second mother to me. She isn't married and has no kids of her own, so she'd be great at looking after us.

I got the plates and came back and put Ty's in front of him, but he was too busy swooning over catalog pictures to notice. I didn't want any pie. I put my dish on my placemat and sat because I couldn't figure out how not to. The poodles who were on the chair next to mine leapt onto my knee and this time I really needed the kisses they plastered all over my face.

Dad ignored the poodles. "We have to sell the house to pay for the trip, Zoey. I assume you're not too happy about it."

I squeezed the fluffy white bundle of fur. "What's to be happy about? I don't want to sell the house and live in a trailer, or move anywhere for that matter. And I don't think I'm the only one." I looked over at Josh's chair, but Dad didn't.

I put the not too happy poodles back on their chair and focused on my plate, shoveling pie in my mouth so I wouldn't have to look at Dad, or even Mom, whose eyes bored right through the top of my head.

"The pictures are great, Sis," said Ty. "I think it'll be fun." He closed the catalog, passed it back to Dad and started into his pie.

I got up with my empty plate and said I'd go do the dishes so everyone else could keep on swooning over the whole thing.

"Swooning," said Dad. "Is that what we're doing? Maybe it'd be a whole lot more helpful if you'd try to swoon along with us sweetheart."

"I'd rather put the dishes in the dishwasher. I'm not into swooning right now."

Later that night Josh did make a loud attempt to get Dad to change his mind. The reason he was so bummed about the whole thing is that at football camp he hoped to be chosen to play quarterback in the fall.

He'll only be a sophomore, but he's that good. Besides I'm sure he's looking forward to making out with at least one of the teeny-boppers who hang around him like he's some kind of movie star. Sure, he's cute and everything with all these blond curls that girls drool over, but football camp, that's the big deal.

I was in my bedroom next to Dad's den when Josh made his point. Both doors were open so it was hard to miss. "It's not fair Dad. I've been by far the best guy on the team this year and I'm only inches from getting the big deal, and now you're saying it's all over. That stinks!"

"Yeah, a lot of things stink, Josh. You're fifteen and you've got a lifetime of football ahead if that's what you want. I'm forty-eight and I've got to make my big deal happen now, while I'm in my prime. If I were you I'd find another tack than a sulky kid who's trying to spoil the whole thing for everybody. Leaving the table in a huff is what stinks, so go and apologize to your mother."

"I'm not apologizing because I'm not sorry. I want to go to football camp and I'm not going to be able to, but that doesn't mean I have to act happy about it. I'm not. I'll be in the trailer because I won't have anywhere else to be."

In the next split second he raced by my room and ran into his own. He slammed the door and I guess the slam got Mom's attention downstairs because she showed up in my doorway. "What was that all about, Zo? Do you know?"

I was sitting in one of my piles of teddy bears working on some words in my notebook about how to tell Amy what was going on. I closed the cover and put the notebook on the floor beside me. "Josh just talked to Dad, and it wasn't nice."

That's when my tears let go. Mom grabbed a bunch of Kleenex and rushed into the pile of teddy bears with me. She handed me a couple, with her own eyes wet, "I'm so sorry you didn't like the surprise, honey. Honestly, it's an adventure. It'll be fun, I know it will."

I shoved the Kleenex in my eyes. "Yeah. I'm sure it will be for you and Dad."

"No, Zoey. It won't be fun for us, not if it isn't fun for the rest of you." She wiped her eyes and scrunched the Kleenex in her hand.

Something popped into my mind that made my tears stay put. "How can it be so much fun for you, Mom? You're this really successful weaver here and you've got so many friends. Why would you want to sell our house and get stuffed in a trailer?"

For years Mom had been sharing a studio with three other weavers and she had a bunch of prize-winning weavings hanging in galleries all over Baltimore. "I don't look at it that way. It's really not about me. It's about Dad."

"Jeez. Are you trying to make me feel bad? Because it's not working. How can anything that involves all of us be only about Dad. That's stupid. It makes me mad."

"Look, and please pay attention and I'll explain what I'm trying to tell you, and why. Will you stop being mad and listen for a minute?"

"I guess if I have to." I leaned back into the tummy of my six-foot teddy bear, the softest and the biggest of the bunch.

Mom got up and sat on the end of my bed. I guess she didn't think sitting in a pile of teddy bears was a good place to give a lecture, and it felt like that's what she was about to do.

"This will probably sound absolutely bizarre to you," she said. "But when I was twenty-one and a new wife, your granny took me aside to share some advice that she thought was very important for a happy marriage. Her advice was, 'You fly on the wings of your husband.' I loved Granny and I thought she was very wise. I know that was way back in the fifties, and it's the seventies now. Women are becoming more independent, but twenty years ago it sounded good to me, so I climbed aboard your Dad's wings, and to tell you the truth I've been riding high ever since." Mom gave me a smile that looked pretty proud.

"Okay," I said. "It does sound weird, that's for sure, but what's it got to do with how you feel about giving up weaving?"

"Well I know I'm a good weaver, but I don't make a lot of money at it, and your father has supported my passion with his financial success.

So I guess that pretty much means I've been flying high on his wings without even thinking about what a responsibility it's been for him. Maybe now it's turnaround time."

"Turnaround, like how? I don't get it, Mom." I started picking on a new hangnail.

She reached over and put her hand on mine. "It's okay. No picking at yourself. Let me finish."

I stuck my hands under my legs and she sat back and kept talking. "Your dad has a dream. He wants to do something important with his life, and I think maybe it's time for you, me, and the boys to spread our wings, let him climb aboard, and give him all the support he needs. I've dropped out of the studio for the time being and I'll put my loom and supplies in storage."

"I guess that means I'll be putting my four poster bed in storage too." Suddenly I noticed how the bedposts framing Mom made her look like she was on stage. My eyeballs filled up all over again. I shoved the already wet Kleenex in my eyes.

"I know it's hard, Zo," said Mom, "and I guess the hardest part is the shock of it all. It was unkind of us to keep this a secret. It at least helps to know we have Ty on board."

It was easy for Ty to get on board because he's always been a loner kind of guy, and he's never been attached to much of anything other than his comic books and his collection of funky marbles.

And also he's no hunk like Josh. He's skinny with knock-knees that rub together when he wears shorts, and stringy hair that for sure doesn't make him cute. He's popular enough but no heartthrob. To me he's a heartthrob because he's the best brother ever.

"Ty was great," said Mom, "and that means a lot to both Dad and me. I know how much Josh wants to go to football camp and I do feel badly about that. But I want to enter a weaving competition next month myself and I know I won't be able to, so I'll live with it. I hope if I tell Josh where I'm coming from, and ask him to spread his wings for Dad, he'll do it."

"I'm not sure any of us have wings strong enough to hold Dad."

"That's just a metaphor, honey. Maybe not a very good one, because the whole purpose of this is for Dad to have a chance to do something that'll make a difference, not just for us, but the world. And he's good, Zo. He's creative, and he's driven, so this change is about believing in him, and I can do that. Can you?"

"Why didn't Dad say anything about having a dream? It's neat that he does, but why do we have to give up our house and move into a stupid trailer for him to make his dream work?"

"Because the whole thing is about exploring what's possible for ideas way beyond just Baltimore. It's hard for me to explain, but you'll see once we get on the road. I promise."

"How can you promise, Mom? There's no way to promise that living in a trailer will be anything but awful. Go talk to Josh and see if you can promise him it'll be better than going to football camp, because that sure is his dream."

Mom gave this humongous sigh when she got up, leaned over and kissed the top of my head. "It'll be fine, Zoey. The poodles are in the yard. Will you go let them in and maybe take them for a walk? I may be a while with Josh.

There was nothing I could say after the "fine", other than I'd go get the dogs.

I went to do that, but obviously Ty had taken care of it because none of them were there. I went back to my bedroom and closed my door so I could work on my words for Amy.

I didn't hear Mom leave Josh's room, but whatever they talked about sure didn't perk him up, because from that night on he wasn't exactly fun to be around.

For that matter he wasn't around at all. He had a bunch of friends and he managed to stay at one of their houses for dinner every night by probably making a big deal out of his sob story. When he was home he was in his room studying for finals, just like Ty and me.

Now Dad, for sure he was around, but neither he or Mom talked about Josh. If they weren't talking about the trip they were talking about getting a buyer for the house.

The whole thing felt like a nightmare to me. I couldn't be in my bedroom without crying, so I studied at Amy's, or in the rec room, and the only way I could even go in my room to sleep was to hide all my bears in the spare room closet. Looking at them hurt way too much. I tried to choose one to take with me, but that was way too hard because I didn't want to hurt the feelings of the ones I left behind. I decided I'd just use the poodles for snuggling when I felt bad. They at least snuggled back.

Once the house was sold, which happened way too fast for me, things got totally turned around. I mean Dad busted out. His business suits and fancy shoes disappeared and he started wearing nothing but sports shirts, jeans, and Topsiders, with no socks. Even his wavy hair that was always brushed flat with hair cream was let loose to be hair doing whatever it wanted. It started flopping on his forehead, and without all the goo on it, it got a lot lighter. The color sort of matches his eyes, that remind me of Ty's favorite brown Tigers Eye marble.

The day he pulled the spaceship into the driveway he came barreling in the house. Amy and I were on the sofa in the living room studying for a math exam. "Come on girls! Take a gander at our new home." He pulled me up, but not before I grabbed Amy's hand.

On the driveway sat this thing that looked just like the picture on the cover of the catalog, a streamlined spaceship. All I could do was gawk.

We went inside and Amy asked out loud what I was thinking, and that was, "Are you all really going to live in here at the same time?" Her eyes were so wide it's a wonder they didn't fall out of her head.

I had told Amy about the whole thing the morning after I found out about it. I'd wanted to tell her that night, but it took me so long to get the right words written down, and then practiced out loud without crying, that it was too late to phone her. I told her on our way to school, leaving out the part about Dad's dream because there wasn't enough time for that.

The whole story sounded like we might be leaving forever, so she about had a fit, the same way I had. I could tell she was trying to be brave and not cry because she knew that's what I was doing. For sure we both knew if we started crying we'd never stop.

Dad skipped over her question, and with this big grin, he went on about how we'd lucked out, that the Airstream was designed for a family of five and at the last minute the family had backed out. I couldn't help but wonder if backing out came when the kids got to see the closeness of their three beds. There was a bunk bed and a single bed with drawers underneath. At least the beds had curtains around them. I knew Josh would grab the single bed. I hoped Ty wouldn't care where he slept, because I wanted the bottom bunk so I could get in and out fast.

The so-called tour consisted of a bedroom for Mom and Dad at the back of the trailer, with a bathroom next to it, and a hallway (with our beds on either side of it) that ran into the living part of the whole thing. There were two arm chairs, a sofa, and a drop-down table with cushioned benches. Up front was the kitchen, with a stove, a fridge, a sink, and some cupboards.

Amy grabbed my hand and squeezed super hard when she asked Dad, "What about everybody's stuff? Where are you going to put it?"

I'd wondered that myself. All I saw besides the drawers under the single bed were some small overhead cupboards in the main room, along with a closet. There was also a closet in Mom and Dad's room with a hanging rod up high, and a chest of drawers on the floor.

Dad lit a cigarette. "It's summer, Amy, and we're heading south. We won't need a lot of clothes."

I was way past where to put stuff. "I sure don't see much room for privacy Dad."

"Don't worry, sweetheart, it'll be great." He didn't get teary when he said that, but he sure sounded like he might. He took a long drag of his cigarette and blew the smoke out over our heads.

"When are you coming back?" Amy asked with another hand squeeze. She didn't seem to notice the look on Dad that I saw. She obviously had worries of her own. "Will you be back in time for school, and what about warm clothes if it gets cold?"

Dad squeezed Amy's shoulder. "Aunt Alyssa has that handled. We've got labels on the boxes, and they'll all be marked and accessible at the warehouse, so she'll be able to ship us anything we need. And if we need more room, there's extra storage on the back of the trailer, so not to worry." I'm sure if we looked worried it was because we were.

"And about school," said Dad, "I've got a friend on the school board and he'll arrange for a correspondence course with individual teachers, if we're still on the road in September."

Well that sure was news, so when our worried look turned into our jaws dropping, Dad made a big grin and added, "It's an adventure, kids. It'll be great!" He took a last drag and then put the cigarette out in an ashtray on the table. "The best kinds of adventures are filled with the unknown. Now c'mon, let's go inside and make a toast. I've got champagne on ice."

"We don't drink champagne, Dad, and Mom said you were giving up smoking." I squeezed Amy's hand back with both of mine.

"I'm working on it, Zo." He made kind of a worn out sigh, like everything he hoped he'd hear from us just hadn't happened.

The following weeks were a blur of activity. With school exams going on I gave up worrying about moving and worried only about passing. The good part about exams was they got me out of the commotion of sorting, tossing, and packing for storage that Mom and Dad took on like pros. I wasn't around when my teddy bears got stuffed into boxes. But once they were packed up, I made Dad put the boxes in the garage so I wouldn't have to look at them.

Dad had the movers booked to come the day before the move so they could pack all the hanging clothes, the paintings, the dishes, and anything else that was breakable.

Once school was out, there was a frenzy of goodbyes, and three going-away parties. The hardest one was mine with all my friends overflowing Amy's back yard. We laughed and cried and I came close to throwing up. I didn't go to the party for my brothers. Josh's football coach said he'd like to be there, so he arranged to have the party in the school gym. And Mom and Dad had a party at Aunt Alyssa's but I only ran in and out of that one. Saying goodbye was really hard, especially since I had no idea how long we'd be gone. Maybe forever.

New Beginnings

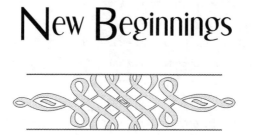

Leaving day was way harder than I ever want anything to be again in my life. Saying goodbye to Aunt Alyssa, like maybe forever, was horrible. We had a really tight hug, but she didn't cry so I tried hard not to. She told me not to worry because wherever we were she'd come. That sure helped.

But when Amy showed up there was no holding back tears. We just about drowned each other and smothered ourselves with hugs.

It seemed like the whole world showed up to send us off, neighbors and friends and people we didn't even know gathered around the space ship, cheering like they do when The Queen Elizabeth takes off.

Once we got going, Amy ran after us for about a block, the two of us waving and bawling like crazy through the window. My heart swelled to watermelon size, and then she was gone.

Dad started singing, "Happy Days Are Here Again" with Ty joining in, even though he messed up the words. The poodles stopped scratching on the windows and huddled together in their wicker basket at the back of the wagon. Josh just slumped in his seat while I kept on wiping my face and blowing my nose. Mom reached her arm over the seat and squeezed my hand.

After a really long drive through a mess of traffic with stops for gas, food, and the bathroom, we finally pulled into our first campground on Cape Cod around six o'clock, all of us so wired we were practically sizzling. Why Dad hadn't chosen somewhere closer to Baltimore I didn't know and it sure didn't seem like a good time to ask. At least enough time and a lot of distractions had made the watermelon in my chest shrink, especially after seeing that our first campground was right on the ocean.

Outside the check-in store, we were sixth in line, behind humongous campers and even bigger trailers than ours. The campground looked really nice, but it was totally packed.

Dad sounded like a snarling dog when he said, "Where did all these people come from? They weren't part of the description of this place in the catalog." He opened the car door and slid out. He shook his legs about a thousand times before he got back in and turned the air conditioner way up.

"C'mon Dad," said Josh, chewing and popping his gum a mile a minute. "Didn't you know this is the big deal for summer vacations? I could've told you that."

"I probably wouldn't have heard you. I wasn't thinking of summer vacations, and let up on the gum. You're making me nuts."

"It's not too late." I said, pulling the bouncing poodles into my lap. "We can turn around, go back to Baltimore and get the Balsams to let us park the trailer in our old driveway until we find another house."

"Not an option, Zoey," said Dad.

Mom said nothing. She just whipped her hand back and forth over her gone curls. Oh yeah, I forgot to mention that the morning before we left home she went to get her hair done, and much to everyone's shock and horror, she came home with all her beautiful curls gone. All she'd said about that was, "It'll be fine for travelling."

"You okay, Meg?" asked Dad. "You're awfully quiet."

"It's been a long day, Sam. I guess we should've had a trial run. Driving this thing around isn't quite the same as looking at it."

"Not a subject worth talking about. This is an adventure and adventures don't come with instructions."

Our turn in line finally came. Dad went into the store and came out carrying a sheet of paper that had all the setup instructions on it, with a red circle around the number showing our campsite. We headed to the far side of the campground with Dad mumbling complaints about how he didn't think he'd ever get the trailer parked.

"The campsites aren't very big," he said, and boy was that right. They were all the same size, a little longer than the length of our trailer, and wide enough to fit the car beside the trailer on one side and the picnic table on the other. Every one of them had some sort of camper on it. The only extras on all the sites, besides wooden tubs of colorful flowers, were picnic tables and barbecues.

Other than pictures in the catalog I'd never seen a campground. But I knew about camping in trailers from Amy's brother who did it once with his friend's family. He didn't tell Dad about it, but he did tell Amy and me enough that I knew there wasn't going to be a lot of privacy.

Backing into the site took all the skills of those guys who guide planes at the airport. Mom swished her arms this way and that to help Dad get it done, and then they studied the instructions on the sheet to figure out what went where.

The yucky job came first and that was sticking a fat drainage hose from the trailer into a hole in the ground. Maybe the job wasn't yucky, but in my imagination it was.

When Dad had that done, he pulled a heavy wire out of a storage place on the side of the trailer and snaked it across the ground to a post that had a big plug-holder on it. He pushed in our plug, Mom flicked a switch inside, and the fancy Airstream turned into a regular home. Well sort of.

The day was really hot, and after the setup was done Dad said he was ready for a shower. But the shower wasn't ready for him. It was full of dog food, game boards, and wooden frames for Mom's new art project, embroidery. Maybe that was a long way off prize-winning weavings, but her plan was to turn the embroidery into pillow covers that she said would at least be useful as gifts.

"Meg, there's a bunch of crap in here," Dad called from the bathroom.

"There's always a shower room at these places, Sammy. Storage was more important. Besides, there's a pool over by the rec center. It'll be fine."

Everything was in the shower because there weren't any closets and drawers in the trailer for extra stuff, only enough of both to store our clothes and private things.

Dad went in his bedroom and closed the door, coming out a few minutes later in his bathing suit. He grabbed a towel and headed out the door. All he said was that he'd be back. The boys already had their bikes off the rack and were checking out the campground.

"That was rude, Mom, him taking off like that. He could've waited for us."

"Don't worry, honey. He'll be fine. It's been a long day. He's tired."

"We're all tired. Why'd we have to drive so far?"

"The campground was recommended." Mom put her arm around me and the right words were there, but her body felt like a rigid pole. "We'll love it. Wait and see."

"Do you want to go to the pool?" I asked.

"No." She headed into the kitchen. "I'm fine. I'm going to feed the poodles and start supper. I'll have a swim when the boys get back. They'll probably want one."

Three "fines" in ten minutes were one too many for me so I said I'd go check out the showers. I wanted to swim in the pool but I didn't want to be around Dad if he was in a bad mood.

The freshly scrubbed showers turned out to be great, with new curtains and fresh bars of soap. I hadn't planned to but I took a shower and it was perfect, with lots of water pressure, even better than in the home I used to have. It took a heap of paper towels to dry myself off so I could put my clothes back on.

Apart from crowded sites the campground was perfect. Everything was freshly painted, with flowers not only in buckets but all over the place. We had close neighbors on both sides, and that was okay because the people were friendly and their kids were polite.

Even though the campground was awesome, there was still a lot of the trailer to get used to, the hardest thing being my bunk. Like Mom had said about having a shot at trying out the trailer before the trip, well that sure was true for trying out the beds. I'd slept in a canopy bed with a cushy mattress all my life, and when I pulled the curtain around my bunk, suddenly what I had to sleep in felt like a tent on the ground.

The first night, after we were all in bed Mom did an imitation of the Walton Family on TV. I guess she was trying to be cute. "Goodnight Zoey," she called. I called back "Goodnight Mom." She did the same with Ty, but not Josh. He interrupted the whole thing with, "Can we get the air conditioning going Dad? It feels like an oven in here."

"Good idea," said Dad. He came out of his bedroom and closed all the windows before he clicked a switch. A contraption on the living room ceiling blasted the whole place with cold air that swept from one end of the trailer to the other. Mom and Dad's bedroom door had an open space above it to let the cool air in with the door closed.

I crawled under my sheet and pretended I was at camp with Amy. That was the first time I'd let myself think about her since we left. What saved me from crying my head off was Jolie who was in bed with me. I pulled her to my face and she licked my eyes as if she was telling the tears not to come out. It worked, because they didn't, so I kissed her eyes back and honestly they were wet. I squeezed her against my chest and suddenly the tent got cozy, even with the rock-hard mattress.

A week of fun exploring Cape Cod almost made me forget the awful feelings I'd had about leaving Baltimore. We went on ferry rides to Nantucket and Martha's Vineyard, and we even got to go on one of the fishing boats where the fisherman was selling the fish he'd just caught. They were piled up on an open ice cooler at the back of the boat. Seagulls squawked overhead while everybody chose the fish they wanted. That part was great, but I hated seeing all those dead fishies with their eyes still open, so I didn't choose one. I just waited and looked somewhere else while the poodles in my arms squawked right back at the noisy gulls.

Riding around on our bikes and stopping at gift stores, where we bought postcards to send home, was really neat because we'd never done that on other trips. Usually wherever we went as a family, Dad had business stuff going on in his head and playing around didn't seem to fit with business. This new dad sure was fun. Not just for me but for all of us.

Even living in the trailer got to be good. Everyone was being super nice, and Josh actually offered to let me sleep in his bed that had a decent mattress. He'd never offered me anything in my whole life without a trade, and he didn't even ask for one. I didn't take him up on the offer because the whole tent feeling had gotten homey. Everything about "New Beginnings" was better than I'd expected.

Well I'd heard the expression, 'Nothing lasts forever' but I'd never thought a lot about what it meant. That is until I got to see it in action one morning when we were supposed to be getting ready for a day of snorkeling in the ocean and Dad wasn't. He was sitting at the table studying the campground catalog with an unopened pack of cigarettes in front of him. The cigarettes sitting there sure was a surprise, because he supposedly stopped smoking the day the house was sold.

Mom picked up the pack. "What's with these?"

"Put them down Meg. They're just a prop to remind me of why I gave them up. Sometimes, like now, I feel like one. But you'll never see the pack opened because even looking at them reminds me of the office and I feel sick. They're done." He took the pack from Mom and jammed it in his pocket.

"You're a masochist," said Mom. "Why would you want to torture yourself like that, and what d'you mean you're not coming? The guys waiting over at the marina. We have it all set up."

"I'm not a masochist, I'm a realist. It's my way of facing addiction head on, so get used to it."

"Well, excuse me. I'm sorry for the name calling, but we do have a date, Sammy."

"You guys go. I'm not coming because I've had enough running around."

"Hey Dad," said Ty. "It'll be fun."

"I'm sorry. I'm not good at sightseeing when I've got a lot on my mind. I need peace and quiet to figure out how all of this works." He patted an open page in the Big Book (his new name for the catalog). "I'm trying to find somewhere to go that's not a tourist trap."

Mom's hair would've stood on end if there'd been any. "All of what works? Can't we have a little vacation before it becomes about work?"

"I'm not sure what it's about Meg, other than a mass of people and a whole lot of commotion. I'm trying to be fun. But right now, like I said, I need peace and quiet."

Dad had bought a bunch of yellow lined notepads a few days earlier and he'd already made a couple of pages of notes. When I asked him what his notes were about, he said he was processing his life.

Mom sunk onto the bench across from Dad. "C'mon, Sammy. There'll be lots of peace and quiet underwater. You'll love it."

"Yeah, Dad," said Ty. "Mom's right."

"I'm not coming, so please just go." Dad didn't even look up from the catalog, he just fluttered his hands.

The hand flutter did it. We left, and on the way to the marina we talked about Dad. Mom said, "One thing about your father is that he's never been one for crowds. We didn't talk about the logistics of camping life. He needed to get away to figure out his next move, and that didn't allow for thinking about masses of tourists. My guess is he's on overload."

Overload sounded dumb to me. "Like you said, Mom, can't we at least have some play time? Doesn't everybody deserve a summer vacation?"

"I think the way Dad sees it is he already had a vacation at home planning this trip, Zoey. And now he's probably worried about not having a job. I'm not sure, because he doesn't talk about his feelings. But after working all his life I'm sure he's got work on his mind, not vacation. All I can say is thank goodness he hasn't resorted to smoking. At least we don't have the cigarette addicted workaholic for a dad anymore. Right?"

"Not so far," said Josh. "But he is looking pretty uptight. I hope he's going to write himself a letter on all that yellow paper and convince himself he ought to go back to Baltimore and find a job so I can go to football camp."

"Don't be like that Josh. As long as we're having fun, eventually it'll rub off on him, so keep the negative comments to yourself."

The car got quiet until we pulled into the marina and Mom pointed out our guy. Across the parking lot a man, with a big smile and a bunch of snorkels and masks, waved.

"Perfect," said Ty. "Let's go!"

The snorkeling was exactly that, perfect. For sure Dad would've loved seeing all the colorful fish up close. When we got home I let him know how much fun we'd had and that I'd go back with him if he wanted. He said we could snorkel down in Florida where there'd be more fish. He grinned as if he knew, just like I did, that what he said didn't make any sense. I let the whole thing go and helped Mom get the shrimp we bought on the way home peeled and ready to cook for supper.

Supper was great. But it was no surprise that as soon as it was over Dad told us we'd be leaving the next day. He opened the campground catalog to his bookmarked page and beamed as he read the description of a state park in the woods.

"But there's no ocean in a state park, Dad," said Josh. "What're we supposed to do with no beach?"

"We're supposed to get into nature where there's plenty of peace and quiet. That's what we're supposed to do."

"Who wants peace and quiet?"

"Can it Josh! We'll check it out and go from there."

The next morning we all piled in the car with our mouths shut in hopes of something great showing up in a park in the woods.

Well what showed up was no hookups, only a lot of pine trees and a lot of boredom coming up. We drove around the park looking for a lake, but all we found were more trees and a whole bunch of tents and kids and other trailers. We didn't bother checking in.

"Okay," said Dad. "So much for a state park. Let's move on and we'll find a woodland paradise on the beach."

The Perfect Campground

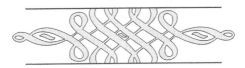

"I don't know why they can't give us some bushes to help make these campsites private," said Dad as we set up our fourth site in seven days, none of them even close to being a woodland paradise.

Driving along the highway that was close to the ocean should've made for finding great campgrounds. But we hadn't planned ahead so anything that was great was already full. The campgrounds that weren't full were awful, even though the catalog made them sound like they'd be perfect. I figured real fast that we must've lucked out in Cape Cod. That is until Dad told me he'd made reservations before we left home.

"Do you think we ought to start calling ahead, Sammy?" asked Mom when we were back on the road one more time.

"Maybe, Meg. But what the ads in the Big Book say, and then what the places are really like, we already know the two don't match."

"Well calling ahead is worth a try. If you get someone on the phone, you can at least ask them about the place. The ad writers and the owners aren't always the same people. That's obvious."

"Okay," said Dad. "We'll stop for lunch and someone else can get some numbers out of the Big Book. I'm not into reading any more phony ads."

"I'll do it, Dad," said Ty. "I like the pictures, even if they're not for real."

"Why wasn't making reservations part of all the planning, Dad?" asked Josh. "I bet the good places are booked at least a year ahead."

"Probably. But when you've never done something before, you don't necessarily get it right the first time."

"No kidding." said Josh.

Dad pulled into Dave's Truck Stop just in time. Josh had a way of turning everything sour, and that's what he was doing until the sign in the window sent him airborne. "Chicken Fried Steak," he hollered. "Now you've scored, Dad. You got it really right this time. I love Chicken Fried Steak."

"That's good. Bring in the Big Book Ty, and you can try to get it right a second time."

Everyone piled out of the car, including the poodles, because the sign in the window said "Dogs Welcome." I'd never thought of truck drivers traveling with dogs, but sure enough there were a bunch of them, big ones and little ones, and all being really good. Jacques and Jolie snuggled right in between me and Mom in the booth.

Ty scoured the Big Book while we were waiting for our fried steak, and just as the plates arrived he landed on a place he said looked hopeful. "It's not right on the beach, but it's only a block away. There aren't any pictures, but the description sounds good though, and maybe this time it'll be the truth. There's even a rec hall. Do you want to call Dad?"

Dad scribbled the number on a napkin and dove into the yummy meal at the same time. He finished it off and wiped away the gravy that dribbled down his chin as he headed to the phone booth outside. Sure enough he came back with a reservation. We finished off the meal with a piece of homemade apple pie and then climbed back in the car.

Well no wonder we got a reservation. The campground was terrible, with absolutely no flowers or trees, and campsites that were jammed together. The beach was half a mile away, not a block. Dad paid for one night and told Ty to try again.

While Dad was attaching all our hookups and the rest of us were doing whatever, Ty came flying out the trailer door. "I've found the perfect one Dad. Sounds as good as Cape Cod. It's called Hyatt Heaven and I bet that means the fancy Hyatt hotel people. Take a look at the pictures. They're awesome."

He spread the Big Book on the hood of the car and we all gathered around. Thick black letters read HYATT HEAVEN CAMPGROUND. There were pictures of flowerbeds, a swimming pool, a rec hall, and even huge shade trees. Best of all was a walkway over the highway to the ocean.

"Fat chance for that one," said Josh. "It's probably booked at least two years ahead."

All Dad said when he scribbled down the number was, "Keep your fingers crossed." He took off for the phone booth.

He came back with his eyes beaming like floodlights. "You won't believe it but they had a death in one of the campers and they're going to have a vacancy. I shared all the sympathy and persuasion I could grab onto, and the manager signed us up for tomorrow."

Josh gave Dad a guy smack on the arm. "Way to go Dad!"

The next morning we packed up in record time and headed to Hyatt Heaven. The day started off perfect. But halfway into the drive the sky turned sour with the blackest clouds I'd ever seen. By the time we got to Hyatt Heaven, buckets of rain had not only flattened the flowerbeds but blurred any view of the ocean. All that saved us from flattening each other was the supersized rec hall that had a colored TV, some table games, and even an extra room for six noisy pinball machines, with a door to close off the racket.

But after three days of pelting rain, all the entertainment in both the trailer and the rec center got old. Everyone in the family was bent out of shape, picking at everything and arguing over nothing. I wanted

Amy. I wanted her to give me a hug, but she couldn't so I decided to get out the notepaper she'd given me and write her a letter. She said the notepaper was a gift so I wouldn't forget her. Ha, fat chance of that ever happening.

Dear Amy:

I know you've probably been waiting for a letter, and I've wanted to write, but it's been so crazy making, what with moving from one bad campground to another, that I haven't known what to say until now. I think Dad pictured this whole camping thing being about sitting beside a babbling brook where he could paddle his feet in the water. Well such a thing doesn't exist in campgrounds, and they're the only place you can park a big beast like ours. So there's no babbling brooks, only a lot of noisy tourists and an extra noisy Dad, hollering that all he wants is peace and quiet. I wish you were here and we could be stupid and silly and have fun like we always do.

We landed at this Hyatt campground a few days ago and it's first class, but the rain hasn't stopped since we got here. Sounds like fun, huh? Do you remember the time you and me and Marj got stuck in that phone booth, and we had to bang on the window to get someone to pry open the door? Well that's what it's like being stuck in here, wondering if the trailer's going to float away in all the rain.

I guess I ought to say it hasn't all been a bummer. I mean, we did have a great time in Cape Cod, our first stop. I sure hope you got the postcards we sent from there with the pictures of the fishing boats and everything. The ferry rides to Martha's Vineyard and Nantucket were a lot of fun. I even had my own lobster in Nantucket. I would've liked his head to have stayed in the kitchen but his tail and claws were deeeelicous. One day we went snorkeling and I loved seeing all the swimming fishies up close. I wish we could've stayed in Cape Cod a lot longer, but Dad got antsy and wanted to find a place without so many tourists. We tried a state park but that didn't work because there was no beach and not even a lake. Nowhere else has been as perfect as Cape Cod until where we are now. Hopefully the sun will come out and then it'll be really great.

Anyway I wanted to let you know I'm still alive. And I miss you loads!
Hugs, Zoey

I'd just signed my name when I caught Josh putting my bra on Jolie. I hardly needed a bra but I made Mom buy me one like Amy's in case I blossomed all of a sudden. Anyway, Josh was supposedly sorting his laundry on the sofa and there he was wrapping the bra around the dog. I had no idea how it had gotten into his laundry in the first place.

"Don't be stupid," I yelled. "That's not funny."

He wound the bra around Jolie twice and was doing it up. "Stop it!" I screamed.

I reached for Jolie and Josh smacked my hand. "You can't even take a joke, Creep." He undid the bra and tossed it at me. Jolie leapt off the sofa and darted into Mom and Dad's room where she'd taken to hiding under the pillows when things got noisy.

"You're a bully," I yelled even louder. "I hate you!"

Dad banged his hand on the table so hard the latch gave way and the top landed on his lap. His papers went flying, and Jacques who'd been at Dad's feet, flew down the hall to hide with Jolie under the pillows.

Dad slid off the bench. He grabbed his raincoat and stormed outside.

"It's all your fault Josh," I said. "Can't you do something with him Mom?"

Mom didn't say a word. She pulled on her raincoat and took off after Dad.

The rest of us picked up the pages, then Ty lifted the table that stayed up. Somehow the Airstream people had figured out a way for the clicking gizmo to repair itself for people like us. He unclicked it and the table dropped down.

I flopped on the sofa. "Do you think Dad's okay? I feel terrible about messing up his work."

"Forget it," said Josh. "He'll get over it."

"You're the one who needs to get over it," said Ty. "Maybe if you'd take time to think about someone other than yourself."

"Shut up," barked Josh.

"Dad's awfully tense," I said. "I'm worried he's going to explode."

"Stop irritating me and he won't have half as much to explode over."

"But you started it this morning."

"See? There you go again. Now shut up!"

"Let's play cards," said Ty.

"Yeah, let's play Go Fish," said Josh. "Sounds perfect with all the rain."

"I like Go Fish," said Ty, "even when it isn't raining."

"Me too," I said.

On the trip, playing cards was like reading. They both took my mind off anyone or anything that bothered me. I played Solitaire a lot, but with the three of us Go Fish was perfect. Ty lifted the table, it locked, and we got right into playing as if suddenly we were the best of buddies. Even the little poodles came running back from Mom and Dad's room to see what all the fun was about.

We were into about our fourth game when Mom and Dad showed up with no leftover signs of the big mess anywhere on their soggy selves.

"We've decided to take off," said Dad. "We're going to Atlantic City. Your mom wants to stroll the boardwalk."

I gasped. "What?" I mean one minute Dad was bent out of shape, and now he was beaming over some place I'd never even heard of.

"Glad to see the table is still working," he said as he looked around to find his notes that were piled on the kitchen counter. He put them in his new file box.

"But Dad," I said, "Do we have to go? This place would be great if it wasn't raining. Shouldn't we give it a chance?"

"You'll love Atlantic City, Zo," said Mom. "Your granny used to get all gussied up and go to the Easter Parade on the boardwalk. She even took me once when I was little."

I didn't bother to mention that it wasn't Easter and it was pouring outside.

"Strolling along a boardwalk doesn't fit your style, Dad," said Josh. "But maybe you can check out the chicks with me and Ty. What's the big deal about a boardwalk anyway? All it is is a bunch of wooden boards."

"It's not just *a* boardwalk, Josh," said Mom. "It's The Atlantic City Boardwalk. It's famous, and besides there's more to do than just stroll. There's a Ferris wheel and historic hotels and stores and game booths."

"Where are we going to stay?" I asked.

"Choose somewhere, Ty," said Dad. "There'll be lots of campgrounds. You look while Josh and I hook up the trailer. I'm not going to bother calling ahead. If everything's full or we don't like what we find, then we'll park on the side of the road. We'll do the strolling for your mom, play some games, ride the Ferris wheel, and come back to Hyatt Heaven when we're finished. How's that?"

"Suits me," said Josh. His mind was already checking out chicks. I could tell.

Our site had been booked for two weeks by whoever had died, so before we left, Dad paid for that night and said he couldn't promise the rest of the two weeks, but he'd let the guy know by the end of the day.

Rain followed the car down the highway, soaking anything worthwhile to look at, including the diner we stopped at on the side of the road for lunch. A row of shingles on the roof were gone and it took two buckets to catch the rain that poured through inside. The waitress wore a raincoat that she didn't need, but the huge smile on her face said she thought she was being funny, especially when she told us the feature of the day was fish and chips because the fish swam in on their own. Dad added to the silliness by shaping a twenty-dollar bill to look like a boat. All the laughing felt really good.

After lunch it wasn't long before the affects of laughter wore off and the drive got boring, with nothing to do but watch the rain beat the windshield. Everything to look at was blurred, which wasn't much, because once Dad got booking ahead figured out, we started driving on a superhighway, and the only thing happening out the window was continuous farmland. Sometimes, sitting in the back seat staring at nothing, I couldn't help but remember all the chatter at the dinner table about things to see and places to go that the Big Book was stuffed with.

Although Dad hadn't said anything, I was sure the reason for no sightseeing was because he was worn out from hauling the trailer, finding the next campground, parking in too-small spaces, hooking everything up, wanting to go somewhere else (which meant dozens of phone calls) and then taking everything apart and getting back on the road for the umpteenth time. On top of all that, there was the note scribbling he seemed to have to do whenever he had a chance.

I hoped that once we landed somewhere we could stay for a while, he'd be different and want to see stuff. But mostly I wished he'd talk more about what he liked and didn't like instead of always hollering, "All I want is peace and quiet!" Dad hollering just wasn't something he ever did back in Baltimore. I could only hope hollering wasn't part of his new personality.

The rain continued all the way to Atlantic City. The first campground we came to that Ty had picked out was close to the boardwalk all right, and it sure had vacancies because it was nothing but a big blob of concrete. There were no trees or flowers, only crabby people who complained about the weather while their kids dropped candy wrappers all over the place. The trailers were packed together so close you could practically hear the people next door breathing.

Dad's patience was about gone. "Let's just do it. We'll spend the night here, and if it's nice in the morning, we'll ride our bikes to the boardwalk, park them, stroll, and then go back to Hyatt Heaven." Everyone agreed.

The rain didn't let up. We lazed around inside the trailer until finally Josh got bored and brought out the Monopoly game. Josh didn't care about reading on the trip like the rest of us. Lazing around for him was either playing some kind of Solitaire or listening to music through earphones with a cord plugged into his cassette player. Sometimes he'd hum out loud without knowing it. We'd laugh and he'd hum anyway.

Josh has always loved music. He even left a set of drums stored away in the warehouse in Baltimore and he probably missed them as much as I missed my bears.

He took the earphones off. "What d'you think, Dad? You ready for another Monopoly defeat?" The last time we'd played, Josh managed to win all the best properties.

Dad actually put his notes aside. He liked Monopoly and that was probably because the money game reminded him of the big business guy he used to be. "Beating me twice isn't in the cards, Josh, so don't get your hopes up."

I've never liked board games. They take forever and make me antsy waiting my turn. But being cooped-up in the trailer with the rain, it seemed like playing games was the best thing to do to keep from killing each other. Mom and Ty were always up for games of any kind.

We played Monopoly right through supper. Mom made sub sandwiches filled with shredded lettuce and chopped olives that spilled all over the board. Nobody cared about the mess with all the action going on. There was no hogging of properties or anything, just a lot of fun. Rain turned out to be not so bad after all.

The next morning, the sky was totally blue and the sun so bright we couldn't get going fast enough. That is, all of us except Dad. We were about to hop on our bikes, but he wasn't.

Mom had the poodles in her carrier and they were wagging their tails like crazy. She stared over at Dad who was unhooking the trailer. "Why are you doing that, Sammy? We're taking bikes."

"I'm opting out of the stroll, Meg. I want to go check out the Atlantic City library. I thought of something yesterday that I want to research."

Unlike the dogs, Mom was definitely not wagging any part of herself. "What're you saying, you're not coming with us. That's crazy. We already talked about how the boardwalk is for couples and families strolling. That's why we're here. You can do the library later. Besides, why didn't you go yesterday when it was raining?"

"What, and ruin the fun of Monopoly? That didn't seem exactly fair, babe."

"And you think it's fair not to come with us today?"

Dad went to Mom and put his hand on her shoulder. "Hey, I'll make you a deal, Meg," he said. "You go check out the boardwalk and find the fanciest restaurant. Tonight we'll have dinner at wherever you choose, and then we'll stroll 'til your heart's content. The kids can fend for themselves, because this campground's too boring to be anything but safe. There's a pizza place down the road, so we'll get a pizza for them, and you and I will have a date."

"But I thought we were going back to Hyatt Heaven after the boardwalk," said Josh. He was sitting tippy-toed on his bike seat with his hands on the grips ready to go.

"Scouting all the things there are to do on the boardwalk will take most of the day, Josh," said Dad. "We'll go back to the Hyatt tomorrow. I'll call the campground."

Josh said nothing, other than, "C'mon you guys. Let's move it."

"Not so fast," said Mom, sloughing off Dad's hand and pushing her kickstand down with her foot. "I'm not ready."

"Picking a restaurant to have dinner out sounds like fun Mom," I said. "You'll have a chance to get dressed up. You'd like that wouldn't you?"

Mom left her bike and leaned against the side of the trailer with her arms crossed. The poodles stopped wagging their tails and stared at Mom. She didn't say anything. She just stood there stone-faced.

"Will you give me some money Dad?" Josh asked. "I'll take Ty and Zoey. We're here to have fun, not get in the middle of a fight."

"I'm not coming without Mom," I said, getting off my bike and pushing down my own kickstand.

"Then just give me the money," said Josh, "and me and Ty'll get outa here."

Dad put his hand in his pocket and brought out a bunch of bills and handed Josh a few dollars. "Make sure you're back by five, so your mom and I can go to dinner."

"It's a deal." Josh stuffed the money in his pocket. "Maybe we'll see you over there Mom." He pedaled off, "C'mon Ty, let's go."

Ty had been pretty silent the whole time, straddling the crossbar of his bike with his arms lazed over the handlebars, picking at his fingers the way I do when I'm nervous. He hopped on the seat and grabbed the handlebars. "Make it soon." He took off after Josh.

"I want to see the boardwalk with you, Mom," I said, "So I'll wait until you two get it figured out." I didn't stay for an answer. I just went in and sat beside the open window so I could hear what was going to happen.

Mom still leaned against the trailer with her arms crossed. "You really screwed that up nicely Sam."

Dad moved closer to her, but not too close. "Look babe, it doesn't need to be this way." He shoved his hands in his pockets like I remembered a guy doing in the auditorium at school. The guy paraded around the stage with a booming voice.

Dad didn't parade, but he did sound important when he said, "You don't need me for the boardwalk right now Meg. You've got Zoey to go have fun with and check out the restaurants. Then when you and I get home this afternoon, we'll put on our best duds, go stroll for a while, and then have all our favorite taste thrills for dinner. You remember them, don't you babe? Double martinis, two-inch filet mignons with friend onion rings? Or maybe a margarita in a salt-rimmed glass? We haven't had a dress-up date for far too long. It'll be great, I promise." He took his hands out of his pockets, but he still didn't move closer.

I couldn't help but picture him back at work, making up fancy words to sell stuff. Mom didn't interrupt him, but she did seem to listen. When he got to the part about the margarita she uncrossed her arms and held her hands in front of herself until he finished.

Then I don't know who was more excited, me or Dad, because Mom stepped away from the trailer and flung her arms around his neck. "I hate you Sammy." She giggled and the giggle sure didn't have any hate in it. She stood back with a big smile. "But dammit, you win, you big smoothie. The steak and the onion rings were pretty good, but it was the margarita that did it. No wonder you won the best P&G sales award for five years running."

Dad laughed. "I'm glad the awards were good for something." Jacques and Jolie, who were still waiting in Mom's basket, barked their approval.

Dad blew me a kiss through the window. "Take your mom, Zo, find us a restaurant, win some prizes, and we'll all catch up later. I'm going over to the store to get library directions. You guys have fun."

"We will Dad." I ran out to a now smiling Mom. Dad headed over to the store and Mom and I didn't say anything about the whole thing. The poodles said it all as they hopped up, perched their little paws on the front of the basket and wagged their tails like crazy. We laughed as we climbed on our bike seats and pedaled away. The doggies cozied down once we got going.

When we got there we parked our bikes in the public stand where we found the boys' bikes. But any chance of catching up with them, or for the strolling Mom had described on the way over, disappeared real fast. The place was jammed with people as far as you could see, and the old hotels that were supposed to be amazing, were practically falling down. A gruff-looking man yelled at people to toss balls for plastic dolls and stuffed animals, "Make the basket, five shots fer a buck!"

My skin prickled for my own stuffed bears. I wanted to toss balls, and if I scored I'd at least have some kind of stuffed animal to hold onto and squeeze when I felt bad, because the poodles didn't like it when I squeezed them too tight.

"Can I toss balls Mom? Maybe not that guy, but further down where it isn't so crowded. The place is huge, and it can't be like this all over can it?"

"It's been over thirty years since I was here the last time. We can try moving on and see if it gets any better, but I'm not too hopeful."

As we pushed forward through the crowd I hung onto Mom's hand and squeezed my eyes shut, picturing the hooped skirts and fancy hats that Mom had described on the way over.

Suddenly Jolie yanked on the leash I was holding. My eyes popped open to see a little kid whirling a cloud of cotton candy in the poodle's face. Jolie leapt around, nipping at the pink fluff until I swept her up and tucked her under my arm. A huge puppy on a very long leash grabbed the candy out of the kid's hand and it was gone in seconds, paper and all.

I couldn't help laughing at the whole thing, but Mom didn't even smile. She scooped up Jacques and blasted in my ear, "No more Zoey! I've had enough."

"But Mom, I really want to toss..." I started to say, but she was already on her way back to the bike rack. I looked to see if I could find the boys and get them to help me toss balls. There was no sign of them, so I had no choice but to go with her.

Mom put the puzzled pooches in the carrier, unlocked her bike and yanked it free. I scrambled to get mine unlocked, and then had a hard time keeping up with her as she raced back to the trailer with her shoulders bent way over.

The car was home so of course Dad was too.

I watched Mom charge inside, almost pulling off the screen door. She blasted Dad with, "The boardwalk's disgusting Sam! The hotels are ugly. There's litter all over the place, with people pushing and shoving. I want to get out of here NOW!"

I'd never heard Mom so upset. I mean, never. I gathered the doggies from the carrier and huddled outside the trailer door. I squeezed the poodles and they both groaned, making me wish I'd begged harder for a chance to win a stuffed animal.

I crept inside and Dad was sitting at the table with his papers, staring at Mom who was slumped on the sofa. "It's gone," she said. "The way it was is gone. All the hotels are destroyed. There's nobody strolling anywhere, only a whole mass of pushy tourists. It's terrible." Then she burst into tears. "I want to go home. Can't we pretend this never happened and go back to the way our life was?" She leaned forward with her arms wrapped around herself. I had to breathe in and out fast to keep from crying myself. The poodles wriggled like mad to get free, so I let go of them and they darted into Mom and Dad's room. If they could've I bet they would've slammed the door.

Dad moved over beside Mom. "Simmer down, babe." He put his arm around her and muttered something about how it was all okay. It sure didn't look okay to me.

Mom pulled away. "Don't "babe" me Sam. It's not okay. It's not fun. We need to go home, get your job back and buy another house." With that, she leapt from the sofa, stumbled to their bedroom and slammed the door. The slam not only rattled dishes in the kitchen cupboard, but everything in the trailer, including me.

"Is Mom okay? I've never seen her that upset Dad. But she's right, the boardwalk was worse than awful. And what about the library? You sure weren't there for long."

Dad sank back in the sofa pillows and leaned his head against the wall. "I wasn't there at all, sweetheart. I drove over and found the place closed for remodeling. I went to the boardwalk, but I knew it'd be hopeless to try and find you guys in the mess of tourists, so I came home."

"I guess the whole thing's a bummer, huh?"

"The closed library was a bummer all right. And your mom, she was in Atlantic City a long time ago, and I guess we should've known nothing stays the same, especially the upkeep on anything as extravagant as the boardwalk scene used to be." He sat up, but his shoulders were slumped. "I know this whole trip isn't easy for your mom. I guess it's not easy for any of us with all the moving, all the tourists, and all the commotion."

"Is it hard to think up a new job to do when everything's so crazy, Dad?"

"I guess you could say that, Zo. It's certainly a lot different than going to an office isn't it?" He laughed, but it sure wasn't a real laugh.

"Are you sorry you quit work? I know Mom wants to go home. Do you?"

Peggy Warren

Right then the door flew open and in charged Josh with Ty behind him. "Hey Dad," said Josh, "There's a guy selling surfboards on the boardwalk. Can I get one, please, pretty please?"

Dad got up and pushed past my brothers and out the door. "Forget surfboards!" is all he said.

"That was pretty snarky," said Josh. "What's going on?"

"Yeah, Sis," said Ty. "Did we miss something? Where's Mom?"

"In her room. She's pretty upset and she hates it here. The hotels were horrible. You saw them. The boardwalk isn't the same boardwalk Mom remembers, so she couldn't get out of there fast enough. I think we're leaving."

"What about the big night out?" asked Ty. "I know the boardwalk bombed, but maybe there's a restaurant in Atlantic City they could go to. And what happened at the library? Dad didn't stay long."

"He didn't get to go in the library. It's being remodeled so it was closed. And if I were you I'd go help him get ready to leave."

The boys went out, and Dad came back in and went to the bedroom. I wanted to go stand outside the closed door to hear what Dad was saying, but that felt too nosy. I kept myself busy by making a bunch of bologna and cheese sandwiches, even though it wasn't exactly lunchtime.

Finally Mom and Dad came out of the bedroom with the poodles in Mom's arms. She'd brushed her hair and put on lipstick, but she sure didn't look like she'd had much fun in there if Dad had tried to get mushy to make her feel better. Usually that stuff worked just as well as all the perfect words he was so good at making up.

Dad took half a sandwich off the counter. He didn't say anything, but he did kiss my cheek before he went outside.

Mom leashed the poodles and said she was going to take them for a walk.

"Do you want me to come?" I asked, practically shaking out of my sandals.

"No, but thanks for making the sandwiches. I'll be back." She left.

— 40 —

I went outside to find Dad. He was sitting at the picnic table with the boys, looking through the Big Book. The bikes were back on the rack and the trailer was attached and ready to go. I squeaked out the question that needed an answer. "Are we going home?"

"No, sweetheart. We're not going home."

I swallowed hard to keep the tears inside. I wanted the answer to be yes so I could be home with Amy and the kids at summer camp. I went back in the trailer and got the letter I still hadn't mailed. It wasn't that I felt like writing any newsy stuff, but I had to get all of what had happened out of me before I burst. It hurt so much to see Mom and Dad upset and I wanted so badly to fix them, but I didn't know how.

Of course writing Amy didn't help. How could it? She wasn't there to give me any ideas. I went on to tell her about all the rain at Hyatt Heaven that made us leave, and how we'd come to Atlantic City to see the boardwalk. I wasn't sure Amy even knew what the boardwalk was, but I let her know that the old hotels were falling down in case she wanted to tell her mom about them. When I was finished describing the whole boardwalk mess, I added on a bunch of hugs and kisses so she'd know I cared a lot more about her than I cared about all the stuff I'd written. I said I'd write again when we got somewhere good, and not to worry about me if she thought I sounded bummed. Then I stuffed the letter in an envelope and stamped it and ran it over to the store.

When Mom came back from her walk she sure didn't look any better. I wanted to ask her if writing letters to her friends back home ever helped her feel better. But then I realized she didn't even do that, or not that I saw anyway.

I was about to ask her when Ty called through the door. "Hey you guys, Dad's in the car. Are you coming?"

Mom covered the whole plateful of sandwiches with aluminum foil and put it in the fridge. "Fine" she said. "Tell him we're coming." So much for talking about letters.

"Where are we going Dad?" I asked as we all piled in the car. "If we're not going home, are we going back to Hyatt Heaven?"

"No, we're not going back. I called and cancelled. We're moving on. The Hyatt's too far from a library, and I need to get doing my job research. We're going down to Jacksonville." He turned on the ignition.

Mom was about to get in the car when she stopped in her tracks and glared at Dad. "Jacksonville is a million miles from here Sam. What're you talking about? You didn't tell me Jacksonville Ty."

"Dad was over calling when you came home, Mom, so I wasn't sure. Sorry. I just knew we were leaving, that's all."

Dad revved the engine. "Just please get in Meg. I need a decent library, and I found a campground in Jacksonville Beach, near the city. I honestly didn't expect to score because the place looks so great, but I called and they happened to have a big expansion going on. They've just finished the first phase so they had a vacancy and I made a reservation. What's a few extra miles anyway?"

Mom dropped down into the seat with a big door slam that made the poodles bark. Dad took off and the doggies leapt from my lap over the seat into Mom's.

"The place we're going looks nice, Mom," said Ty. "Wanna see a picture?" He held the catalog out to her but she didn't take it.

We drove out of the campground and onto the highway without saying a single word. Mom's body looked so tight I could feel it squeezing me. I would've reached my arms over the seat and given her a hug, but I didn't want to make a big deal out of what I couldn't change. The boys set up a game of magnetic Chess in all the silence and it was weird to watch them playing without arguing. Dad turned on the 'oldies' station with the volume way down. I put the pillow against the window and stuffed my head into it, hoping I could fall asleep so everything would go away.

Suddenly Dad shouted, "Fried clam strips everybody! Did you see the Howard Johnson billboard? I know it's a bit of a detour, because the sign says it's over on the beach, but I think we can handle that for a taste thrill like those clam strips. Everyone agree?"

Dad's booming voice scared Jolie and Jacque, and they leapt from Mom's lap over the front and back seats, landing in their basket. They snuggled tight. As well as needing to comfort us at just the right time, sometimes they needed to comfort each other.

For me, all the comfort I needed was the clam strips. I loved them a lot, but the whole family knew no one loved Howard Johnson's fried clam strips more than Mom.

For sure no one knew that better than Dad. "It's not maybe as good as a steak and margarita, babe, but I know it comes close. What d'you think?"

Maybe Dad didn't win Mom over in the bedroom after the boardwalk mess-up, but right then I watched him back in full swing with all the right words. Mom didn't say anything. She did look over at Dad though, and I saw a smile inching its way across her face.

"It's just going to make the drive that much further," said Josh. "Are clam strips really that important?"

"Clam strips are really that important, Josh." Dad smiled back at Mom and reached his hand across the seat to take hers. I could feel her tightness unravel just the way her weavings would with one tug of a loose end. Dad sure knew how to get at Mom's loose ends.

The drive was longer than I wanted it to be, but when we finally got there, Dad pulled the trailer into the lot and parked as close to the front door as he could.

He opened his door and told Mom not to get out. He closed it and ran around to Mom's side. He opened hers and reached out his hand that she took. "C'mon babe. It's not quite a filet and margarita, but the sentiment's the same."

Mom smiled big as she got out and stuck her arm through Dad's. We sat in the back seat staring as the two of them schmoozed their way into the restaurant.

"Oh brother," Josh muttered. I smiled to myself and I bet Ty did too. I couldn't see his face because he and Josh got out while I was promising the doggies a treat.

Once we were all inside and sitting, Dad ordered a dozen baskets of clams. When they came, Mom shoved in mouthfuls with such gusto that she had herself covered in coating crumbs in seconds. Dad put his arm around her and even I could feel the big squeeze he gave her as he kissed her cheek. We all stuffed ourselves with way more than we needed, making the whole thing the best fried clam spree ever.

"Let's take a walk on the beach," said Dad. "I can't drive with a stuffed gut."

The restaurant wasn't exactly on the beach, but it did overlook a great view of the ocean. "How do you get to the beach?" I asked. "There's nothing but sea grape bushes."

"We'll drive down the coast until we find a parking space and a walkway to the beach, that's all," said Dad. "And then me, the poodles, and whoever else wants will take a stroll." Dad put his arm around Mom. "The stroll we didn't have on the boardwalk, Meg." He laughed.

"Not quite the same, Sammy, but I'll take whatever I can get." She kissed Dad's cheek.

We piled in the car and I gave the poodles the clam strips I'd wrapped in a napkin. "That was so much fun," I said. "Can we talk about other fun stuff now that we're all in a good mood?"

"Who's in a good mood," said Josh. "We've got a million miles left on the road before Jacksonville."

I wanted to smack him, but instead I just said, "Why can't we talk about other vacations, y'know, like fun ones? That should take up lots of time. Anyone got any good stories?"

"Sure, I got a doozie," said Dad. "Actually we had our first Howard Johnson fried clam strips on that vacation. Remember, Meg?"

Mom laughed. "How can I forget."

With that, Dad went on to tell us about the ski trip he and Mom took to Colorado before we were even born. On their very first day at the ski resort the ski lift broke down halfway up the mountain. After almost an hour of sitting there, Dad got impatient and jumped off, landing in a deep pile of powdered snow.

"Everyone on the lift gasped," said Dad, "and you should've seen the look of horror on your mother's face as the lift took off and I sank deeper and deeper in the snow. I know that probably sounds scary to you kids, but I didn't feel any horror. The powdered snow was so soft it was like being buried in a cloud. Honestly," he said, laughing, "the whole thing was heavenly."

With more laughter Mom took over the story and described how Dad got buried so deep that only his head and the tips of his skis were sticking out by the time the ski patroller got her to him.

For sure it felt good to me hearing my parents laugh like that. Dad added extra laughs by describing the ride he got on the rescue toboggan, with Mom sitting up front, looking like a cocky pilot with her goggles all steamed up. Nothing bad happened to Dad, but I guess the ski patrollers decided to put him on the toboggan before he got into any more trouble.

"I think we ought to get back on the thruway, Sammy," said Mom, once the memory story was over. "I'm not sure there's any access to the beach. The sea grapes are so thick you can hardly even see the ocean."

Well miracle of all miracles, out of the blue, not only a walkway showed up, but a huge campground that had been cleared out of the thick sea grapes. A guy on a ladder by the road was adding letters to a sign that so far read VIRGINIA BE…

Dad headed the car straight into one of the sites. "An oceanside campground is as close to a woodland paradise as we're going to get. What d'you think, Meg, kids? Like it?

"Sure beats driving to Jacksonville," said Josh. "Does this mean we're making a plan change Dad?"

"For right now I guess it does. An almost empty campground on the beach is too good to pass up. I'll call and see if I can delay our Jacksonville reservation. Seeing as their expansion is about making new campsites, it'll probably be okay. Would everyone like that?"

A big hooray and a couple of poodle whoops filled the car as our eyes bugged at the massive empty beach in front of us, with the ocean spreading out like a huge blanket of blinding light, all calm and sparkly. There were still some sea grape bushes between the campsites and the beach. But the sand and the water were awfully close compared to anywhere else we'd been.

Dad turned off the ignition and Mom leapt out of the car, kicked off her sandals and flew down the path between the sea grapes and across the sand to the water's edge, throwing her arms in the air.

A man came running from the campground store. He yanked open Dad's door. "Hey, what're you doing? Didn't you see the sign in the store window? You've gotta check in first. You can't just park here."

"Sorry, fella," said Dad. "My wife needed some air."

"What's the big deal?" asked Josh. "There's no one here."

"Well, there's going to be. We just opened. And don't bother with the lip, Sonny."

"It's really nice," I said. "Can we stay, please?"

The guy peered in the car. "Cute dogs. If your dad comes with me, y'can can stay."

"Go for it Dad," said Josh. "This place is cool."

Dad got out and took off with the guy.

"Phew," I said.

"Yeah, phew," said Ty. "You almost ruined our best score yet Josh."

"Shut up little brother."

On The Beach

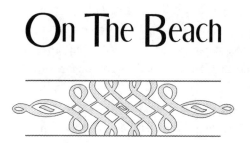

The weather at Virginia Beachside campground was so perfect that we spent all our time on the beach. Even though we had a big new barbecue and a picnic table on our campsite, Dad rented a portable barbecue at the store and we set it up on the sand. We cooked lots of hot dogs and hamburgers and roasted a ton of marshmallows. Almost right away all the horrors of Atlantic City, and any of the other awful places we'd stayed, faded. Even Dad hung out with no yellow sheets of paper, only playing in the surf with Ty and me, cuddling Mom, and tossing balls for the poodles. A guy with a truckload of surfboards showed up and Dad bought Josh exactly what he wanted, a board with a picture of a girl in a bikini stretched out from one end to the other.

All I could think was that Dad had decided to try and turn the whole thing into a vacation after all. Maybe it was the laughing over the ski trip, or maybe it was just him wanting to do something nice for Mom after the boardwalk. I sure had no way of figuring out the change, but it was really great to see Dad having fun. He'd even stopped hollering about wanting peace and quiet.

Then after about a week, things began to change. The campground had definitely been discovered and people were pulling in all the time, which made for a lot more commotion and a lot more racket. Dad stopped playing and started spending more time at the library. Although the Virginia Beach library couldn't have been all that big, it seemed to have enough of what he was looking for to keep him busy writing on his yellow pages.

It wasn't long before he began to get antsy the way he was after we'd been in Cape Cod for a week, with peace and quiet hollers shooting out of him like crazy as the beach filled up and the flying Frisbees swooped overhead. The library days got longer, and Dad started to get really impatient.

One day when Mom, the poodles, and the boys were over checking out the new rec center, I opened the trailer door and found Dad sitting by himself with his head in his hands and his closed cigarette pack sitting on the sofa beside him. I could've sworn he was crying.

"D…Dad?" My voice caught in my throat.

He didn't lift his head, but he did flutter his hands for me to leave, so I let go of the door and bolted. I leapt through a tangle of sea grapes and raced along the beach, away from the campground to a beach where a bunch of kids were roasting marshmallows on a portable barbecue just like ours.

The memory hurt so bad I fell down. My head spun like an out-of-control top, with Dad's tears flooding my insides. I wrapped my arms around myself and squeezed until the spinning gave way to a burst of tears.

"You okay?" I heard.

I looked up into a mass of long blonde hair, and a big smile on a lady's face. "Would you like a cup of lemonade? You must be thirsty from all that running."

I tried to speak and nothing came out but choking sobs.

The lady crouched beside me. "The lemonade is cold. It's good."

I rubbed my face, smearing the tears all over the place.

"Wait a minute," she said. She got up and ran over to her blanket. She came back with her towel and handed it to me. "Here, wipe your face with this."

I did that, and then I let her pull me up. I put the towel over my head to hide the gawking faces while she led me to her blanket. She poured the lemonade from a thermos, and nobody seemed to be gawking anymore so I handed her back the towel. "Thanks. That was nice of you."

"Hey, my pleasure. I'm glad I could help." She stretched the headband that was around her neck up over her hair, holding it back from her face. She sat down and crossed her legs. "Why don't you sit a minute and catch your breath."

I knew I ought to go home before I was missed. I sat anyway. I gulped the lemonade, all of it.

The lady emptied the thermos into my cup. "Are you staying at the campground?" she asked.

I nodded.

"Anything you want to talk about? You looked pretty upset."

"It's just that five of us are all crammed together in a trailer and my dad's freaked. We got here when this place first opened, and now it's crazy with so many people, and I think he wants them gone." There was no way I could tell her about finding him crying without crying again, so I kept those words to myself.

"Getting rid of everybody, that's a tall order in the middle of July," she said. "Is your trailer a big one?"

"Not big enough I guess." I didn't want to talk about the trailer or me or Dad or any sad stuff that nobody could fix, so I changed the subject real fast. "Are you staying here too? It sure is a big campground isn't it?"

"It is, and I have been staying here, but I'm leaving later today. I'm in a VW camper by myself, so there's no crowding. My name's Melinda Geary." She smacked her palm against her forehead. "No, that's not right. I won't be Geary anymore. I'm getting divorced and

I'll be Melinda Spratt again. You like that? Melinda Spratt, like Jack Spratt? Only I can eat fat." She laughed as she rubbed her flat tummy.

Getting divorced didn't seem like something you'd want to joke about, but I made myself laugh along with her.

"I'm glad you liked that," she said. "You look a lot better with a smile on your face."

"I haven't wanted to smile much, or not today anyway." As soon as I'd said that I knew we were headed right back into the pits. So before Mrs. Geary had a chance to ask me why, I said, "I think I'd better go. My mom's probably wondering where I am." I got up.

"I'm sure she is. Are you going to be okay?"

"I hope so." I made up another sort of smile. "Thanks again for the lemonade."

"You're welcome." She put on her sunglasses and bunched her towel into a pillow. "I think I'll catch some rays now, but you take care of yourself."

"I'll try," I said. I wanted to say I would, but I had no idea how to do that.

I walked back along the beach wondering how I could ever take care of myself if Dad was a mess, especially since there was no way I could ever tell anyone what I'd seen. Mom would freak and the boys would probably feel even worse than I did. After all, guys weren't supposed to cry, and for sure not your dad.

The top in my head started spinning again. There weren't any tears coming out this time, but I was sure my brain was going to fly through the top of my skull. Everything was such a blur that I didn't see Mom, or not until this person with flailing arms coming at me turned into her.

She grabbed hold of my shoulders. "Where have you been Zoey? Don't you ever, ever disappear like that again. You had me crazy."

The strain in Mom's face squeezed my heart almost as hard as Dad's tears had. She pulled me into a hug so tight I could feel her heart beat right through my tank top.

I hugged her back just as tight. "It's okay Mom. I just walked further than I meant to. I'm sorry if you were scared."

She backed out of the hug and put her hands on my shoulders again. "Well, don't ever do that again. Will you promise?" She squeezed, probably to make sure I got the point.

"Honest and true, Mom, I promise to never do that again."

"Honest and true? That's quite a promise. Your granny loved that expression, and I haven't heard it in years."

Mom smiled, and seeing the strain on her face go away sure made me feel better. I pictured granny up in heaven, smiling at us, but I didn't say anything. I just let Mom put her arm around my shoulders and steer me back to her blanket.

She dropped down on the blanket, crossed her legs, and reached for my hand. "Sit with me honey. I just want to look at you."

I couldn't take her hand because I really had to go to the bathroom. "I can't Mom. I gotta pee before I wet my pants."

She laughed. "By all means. Go! We wouldn't want that."

First, I had to ask, "Where is everybody?" Of course everybody was only Dad.

She told me the boys and the poodles were at the rec center playing pool. "I was there too, and I saw Dad drive out of the campground. He was alone so I figured you were probably at the trailer. But you weren't, and you weren't at the store or the laundry room, and that's when I checked the beach and realized you were missing." She put her hand on her heart. "But thank God you're not. So just go, but don't disappear."

"I won't. Honest and true." We both laughed this time, and I sped back to the trailer.

After going to the bathroom, I sprawled on my bunk while I tried to figure out why Dad was crying. I knew he was frustrated with all the racket, but I'd hoped the research he was doing would make him feel better, not worse. Obviously it wasn't fixing anything. I wished there was some way I could do research on how to fix a dad. I was good at fixing Amy when she was sad, but Dad, well I guess I wasn't even supposed to know he was sad.

Mrs. Geary had said Dad wanting to get rid of everyone in the campground was a tall order. I was reminded of a sign on the outside of McDonalds in Baltimore. It said, "A TALL ORDER", and under the sign was a skinny picture of cheeseburgers piled high up the side of the building. Maybe I was just hungry or something. Of course I couldn't order up a cheeseburger and fries, but then another idea blasted me right out of the bunk, like Fourth of July fireworks. I clapped my hands together to make the sound real.

What if I ordered up peace and quiet for Dad?

I flopped back down on the bed. The fireworks fizzled real quick as I realized there was no way I could order up something when I didn't even know what it was, especially the way Dad hollered that it was something he really wanted to *get*. For sure the peace part was mostly what he wanted, because there was always lots of quiet in a library.

I stretched out and covered my face with my arms, hoping something smart would show up in my head. I didn't see pictures or anything. But I did think something that made me sit up fast, and clap my hands even harder than before.

What if I was to talk to people in the campgrounds, and ask them what peace and quiet meant to them. I'd probably get really neat answers, and more than that, if I got the perfect answer, I could turn it into a gift for Dad's birthday. I wished I'd thought of my idea earlier. Mrs. Geary would probably have had great stuff to say about peace and quiet. With Mom so freaked, and with Mrs. Geary leaving, I knew I couldn't go back and find her. But I was at least glad her tall order thing had given me the idea.

Coming up with presents for Dad was always hard, but this would be a super special one. The birthday was still more than a month away so I wouldn't be able to give it to him as fast as I wanted. But that was okay because finding people I could come right out and talk to about stuff like that would take lots of time anyway.

I decided to write my plan out in a letter to Amy to see if it made sense. I didn't tell her about Dad crying. Writing those words would only make me cry again and sop the page. So I just told her that Dad was so frustrated with all the moving around and tourist racket that he was hollering even more about wanting peace and quiet, and I'd decided if he wanted it so much, I was going to find a way to get it for him. When I got to the end of describing how the whole thing worked, I told Amy I was going to call the plan 'my assignment' because it felt more important than just an idea.

Writing all that down made me want so badly to see her face and hear what she'd say. All our lives we'd planned everything together. But she wasn't there so I wouldn't be able to get any reaction from her. I was wondering whether to crumple the letter up when I heard the trailer door open, and then, "Hi, babe. How about a swim?"

"Wow!" said Mom. "What a surprise. It's not even noon. I was just going to make lunch." I'd been so busy writing Amy that I hadn't even heard Mom come in.

"I know what time it is," said Dad with his voice all mushy. "I thought it'd be fun to surprise you. C'mere."

I heard a scuffle and Mom giggling. "Hey Zoey," she called. "Surprise! Your dad's home." I could picture her pointing at my bunk to let Dad know they weren't alone. "Want to go swimming with us before lunch?"

I had no idea Mom knew I was there, but of course she did. Moms know everything. "Okay. I'm just finishing a letter to Amy."

On the way to their room to get on their bathing suits, Dad stopped by my bunk and planted a kiss on top of my head. "I'm fine sweetheart," he whispered.

That was Mom's word, and I figured maybe it was getting to be Dad's too. I didn't have one of those, so I said nothing.

We all went to the beach like the happy family we were supposed to be. I didn't crumple the letter before we left. I stuck it under my pillow because I knew I'd have to send it just so Amy would know what I was doing. Her somewhere else support was better than no support at all.

The next morning Dad took his yellow pad and went to the library the same as usual. To keep from trying to figure Dad out I decided to picture him as the dad he used to be, like a working dad (without the shirt and tie) who now had the library for his office. I knew that would help me not see tears every time I looked at him, even though I didn't get to look at him much. He was practically always gone.

Nobody had said anything nasty about that until a few days later when Josh exploded with words that said it all. He and Dad were out by the picnic table, Josh with his board, ready to go to the beach, and Dad with his pad, on the way to the library.

The rest of us were in the trailer cleaning up the breakfast stuff when Josh's voice came through the windows and door. "I think it's mean the way you leave Mom alone all the time, Dad. That doesn't seem fair to me."

Mom and Ty and me, we stopped what we were doing and stared out at them.

Then Dad said, "There's no way I can put together any plans for our future with all the commotion going on around here. Your mother understands what I'm doing, and you'd better understand too, if you want a life that includes something more than floating around on that surfboard."

"Well if I didn't have the surfboard, I'd be on the highway hitching a ride back to Baltimore and football camp. That's how much fun this trip is with you gone all the time. The rest of us, we don't go anywhere, we don't see anything other than the car taking off in the morning. You say Mom understands and I'd better too. So tell me what I'm supposed to understand, because I don't know anything."

"You know I'm researching a new career. Isn't that enough? I go to the library to get information. I'm researching what's not being done in the world so I can come up with a new idea. To get any of that done I need peace and quiet, that's what I need."

My heart just about exploded with those words.

"So why couldn't you have done that in Baltimore? They have a great library there."

"It's not just the library, Josh. It's the travel, and all the different people I meet and talk to in the towns, the coffee shops, the restaurants, and of course the libraries. I need new, fresh ideas, and I can only get them by listening to people and studying different attitudes and lifestyles. It's called research."

"I know what it's called, Dad. What I don't know is what you're researching. I only know you drive off, are gone all day, come home and don't say anything, just write away on your yellow paper. How would I know that you're meeting people and getting ideas that way? Who knows anything about any of it, other than you?"

"I've told your mom what I'm doing, but I guess maybe I didn't think you'd be interested. Your only interest seems to be that board."

"Well maybe that's because there's nothing else to be interested in. I'm going surfing!" He headed to the beach.

"Of course you are." Dad jumped in the car and took off.

Ty sure liked what he heard. "Wow! That's news. Something that's never been done before! That's great!"

Mom plunked herself down at the table. "I'm sorry Josh had to make a big scene of it."

"He didn't, Mom," I said. "He just got Dad to say out loud what he's doing. I'm glad Josh did that."

Ty sat across from Mom. "I am too. And Dad quitting work like he did, he must've really hated his old job."

"It wasn't so much that he hated it, Ty. He just hated what he'd become."

I slid in beside Mom. "What's that supposed to mean? He became rich, and what's not to like about that?"

"Exactly, Zo. He became rich. But meeting and even exceeding corporate expectations turned him into a workaholic. That's not what he wants to be. That's not the dad you guys deserve."

"That's the only dad I've ever known, Mom. And now that he's not working, well to tell you the truth, he's kinda scary, like he seems to be having a really hard time on this trip, always hollering he wants peace and quiet and everything. I know Dad has a dream, but honestly, sometimes it seems like more of a nightmare for him.

Mom looked like she was stuck in a knothole when she said, "I hate that it's so hard when it was supposed to be fun, Zoey."

"We all hate it Mom. But at least it was good to hear him say out loud what he's been doing. Sure makes the whole thing sound a lot more fun, hanging out in coffee shops and stuff. Can I go with him?"

"Maybe that's why I haven't told you, honey, because I knew that's what you'd want to do, and of course you can't go with him.

I couldn't help but wonder what peace and quiet meant to Mom, and if she even had room for it in the mess of private stuff she kept in her head.

Ty broke through my thoughts. "Well good for Dad. It's true what Zoey said, that he's the only dad we've ever known. I like that our new dad wants to make a difference, to do something that's brand new. That's great." He slid off the seat. "By the way, talking about brand new, they're putting in the TV at the rec center this morning. I'm going over. Do you guys want to come?"

"Sure, I'll go," said Mom. I got up to let her off the bench.

"You coming Sis?" he asked.

"Nope. I want to finish a letter to Amy." I was sure glad I hadn't crumpled it because I needed to tell her about more than just my assignment. I needed her to know about everything that had just happened.

"Okay," said Ty. "I'll see you later. C'mon Mom." He headed out the door.

"I'll be there in a minute," she called after him.

Mom stayed behind long enough to say, "Keeping things from you kids has always been something I do to protect you, Zoey. I guess it's a mother thing. But you're growing up a whole lot faster than I expected, so I guess you don't need a lot of protecting anymore. You'll have to be patient with me though, because I've spent a lot of years keeping things to myself, not just to protect you, but well I guess sometimes to protect myself. " She reached her arms around me. I wasn't any taller, but I sure did feel more grown up hearing Mom say that. It helped me sort of get why she said "fine" as much as she did. I hugged her back real tight and I could feel her springing right through the knothole.

She left and I got right into Amy's letter so I could try to untangle everything about Josh and Dad and why Mom kept things to herself by saying "fine" all the time. That was way harder than I hoped it'd be. I did my best, but mostly what came out of my pen was how badly I needed her to help me figure things out. I told her I could hardly wait until we stayed somewhere long enough for me to get a letter back from her. We'd already been in Virginia Beach long enough for that, but with Dad being like he was, I was never sure when he'd want to take off. I didn't want to write anymore after that, so I just added a bunch of kisses and stuffed the letter into an envelope and ran it to the mailbox at the store.

On the way home I decided to go on a search for my first assignment person. I'd kind of been putting it off because it was really hard to get up the nerve to barge in on people.

I wandered from one end of the campground to the other, and everyone was either busy doing something that I couldn't interrupt, or hanging out with other people, or just plain not home. There weren't even any kids my age who looked like they might want to be my friend. I mean on the trip there never had been any kids my age, which seemed pretty weird. I decided maybe eleven-year-olds didn't like camping with their parents, and it wasn't hard to figure out why, especially when there were certain kinds of brothers included. Whatever the reason, I finally just gave up and went to the rec center to watch TV and forget everything.

That night, right out of the blue, finding people fixed itself, because what looked like the perfect first assignment person pulled into the campsite right next to ours. He was on a big black and silver motorcycle with a dog carrier on the back fender and some kind of contraption being hauled behind.

The guy hopped off the motorcycle, unattached the carrier and put it on the table. He opened the door and out popped the cutest little windblown dog with a mop of hair the color of butterscotch. The little thing jumped off the table and darted in circles so fast you couldn't see any feet. Jacques and Jolie went crazy on the end of their ropes, and before the guy had a chance to catch the pooch it was at our picnic table playing with the poodles. The guy ran over and scooped it up with one hand and yanked off his helmet with the other.

"Sorry, folks," he said. "We've been on the road too long and Charley's got a lot of pent-up energy going on." I could barely see the pooch's face through all the hair. The guy himself, who looked to be around Dad's age, had a buzz cut.

"I'm Eli," he said, "and Charley and me, we're on our way to a bike rally in Atlanta."

"Nice Harley," said Josh, ogling the motorcycle. "Can I have a look?"

"Sure you can." Eli turned to Mom and Dad. "Is it okay? I'm not bothering you guys am I?"

"Not at all," said Mom. "You give the place a little color."

"You're right about that," said Dad, supposedly under his breath, but I heard.

Eli definitely gave the place color, done up in black leather, boots and all. When he turned to go back to his place, my eyes bugged out of my head at the sight of the beautiful painted eagle on the back of his vest, with *SOAR LIKE AN EAGLE* painted underneath it in gold letters. His tanned skin was bare under the vest.

I would've liked to look at the motorcycle but I could tell that was Josh's thing, and I guess that's what Ty thought too because he didn't go either. But really I didn't care about the motorcycle, I cared about getting rid of everyone so I could talk to Eli.

I watched him show Josh everything, including how the contraption he was hauling came apart and turned into a tent. At least I got to see he was staying for the night.

Josh must've asked for a ride because suddenly all of them, including Charley who was tucked down the front of Eli's vest, were riding around the campground with Josh on the passenger seat, glowing like a Halloween lantern. It was pretty cute.

Nobody else got to have a ride, but we did get to spend some time hanging out at the rec center with Eli and Charley that night. Eli said he'd be leaving in the morning so I did everything I could to try and get him alone. Nothing worked because Josh was pretty much hogging him the whole time. He did have a game of pool with Dad and that was fun to watch, seeing as the two of them were really good. I think Dad won, or probably more like it, Eli let him win. Eli seemed like that kind of guy.

In the morning while I was washing the breakfast dishes I saw Eli out the kitchen window sitting at his picnic table. He was whittling on a tree branch with Charley curled up in front of him. My head was working like crazy to figure out how I could get over there to talk to him, when suddenly out of Dad came a bunch of swear words.

I turned to see that Josh had knocked over Dad's coffee mug with his surfboard. He kept the thing in the trailer at night, because he was afraid someone would steal it outside. All of us bellyached about that, but Josh did it anyway.

Dad crumpled his soggy notes and flung them at Josh. He missed because Josh was out the door already. Jacques and Jolie did a good job of supporting Dad's hissy-fit along with Charley from over at Eli's place. Mom put the leashes on the poodles and took off. Ty picked up the wad of pages and flattened them out while I sopped up the spilled coffee.

Dad had his head in his hands, and I bet there were more tears behind the growling sound he made when he told Ty and me to leave him alone. You can be sure we did.

Ty went to the beach, and without even thinking about it I went next door.

When Charley saw me he popped up and wagged his tail, which meant his whole body because the wag wiggled him from front to back.

Eli turned and smiled. "Well, hi!"

I said "hi" back. "I don't want to bother you, but can I see what you're making?" I ruffled Charley's fur. He collapsed and rolled onto his back.

"You're not bothering me." He handed me the carving. "Belly rubs are Charley's favorite." He gave Charley a real belly rub while I ogled the carving.

Charley was cute, but the carving was amazing, the most perfect eagle's head ever. A smaller branch out the side of the big one formed the beak that was curved like a real beak. Eli had even cut back into the branch to make the neck. I turned it around and around so I wouldn't miss any of it. "How long did it take you to make this?"

"Oh some time here, some there. It's hard to figure time. I've had this one going for a while so it's about done. But time's not important. What's important is I whittle to feel good, get my day started right." He gave up the tummy rub and Charley sprawled on the table in front of him. "Whittling and Charley, they're my feel good buddies."

I handed Eli back the carving. "My poodles are my feel good buddies too. Did you paint that eagle on your vest? It's beautiful."

Eli laughed. "I'm no artist, kiddo. It was painted by one of the guys in our biker club. What's your name anyway? I didn't get it last night."

"I know. I'm Zoey. Is it okay if I call you Eli? You didn't tell us your last name."

"Sure. Just call me Eli, 'cause that's who I am. I dumped my last name years ago. It's German and I'm not a German guy anymore. I'm an American guy and proud of it!"

I am too," I said, feeling just as proud.

"Hey," he said. "Why don't you sit down over there across from me so I can look at you without straining my neck."

"Okay." I went around the table and climbed over the bench. I had no idea how to get to my assignment, but what he'd just said at least let me know I wasn't bothering him. I didn't want to just spit out the question though, so I asked, "What's a biker club?'

"Well for starters, it's a bunch of dudes getting together to hang out and be dudes and show off our bikes."

"Does everybody take their dogs?"

"No way! Charley's going to visit my sister, his Aunt Molly. She lives in Atlanta. He'll stay with her and she'll get to brush out his tangles while I'm at the rally."

"Does the biker club have a name?"

"Yeah. We're called 'Soaring Eagles' because that's what we do." He shifted around to show me the words on his vest that I'd already seen. "The guy who painted the eagle, he painted the slogan too. Have you ever seen an eagle?"

I remembered the eagle in a National Geographic magazine at school. In the middle of describing to Eli how the wingspan spread across the middle pages, my question fell right out of my mouth. "Do you know what peace is?"

Eli's eyebrows shot up his forehead. "Weren't we talking about eagles?"

"We were, but I know you're probably leaving soon and I needed to ask the question."

"Well for one thing," he said, with his eyebrows back in place, "it's the other side of war, and I know that because I was a fighter pilot in Vietnam."

"Oh my gosh. I'm sorry. I hadn't even thought of that kind of peace."

"Hey, don't be sorry. I got my slogan up there soaring with the eagles, and I got back from the war in one piece, so there's nothing to be sorry about." He set the carving on the table. "Now, tell me what kind of peace you're talking about exactly."

I told him I wanted to give Dad the peace and quiet kind.

"You want to what?"

That wasn't what I'd hoped for and I knew I was blushing.

"Hey, it's okay," said Eli. He took a drink of orange juice from the carton on the table. "It's just the kind of peace you're talking about, well I don't know if you can give that to anyone. They probably have to find it on their own."

"But my dad hasn't found it." I turned to get off the bench.

"Wait a minute! Don't go anywhere. I know I'm not helping you at all and I'd like to, so just stay here and tell me more."

I knew all I could do was start over or leave, and I didn't want to leave. I turned back and crossed my arms over my chest. I'd seen people do that when they were making important speeches. I wasn't about to make an important speech, but I did feel ready to start over.

"My dad, he's not used to traveling around in a trailer all the time. He keeps hollering all he wants is peace and quiet, and I know you said people have to find it for themselves, but he hasn't. What I want to do is ask people what they think peace is, and maybe I'll hear something I might be able to turn into a gift for Dad's birthday. The quiet part's easy, it's just the peace I need to know about."

Eli didn't say anything. He took another drink of orange juice.

He offered me some, but I didn't want any. "Does that sound stupid?" It sure sounded stupid to me the way it came out, so I added, "I watched you whittling out the window this morning and because you were all alone I decided to ask you. It's hard to find people to talk to."

From the way Eli squeezed his eyebrows together I hoped maybe he was making up words to tell me. It seemed like a long time before he finally said he didn't have a good answer.

I'm sure I must've looked like I felt, because he said, "I guess that's not what you want to hear is it?"

I shrugged my shoulders.

Eli finished off the orange juice and squished the two sides of the carton together. "Well maybe I can't figure how you'd give peace to your dad, but I guess I could try to tell you how it works for me." He tossed the carton in the trashcan. "Would you like that?"

"Yeah. It'd be really neat to hear how it works for you."

"Okay." He picked up the branch and twirled it between his fingers. "What happens for me is that I usually start most days by whittling, and when I'm whittling, that's when I get the peace." He looked right at me. "But this morning, well the peace got a little broken up after I'd been at it for a while, if you know what I mean."

Just then I watched Dad take off in the car, no waving, no nothing. I began to squirm.

Eli turned to see what I was looking at. He saw the car driving away, and then turned back to me. "It's okay. It wasn't your fault. Your dad was bummed, right?"

I tried to describe what had happened, but it all sounded stupid. "If it's okay I don't want to talk about my brother and his surfboard anymore. I want to talk about what you were going to say about peace."

"I know you do." He studied the carving and really seemed to study it before he said, "So, to get any peace from whittling, I have to clear my head of the day-to-day crap of who's doing what to who, and why. Once I get quiet, then I bring out my knife and allow my creative spirit to take over and express itself." He looked at me again, and this time I swear his face was glowing like there was a light on inside him. But the glow went away real fast when I told him I didn't understand what he meant.

He put the eagle's head down and reached over and picked up Charley. He put the bundle of fur to his face and pressed the little body against his cheek. "I'm messing up here, Charley boy. I need your help." Charley lifted his head and licked Eli's nose. Eli cuddled him for a minute before he set him back on the table and gave him a doggie biscuit from his pocket. "I don't know about your little poodles, but Charley, he gives me help when I get into trouble trying to talk about touchy-feely things. I know what I think inside, but talking about how what I think works, well that's not easy for a biker dude, y'know? We need Sara, my girlfriend. She's the one who talks easy about the creative spirit." He ruffled Charley's fur. "But we don't have my girlfriend, so I'll give the whole thing my best shot and we'll see how it goes."

"That'd be nice, because what I'm trying to do is really important." I hated that I could feel tears coming. I tried taking deep breaths to make them stay away but that didn't help much.

"Well, now I *really* need my girlfriend. Why the tears?"

I was lucky enough to have a Kleenex in my pocket, so I pulled it out and stuck it in my eyes. "I hate that everything is so hard for Dad. He had this big plan for traveling around. He was all excited about it, and it's not being the way it was supposed to be."

"Well, for starters, I know you're only a kid, but you have to know that nothing is the way it's supposed to be. There's no such thing as 'supposed to be' in life."

"But there is 'trying to be' isn't there?"

Eli smiled. "Well yeah. I guess there is that."

"I think Dad's trying to be happier, but it doesn't seem to be working. That's why I need to find a way to give him the peace and quiet he keeps saying he wants. Talking to people like you is the only way I can think of to do it."

Eli stared at his carving, twirling it a few times. "I got that, and I'm going to try my best to help. Okay?"

I nodded my head. The tears had stopped and I tossed the Kleenex in the trashcan.

"So, here goes." He squeezed his hands around the carving. "Well first of all I want to make sure you get it that the creative spirit I'm talking about is the part of me that turned this branch into an eagle's head. And that part, the part that communicates with Charley and the tree branch, is the best part of me. It's not the guy who races around on a Harley that gets what you're looking to give your dad. It's my creative spirit that takes me where you want your dad to go."

"What's a creative spirit? Like where exactly is it, and does everyone have one?"

The glow came back to his face. "They sure do. It's like Sara says, your creative spirit lives right in here." He tapped his heart, and then he kept patting other parts of himself, "and here, and here and here, all over, inside and out. She taught me to see it as being the part of all of us that makes us unique, y'know, gives us qualities that other folks don't have, like whittling for me, and sculpting for her, and other things for other dudes, like painting or growing flowers or playing the piano, or even being a very caring friend. Now what that is for your dad I don't know, but I do know that everyone has their own unique creative spirit. And when I hang out with mine, that's when I get to have peace." He twirled the branch. "And if I'm lucky, I get a bonus like this when I come back to being Eli, the Harley guy, again."

"And does having peace last when you're not hanging out with your creative spirit?"

"You're a real trip, kiddo. I don't want what I'm going to say to be a downer, but no it doesn't last. I get that you want to give peace to your dad and you want him to have it all the time. But it doesn't work like that, or not for me anyway. It's something I get when I hang out with my creative spirit. But I can't be there all the time, because life moves in and takes over. I guess you're worrying about life taking over your dad all the time. Is that it?"

"Yeah, I guess so."

"What about your mom? Does she want peace too?"

"I don't know, and I don't want to ask. I'd probably end up ruining my secret if I asked her that. For sure she'd want to know why, and I want the gift to be a surprise, so I'm not telling anyone in my family. And Dad, well I don't know whether he even has a creative spirit because he doesn't do anything but work."

"Hey, c'mon now kiddo," said Eli, running his hand back and forth over his buzz cut. "You don't make the big bucks needed to buy one of those fancy travel machines without being some creative guy. Maybe not the peace and quiet kind of creative, but creative, big time!"

"What's the difference between the peace and quiet kind of creative and Dad's kind? I don't understand."

"Boy, oh boy! We need a lot more time, as well as my girlfriend to pull this whole thing together. I'm no businessman, and I'm not really that hot an artist, but I do know that what you're after is about getting in touch with a part of yourself that's unique to you. I sure didn't know anything about being unique until I met Sara, and she's the one who helped me figure it out. So that makes me one lucky dude, doesn't it."

"It sure does. But I wouldn't have any idea how to do that for my dad."

"Well, maybe you can, or maybe you can't. But what you're *trying* to do, that's way past unique, and when your dad gets to find out what you're up to, he's going to think so too, whether he gets to have peace and quiet or not."

Eli swung his legs over the bench and closed up his knife. "Now it's time I got on the road, so me and Charley gotta get packed up."

With those words Charley hopped off the table and shook his thousand strands of hair. He ran over and lifted his leg on a bush and had a long stretch before he raced to his carrier that was on the ground by the motorcycle. He barked for Eli to open the door. Eli did and Charley jumped in. We both laughed.

Eli handed the carving to me. "This is for you, kiddo. Maybe I can't give you the answers you want, but I can give you the result of the answers I get when I'm hanging out with this thing you want for your dad."

I took the carving and squeezed it tight. "It's really beautiful. Are you sure you want to give it away?"

"I wouldn't give it to just anyone, but I do want you to have it for remembering me and Charley, because we aren't going to forget you." He reached into his tent and pulled out a few branches that he handed me. "These are for giving whittling with your dad a try. You never can tell how or when his creative spirit is going to show up."

There were too many to hold in my hands along with the eagle head, so I stuck them under my arm. "Thanks a lot. You're the first person I've talked to about peace and you sure made talking fun. I wish I could've met your girlfriend."

"Maybe you didn't meet her for real, but you got to meet her through the eagle's head. I'd never have been able to make something like that without her. Having a creative spirit was all hooey until I got to be with Sara, and now it's the best part of me."

"Wow!" I twirled the carving between my fingers like he did, and it almost looked real.

"It's the best part of you too, kiddo. What you're doing for your dad, that's about as creative as it gets. Now get out of here before I get all mushy."

"I bet motorcycle dudes don't get mushy much, do they."

"You're right about that. You're a definite first for me. Now scoot!"

I scooted all right, like about four feet off the ground. Eli hadn't only made my assignment fun, but he made what I was doing feel sort of important.

I put the eagle's head carving at the back of my private drawer beside the special seashell that Aunt Alyssa, had given me. At the time she told me it meant 'luck', along with 'happiness near water'. I'd sort of forgotten about it, but right then I decided to take it out of hiding and put it on the shelf at the end of my bed. That way I could look at it every day and be reminded of luck and happiness. For sure, both those things had happened with meeting Eli.

I'd like to have put his carving out too, but the whole thing was so special and so private and I didn't want any questions about where it came from or why, like I knew Josh would try to get out of me. Not that he cared or anything, but he sure liked to niggle me.

I put the other branches in the drawer for when the right time to bring up whittling with Dad showed up.

I got out Amy's notepaper and sat at the table and wrote her about the whole thing as best I could. As I wrote about being unique, I wondered whether there was anything in Dad's notes that would show me something unique about him.

His file box was behind the chair. My heart skipped like crazy as I got up and slipped a few sheets from one of the folders. But it about stopped altogether when I realized the scribbles were way beyond deciphering. Maybe there was something unique about Dad in there, but whether it was creative or not I'd never know. I felt too guilty peeking, so I put the papers back and went to finish Amy's letter by telling her that making me her best friend was a perfect expression of her unique creative spirit.

That afternoon, when I came home from the rec center where I'd left Mom and the boys watching a game show I didn't want to see, I was totally surprised to find Dad sitting at the table, copying something from one of the magazines he had piled beside him. He didn't look up when I came in, he just went right on copying.

"Hi Dad," I said. "You're home early."

"Hmmm," was all that came out of him.

I plunked myself on the chair. Being alone with Dad was pretty unusual, and after spending all day thinking about Eli and the creative spirit, my brain started digging for words to ask Dad that might tell me something unique about him, seeing as the note-peeking hadn't worked. One thing for sure, Dad hated being interrupted when he was working.

I guess me sitting there saying nothing was hard to ignore because he looked over, and with a big frown that dug grooves in his forehead, he asked, "Did you want something?"

"It's okay. I don't want to interrupt, but I was wondering if you'd ever done any whittling."

"What? Did you say whittling?" His frown didn't go away. It got bigger.

"Never mind. We can talk about it later if you're busy." I got up.

Dad stared at me like he was studying me for an exam. "Wait a minute." He looked back at his work. He slid his papers and magazines over to the window. The frown on his forehead went away as he patted the table across from him. "Sit down, sweetheart. We don't have to wait for later. I'm never too busy for you. Sometimes I get my priorities out of whack, and you, well you've got a great way of bringing them back to center."

I sat fast.

"When I was a boy scout I used to whittle, but I wouldn't say I was good at it. Why do you ask?"

I couldn't believe how fast everything had spun around. The frown was gone and Dad had just said he was never too busy for me. I didn't know what had happened, but I honestly didn't care about the creative spirit or anything else. I just cared that I was sitting with my dad who was talking about whittling as if what I thought mattered.

I said, "Eli, the motorcycle guy, I watched him whittling this morning and it looked like fun."

"I saw that. Was he any good? He seemed like a nice guy."

"He was." Suddenly I felt like I had to show Dad the carving. He'd said Eli was a nice guy so I knew that was enough reason, and

I wouldn't have to explain why. "He gave me what he made, Dad. It's really good. Let me show you."

I knew Dad had other stuff on his mind but I really wanted him to see it so I ran and got it.

He twirled it around. "Wow, I'll say he's good. This is beautiful. Why don't you put it out for everyone to see."

"I don't know. I want to keep it in my private drawer, but I wanted you to see it."

Dad reached into his pocket and brought out his key ring with a pocketknife on it. "I've got this knife that'd be good for whittling if you want to give it a try, that is if you can find any decent branches to whittle on."

"Eli gave me some of those too." I jumped up and ran to get one.

"Great!" Dad had a look, and then he took the knife off his key ring and opened the blade. He slid a shaving off the side. "This branch is perfect for whittling."

"Eli gave me more, so you can use that one if you want to make something. I'd like to watch."

"Not right now, sweetheart. I'm in the middle of something else here." He patted the magazines. "I've only borrowed these from the library overnight."

He closed up the blade and handed me the knife along with the branch. "If whittling turns out to be what you like to do, I'll get you a knife of your own. In the meantime use mine but be careful. It's sharp."

"I will, and thanks Dad." He didn't know it, but the thanks wasn't for the knife. It was for telling me I had a way of bringing him back to center. I sure hoped my assignment worked so he'd be back to center all the time.

I put the carving back in my drawer and hung on to the knife and branch. "You can get back to work now, Dad. I'll go outside and try whittling myself."

"Good." He slid his magazines in front of him. "Maybe we can take a whirl at it together later. Work overwhelms me sometimes, so thanks for the distraction."

"You're welcome." I said that to be polite when what I really wanted to do was give him a hug, but he was already back to the magazine.

I went outside to Eli's table instead of ours, hoping there might still be some of Eli left there to help me figure out how to do it.

I sat down and opened up the knife and studied the branch to see if anything showed up on it. Nothing. I sliced off some shavings and then kept shaving, but in the end all I got was a pile of shavings and a destroyed branch. Eli had already told me my creative spirit was busy trying to help Dad get peace, so I decided maybe it wasn't supposed to do more than one thing at a time. I cleaned up the mess and put the knife in my pocket. I went back to the rec center.

New Friends

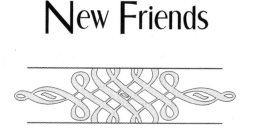

Early the next morning Dad took off for the library, but he was back in less that an hour. He said he'd only gone to return the magazines and he wanted us to pack up because he'd finished researching in Virginia Beach and needed to get closer to a big city. None of that was a big surprise to any of us because Virginia Beach wasn't all that big and the campground had gotten pretty stuffed. Dad said he wanted to go to Jacksonville, to the campground he'd booked earlier.

I went with him to the store to call for a reservation, and when he did, he found out the added campsites were finished all right, but already full. The campground owner said there'd be more coming if he could wait at least another week.

The guy who owned our campground was in the store at the same time, and I guess he'd been listening, because when Dad hung up he told Dad he had a friend who owned a campground in Myrtle Beach. He knew Dad was researching stuff, and he said Myrtle Beach didn't have much of a library, but it was close to decent-sized towns.

Well, with that, all the disappointment went away as Dad got right into doing his big selling thing, and before long our owner was ready to call his friend to see if he'd let us stay there.

"The guy owes me big time, so if nobody's staying on his guest campsite I'm sure he'll let you have it." He picked up the phone and said not a whole lot of words that made much sense to me. Then he hung up and smacked Dad on the back. "You're in, my friend. Go right on down if y'want."

Dad laughed. "Thanks, pal. You're a real savior." He stuck out his hand and they shook like crazy.

When we got home, everyone checked out the Myrtle Beach campground in the Big Book. It wasn't on the beach, but there was a bridge across the highway and a fancy restaurant at the end of the bridge. The campground had a rec hall and a pool, with lots of trees and buckets of flowers.

We took off right away, and when we got there everything the Big Book said was true, and even better than that, the guy treated us like long lost friends. I mean the favor he owed must've been huge to get that kind of greeting. His guest site was right next to the store, which didn't make Dad too happy with all the people running around, but it was a total lucky break because for sure there were no other empty spaces.

It was way past lunchtime so I suggested to Dad that we splurge and have lunch at the fancy restaurant. All he said was, "This place is a zoo. I think we should've tried for somewhere more remote."

"Like where, Dad?" Josh asked. "Why don't you just ignore what you don't like and take all of us to the restaurant. You can have a shot of whisky and pretend you're on vacation just this once."

"I don't pretend, Josh. It's not my style."

Of course I had to practically bite my tongue off to keep from asking him what he'd call what he was doing when he was acting so happy just before I caught him crying.

"I'll make tuna and pickle sandwiches while you do the hookups Sammy," said Mom.

"Bummer," muttered Josh.

I had another idea. "Why don't you take me to the restaurant Josh? I'll be your date. I'd be a good date."

"Yeah, that'll be the day. I'd rather have tuna and pickles thanks."

"Okay," said Mom. "Everyone be nice."

Ty didn't say anything, but he did add a bunch of cheese slices to Mom's tuna sandwiches. We all knew that those two things together made Dad happy.

We were just finishing our lunch at the picnic table when into the campground came what looked like an old school bus, all painted up in crazy colors. The driver stopped at the store, went in, and when he came out he drove right into the campsite next to ours that had just emptied.

"Wow!" said Josh. "There's a hippie setup if I ever saw one."

The bus was painted blue and red with purple, orange and white stripes across the top and the bottom. The inside curtains were the same colors as the bus. I figured they were tie-dyed to match.

The driver was hardly parked when the door burst open and out spilled a couple of kids, a really cute girl around Josh's age with a whole bunch of curly hair (like Mom used to have, only hers was black) and a younger boy with red hair and freckles, who looked to be around nine or ten. After them came a neat-looking lady with long, silky black hair. She looked like a real Indian, wearing a gauzy skirt that came to just above her bare feet. She had on an embroidered blouse, with long strands of colored beads around her neck. Behind her was a tall, skinny guy with brown hair pulled back in an elastic band, with a beaded headband around his forehead. He and the kids were all wearing tie-dyed t-shirts, just like the curtains, only different colors.

Questions began spinning in my head for the lady, but not the man. He only looked around for barely a minute before he went back in the bus.

"Why don't I go see if I can help them get set up," said Josh. It wasn't hard to see he was eyeballing the girl.

"Good luck," said Mom with a laugh that pretty much everyone shared. Josh hardly knew how to put our trailer together let alone what went into making everything work over there.

"I'm going fishing," said Dad. "Anyone coming with me?"

Dad was home because it was Sunday and the library was closed. Ever since he'd started going to the library he had tried to be a regular dad on Sundays. Regular stuff for him was fishing, mostly with Ty, watching TV, and playing pool or pinball with whoever wanted, and sometimes board games, like Monopoly or Sorry, with all of us. That was also shopping day for Mom with the car there, and sometimes Dad would even go with her to help with the bags. Some Saturdays he'd work at home, and that was another good day for shopping, so occasionally I'd go with Mom.

I particularly liked the Sundays when all of us would go out for lunch and then maybe even a movie, which didn't happen often. As long as we didn't want to go to touristy places, Dad was happy to do almost anything we wanted.

"Sure," said Ty. "I'll come."

"I'll come too," I said. "I don't want to fish, but I'll catch the sand fleas." What I really wanted to do was talk to the bus lady. But with all the commotion going on over there I knew that wasn't going to happen any time soon. Besides, I loved digging for sand fleas. Dad had a collapsible pole, with a metal basket on the end, that he kept in the trailer storage box. It worked great for digging up the crusty little critters who lived under the wet sand. Sometimes I'd get dozens with one scoop and other times I wasn't so lucky, but it was still fun. A lot of them were almost an inch long.

The fishing part was okay until I caught a fish, and then I hated what followed, like taking out the hook and then killing the poor thing. Both Mom and me, we preferred collecting shells on the beach after the live parts had left.

Mom said she wanted to meet the new neighbors, so Ty, Dad, and me took off.

When we got to the beach I noticed an old fisherman a little way down from us. That was the first time I'd ever seen anyone fishing alone, and being that he was such an old guy, I figured he'd have ideas for my assignment.

After I'd gotten a pile of sand fleas, I said I wanted to go see if the old guy had caught anything. Dad seemed okay with that as long as I wasn't a bother, so I went and stood behind him while he put a shrimp on his line.

I looked in his pail and it was empty. "Nothin' in there yet," he said. "Will be soon though." And then he went out in the water a little way before he cast the line. He reeled it in and cast it again about three more times in different places. When he got that done, he backed up and stood beside me.

"Did you aim somewhere in particular?" I asked. "My dad doesn't do that."

"Sure did."

"Do you mind if I watch?"

"Nope. Don't mind."

I pointed at Dad and told him that he wasn't much fun to watch, seeing as he wasn't too lucky catching fish. "Do you think he should be aiming somewhere special, and maybe even using shrimp instead of sand fleas?"

He looked over at Dad and Ty who were just standing there holding their rods with the lines out in the water. "Fishin's got a lot more to it than luck, little girl. I'm aimin' for the troughs 'cause that's where the flounder are. They cruise the troughs lookin' fer good bait, and if they see my shrimp, then whammo, I got me one."

I told him my name was Zoey if he'd rather call me by name. I didn't like the "little girl" thing.

"I'm Ollie," he said. "Ollie Watts. Y'can call me Ollie if y'want. Everybody does."

I asked him if telling me his name meant I could talk to him.

"Depends what's on yer mind, and somethin's in there, so might's well get to it."

With that opening, I leapt right in. "Do you get peace from fishing Ollie?"

Either he didn't hear me or I'd thrown him for a loop. "Pardon? Do I get peace? Is that what y'said?"

I told him yes.

He yanked his rod up in the air as if maybe he had a fish on it. He tilted his head toward the rod like he was listening to the line. He told me to wait a minute while he checked the bait. He reeled the line in and the hanging shrimp looked the same as before, so he went back in the surf and cast the line out a few times again.

Once he got everything where he wanted it, he said, "Ain't never thought 'bout that, little girl. Where'd y'come up with it anyway?"

Well that was the perfect chance to tell Ollie about my assignment, and seeing as Dad never fished for long I figured I'd better get on with it. I didn't tell Ollie about what Eli had said, just about Dad and how hard the trip had been for him so far, and what I wanted to do to help him. Ollie kept watching his line while I kept talking. When I finished, he turned and stared at me without saying anything.

He swished his line here and there before he finally said, "Well, if that ain't 'bout the cutest thing I've heard'n ages, peace 'n quiet fer your daddy's birthday. How y'plannin' on doin' that, if y'don't mind me askin'?"

"The quiet part's easy. We'll just get out of Dad's way for the day. But the peace part, well I haven't got that figured out yet. Would you have any ideas?"

Ollie held the rod in one hand while he pulled the brim of his hat down and wriggled it from side to side. I remembered Eli being quiet like that, and then saying he didn't have any ideas. My heart felt like a shriveled prune. "I'll go if you want me to. I don't want to bother you."

"Y'do too!" He grinned at me. "Can y'be quiet a minute'r two fer me t'think some?"

I looked over at Ty and Dad. They didn't seem to be going anywhere, so I told Ollie I could be quiet for as long as he wanted. I sat down and tried to build a castle, but the sand was too wet.

Ollie worked his rod up and down, swishing it this way and that so busily I thought I might have disappeared for him.

Then the line tugged hard, and for sure Ollie had himself a fish. I jumped up to watch him whip his rod in the air, jerking it real hard.

He started cranking the winder, heaving the rod up with lots of jerks. I could tell the fish was huge from the way the rod bent almost in half. Ollie had to work hard to reel the fish in. He managed to do it though, and the thing was a big sucker.

"Here, hold this." He handed me the rod. He lifted the line and set the flapping fish on the board, and before I had a chance to look away he clobbered it over the head with a piece of wood. I guess he had to do that to make it quiet enough to get the hook out of its mouth. It was horrible, especially since the fish kept twitching.

Ollie stuck his fingers through the gills and held the fish up in front of him, bobbing his head up and down. Dad and Ty, and all the other people who'd been watching, clapped. He dropped the fish in the pail. He took the rod from me and reeled it tight before he put it in the holder. "Thanks, little girl. Y'sure came in handy. It's good t'have someone along t'share the fun with." He sunk into his sagging beach chair.

"I'm glad. And that's a really big fish!" I sat back down on the sand beside Ollie, hoping he'd remember the minute or two he'd said he wanted for my question.

He closed his eyes, but in a few seconds he opened them and looked at me. "Y'know what, little girl? That there gives me sucha good feelin', catchin' a biggun. That's a real feelin' of satisfaction. Plannin' somethin' and havin' it happen. That'sa feelin' that surely does give me alotta pride. These guys are hard t'come by, but if y'do the proper plannin', y'can count on it payin' off."

"And does all that maybe give you peace, all that planning and stuff?"

"Don't know 'bout peace, but sure does give me lotsa satisfaction. But maybe the two things're the same anyway."

"Dad doesn't have much patience. So he'll never get satisfaction from fishing. But he is doing a lot of planning for a new job. Do you suppose if he finds a new job, he'll get satisfaction, and maybe even peace, all on his own?"

Ollie snickered. "Y'mean, ruin yer birthday present? That'd be no fun."

"It's not supposed to be fun Ollie. It's serious. Do you think it's silly?"

"No! 'Course I don't think it's silly. I just ain't never thought 'bout it. It's swell that y'made me think 'bout what's goin' on inside me when I'm fishin'. Real swell." He yanked on the hat brim again and swiveled it some more.

Then he looked at me again. "D'you know what, little girl? If I were t'take a guess here, I'd have t'say the best peace yer daddy ever got was the day he got you. Havin' you would be better than catchin' the biggest fish in the world."

I didn't know what to say to that, but I knew for sure my cheeks were red. I managed to get out a squeaky, "Thanks" before I looked over and saw Dad and Ty packing up. "My dad's getting ready to leave, so I guess I better go."

"Looks that way, but it's sure bin fun talkin' t'ya, though. Yup, sure has."

"Are you staying at this campground? Maybe you could teach Dad and Ty about fishing in the troughs, that is as long as you don't tell them what I'm doing. Would that be okay?"

"That'd be swell. I'm not stayin' here, but I do fish here lots. This beach works great fer catchin' flounder."

Not knowing if and when Dad would want to move on, I wasn't sure we'd be around long enough for Dad or Ty to learn what Ollie had to teach. I didn't tell Ollie any of that. I just thanked him and took off.

Dad and Ty hadn't caught any fish, and even though they hadn't been trying for all that long, I didn't bother to say anything. I made sure Ty emptied the can of sand fleas in the wet sand so the little critters could squiggle their way back to safety.

We headed home, and when we got there we shoved everything under the trailer and went to sit with Mom and Josh at the bus peoples' table, along with the lady and the kids. They turned out to be Lauren who was fifteen and Jesse who was nine. The lady was their mom, and her name was Maya McLean. She told me and my brothers to call her Maya, which surprised me, because I didn't call many adults by their first name. It felt really friendly. Her husband, the kid's dad, wasn't there, but his name was Zack.

Maya told us about how she'd inherited money from her grandfather and bought the old bus. She said that Zack had just come back from Vietnam, and although he wasn't wounded physically, he sure was mentally, and he needed to transition into the real world before going back to work as a car salesman. She was a teacher, so they decided to take the summer to give travelling in the converted bus a chance to heal Zack and show the kids the country. The plan was that if everyone loved travelling, she'd take a leave of absence from the classroom and homeschool the kids.

She was like a little kid, telling us about the two months of fun they'd had ripping out the old bus seats and painting and fixing the thing up to live in. "Zack's always been good at do-over projects. But after ten days on the road, I'm not too sure about him as a bus driver."

Except for the awful war part about Zack, the story was good, but all I could think about was the great stuff a teacher would have to say for my assignment.

Josh got up. "Want to go check out the beach, Lauren?"

Obviously he wasn't paying any attention to Maya's story, and I figured Lauren wasn't either, because she said, "Sure," and the two of them took off. That was fine with me. It meant there'd be two less people to get rid of so I could talk to Maya.

Well that didn't happen. She and Mom hadn't stopped talking and it didn't look like they were going to. I knew Mom was missing her friends, but I had no idea how much until I watched her bubble and glow at the same time.

Seeing as Dad was looking bored, I figured it was my chance to get him to whittle with me. Ty and Jesse were into Jesse's Legos and Dad didn't seem to care about Legos. Neither did I, so I asked him if he'd like to try whittling.

"Sure," he said as he got off the bench. "Let's go over to our table because there's enough going on here." He put his arm around me. "But there is a problem, sweetheart. We've only got one knife."

"That's not a problem, Dad. I don't want to whittle, I just want to watch you. Maybe I'll learn something. I already tried, but I really need a lesson."

"Okay. Don't count on anything close to Eli's talent, but get the knife and the branch and I'll give it a try."

I ran and got them, and once Dad got started he hardly had any shavings off the branch when the knife slipped and cut his finger. "Jeezuz!" he hollered, dropping the knife and tossing the branch across the campsite with his finger spurting blood.

Then all the commotion between Maya knocking the boys' Lego building over on her dash to get paper towels, and Mom darting into the bus for a first aid kit, as well as Dad's swearing up a storm with Jacque and Jolie supporting him, the whole thing was unique all right, but not in a good way. I closed up the knife and stuck it in my pocket for another time, even though I really didn't expect another time to show up.

Finally things settled down, and a rattled Mom, a bandaged Dad, and the yippy poodles took off for a walk on the beach. Ty and Jesse packed up the Legos, and Maya, acting calm the way teachers do, said she thought we all ought to go explore the rest of the campground.

"Can we go swimming in the pool?" asked Jesse.

"Not right now, Jess," she said. "Why don't we go check out all of what's here first."

"No argument there," said Ty. "Let's do it."

So we did. The restaurant at the end of the bridge was super fancy, with huge windows that looked out over the ocean. It was built on tall stilts that were stuck in the sand, and the beach spread out a long way before it reached the water.

On the campground the rec center was great, with lots of table games and a big color TV. There was even free popcorn in a glass popper. The only trouble with all the fun we had exploring was that I didn't get a single chance to be alone with Maya.

Moving On

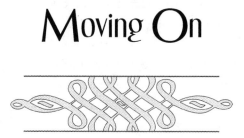

Just like I thought they would Mom and Maya got to be really good friends. Maya did turn out to be part Cherokee Indian, and her beaded necklaces that she made herself for sure showed off her unique creative spirit.

Mom was quick to get into stringing beads and I figured that was partly because of the friend thing, but mostly just to learn something new. Maya's plan was to sell the necklaces, so she was really happy to have Mom's help making them, and the big trade was that Mom got to keep whatever she wanted for herself.

Although Dad sure didn't like all the racket in the campground, he did find lots of places for his research in the close towns, enough that he was gone even more than before. I wished I could've gone with him and had some of those people to talk to. I wasn't finding anyone who looked like they wanted to talk to me, let alone answer my question, and there still weren't any girls my age anywhere. At least Ty was having fun with Jesse. And Josh, well Lauren had finally gotten her own board, so they were into nothing but surfing and each other.

I'd about given up on talking to Maya. If she wasn't with Mom, she had Zack wanting her for something or other, or Lauren wanting to show off the surfing skills that Josh was teaching her. Not that he was all that good himself, but he was sure getting a lot better every day.

The good part about Lauren having a surfboard was that Josh finally put his under the trailer. He only did it after he saw that hers wasn't stolen from under the bus.

Anyway, I got to see real fast that if I was ever going to get Maya to myself I'd better start stringing beads. I'd done some of that at summer camp so I pretty much knew how it worked, but Maya's beads sure were way more beautiful than anything I'd ever seen. Making neat designs with them was really fun and I turned out to be pretty good at it. But as far as getting Maya alone went, that wasn't working because Mom was there too. All I hoped was that at some point she might want to do something else.

Well none of that happened, and what was even worse was that Ty and Jesse got into the necklace thing too. They weren't very good at it, but what they were good at was sorting all the beads and trinkets that were jumbled together in ten different drawers of Maya's wooden box. She knew what was where by memory, but it sure helped Mom and me to have the drawers organized.

While we were all at it one morning, Ty came across a tiny silver dagger that about sent him over the moon. He strung it on a leather cord and put it around his neck with a very loud "Whoopee!"

"Perfect," said Maya. "I knew there was a tough guy in there somewhere. Good choice, Ty." He grinned so wide that we all hooted, which of course made the dogs hoot too.

"Keep it down over there," came Dad's voice from the trailer. We hadn't thought about Dad working because most Saturdays he'd go somewhere and talk to people who worked during the week. If we'd been looking, we'd have seen the car was still home.

A few minutes later he showed up with his yellow pad. "I'm going to the library to get something Meg. I won't be long, but I need you guys to pack up. We're leaving."

"What?" Mom gasped.

"Why, Dad?" I asked. "We're having fun. Why can't we …"

My words got cut off real fast. "Sorry, but I've got to move on. I've been everywhere and met everyone from around here, and now I need a city library, as well as city people to talk to."

"That old fisherman's back." said Ty. "Can we at least get some of the pointers he told Zo he'd teach us?""

"His name is Ollie," I said. "It'd be fun, Dad. You can come with us."

"Me too," Jesse said. "I hate fishing, so maybe pointers would help me like it better."

"You go if you want," said Dad. "But count me out. And before I get back, find us a campground Ty. Look for one off in the woods, maybe another state park. Just make sure it's near a city, that's all.

"But you can't have woods and beach at the same time Dad," said Ty. "And the rest of us want beach. We already got that figured out."

Dad slapped his pad against the side of the trailer. "Then don't worry about woods. Call the campground in Jacksonville Beach Meg. The guy said the extra campsites would be finished soon, and we've been here long enough that soon could be now. The number is circled in the Big Book."

"Fine," said Mom.

Maya gathered up the beads. "I'm going to put these away and go stretch out on the beach," she said.

Without saying a word, Mom headed into the trailer.

Ty got the fishing gear. "I'll go see Ollie. What about you, Zo? You coming?"

Mom worried me, so I said "I'm not ready yet. You guys go."

"Ready for what?" said Ty. "This is it Zo. There'll be no more Ollie."

I poked my head at the trailer and mouthed "Mom's upset."

Ty shrugged his shoulders. "C'mon Jesse, let's go." They took off.

I took the poodles inside and it was no surprise that they flew right past Mom into her room and under the pillows. She was in the kitchen cutting a salami roll in chunky slices that sure didn't make for sandwiches. "What're you doing Mom? It's too early for lunch." I was scared the end of one of her fingers was about to disappear.

"You butter the bread Zoey," she said. "I don't care if it's too early. We'll eat when your father gets back."

I dumped the bread out of the bag and slathered it with a whole lot of butter and mustard. "Are you okay, Mom? I mean you and Maya are really good friends, and all the bead-stringing is so much fun. Do you think there's anything we can do to change Dad's mind?" I knew I was babbling.

Mom didn't look up. She was into a third roll of salami and kept right on slicing, even though she already had more than enough. "I'll talk to him," she said, but her words were aimed more at the breadboard than me.

My insides cramped. I knew when Mom got weird, there was nothing I could do about it. I finished making the sandwiches with as much salami as I could stuff in them, and then I put the pile on a plate. I grabbed one for myself even though I sure wasn't hungry. I told Mom I needed to go get Ollie's pointers.

"Fine." The word was maybe even louder than before.

I left, and outside I had one bite of the sandwich and ripped up the rest and threw it in the air for the gulls. They snapped up the pieces in seconds, squawking like crazy. I watched them fly off, and suddenly I wanted to fly off with them. I'd fly way out over the ocean and land on a boat that was headed to the other side of the world where trailers didn't exist. Right then I hated everyone in my family, all of them except for maybe Ty. I'd go get him and he could fly away with me.

With that picture flooding my whole body I raced down the beach.

"Hey Zoey, will you come put some lotion on my back?"

Maya's voice smashed me back to earth so fast I lost my balance and teetered for a minute. I wanted to scream NO! I wanted Ty, and I wanted us to fly off. But now the seagull picture was gone, and there was Maya stretched out on her towel in the sand. I hadn't even seen her.

"Hey," she called again.

I tried to bring back the seagull by squeezing my eyes shut and picturing an eagle soaring. I saw the eagle all right, but at the same time a voice inside my head screamed, "MAYA'S ALL ALONE. YOU'RE LEAVING AND YOU'LL NEVER GET A CHANCE TO TALK TO HER IF YOU DON'T DO IT NOW."

I wanted to ignore that voice. I wanted to get Ty and disappear. I didn't want to spread lotion on anyone. But again inside my head I heard NOW. And before I had a chance to figure out where the voice was coming from, my legs steered me over to Maya and plopped me on the sand beside her.

Lying on her stomach, Maya reached around and undid the top of her bikini. She handed me her open bottle of lotion. She dropped her head on her folded arms and closed her eyes. I knelt beside her and spread the lotion on her back and legs while my head throbbed with the echo of the voice. I'd never heard voices in my head before, and I'd also never imagined doing stupid things like flying away. I wondered if maybe I was going crazy.

I put the top that was on the towel back on the bottle and sat down in the sand. Maya thanked me. Then she put her arms out, with her head on the blanket and her eyes closed.

I shifted around, wishing my other voice would command words out of me, because my regular voice was strangled.

Maya lifted her head. "Why all the wriggling? You're squirming like a scorched eel. Stretch out." She squiggled over on her blanket to make room for me before she put her head back down and closed her eyes.

I didn't move. My legs started to itch and I scratched like mad, even though nothing was there other than sand. Finally I forced out, "Do you know what peace is?"

"Mmmmm," she mumbled.

I held my legs against my chest to keep from kicking sand at her. "Did you hear me?"

Her eyes stayed closed. She felt around beside her, picked up the lotion and tossed it my way. "Here. If you're not going to stretch out, then at least give your scorched eel some relief."

"I don't want any." I tossed it back.

She lifted her head and glared at me. "What's going on? You're acting very strange."

I fell onto my back and blew out a huge breath.

She reached behind herself and did up her bikini before she hiked onto her elbow. "Okay. I surrender. So what's this about peace?"

Right then Ty and Jesse came running with Ty's fishing stuff, and a big flounder hanging from a rope. "Ollie gave me this. He told me it was for you, Sis. Isn't it a beauty?"

"I love it," said Maya. "But get it out of my face."

"Yeah, and you go clean it Ty," I said.

"You might tell Ollie thanks."

"I can't. I'm busy."

"Sheesh," said Ty. He and Jesse took off.

"Being surly, that's not like you, Zoey," said Maya. "What's going on?"

"It…it's no big deal." I got up.

Maya flipped onto her seat. "Hey, wait a minute. I'm sorry. You're serious, aren't you?"

"It doesn't matter. I've gotta go."

Tears came barreling from out of nowhere. I took off before Maya could see them, and I ran down the beach so fast my heart about burst through my chest. I finally dropped to the sand and spread out like the scorched eel I was supposed to be. I put my arms over my eyes and lay there trying to catch my breath. I rubbed my eyes dry, but I was afraid to open them in case a million people were staring at me. I stayed that way for a long time, with my mind running circles around itself.

Something touched my arm. My eyes popped open and there stood Maya. "I'm sorry. I didn't handle that whole thing very well. Are you okay Zo?"

I felt more tears coming, but I made them stay away by thinking how nice that was of her to find me. She asked if it was okay if she sat. I didn't say anything and she sat anyway. "Is it about leaving? We're leaving too y'know."

I sat bolt upright. "You are? Honestly?"

"Honestly. After I saw how upset you were, I went and told your mom. She was pretty upset herself, so I told her there was no way I was going to let any of you out of my sight. We're buddies, all of us. We won't be able to go today though, because Zack's got work to do on the bus engine. But we will be coming tomorrow."

"Wow, that's great" Boy, was that ever a good surprise.

"So that was it? You're all better now?"

"Yeah, I'm really glad."

"But what about the peace question?

"I was just wondering what peace means to you, that's all."

"That's all? Peace is a whole lot more than 'that's all,' isn't it?"

"I don't know. That's why I asked."

"Well to tell you the truth I'm no authority on peace, because I don't spend a lot of time thinking about it. I have my hands full with this 'on the road' life change, just like you guys. Peace is so far off the radar for me that I'd have to pull it in and examine it before I could tell you what it means. But I think we'll have to wait until we get where we're going to talk about it, because right now we'd better get back. Your dad is hot to trot, remember?" She got up. "So would later be okay?"

I said it would, but all I could think was that I should've paid attention to the voice inside my head instead of freaking out. I knew getting Maya alone again would be hard.

When we got home Dad wasn't there, but an excited Mom came running with news about getting two reservations at the campground in Jacksonville Beach, one for us that day, and the other one for the bus the next day. Ty had the Big Book open on the table and everyone was eyeballing the pictures that showed the campground on a huge piece of property on the ocean side of the highway. There was not just a rec center, a pool and store, but even a small park. The best part of all was that we didn't have to cross the highway to get to the beach.

"Hey, Lauren," said Josh, with his arm around her. "If we're leaving today and you're not, I think you oughta come with us."

Lauren laughed. "Sounds good to me."

"Yeah, like where are you going to put her?" I asked.

Josh gave me one of his arm punches. "Why don't you stay behind Creep, trade places."

"I wish!" I would've loved to have traded places with Lauren, but I sure didn't want to ride in the bus.

And I didn't want to talk about it either. I was mad that Dad wasn't home, because if I'd known, I could've had more time to talk to Maya, and now she and Mom were all tied up, babbling over the fun of going somewhere else.

I went in the trailer and pulled out the letter I'd started to Amy so I could tell her what had just happened. But before I could get into that, I had to bring her up to date on Ollie and the bus people and everyone getting into stringing beads. I scribbled on about everything, right up to where I wanted to fly off with the seagulls and how a voice inside me yelled that I had to go tell Maya about my assignment.

As soon as I wrote that, I realized I couldn't tell Maya about my assignment. She and Mom were like best friends, and if I told Maya, she'd have to tell Mom. Amy and I both knew that best friends didn't keep secrets.

I didn't bother writing about that because I knew Amy would be stuck on the part about my other self anyway. So I asked her to write me and let me know if she thought I was going crazy. I said we were just leaving for Jacksonville, where there'd be a huge library and hundreds of research chances for Dad, so we'd probably stay long enough for her to get the letter to me. I let her know I'd send the address as soon as I knew we'd be staying.

The road trip was as boring as usual, that is until Ty came up with the best idea ever. "Now that we're headed to Florida, Dad, how about you get a bunch of research material from the library, and while you're working at home, we'll take the car and go to Disney World. They opened The Magic Kingdom last year. Our teacher went and he said it was great!"

It only took a second for Dad to say he liked the idea.

"Disney World's got to be a lot better than the boardwalk," said Mom. "At least the buildings aren't falling down."

"The Magic Kingdom. Wow! That'd be fun," I said. "But are you sure you don't want to come with us Dad? Maybe there's no snow, but you could jump off the roller coaster."

"Now there's an idea. Then I'd be gone and we wouldn't have to worry about finding me a new job."

"That's awful. It was supposed to be a joke, and now you've made me really sad." I sunk back into my seat.

"I'm sorry, sweetheart. I've made me sad too. There's nothing I'd like more than to play at Disney World, and believe me, playing is exactly what I'm looking to do at whatever I come up with for my new job. Count on it."

"Okay," I said. "I will count on it."

"Me too," said Ty.

"Yeah, me too," said Josh.

"Have you guys noticed all the signs for Savannah?" asked Ty. "We studied U.S. cities last year and it's one of the most historic, so it'd be great for sightseeing. How about we pull off the highway and take a tour, Dad? It doesn't have to be a big deal. We can park the car and catch a tour bus."

That idea sure pumped me, and probably Josh and Mom too, but all Dad came out with was, "If you think Cape Cod was overrun with tourists, you have no idea. Savannah, well no, Ty. I'm not stopping in Savannah."

"Thanks for all the consideration, Dad," said Josh. There are four more of us y'know!"

Boy, my brother didn't need an inside self to say the bold stuff. He was just outspoken naturally.

"That's right," said Dad. "And it's the four of you that have me wound in knots. It's you I'm thinking of every second, and that's why I can't go making myself crazy in a mob of tourists. I have to keep centered and focused. Mayhem and madness, that's what Savannah would be like in July."

"Okay," Ty sighed. "It was worth a try, that's all. I'll be driving in a few years, and then I'll take whoever wants to go."

"Now there's a plan," said Dad. "Thanks, Ty.

Mom rested her head on Dad's shoulder, squiggling it in closer to his neck. With my head on my pillow against the window I imagined what it would've been like to have flown away with Ty. I pictured us soaring through the sky and I even saw us landing on this huge boat with billowing sails. I'm not sure what happened next because I drifted off to sleep and stayed that way until Mom announced we'd landed at the new campground.

I threw open the car door and leapt out. I flung my cramped legs into jumping jacks while the poodles whipped around in circles. I leashed them.

"Wow!" said Josh, taking in the place. "Looks good, huh Dad?"

"Shows promise," said Dad, heading into the store.

It showed more than promise to me, being right on the ocean. There was a line of huge palm trees next to the highway, and behind them was the check-in store where we were parked, with a pool connected on one side and a rec center on the other. I couldn't see the promised park, but I looked forward to finding it.

"Nice place," said Mom.

"Let's go check out the rec center," said Ty.

"I'll do it," said Josh.

I wanted to see inside the store so I handed Mom the leashes. She followed the boys and I went to check in with Dad.

The big expansion must've included the store because the shelves were stocked high and everything looked brand new. One wall was total paperback books and another one was total cooler and freezer.

The store lady was talking about books with a couple over in that section, and the registration sheets were on the counter. Dad looked at one, filled it out and then wrote a check.

I couldn't help staring at the lady. She was about Mom's age, but definitely not like Mom. This lady had short, pitch black, spiky hair with shots of purple thrown in. I'd never seen anyone who looked like that and I thought of Morticia on *The Addams Family*. The people on that TV show were a spooky bunch. This lady didn't look exactly spooky, but she did look like she and Morticia could be friends.

She came back to the counter to take care of us while the couple stayed with the books. "You folks come a long way today?" Her wide smile showed off a gold star in her front tooth.

Dad didn't say anything about that. He handed her the sheet and his check. "We have a reservation." His voice sure wasn't friendly.

"We came from Myrtle Beach," I said, hoping the long drive might explain Dad being like he was.

She looked at both the check and the registration sheet, and then at a list from under the counter, before she ripped off the carbon copy and handed it to Dad. "You're right, you do have a reservation for it looks like a week. Welcome."

She took a map of the campground from a pile and circled our campsite. She handed it to Dad, and I couldn't help but notice her nails were the same dark purple as her lipstick. "Nice nails," I said.

"Thanks, babycakes." She gave me a big gold-tooth smile.

"C'mon Zoey, let's go." Dad headed out the door.

Outside I asked, "Why were you like that in there, Dad? I hope you like the campground better than you liked her. You sure were rude."

"I wasn't rude. I just wasn't interested. She's too wacko for me. Now let's go and get set up, and if we decide we like the place I'll come back later and pay for a year. How would you like that?" He put his arm around me with a squeeze.

"Not funny Dad."

Our new campsite turned out to be wider than usual which sure made Dad happy.

When the hookups were all done, the bunch of us went for a cool-off in the pool, and when we got back to the trailer Dad turned on the radio to the 'oldies' station. For the first time on the trip my parents danced. Karen Carpenter was singing "Close To You". There was hardly enough room for the two of them to stand together, let alone dance, especially with little poodles skittering between their feet. The rest of us pretty much gawked.

After we finished Ollie's flounder dinner that was really good, the boys went to the rec center and Mom gave me a dollar and asked me if I'd go to the store and get a loaf of bread for breakfast. I hadn't noticed we were short of bread, but it wasn't hard to figure out after watching them snuggle on the sofa, that what she wanted was some alone time with Dad. She made that totally obvious when she asked me to go check out the park I was so excited about. I said I would. I mean all of that was okay with me because I was dying to talk to the store lady. I figured with the gold star in her tooth and her spiky hair and all that purple thrown in, she'd probably have lots to say for my assignment.

When I got there she was reading a book at the register, so I picked up a loaf of bread and took it to the counter. She folded down a corner of the page and put the book on the windowsill behind her. She smiled a big gold-toothed smile. In a sing-songy voice she said, "Hi, good lookin'. What y'got cookin'?"

Boy, that sure caught me by surprise. "What's that supposed to mean?" I tried not to laugh in case that wasn't supposed to be funny. Actually it seemed more silly than funny.

"It means, how y'doin'?"

I told her I was doing good. "How'd you get the star in your tooth?" She looked real proud of it.

"A lot of bucks. That's how I got it." She smiled real wide to show it off. "Y'like?"

"Yeah, it's neat." It was more than neat the way it fit into the tooth so perfectly.

"Those words," she said, "they're from an old favorite of Granny's. I dig old-timey music. D'you?"

"I don't know anything about old-timey music. I'm only eleven, and my name's Zoey, if it's okay to tell you that."

"Of course it's okay. Do I look like you're not supposed to tell me your name?"

"No. But sometimes bosses don't like to talk to kids. And you look like the boss of this store, so I don't want to bother you if it's not okay. Are you the boss?"

"Nope. I'm just Angie who works here, so you can talk to me anytime." She put out her hand and I shook it.

"Should I call you Angie, because usually I call Mom's friends Mrs. whatever." I gave Angie the dollar bill I was clutching in my other fist. She put the money in the register and handed me the change that I put in my pocket.

"Well," she said, "I'm not your mom's friend. Or not yet anyway. So, Angie it is."

Although she was easy to talk to, I wasn't too sure about bringing up my assignment. Somehow it didn't seem to fit with old-timey music. "What's old-timey music?" I asked. "I mean, how old is it?"

"Old as my granny. So that's way up there, and she's a real swinger. That's what they called gals like her back then. She's got a record collection that'd blow your socks off and an old gramophone we play them on. She taught me swing dancin'. Wanna see?"

She came around the counter and grabbed my hand and whirled me around while she sang what sounded like more of the other song. Her striped purple mini-dress hugged her body tighter than a rubber glove.

I stumbled. "It's okay. I'll take your word for it."

"Sorry." She let go of my hand. "I didn't mean to upset you, babycakes. I get carried away sometimes." She went back around the counter and sat on her stool.

"You didn't upset me. I was just surprised because I don't know anything about old-timey music like you do. Is swing dancing fun? It looks like it might be."

"In the right place and at the right time it's fun all right." She stretched her arms across the counter and locked her fingers together. "I guess this isn't the right time though, so put that bread down for a minute and tell me what it is that you dig. I liked the way you covered for your surly old man earlier."

I felt my face redden. "My dad's not always surly, and he's not that old either."

She didn't say anything about me blushing. She just said, "That doesn't mean he's old, it just means he's your dad, so we won't talk about him. Like I said before, let's hear what you dig. You're overflowing with curiosity in there, and it's pouring out your eyes a mile a minute."

Before I could say anything, the bell over the door jangled and a bunch of people came in.

Angie hopped off the stool.

"Hi there," she called. To me, she said, "You better come back tomorrow babycakes, because things get ragged around here at night. Okay?"

"Okay." I said that, but I didn't feel okay. I felt all tangled up inside. After what Angie said about Dad, I wasn't sure I'd ever be able to talk to her about my assignment.

I didn't want to go back to the trailer in case Mom and Dad were still doing their thing, and I didn't want to go check out the park, so I went to the rec center.

The boys and a bunch of other people were watching *Bonanza*. I slouched on the sofa and stared at the TV, but I couldn't concentrate. All I wanted to do was write Amy about Angie. To kill time I sat through *Bonanza* and half of another show I didn't care about. Then I'd had it. I couldn't sit a minute longer, so I got up and went back to the trailer, hoping Mom and Dad were finished doing whatever.

On my way, I saw them headed to the beach with their arms around each other and the leashed poodles scampering along beside them. I got out Amy's notepaper and started to scribble.

Hi again:

I know I just wrote, but I have to tell you about this lady I met who works in the store at the campground we just got to in Jacksonville Beach. She's a combination of fun and neat and weird and outrageous all in one. I just wish there was some way I could take a picture of her for you but Mom dropped her camera the second day out and broke it. It wasn't a good one anyway and she's never bothered buying another one. She says with all the moving around, getting pictures developed would just be a hassle. Mom's never been much of a picture taker and that's probably why none of the rest of us are either. Postcards, like the ones I sent from Nantucket, show off most of what the good stuff looks like, and seeing as we don't do any more sightseeing, there hasn't been all that much good stuff. As for people pictures, up until the bus people and now Angie, the store lady, there hasn't been anyone I wanted you to see. Maybe Maya, the bus lady, has a camera and will take pictures of everyone for me. I'll be sure to ask her, just for you. But for me, my memory's the best camera in the whole world because what I see will be in there forever and I can look at it whenever I want. I know you'd like to actually see what we're doing but you can't, so just make up your own pictures from what I write and I'll try to make the words into good pictures for you. Okay?

I'm not going to write anymore now. I thought I was but I'm really tired so I'll tell you more about Angie after I talk to her again. And I'm not sure how long we'll be staying here yet, but my best guess is for a long time, so I'll let you know as soon as I do, and then you can send the letter I hope you've already written.

I'll leave this letter unfinished and pick it up later.

Getting To Know Angie

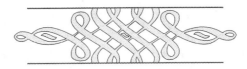

The next day was Sunday. Dad and Mom were in the trailer with me, and the boys and the poodles were at the rec center. Dad said we should go have a swim in the pool while a lot of the campers were at church. "I love having the pool to myself."

He was sitting on the sofa with his arm around Mom's shoulder. "Does that mean you want to go alone?" I asked.

He pulled Mom closer. "No, sweetheart. It means how about you and me and your mom have some pool time? Some exercise would be good. Agreed? Mom agreed. I did too.

When we got there, Dad was right about having the pool to ourselves. There were people sprawled out on lawn chairs and little kids in the baby pool, but the big pool was empty. We did the lap thing, but me, only as long as I could, because my legs weren't into kicking. They were into seeing Angie.

When Mom came up for air I told her I was going to get a look at the books. She waved an okay, so I picked up my towel, dried myself off and flung it over my shoulders.

In the store Angie was behind the counter sorting papers. "Hi, babycakes." She pushed the pile aside. "I'm glad you're back."

"Are you really? You look busy."

"Hey, I'm never too busy for a kid like you. You're a feel-good kid. So while it's quiet in here, let's get to talking about this thing you dig."

"Are you sure you want to hear? Because what I dig is about my dad and you called him surly. So if you don't like him you may not want to hear."

"Who says I don't like him? Calling him surly doesn't mean I don't like him. That only means he acted not too nice, that's all."

"What I dig is supposed to make him act nicer, or that's what I hope anyway. He used to be a big-shot businessman and now he's just my dad with no job who hauls our home around on wheels. I don't think that makes him happy."

"Well, whoopteedo! What's not to be happy about that? Sounds like a blast to me."

Angie slid off her stool and told me to wait while she got another stool from the storeroom. I watched the polka dots on her turquoise miniskirt pop up and down as she walked with a bounce. Her sandals that were laced up her tanned legs looked uncomfortable, but what did I know. My feet were bare.

She put the stool in front of the counter and went around back and sat on hers. "Now I'm ready, so sit yourself down and tell me more."

I sat. "I don't think babycakes sounds like you're ready Angie. That sounds silly, and what I'm trying to do isn't silly, or I hope it isn't."

"Hey, hey, No judgments here. Babycakes is a compliment. I only call the people who make me feel good babycakes. And like I said, you're a feel-good kid, and I'm going to call you the names that go with feel good. Okay?"

I told Angie I'd never been called anything like that so I wasn't sure whether it was good or not.

"Now you have," she said. "And before someone comes in here and messes up our time together, let's hear what you have to say."

"It's an assignment I gave myself. I want to give Dad peace and quiet for his birthday."

Angie's eyebrows shot up her forehead. "Why in blazes would you want to do that? A rocket ship to the moon sounds more like what he needs."

"You don't like my idea." I slid off the stool. I should've known she'd think it was dumb.

"Hey, I didn't say I didn't like it. So don't go anywhere. It's just that I guess I don't understand where you're coming from."

I sure didn't want to go, so I sat. "I don't know where I'm coming from. What does it mean anyway? I know people say it all the time, but what does peace and quiet really mean?"

"It's just one of those phrases people throw around like Frisbees. I've never been too good at catching Frisbees, and it feels like I'm not too good at catching your drift either. What're you after exactly?"

"Well peace and quiet, it's more than a phrase to my dad. He's always hollering that he wants it, like it's something he wants to get really bad. And I figure if I could find a way to get it for him, then maybe he'd be happy after he had it. That's all."

I told her I planned to talk to lots of people and ask them what it meant to them. Then I told her about Eli and everything he'd said, or as much as I could remember anyway.

I was about to tell her about Ollie too, but suddenly she got a teary look on her face. She reached under the counter and brought up a napkin that she stuck in her eyes. I felt terrible. I had no idea what I'd said that made her sad.

I told her she didn't have to talk about my assignment if she didn't want to. I slid off the stool again.

"Hey, not so fast." She scrunched up the napkin and tossed it in the trash. "I do have to talk about it, because I wish I could've used some of what Eli said on my ex, y'know, gotten him to calm down. He's a great sax player, and a real different guy when he's playing the sax. It would've done him a lot of good to know about his cool creative spirit, maybe expanded on that, instead of letting his demons get the best of him."

"That's terrible. What were his demons? I don't know much about demons except from church and the devil and stuff."

"We're not getting into my exe's demons, 'cause that's way off track. But I did learn to do something from being with his demons that might fit somewhere in your assignment. I'm not sure how, but if you sit back down I'll tell you about it."

I sat.

Angie clasped her hands on the counter pointing her two purple fingernails right at me. "What I learned, it might sound kinda crazy to you, but I learned to leave my body." She grinned so wide her ears wiggled.

"Are you kidding me?"

"No, I'm not kidding you. My ex had a real nasty temper that didn't show up until after we were married. So what I finally did, instead of freaking out and yelling back was, I'd leave my body. He'd be standing there with nobody present, and in the end, he'd shut up because there was nobody fighting back."

"So why aren't you still married if you got that figured out?"

"I got it figured out, but he didn't. So I just got tired of the ritual, and he wouldn't get help. I deserve better than that, sweetface, so the last time he yelled, I left him standing there yelling, and I was out the door for good."

"I'm really glad you got away from him, Angie, because you sure do deserve better. But I don't see how that has anything to do with my dad. He's not mean or anything. And how do you leave your body anyway. I mean where do you go?" I shoved my hands under my thighs to keep from yanking off a hangnail that I'd been picking at.

"I go different places. Wherever I picture in my head, that's where I go. It's a choice thing. I go wherever I want to go to get away from whatever's happening that I don't want to be a part of."

"But you can't go to a picture. I go to pictures in my memory, but they're real pictures. You can't go to made-up pictures can you?"

"Sure you can. You can go wherever your imagination takes you. With my ex, I imagined myself on a rainbow. I set myself up there in the cloudy sky, dangled my feet and let myself float out of the clouds into a rainbow colored sky." She reached over the counter and pinched my cheek. Not hard enough to hurt, but I know I blushed. I mean that was *really* weird.

Actually it reminded me of the time I pictured me and Ty flying out over the ocean with the seagulls. I wondered if that was what Angie was talking about.

Angie crossed her arms on the counter. She had that eyebrow-twitching confused look when she asked, "What's going on? You're blushing. Is that 'cause you don't believe me?"

"I do believe you. I tried imagining something once and it was neat until someone messed it up." Even though Angie looked confused, I didn't feel like talking about my other self.

"You're a trip, babycakes. I like what you're doing for your old man. It's real sweet. The idea that you care that much about making him happy, I'd say that's way past sweet. It's awesome."

"But if you're saying Dad has to leave his body to get peace, there's no way I could ever teach him to do that. He'd think I was crazy."

Angie laughed with her gold star sparkling. "You're not getting it, and that's my fault. I guess I forgot for a minute that you're a kid. You're like this little octopus, all the wigglies reaching out, grabbing on." She put her elbows on the counter and stuck her chin in her hands while she stared at me. "You are a normal kid, right?"

"I think so." Maybe I said that, but honestly I didn't know what I was. I liked the idea of being an octopus with a bunch of wigglies. I could almost feel them.

Angie uncrossed her arms, put them back out front and tapped her fingernails on the counter. "So, in normal language, here's the way I see it. This life we're living is a play we're in, and it's our play, so we make it up. The way we behave, we make that up too. We make it up good or we make it up bad. And me, well I choose the good way, and leaving my body is a made-up good way for my life to be the way I want it to be."

Suddenly I saw Dad crying after making up he was this happy guy. I told Angie I hated how people made up being what they weren't.

"Hey, hey! I never make up anything for myself that's not me. I only act out made-up scenes so I can feel better. Leaving my body is one of them. What I'm doing when I do that is a lot different than pretending to be what I'm not. What you see with me is who I am. Always."

I tried to swallow back the words I knew were coming but they slid out anyway. "My dad, I caught him crying when just before that he'd been acting like he was having such a good time with all of us."

Angie leaned against the wall and crossed her arms. "Well, what your dad did isn't far off what I'm saying. Only in your dad's case the acting didn't work, probably because he wasn't sincere about it. Making up what you want in life only works if you're sincerely going after what's good for you. Playing around wasn't good for your dad with everything on his mind. So maybe what you're doing for him, maybe that'll help him feel good naturally, doing whatever he's doing."

"Do you think so? I mean that's what I want anyway. Is your dad fun?"

"Yeah, he's fun. I don't get to see my folks much. They live in LA, and I came here last year to take care of my granny. Grandad died, and she didn't want to go to LA, and they didn't want to come here. So me, being the only kid, I volunteered to take her on. I guess I'm no kid at 39, but I was ready to leave Brad, get out of my boring job in a hair salon, so coming here to look after Granny was perfect. Granny's ninety, almost blind and pretty much lives in a wheelchair. My folks are fun, but not half as much fun as my granny. She's the one who loves old-timey music. We play her gramophone a lot and I whirl her wheelchair around the apartment, pretending we're dancin' to the beat of her favorite songs. The neighbors think we're crazy, but we don't care. We invite them in for popcorn and beer, and before they leave most of them are dancin' right along with us."

"The way you do all that stuff with her you must love her a lot."

"I do babycakes. I love her heaps. But enough about Granny and me. Are you ready to hear more about feeling good naturally? Because I hate that your old man's feel-good effort backfired. There's no way he'll ever get what you want to give him if he doesn't feel good. We need to figure out a way to make him feel good. That's the number one priority here. Right?"

"You're nice to care about that, Angie. Most grownups don't care about what kids think, so I've had a hard time finding people to talk to about my assignment."

"I don't know about most grownups. But I'll tell you something. You're no ordinary kid and you've got a big problem going on, so as long as we don't get interrupted again, let's see if I can help. I love solving problems."

"Are you saying you think Dad has a big problem that made him cry besides wanting peace and quiet?"

"I'm saying I think what we want to take a look at here is what's going on with him that's got him bent out of shape. And I've got an idea about that. Wanna hear?"

I nodded my head really hard.

"Do you play baseball at school?" she asked.

"Nope. We play softball."

"But you know how to play baseball. Right?"

"Yeah."

"The idea's the same. So it should be real easy for you to understand. Are you ready?"

I was just about to tell her I was when the bell over the door jangled. Angie asked the man who came in if she could help him. "I'm after a book," he said. "Have you got any recommendations?"

"Maybe," said Angie. She hopped off her stool and tapped my shoulder. She told me to wait while she took him to the book wall, which was super hard because I was sure Mom would show up any minute and ruin everything.

Angie and the man chattered on about the bestsellers. He finally picked three books. They came back to the counter and Angie rang the books up and gave him his change. He took off, waving the books with a big "Thanks."

"Sorry for the interruption, sweetface. I'm glad you didn't split because we've just got started."

"I hope no one else comes in, including Mom and Dad. They've been at the pool a long time."

"You want to check on them?"

"NO!" The word came out a lot louder than I meant it to. "I want to hear about baseball if it'll help me with my assignment."

Angie clasped her hands together on the counter so I clasped mine in my lap and squeezed them real tight.

"Okeydokey," she said. "Are you ready to hear how it works? You're looking kinda jumpy."

"I'm just scared with Mom and Dad out there, and you, well, I'm not sure. But I do know I'm ready." I wriggled around on my stool to get comfortable.

Angie gave a little chuckle. "That's better. You're at least looking ready, so here's the way it works. For starters, we all come into life as babies full of trust, wanting only to love and be loved." She looked hard at me, sort of studied how my face looked. "You with me?"

I nodded pretty hard.

"Okay. So what happens is we grow up, and then we get into what I call 'the ball game of life'. We take our place on home plate where we're all pumped with love and trust. We're clutching the bat tight, when here comes a ball hurtling our way. If we're lucky, we slam that sucker, whack it out of the park and have a home run. Everyone cheers, and love and trust flourishes."

"I'm a big hitter so I get lots of home runs. Does that mean love and trust flourishes in me?"

"You've got that right, but you're still a kid. Once you get into the grownup ball game, hanging on to love and trust, well that isn't always easy. More often than not, balls come your way with curves and shin-hits. You swing like crazy, miss the curves and the shin-hits hurt. If you miss the balls too much and get hurt a lot, love and trust slides away, and you don't even want to play the game anymore."

I stuck my hands back under my thighs because I sure felt like picking. "What're you saying Angie? Are you saying Dad's love and trust slid away and that's why he quit work?"

"I don't know what your dad was doing before the trip. But my guess is that something mucked up his love and trust in whatever he was doing, or he wouldn't be out here looking for a new ball game."

"Is love and trust the same as peace and quiet? I mean if Dad gets love and trust back will he have peace and quiet too? I guess I don't understand."

"Now hold your horses. It's not half as complicated as you think. But it may be a whole lot more information than you need right now, so how about we try something a little easier."

The bell over the door jangled. I turned and it was Mom. She asked me if I needed any money for books. I'd almost forgotten I was supposed to be looking at books. I told her I didn't. I said I wanted to stick with *Nancy Drew.*

"We're going home for lunch. Are you coming?"

Of course I wanted to say no, but Angie looked at me and winked. "I think you better go. I gotta get back to work anyway." She slid her pile of papers in front of her so I told Mom I was coming.

"When can I come see you again Angie? I need to hear about the easier thing."

"I know you do. So come anytime, and don't take too long, because you're a breath of heavenly air."

I liked being heavenly air. I liked that better than babycakes or even an octopus. But most of all I liked Angie a lot.

Outside the store, Mom asked, "What did you and that strange lady have to talk about?"

"Strange is right," said Dad. "Did she tell you about her life on Mars?"

He laughed, but I didn't. "She's nice. If she comes from Mars I'd like to go there."

"Not anytime soon," said Mom. "C'mon, let's get lunch. I'm hungry."

"Sounds good to me," said Dad.

The two of them sped ahead and I trailed behind, wondering if there wasn't some way I could get to move in with Angie and her granny. I was sure they'd be more fun to live with than my family. I knew I should've stood up for Angie and told Mom and Dad about how she took care of her granny. Then they'd know she wasn't as strange as she looked. But honestly I was too mad at Dad's stupid comment to bother.

While Mom made lunch I hauled out the letter to Amy I'd started and added on a description of my time with Angie. Describing all the things that Angie said was not easy. Along with the other news I'd already written, the thing ended up being three pages. I stuffed it in an envelope and ran it to the mailbox before lunch.

We were just finishing up our sandwiches at the picnic table when the bus people pulled into the spot next to ours that Mom had reserved for them. Josh was up and over there so fast it was a wonder he didn't land under the wheels. Lauren appeared just as fast, and the two of them ran to the beach, laughing, hanging on, and tripping over each other all at the same time.

"I'm going fishing," said Dad. "I feel like a fish fry for supper."

"Good idea," said Ty. "I'll come with you. But Ollie uses shrimp instead of sand fleas and he says that's important for catching flounder in the troughs. Do you know about troughs?"

"No," said Dad. "But I do know about flounder. They taste great. We'll get some shrimp at the store."

"Okay. Then I'll come too," I said.

"Wait a minute," said Mom. "I need someone to hang onto the dogs while I take them to get their itchy rashes checked out. The vet's closed, but the drugstore's open and the pharmacist can probably help."

"Okay, I'll come with you," I said, suddenly changing my mind about fishing with live shrimp. I didn't want to stick hooks in them. At least sand fleas didn't have eyes that stared at you. I didn't bother to say anything about that, I just said, "You guys go, and catch us a monster flounder."

"We'll do it," said Dad. He and Ty took off just as Maya and Jesse showed up at our place. Maya put a bottle of beads on our table, and she and Mom hugged like they'd been apart forever.

"I'm going into town," said Mom. "Want to come along?"

"No, I'm bushed," said Maya. "I've had enough driving. I'll be here when you get back."

I couldn't get my eyes off the new bottle of beads. I asked Jesse if he was too bushed to go with Mom and hang onto the dogs. "She's taking them to get some stuff for their itches?"

"Sure. I'm never bushed," said Jesse. He swept the poodles up and raced to the car.

Mom laughed. "So much for that. I don't care who comes, as long as the poodles aren't loose in the car."

As soon as they drove off I picked up the bottle and swirled it around. "Are these new, Maya?"

"They are. And I guess that means you're into stringing. Am I right?"

"Yeah." I swirled the bottle again. "Where'd you get them?"

"I got them from a trader on the side of the road outside of town. Didn't you see him?"

"We only drive on super highways so we never see anything. Dad goes right from one place to the next without stopping to look at anything. Isn't that stupid?"

"I don't know about stupid. Remember, I'm a teacher so I like all the tourist attractions, and Zack will stop whenever I want him to because he knows the kids like looking at anything interesting. But your dad, well he's on a mission with the job search, so that's a whole different story."

"I guess it is. Are you too tired to start stringing the beads now?"

"I'm never too tired. Any time's a good time as far as I'm concerned."

"Goody." I said that because it was way more than just good to have something fun to do, especially after a couple of bummer days. Sure, the idea of Disney World was fun, but I didn't want to think about that. The way things worked with Dad, it might never get to be more than just an idea.

Maya went to the bus and got all her supplies. She emptied the bottle onto a white towel and for sure the beads were totally special. There were lots of real turquoise ones and some colored stones I'd never seen before. Maya gave me the names for a bunch of them, but mostly I just liked looking at them and feeling them while I was stringing.

We sat and I'd just gotten the beads I wanted sorted when Maya put down the partly done necklace she was working on. "I've been thinking about your peace question, Zo. Can you elaborate, tell me why you want to know, so maybe I can give you a decent answer instead of hurting your feelings like I did yesterday?"

"You didn't hurt my feelings. I'm fine." That was the perfect time for Mom's word, because I'd already decided I couldn't tell Maya about my assignment. I threaded like crazy with my head down so I wouldn't have to look at her. All I could do was change the subject. "Will you tell me about the trader?"

"I guess I can do that." Her voice sounded like people do when they can't get what they want, like sort of fed up. But as she went on to describe the trader who lived on an Indian reservation, and set up tents for selling all over the place, she got right into how she traded some of her beads for the ones she got. She even told me about all the other things the trader was selling, like blankets and clay pots that she didn't buy.

But as soon as the trader story was over, she about knocked me off the bench with, "So we're not going to talk about peace anymore? I'm curious, Zoey."

Suddenly I felt trapped, just like I did when the teacher picked me to say something smart about what I felt dumb at. I felt really dumb right then, and what came out of my mouth was even dumber. "You don't have to be curious, because stringing beads is more fun than talking about hard stuff."

Maya's eyes totally bugged. "Peace is hard stuff? Now you've *really* got me curious."

I tried to keep my mouth shut, but my other self didn't care. Words I'd been trying so hard to hide came barreling up my throat and out of my mouth, "Peace is hard stuff when you want to give it to someone. And I want to give it to Dad. He's always saying he wants peace and quiet, and he needs it so he can have love and trust."

Maya bunched her eyebrows and stared at me. "What on earth are you talking about?"

I couldn't ignore Maya's bug-eyed stare, so I stared right back at her. "I don't know what I'm talking about. Can we just string the beads please?" I dropped my head and started threading like crazy.

Maya reached over and stopped the action. "Hold it a minute, young lady. You're talking in circles and I can't keep up. For starters, giving peace to your dad, that's not your job, that's not anybody's job. If he wants peace or love and trust, it's his job to get them for himself. You're only a kid. Your job is to have fun."

My whole stomach cramped. "That's why I want to string beads, so I can have fun." I said that even though what I wanted to do was dig a hole beside the bench and bury myself.

Maya sighed. "Maybe you're worrying too much. Let me tell you something I learned from an Indian Wise Woman many years ago when I first started teaching. Would you like that?"

"I guess so." I really wished I was the one hanging onto the poodles in the car.

Maya went in the bus and came out with a couple of glasses of water. "Here." She handed me a glass.

I didn't want any water but I took a drink anyway. I put the glass down.

Maya put her glass on the table and sat down. "I think you'll like this. It's a great way to keep from trying to change people."

"I'm not doing that with Dad am I? I just want him to be happy."

"Of course you do. I'm a teacher so I want everyone to be happy. But that's not the way it works Zo. Everyone is the way they are, and our job is to accept them just as they are, and that's where my Indian Wise Woman's advice comes in. Do you want to hear more?"

This time I nodded hard, hoping that what I was going to hear wasn't weird, like leaving my body or something.

"Now," said Maya, "what I want you to do is turn your colorful imagination inside out and picture people as flowers. Think of lots of different kinds of flowers, and see each person in your life as one of those flowers." She smiled. "Are you with me so far?"

"I don't know. I mean what's that got to do with letting people be like they are? I guess I don't get it."

"Believe me. You'll get it if you let me finish. So hang in there." She reached across the table and squeezed my hand. "How it works is that the flower you pick for that person is who they will be for you from now on. Remember, each one will be different. For me some people are roses with thorns, and others are sunflowers, towering over all the others with their bright open-wide faces."

My head filled to the brim with the pictures Maya was making, and out of nowhere I saw her as a bright red poppy. I didn't tell her because she kept talking. "What happens is that if I see them as a thorny rose, I don't try to make them a smiling sunflower, but just accept and enjoy them as a rose, thorns and all. In my mind you're a multi-colored pansy with many shades of purple melding together in a blend of curiosity." She squeezed my hand extra hard. "Right now, I want you to simply savor all the shades of the precious pansy that you are to me."

Suddenly I felt ripples flutter through my whole body like I'd been brushed by butterfly wings.

"Hey, did I lose you?" Maya asked. She let go of my hand. "Was it the precious pansy, or the whole thing? What's going on in there?"

"You didn't lose me at all. I got shivers. That was so nice. And you know what? You've turned into a bright red poppy. Every bit of you is red. Honestly, I'm not making that up."

"Wow, I love it. A poppy is one of my favorite flowers, and the deep purple center of the poppy, that's my heart!" She put her hand over her heart, popping the hand up and down. "See? My heart's beating right through my blouse."

"That's just because you've got a really big heart."

"Well let's not get carried away."

"What flower do you think my dad would be? Dad changes all the time so he wouldn't be just one kind of flower."

"Sure he would. The perfect flower for your dad would be the African daisy. It closes up in the dark and opens in the light. Maybe that's what your dad does, he closes up when things are dark for him and opens up when they brighten. Everyone has moods, and your dad, with all that's going on for him, I'm sure he has open and closed moods all the time."

"We have daisies in our garden back home but they're just regular daisies. They don't close up."

"The African one looks pretty much the same as the regular daisy only smaller. If it's easy for you to picture a regular daisy, then do that for your dad. You want to see him open anyway, not closed, and if he knows you see him that way I bet he'll feel better. It's amazing how our attitude rubs off on other people."

"He went to Africa once, he and Mom, and they loved it there. They didn't say anything about daisies, but they sure loved the giraffes and lions."

Right then Maya looked over my shoulder. "Oops. Don't look now, but here comes your dad and he's looking pretty closed."

I didn't turn, but I heard, "Go fish with Ty, Zoey." I shifted around as Dad went in the trailer. No explanation, only a click of the screen door.

"If I were you," said Maya, "I'd go see what's happening with your brother. You can finish your necklace later."

"I don't want to finish." I slid all the beads off and swept them into the pile. I got up.

"Before you go, Zoey, I just want to say one more time that it's not your job to worry about your dad. Your job is to be a kid, so be one for all of us. Okay, you purple pansy you?"

"Okay." I could feel tears behind my eyes and the last thing I wanted to do was cry. I took off without bothering to put on my bathing suit.

When I got to the beach, Ty was standing there holding his rod with the line way out in the ocean. Dad's rod was still in his holder, stuck deep in the sand with a shrimp dangling from the line.

For some reason the flower that came to mind for Ty was a white lily, the kind Mom always had in the house at Easter. Not that Ty was exactly white or anything but that's how I thought of him, with soft petals. I wasn't about to tell him, especially after he'd chosen a dagger to wear around his neck. Maybe the dagger idea was cute, but it wasn't fooling me. Ty sure was no gangster.

"So much for Dad's fish fry," I said to his back. "What happened?"

He turned around. "Yeah. So much for Dad's anything. He was all excited, but as soon as he got here he had a fit about the tide being too low. Sure it's way out there and who cares. I bet people catch fish at low tide. You just have to go out further to cast. Big deal. We did that, with him complaining the whole time, and finally after enough unsuccessful tries he plunked his rod in the holder and flung his arms in the air. I don't know, but why couldn't we have just had fun doing something together, seeing as we never do. He said he was going to get you, that he had other fish to fry. I guess he thought that was funny, but I wasn't amused. So much for spending time with his son."

"Don't be mad at him Ty. It's really hard for him to have fun when he's got all that business stuff to worry about. It's too bad he didn't think about where the tide was before he came."

Ty didn't answer. He reeled his line in and shoved the rod in the holder, tilting the thing way over. He headed down the beach.

"Wait!" I hollered. "You're scaring me!"

He stopped. He stood for a minute before he turned and came back. "I'm sorry. It's too much, this stupid trip. It's too much!"

I couldn't see Ty's eyes behind the sunglasses, but his weird behavior really scared me. "You're the one person I count on for happy. What's wrong?"

"The trip's a bust is what's wrong. Right now was supposed to be fun. Dad didn't have to get all freaked out."

"Well we're going to Disney World and that should be fun."

"Yeah, like when? I don't see anyone making any plans."

I wanted to tell Ty about my plan for Dad but I couldn't, so I told him I'd race him to the pier that was practically out of sight.

"You're crazy. You can't beat me."

"Wanna bet? Who's the champion track star? Have you forgotten already?" Maybe he didn't remember I'd won first place ribbons in all the track events on Sports Day at school.

"Okay. Let's go."

I scooped the shrimps out of the container and ran out and tossed them in the ocean.

"What're you doing Sis? Dad'll have a fit. Those were live shrimp and they cost money."

"I don't care. Maybe we don't have freedom, but I want them to. Get rid of the ones on the hooks. I hate looking at them."

"They're dead, and you're nuts!" He ripped them off and tossed them in the air. "C'mon. Let's go get some of our own freedom. The race is on."

He took off running and I sped after him. I knew he was slowing his long-legged stride to let me win, and in the end I did.

By the time we reached the pier we were both panting and sweating. Ty's hair was plastered to his head and my ponytail was stuck to my neck. Lots of people were on the pier, sitting with their legs dangling over the edge. I wished I could've done that instead of running myself out of breath to keep from worrying about my brother.

"Thanks Sis," he said. "That was good, a lot better than complaining. We can't do anything about Dad anyway."

"Not yet. Right now we might as well go back, don't y'think?"

"Yeah. We might as well do something, because complaining is doing nothing. I'm not into doing nothing. So c'mon."

We walked the long way back to our fishing stuff, without saying much, and packed it up before we headed to the trailer. When we got close, we could hear Josh yelling, but not what he was saying, only Dad yelling something back. Thank goodness there was no one around. Even the bus wasn't there.

When we got right up to the trailer, they were still going at it, and I heard Josh yell, "It's just down the beach by the pier. The surfing's better by the pier. I'm not asking to drive to Miami for God's sake." Josh sure was no flower. I saw only a firecracker for him.

Then Dad said, "You know you can't take the car out of the campground, so forget the swearing and get used to it. You'll have plenty of time for driving once you're sixteen."

The trailer door flung open and Josh leapt out over the stairs, almost knocking me down. He hopped on his bike and took off.

We shoved all the gear under the trailer and went inside. Dad was slouched on the sofa with his head on his chest, and Mom was sitting beside him with her arms crossed, looking like a drooping daffodil. Maya had said that if I pictured Dad's closed African daisy open, that maybe he'd know and feel better. I didn't see that happen when I tried, and I tried with Mom too, but her daffodil still drooped.

"What's happening with Josh?" I asked.

"I bet I know," said Ty. "I bet he wanted to take the car and go necking with Lauren."

"That really helps," said Dad. "Keep your comments to yourself." He got up. "I've had enough. Let's go to that diner on the highway and get a burger."

"It's too early for supper," I said.

"Who cares," said Dad. He pushed the door open.

"Shall I go find Josh?" I asked.

"Forget Josh," said Dad.

"What happened with the dogs Mom?" I asked. They were sprawled on a towel at the end of her bed. I pictured dandelion puffballs.

She said the pharmacist told her the rash was from flea bites and he sold her some powder. "It smells and they're not happy, " she said."

"So we'll bring them back a treat. "Bye, babies." She blew them a kiss.

In the car there was no talk of Josh. To try and get rid of the knot in my stomach I asked Dad when we were going to Disney World.

"We've got our own Disney World, and your brother's the wildest ride in the park."

"Maybe Disney World would be good for him Why don't we go, like tomorrow?"

"I'm not ready to give up the car yet, Zoey. I've mailed away for some research material and when I get what I want I'll let you know." He pulled into the White Castle parking lot, which ended that conversation.

The White Castle was what Dad called a classic diner from the forties. It was painted white with black trim. The floor inside was covered in checkered black-and-white linoleum. Red plastic booths in front of the windows ran the length of the diner that was about twice as long as our trailer.

We sat in one of the booths and ordered from a sign over the kitchen that said the place was famous for inch-deep hamburgers, shakes too thick to budge a straw, and crunchy fries piled a foot high. I ordered an extra burger.

Dad was in the bathroom when the food came. I took about a dozen napkins out of the holder and wrapped the extra burger I'd ordered. "For the poodles," I said, probably not fooling anyone.

When we got home, Josh wasn't there and neither was his bike. The bus was still gone which meant he wasn't with Lauren. I put the wrapped burger under his pillow while Mom gave the dogs the fries she'd brought for them. They lifted their heads and took them, but they didn't even wag their tails. Ty suggested we all go swimming.

"Good idea," said Mom.

"I don't know why Josh has to make everything so difficult," said Dad. He followed Mom to the bedroom and closed the door. I put my ear to the door to hear what Mom might say about that.

"I don't think you're being fair, Sammy. Have you forgotten what it was like to be fifteen? Can you even imagine your parents doing what we've done? The kid's hormones are raging. He's been torn from his safety net of popularity and he's madder than hell. So let up on him."

I didn't hear anything from Dad, but I wanted to scream "Hooray for Mom!" Everything she said made perfect sense. I found myself feeling sorry for my brother for the first time.

I got in my bunk and pulled the curtain. I put on my bathing suit while Ty was above me in his bunk doing the same. "Do you think he'll be okay Ty?"

"Who?"

"Yeah right. What do you care if your brother gets squashed by a monster truck."

"You're right. What do I care." He yanked back his curtain and jumped down. "C'mon. Let's go drown the lousy mood in the pool."

We went to the pool but I didn't really want to swim. I wanted to sneak in the store and see Angie. But there was no sneaking anywhere because a bunch of people were already there. "Rats!" I said to myself as I jumped in the pool.

After the swim, we took the powdered and pouty poodles for a long walk on the beach, and when we got back, there was still no Josh. We changed into our clothes and went over to the rec center to watch some TV. The regular *Sunday Mystery Movie* was coming on so we stayed for that, and when we got home, only the poodles were there.

"I'm turning in," said Dad.

"What about Josh?" I asked.

"What about him? He'll show up when he's good and ready. C'mon Meg. Hanging around worrying about him isn't going to bring him home any sooner."

Mom gave me a hug and whispered that Dad was right. She followed him to their room.

Ty and I sprawled on our bunks to read but that didn't work for me. Nancy Drew was good at getting my mind off stuff normally, but not this time. I shoved my head under my pillow and counted about five hundred sheep leaping fences before I finally fell asleep.

Mom's door opening woke me. I peeked through my curtain and saw her checking Josh's bed. He wasn't there. She went back in her room and closed the door.

At the same time, I heard the trailer door open. I got out of bed and of course it was Josh. Mom didn't reappear, but she had to have heard the door so she probably felt as relieved as I did. Ty didn't say anything. I figured he was pretending to be asleep behind his curtain.

I went in the kitchen where Josh was in the fridge getting some milk. "Are you okay?"

He took a gulp and stuck the carton back. "Yeah, I'm super."

"I've got a surprise for you." I ran and got the burger from under his pillow. I unwrapped it and gave it to him. "Sorry it's cold."

The burger was gone in seconds.

"So where'd you go?" I asked.

Josh went and slumped on the sofa. "None of your business."

I followed him, but I didn't sit. "Then don't tell me." If he was going to be nasty I'd be nasty too. "See if I care."

He let out a big sigh and sunk back into the cushions. "If you must know, after I rode my butt off, I shot pool over at the rec center with some old guy, had a couple of overdone hotdogs at the store while I hung out with the lady over there, and thanks for the burger. I like cold burgers better than overdone hotdogs."

"You hung out with Angie?" That news flopped me on the chair across from him.

"How'd you know her name?"

"I've talked to her. Did you like her?"

"Yeah. The star in her tooth's pretty far out, but apart from that she said a lot of cool things about people loving each other and about people listening to each other and understanding each other. The kind of things that don't go on a lot around here."

"Did she offer you her car so you could take Lauren out to neck? Ty said that was what you wanted to do."

Josh took a deep breath and blew it out. "No, Creep. She didn't offer me her car. She took a lot of time to explain that trying to get Dad to loan me the car was stupid, that fighting with Dad is stupid, and that taking deep breaths when I get frustrated will help me keep from blowing up. She said that not letting myself react to dumb comments, like the one you just made, will keep me from losing it."

"Wow. She taught you all that?"

"Keep it down," Ty called. "We're trying to sleep back here."

"What else did Angie say?" I whispered.

"I'm not into whispering," said Josh. And with that he jumped up. The bus was pulling in and he was out the door.

I leaned back and tried to imagine what flower Josh might be. All I saw was another firecracker.

Disney World

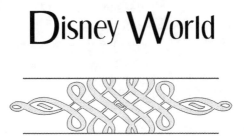

The next day life in campville was back to normal, if such a word applied to our family. There was no talk of where Josh had gone, and I didn't bother bringing it up. Ty was quieter than usual and nobody talked about that either. All of it seemed weird until I remembered that weird was what *was* normal in our family.

Jacksonville definitely worked for Dad and his yellow papers. He said he'd paid to stay on in the campground for another two weeks and that the library in the city was the best he'd seen so far. He'd discovered an organization called The World Future Society, where people supposedly shared ideas to make the world a better place.

I dashed off a note to Amy to tell her I was right, and that we'd be staying in Jacksonville Beach long enough for her to write me. I gave her the address and ran the envelope over to the mailbox.

While I was there I decided I'd see if I could get Angie to tell me about her easier idea for my assignment. But when I went in the store she wasn't there. A burly man with a big frown sat behind the counter looking at some papers. He didn't even look up when I asked where Angie was, he just said she was at the dentist. I figured he must've been the owner. For sure no one that rude would ever be hired to work there.

When I got back to the trailer Dad was just leaving for the library. He hadn't gone first thing because the plan that day was to take everyone to get haircuts, everyone being Mom, Josh, Ty, Lauren and Jesse. Maya and I didn't want one. He said the library was in a different direction from the haircuts, so he'd take a quick run to the library and be right back to pick everyone up.

While he was so pumped about everything I decided to try for a way to get Ty pumped too. "Why don't you take Ty with you? He could do with more to read than his comics, and besides I think he's bored."

"There's an enormous wall of paperbacks at the store, Zo. I haven't heard Ty complain about being bored, and he's never said a word about wanting to go to the library."

At that moment Ty came in. "Sorry. Am I interrupting?" He turned to go. "Mom's over in the laundry room and I'll go give her a hand."

"Wait a minute," said Dad. "Do you want to take a run to the library with me and maybe get a real book to read instead of the comics? I know we're going for haircuts, so I won't be there long, but long enough for you to get a book."

"I like the comics. But yeah, that'd be great."

On their way out, Dad kissed my cheek.

While they were gone I went by the store and peeked in to see if Angie was back. She wasn't, so I hung out at the rec center, watching TV with some other people.

When Dad and Ty got back, Ty had three books called *The Lord of the Rings Trilogy* that came in a case. He had one of them out with a bookmark in it, so he'd obviously already started reading on the way home.

"I think I'll skip the haircut, Dad," he said. "I'm into reading, okay?"

"No, not okay. Your hair's a mess. Mom's in the car, ready to go. And Zo, she wants to know if you'd like to ride with us. We're going to McDonalds for lunch."

"Nope," I said. "But you can bring me back a cheeseburger. That'd be nice."

McDonalds did it for Ty. He tossed the book on his bed and Dad promised to bring me a burger.

After they'd gone, I started poking through Ty's book, and before I knew it I was sprawled on my bunk reading, with the poodles snuggled next to me.

I was hardly into the story when I heard Zack yell, "Goddammit Maya. What the hell do you want from me? Maybe you like hanging around these shit holes but I don't. It's hotter than hell and it's a waste of time."

Jacques let out a yip. I held him and raced to the window. The bus looked quiet enough.

Then I heard Maya yelling back, "Turn on the air conditioner. Get out, go somewhere, do something other than sitting around all day getting stoned. You're not even trying." Her voice sounded awful. I could've sworn she was crying.

"And I don't intend to try either." yelled Zack.

"Well that's just great. What kind of example are you for Lauren and Jesse? Maybe you don't care about yourself, but you have to care about the kids."

"Get the hell outa here. Quit your sniveling and go play with your stupid friends."

I tried to picture a decent flower for Zack, but all that showed up was a black widow spider. I didn't know much about getting stoned, other than that's what happened when hippies smoked pot, or at least that's what I'd heard at school, and I'd also heard that it made people mellow, not ugly like Zack sounded.

There was a rustling and a banging and then the door of the bus burst open. I hid behind the window curtain and peeked out. I couldn't see Maya's face as she charged toward the showers, and I didn't know whether Zack had actually smacked her, but I imagined a bloody nose and black eyes.

I started shaking. I'd hardly ever seen Zack so I had no idea what he was like. He sure sounded scary.

Through the chattering of my teeth, I heard GET HELP inside my head.

I didn't know anyone in the campground to get help from other than Angie. So with a big kiss I dropped a puzzled Jacques on my bunk with Jolie and put Ty's book back on his bunk. I flew out the door, tripping over my feet to get to the store. I could only hope Angie was back from the dentist.

When I got there, a bunch of people were going in and I couldn't see whether Angie was there or not. Without taking time to think of a next move I rushed into the phone booth outside the store and yanked the door shut. I dug for a dime in my pocket and dropped it in the slot and dialed O.

"This is the operator."

I cupped my hand over the mouthpiece and whispered, "I need the police. Can you get me the police?"

The operator said she couldn't hear me, and that was a good thing because I suddenly realized if the police came I'd be making terrible trouble for everyone. I slammed the receiver in the holder, yanked open the door and practically collapsed on the curb. I put my head on my knees and wrapped my arms around my legs.

The voice I heard next wasn't inside my head, like a message for what to do. It was Maya's. "What's wrong, Zo?"

I looked up. She stood there with no black eye, no broken nose, no tears on her face, but no red poppy either. All I could say with barely enough breath to get it out was, "Nothing. But are you okay?"

She dropped down on the curb beside me. "Yeah, I'm okay, but what's wrong with you? You don't look so good."

I never lie, but out of my mouth came a biggy. "I just got my first period and Mom's not even home. I figured it out by myself, but it feels weird, Maya."

She dropped down beside me and put her arm around me. "Well, I'm here, Zo, and believe me, it's not weird at all. All it means is that you're now a woman."

"I sure don't feel like one. Is that supposed to be a good thing? How old were you?"

"I was probably at least twelve, but hey, lots of girls start early, so of course it's a good thing." She got up and put out her hand. "Now c'mon inside and I'll buy you a Coke or a candy bar or whatever you want. I need some butter."

I took her hand and she pulled me up. Maybe I was supposed to be a woman, but I sure wasn't hungry. My stomach was far too tangled to put anything in it.

Inside the store Angie was busy with customers over in the book section. "I'll grab the butter," said Maya, "and you get whatever you want."

"I don't want anything thanks. I'd just like to talk to Angie when she's finished."

Maya got the butter out of the cooler and came to the counter. "Are you sure you're okay, Zo? I'm making cookies so I need to get back." She tore the top off the box of butter and put the money on the counter.

"Yeah, I'm okay, but I'd sure like one of your cookies." I pretended a smile, but all I could think was that making cookies seemed awfully weird after what I'd heard.

"Good, I'll make extra for you guys and I'll see you later." She took off.

I watched Angie chatter away, smiling her big gold-tooth smile. I tried to shut off what I'd heard by imagining what kind of flower she'd be. I didn't know a lot of flower names. But Angie, I decided she wouldn't be only one flower. With so many parts to her personality she'd be a lot of flowers. I remembered a bunch of wildflowers in a field where we'd gone for a picnic once, and Angie became those flowers. All the colors were so brilliant they made me shiver.

Angie rang up the books for her customers and patted the stool that was now beside hers. "You better sit yourself down. From way across the store you had me worried. You look awful?"

I didn't move. "That's 'cause I'm scared. I heard something awful."

Angie checked the top of the butter box, threw it away and dropped Maya's money in the register before she came around the counter and put her hands on my shoulders. "So tell me what this something awful is about. What's going on?"

She had on a white tank top with *LIFE IS LOVE* in big purple letters across the front. As I read those words up close, other words sounded off in my head. "TATTLETALE, TATTLETALE". Then a picture of a stupid kid at school flooded my brain. She always squealed on everyone and nobody liked her. My own tattletale words got caught in my throat.

Angie took my hand and squeezed it. "Speak up."

I took a big breath and blew it out right in Angie's face. She laughed, and although nothing was particularly funny I laughed too.

"You looked pretty gone right then, sweetface. Why don't we both sit down and you can tell me what's going on inside that cute little head of yours." She went behind the counter and flopped on her stool. I followed her and did the same on the other one.

"So," she said. "What did you hear, pray tell."

I told her that after reading *LIFE IS LOVE* on her top I didn't want to talk about what I'd heard.

She held the top away from her chest. "Does that mean you know how special these words are?"

"No. Why? How special are they?"

"They're special, because in Greek your name Zoey means 'Life', and so that means you read Zoey is Love and all the awful thoughts went away. Right?"

"How do you know that, Angie? You're just making it up like you do everything else."

"Now let's not get huffy here. I'm not making it up at all. The fact is that I'm Greek myself. My name is Angela Stephanopoulos. But to tell you the truth, I didn't know about Zoey meaning 'life' until Granny told me. We talk a lot about you at my place, so how about we get another tank top made for you with Zoey is Love on it. That'll get rid of any awful thoughts you have for good. What d'you think?"

"What I think is that you're really funny. Did you know you're a field of wildflowers?"

"What? Where in the world did that come from?"

"Maya, the lady who bought the butter, she sees people as flowers, and she told me to do that so I could accept the way people are without trying to change them."

Angie laughed. "Are you saying you want to change me?"

"No, I sure don't want to change you, and I don't want to talk about flowers, or my name or anything else anymore. It's all way too weird. What I want to talk about is the other thing you said you'd tell me for my assignment."

"Well if you're not going to tell me what you heard, and my other idea will maybe make you feel better, then I can do that. Are you sure that's what you want?"

I wished Angie could see inside me and she'd know how sure I was. My heart was beating like crazy. "Yeah. I'm really sure."

"Okey, dokey. The assignment idea, it's called a joyride."

"Peace and quiet is a joyride? Isn't a joyride noisy?"

Angie laughed. "I suppose it can be. But my kind of joyride, most people call it meditation. I get a lot of joy from meditating, so I like to call it a joyride. Have you ever meditated?"

I told her I'd heard the word but that was all. "It's not like leaving your body is it? I know I could never teach Dad to leave his body."

"Nope. They're altogether different. I leave my body to get away from what I don't want to be around. I go on a joyride to be with just me, like your friend Eli when he's whittling. But me, I don't *do* anything. I only quiet the chatter inside myself by repeating *Life is Love* over and over enough times so there's no room in my mind for anything else. From the look of your old man, there's not just chatter going on inside him, there's real racket. He feels like a time bomb about to go off every time he comes in here. So if you can teach him how to get rid of all that chatter, I'd call your assignment a huge success. You want to give it a go?"

"Sure." My whole body tingled.

"Well the first thing you have to do is close your eyes, and I want to watch you do that before I close mine, because you look like you might split if I'm not watching."

"I'm not going to split. I'm just kinda nervous. I mean why are you going to close your eyes?"

"That's what you do when you meditate, you close your eyes, and all the distractions around you disappear."

"I don't know anything about meditating. I've never done that."

"Exactly. That's why I want to teach you. So I'll watch you close your eyes, and then I'll close mine."

I did. "Do I do something else now?"

"That's right, sweetface. Now what I want you to do is clear your mind of all thoughts, sort of like rubbing everything off a chalkboard. Make your mind a blank slate."

I squeezed my eyes tight but my mind wouldn't go blank. I tried picturing a chalkboard and rubbing stuff off, but Maya's black eyes and Zack yelling at her wouldn't go away.

In a real calm voice, Angie said, "Take a few deep breaths and at the same time repeat *Life is Love* over and over inside your head.

I took three deep breaths and repeated the words, but I didn't feel anything. I kept peeking at Angie to see how she looked. All her wildflowers were practically glowing. Watching them snuggling together was more fun than trying to get rid of pictures of Zack and Maya. I squeezed my eyes real tight again and began taking more breaths.

I'd hardly gotten started when the bell over the front door jangled. My eyes jerked open and I jumped off the stool. Angie didn't. She just kept that same calm look, as if she wasn't even there, so maybe she'd left her body. I asked the man who was staring at her if I could help him.

"A pack of Marlboros." A frown carved two big grooves between his eyes. "She okay?"

I told him she was meditating. I had no idea what she was doing, but I puffed my chest for at least knowing the word as I handed him the cigarettes. He dropped his money on the counter and darted out without waiting for change. Angie still didn't move a muscle.

The door burst open, practically ripping the bell off the wall. The same burly man who'd been there before stormed over to the counter. "What the hell's going on in here?"

This time Angie jumped off the stool and shook her head a few times. "Why, hi Al. Long time no see."

"Don't give me any of this "long time no see" crap. What the hell you doin' meditating? You should be takin' care of the customers for chrissake. That guy out there says we're runnin' a nuthouse in here."

He was so ugly, and there was Angie, with no reaction to how mean he sounded. All she said was, "A little meditation never hurt no one. And for your information, my friend here waited on that guy like a real pro."

"Well I ain't payin' her, I'm payin' you. So get your fanny back in gear." He turned and charged out the door without looking back.

"Sorry," she said. "That's Monster Man. He's my boss and he's a planet away from loving thoughts. There's no point in trying to communicate with him."

"How come you didn't even seem to notice the cigarette guy coming in?"

"I heard him, but my mind was busy with *Life is Love*, so I chose not to break the spell. Besides you were handling the thing real well."

"But you got into trouble. Isn't that awful?"

"Nope. Nothing's awful unless you make it that way. The only awful part is I guess we're over for today. How'd it go for you? Did you get to feel anything?"

"No. I wish I did, but all these pictures of stuff I don't want to talk about kept popping up and getting in the way."

Angie laughed. "Well we can't expect perfection right off. It takes practice, and unfortunately practice is over for today. I bet you anything Monster Man's hanging around out there, ready to pounce again."

"You think we can do it later, when he's not around? I see him as a real ugly weed, Angie. Do you think we could put some weed killer on him and get rid of him?

"Now don't get carried away with the flower imagery. Focus on one thing at a time, and for now it's *Life is Love*, or better still, *Zoey is Love*. Y'got that?"

I told Angie I did, but it sure was hard to leave without getting a joyride. I didn't let myself think about that. I just focused on trying to figure out how the whole thing worked.

When I got home I could hardly wait to write Amy about Angie, and how she told me Zoey meant 'Life' in Greek, and then about the joyride lesson that hadn't worked. I started to write about Zack and Maya but that was too hard so I scribbled it out.

I did tell her about the flower people though, and who I saw as what flower and why. That was fun to write about. I said I wanted her to be a pansy too.

Just as I got to the end of the letter, everybody came back from wherever they'd been to get haircuts. I tucked the letter under my pillow and pulled the sheet over my head pretending to be asleep. I sure couldn't talk about what had gone on with me while they were away.

The dogs leapt off my bed. Mom must have seen me under the sheet because she shushed everyone. I heard some muttering about fishing from Josh, but nothing that made sense seeing as Josh never fished. And then I couldn't make out what anyone else was saying. Before long all was quiet, that is until I heard the fridge door open and close.

I got up and Mom was in the kitchen pouring iced tea into glasses. She looked over at me and I gasped. She'd done a Joan of Arc thing to her hair.

"Did I wake you, honey? I'm sorry. Would you like some tea?"

Honestly, I couldn't think of a thing to say. I mean her hair was even shorter than when we left home. She looked like one of those mushrooms with the fuzz on top. "Uh, no thanks."

Mom put the pitcher down, looked at me and whisked her hand back and forth over the mushroom fuzz. "You don't like it, do you?"

"I guess I'll get used to it Mom. I mean why…" I started to say, and then my stupid other self came out with, "Do you ever leave your body?"

Mom's frown squished her eyebrows together. "I beg your pardon? What makes you ask that?"

"Angie over at the store, she leaves her body."

Mom put the pitcher in the fridge. "I bet that's not all she does."

I wanted to smack my other self. I sure didn't want to talk about Angie, and fortunately Mom headed out the door with the tea so I didn't have to. I could hardly wait to take a look out the window to see if Dad's hair was gone too. It wasn't. It was just shorter, like normal haircuts. Phew!

Mom came right back in with the cheeseburger Dad had gotten for me. "Do you want me to warm this in the oven?"

"No thanks, I like it cold." Normally that wasn't true, but right then I needed to stuff my face to keep my other self from coming out with something else.

"I wouldn't spend too much time with that woman at the store, Zoey. She's liable to fill your head with a bunch of nonsense."

"It's not nonsense. She's…"

Ty cut my words off mid sentence when he came in. "It's dinner time at the zoo." He let the dogs down, and then he picked up a lemon that was on the counter and rolled it across the floor. The poodles scurried after it and Jolie got there first. She put her teeth right into it before she dropped it, shook her head, sneezed, and ran to Mom.

Mom whisked her up. "What're you doing? That was mean, Ty." The tone in Mom's voice was far too close to what I'd heard next door.

"Sheesh. All I was doing was fooling around. A little testy are we now that we don't have any hair? I feel pretty good about mine." Ty's hair was almost gone too, but on him it looked good.

"Just feed them," said Mom. "I'm going to make peach cobbler. So get the lemon, I need it."

Ty picked up the lemon and tossed it in the sink. He told me to feed the dogs. "I'm going over to shoot some pool. I don't think I'm too welcome here." He flew out the door.

Mom squished Jolie under her arm and took a can of dog food out of the cupboard. I told her I'd do it, but she had the top whipped off and scooped into their bowls in seconds. Jolie wriggled free, dropped to the floor and gobbled up her food. Jacques sat there looking baffled by the whole thing. He nosed his bowl over closer to Jolie's before he began to eat. When her food was gone, he let her put her face into his dish and nibble along with him. Pretty cute, is what I thought.

But I didn't feel cute, I felt stuck and I wanted out of there. "I'm going for a swim Mom. Would you like to come? It'd make you feel better."

"I feel fine. I'm going to make the cobbler. You go have a swim. I'd like to be quiet. That's what I'd like."

The "fine" was all I needed. I left.

I swam about a hundred laps and by the time I was finished I was too tired to care about anything any more. I didn't even have the energy to look and see if Angie was in the store. I just put one foot in front of the other and dragged myself home.

Mom was stretched out on the sofa reading, and I knew the yummy smell meant the peach cobbler was baking. I didn't know much about Mom's books other than she used to belong to a book club that read only inspirational books. She had a few on the table by her bed, but I'd never paid too much attention to them.

I could see the title on the one she'd just put on her stomach, and it was called *Your Erroneous Zones*, which sure didn't make much sense to me. I guess it did to her though, because her eyebrows weren't squished anymore. She looked up at me, "How was the swim?"

"Great. I'm sorry for how I was before, about your hair I mean. It was a shock, but it looks nice. Just different, that's all."

"Thanks, honey. That means a lot. I know it was a shock. It was for me as well."

I started to say, "Then, why…" but cut myself off real fast with, "I swam a million laps and I'm beat so I think I'll stretch out."

"Good idea. Your dad took the poodles to the beach and it's nice and quiet."

I stretched out on my bunk and closed my eyes, trying to picture myself up on a rainbow, like Angie when she left her body. I saw the rainbow all right, but my body wasn't going anywhere. My mind was far too busy worrying about Mom to think about body-leaving. I knew Dad needed peace and quiet and I was going to get it for him, but Mom, she needed something too. I wouldn't be able to even *try* getting it for her seeing as I had no idea what it was.

I put the pillow over my face and tried smothering myself but that didn't work. I didn't want to die anyway, but I did want to sleep so I started counting sheep. I guess that worked, because the next thing I knew Mom was telling me dinner was ready and she wanted me to set the table. I blinked my eyes about fifty times before I hauled myself out of the bunk.

I was so surprised at how much time had passed. The finished cobbler was on the counter along with the salad bowl that was piled high with lettuce and veggies. Dad was working at the table outside and Ty was putting the steak on the barbecue with the poodles drooling at his feet.

I gathered up all the place settings in a total daze, went outside and plunked them on the picnic table. Dad picked up his papers and stuck them in his file box just as Josh came back from the beach with two fish in his pail. I didn't care a lot about the fish, but I sure cared that Josh's blond curls were still there, a little shorter than before but that's all. I couldn't help but wonder what he and Dad thought about Mom going bald, but I bit my tongue to keep from making a big deal that I knew wouldn't get me anywhere.

"Good for you," said Ty. "You've got better luck than I do. Where's Lauren? Did she catch anything?"

"Neither of us caught anything. She got bored watching nothing happening on our lines, and when I got talking to the guy who was having all the luck, she took off. He got more bluefish than he wanted so he gave me these."

Mom put the salad and a plate of buttered bread on the table. "Why don't you take them over to Maya's seeing as we're having the steak. Where is Maya anyway? I haven't seen her since we got back."

I should've attempted an answer, because what came out of my mouth for sure wasn't from my regular self, and it wasn't good. "Zack smokes pot all day."

Whap! Josh whacked me.

Dad grabbed Josh's arm. "Don't you ever smack your sister. Tell her you're sorry. Now!"

"Yeah, sorry," Josh muttered. "I'll take the fish over there." He shoved the fishing gear under the trailer and took off.

"What made you say that, Zoey?" Mom asked.

I hadn't meant to tell on Zack, but my other self spilled the beans, so I pretty much had to try and clean the mess up. "It's just that I heard them fighting about him being stoned, but it was probably nothing. Just forget I said it."

"Well, it's not our business anyway," said Dad. "What Zack does is no concern of ours."

Mom told me to get some water for the table, but I knew it wasn't water she wanted. It was saying something private to Dad, even though Ty was out there cooking the steak. My head was already full, and it didn't have any room left for whatever Mom was going to say. So I closed my ears while I went in and took more time than was needed to fill up a bunch of glasses.

"Steak's ready, Sis," Ty called. I looked out the window and Mom and Dad were sitting there saying nothing at that point. So I went out with the water, and that's when Lauren showed up with Josh. Mom and Dad got all gushy and polite with her, like everything was hunky-dorey.

Ty put the steak platter on the table. "Have at it." He didn't look even a little bit like everything going on was way past weird. I wished I could get whatever Ty had that made him so easy-going about everything.

Actually Ty maybe wasn't as easy-going as he was just not nosy. I mean he probably wasn't even listening to what was being said. As a matter of fact he didn't even seem to care that Zack stayed in the bus or smoked pot or whatever. He told me once that minding other people's business just got you into trouble, and he swore he'd never do it. For sure, he paid a whole lot more attention to himself about that than I did.

Dad carved the steak and put slices on the plates and passed them around just as Josh showed up with Lauren.

"I want to share mine with Lauren," he said. "I left the fish over there and she wants steak."

"Is that okay?" asked Lauren.

"Fine," said Mom, which obviously meant the messy thoughts from what had happened before were still bothering her. She went ahead and doled out the bread and gave the empty plate to Josh for Lauren. The two of them sat practically glued together while Josh took some extra steak off the platter and put it on Lauren's plate with the salad Mom had given her. The plate wasn't half big enough, but nobody did anything about getting her a bigger one, and with my new plan to mind my own business, I didn't either.

"Where's Jesse?" I asked. "Wouldn't he like steak? He can have some of mine."

"He and Mom are working on a puzzle," said Lauren. "They'll have the fish when Dad gets it cleaned. Mom has a plate of cookies cooling for you guys if you want them."

"We've got a cobbler for dessert, but I'd be happy to get them later. Her cookies are great. Thanks, Lauren."

I couldn't believe Jesse would rather do a puzzle and have fish instead of steak. I wondered what kind of flower I ought to choose for

Jesse. Nothing showed up, and besides I was tired of trying to figure out the bunch of them. I finished my steak and took my plate inside.

I brought out the cobbler with some plates and put it on the table, but I didn't want any.

"Do you mind if I take the poodles to the park and have dessert when I get back, Mom? They don't look too happy." They were kind of huddled in a heap, and I knew they probably wanted under the pillows, but I needed to get out of there.

Mom piled the empty steak plates and headed into the trailer. "Suit yourself," she said.

"Thanks for the steak, Ty. It was great." I said that, but what I really wanted to do was scream bloody murder.

"You okay Sis?" asked Ty.

"I'm fine."

For the first time ever, I really got it how that word worked for my mother.

Discovering Buddhism

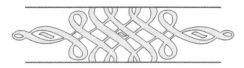

Next to being with Angie, the park was my favorite hang out when things got messed up at my place. It was so stupid how everyone in my family kept bad feelings inside, that is except for Josh, and all he did was make things worse by spouting off. For sure I couldn't have been the only one who wanted to scream bloody murder with all the tension going on over there.

I mean a lot of times on the trip I felt so totally alone, and other times I felt totally crowded out by everyone's stuffed feelings. I hated stuffing mine, and sure, having Amy to write to about them sure helped, but talking about some of them, well I just didn't know enough words.

Angie had said that we make up our lives the way we want them to be, and that I should remember Zoey is Love when I felt bad.

I could remember all of that easy enough, but feeling it sure didn't work for me. I mean I could make up, and even feel all kinds of good stuff when I was by myself, but making it up and feeling it, while being stuck in a trailer with my whole family, well it was no wonder there weren't any other kids my age in the campgrounds. They were probably all at summer camp like I was supposed to be.

At least the park gave me a place to go and get away without Mom freaking out. Ever since that day on the beach, she watched me like a hawk, but the park, it was right there, and you could almost see me in it from our trailer.

Me and the poodles, we liked to sit on the bench and daydream about how we wanted life to be the way it wasn't. I know that sounds crazy to say about the poodles, but honestly I knew they daydreamed as much as I did, and for sure hurt even worse than I did when things got messed up. They didn't have words for how they felt, but they sure knew how to show feelings. I bet Eli would say they were totally unique in the doggie world.

Well, for the first time ever, there wasn't going to be any daydreaming for me and the poodles, because there was a lady sitting on the only bench in the park. She looked to be somewhere in her twenties, but it was hard to tell with the big sunglasses she was wearing. She had a black lab curled up at her feet. She was sitting at one end of the bench reading a book. I decided I could sit on the other end without bothering her.

I hadn't planned on how dogs don't care about manners, and suddenly there was lots of commotion with the three of them discovering each other. The lab started sniffing the poodles as they nipped at his huge feet. In minutes the bunch of them were tangled in the poodles' leashes.

I tried to yank my dogs out of the mess, but nothing worked until I undid the leashes. All three dogs took off with the lab poking the poodles' bodies as they tumbled and rolled and popped up for more. The lady and I didn't say anything, but we did laugh, me a lot harder than her.

"I'm sorry," I said. "The poodles don't get to play like this with many dogs. We're usually the only ones here. I think most people take their doggies to the beach to play, but me and the poodles, we like being quiet sometimes."

"Not to worry. I think it's pretty cute."

"Do you mind sharing the bench?"

"Of course not. My name is Emily, my lab is Barney, and you're…?" She turned down a page corner and closed the book she'd been reading "I'm Zoey and the poodles are Jacques and Jolie. We're staying at the campground. Are you?" My eye caught the title of her book, *Knowing Peace.* I had to look twice to make sure I wasn't seeing things.

"I'm not, no." She didn't say where she was staying, she just got right into asking me about my family.

I told her we were traveling around the country looking for a new job for Dad. But I didn't want to talk about my family, I wanted to talk about the book, so I didn't waste any time asking, "Are you reading *Knowing Peace* because you don't have any?"

She put the book to her face and I wasn't sure why, that is until I heard my own words played back. "I'm sorry. I guess that sounded nosy. Sometimes I say stuff that comes out different than I wanted it to. What I meant to ask is if the book is good at describing peace."

She put the book in her lap and stroked it. "That wasn't nosy, it was honest. But about the book being good, I guess that depends on who's reading it. You seem intrigued. Tell me why the intrigue and maybe I can answer better."

Something about Emily kept me from coming right out with my assignment. She was full of another kind of mood that I didn't feel like interrupting. But I didn't want to go away either. I mean me finding someone reading a book about peace was way too weird to leave behind.

I forced myself to spit out, "I'm looking for what peace means to people so I can come up with a way to give my dad peace and quiet for his birthday. He doesn't have it and he wants it badly. That's why the book looks sort of promising, if that's the right word."

"My, Zoey, I'd have to say that's quite a gift."

"It would be if it was working, but so far I haven't learned anything I could make a gift out of."

Emily picked up the book and held it to her chest. "Well, promising is a perfect word for this book, so let's talk about what might be promising in here for both of us. But first of all, why are you wanting peace and quiet for your dad? He's not sick, is he?"

"Oh no. He's just out of whack from all the trailer stuff. And if it's okay, I'd rather not talk about him. I'd rather just hear about what's promising in the book for you, and then I can think about how it might be helpful for Dad. It's too hard to talk about Dad and all the things that make him want peace and quiet. I just want to get it for him. That's all."

"Okay. That's fair. So before we go any further, let me tell you that the book is about Buddhism. Do you even know what Buddhism is Zoey?"

I remembered a fat clay Buddha on my teacher's desk at school. I told Emily how Miss Miller had tried to explain what the Buddha was all about, but my mind had wandered. "I'll listen this time if you'll tell me again."

She opened the book to a page she had marked with a bent corner and read,

The root-word 'Buddh' means to wake up, to know, to understand. And he or she who wakes up and understands is called a Buddha.

Listening to Emily wasn't a whole lot easier than listening to my teacher. Waking up, knowing and understanding all at the same time didn't make a lot of sense to me. I told her I thought it was hard to do all those things at once.

Emily said, "It's a different kind of waking up than the sleeping kind, Zoey."

I felt like she was getting impatient with me because she sighed when she said that. "Do you think I'm not old enough for Buddhism?" I asked. "And maybe the book isn't what I hoped it'd be?"

"Of course you're old enough. Buddhism isn't complicated. What those words mean is that by 'waking up' you become aware of your thoughts. Then you can take time to understand them. That's all."

"So waking up is like understanding something? It's not like the opposite of being asleep?"

"Well it is, but not literally. 'Waking up' is just understanding that if you have bad thoughts, applying Buddhist principles can help wake you up to the power of how those bad thoughts are making you *feel* bad."

"Do you have bad feelings about your job, like my dad does about not having one? Is that why you're reading the book?"

"No, that's not why I'm reading *Knowing Peace*." Emily clasped her hands on top of the book so tight her knuckles got white. "My peace is different than the kind you're after. I'm trying to find a way to turn sadness into peace. I think that might be more difficult than what you're doing." She wrapped her hands around the book.

My heart gave at least a dozen extra beats. I'd known something was wrong with Emily right from the beginning. "Do you want me to go away so you can keep reading? I can go sit under that palm tree over there. I usually come here to daydream anyway and I can daydream just as easily over there."

"No, I don't want you to go anywhere. I like having you here and besides, look at the dogs." Barney was sprawled out beside the bench with the poodles nestled into his chest. "Who wants to disturb that." She slid her sunglasses up on her head. "How old are you anyway, Zoey?"

The red rims around her eyes told me she'd been crying and I wasn't at all surprised. The sound in her voice had been sad all along.

I told her I was eleven. "I don't think I'm old enough to say anything that'd fix being sad, like the stuff in the book might, but if listening would help, I can do that. I do it all the time with my best friend when she's sad."

Emily started patting the book. There was a long silence while she kept patting. I started staring at the dogs because watching Emily was making my heart ache.

Finally she whispered, "My daughter, my baby girl, was killed in a car accident. She was three."

I gasped. I'd known something terrible was coming but not that terrible. I wound the dogs' leashes around my fingers so tight they burned. All the blood in my body charged to my face.

Emily put her hand over mine. "I'm sorry. I didn't mean to scare you."

"That's so awful. I wish I could say or do something. Can I?"

"No. There's not much anyone can do, except hopefully myself." She pulled a pack of tissues from her purse and took one herself before she handed me the pack. I pulled one out. She wasn't crying, and I didn't want to make her feel worse so I made myself not cry either. She folded the tissue over and over again until she'd made a tiny square out of it.

She said, "Let's talk about your peace gift instead of me." She stuck her little square into the pack and put it back in her purse.

It felt to me like she was doing the pretend thing, going from something horrible right to my gift idea. Myself, I couldn't shift that easily. "I feel too awful to talk about my gift right now. Is it okay to tell me when that happened?"

"Of course it's okay. The accident happened six months ago tomorrow. We were on the way home from her nursery school and she was telling me about all the things that'd happened at school. And out of nowhere a man ran a red light and rammed right into her side of the car. He wasn't hurt and neither was I, but little Beth, she was killed instantly."

My whole body froze. Emily kept on talking, without crying or anything. The way she described the whole thing sounded like she was a news reporter, going back and forth from the beginning to the end, over and over. It was eerie the way she did that. She sure didn't sound like her baby's mother. If my whole self hadn't been frozen, I probably would've cried my head off just watching her talk.

When she finished the story she picked up the book. She didn't look at me, just at the book. And in another voice, one like my teacher announcing something important, she said, "I'm hoping that reading this will put me in the process of waking up to not only accepting what happened, but understanding how my negative thoughts are affecting my ability to move on."

Emily shifted around for a minute before she looked at me, like I was suddenly there and she was seeing me again. "I know all of this is difficult for you, young Zoey, but you're helping me by being here. Do you understand that?"

"I hope I'm helping you. I guess I don't know what else to do." I was being honest about that. I didn't want to pretend anything. But I did want to see a flower in Emily. No flower showed up. But what did was a butterfly, and that might've been from the way her short hair was being pushed out from the sides of her head by her sunglasses, sort of like wings.

"Talking to you," she said, "and hearing myself, is definitely waking me up to how I've trapped myself in painful feelings. Perhaps understanding that will help me free them and let them go."

"Like a butterfly, when it comes out of a cocoon." Honestly, where that came from, well I didn't even want to think about it, but it sure sounded neat.

"Pardon?" Emily popped her eyes real wide, red rims and all.

I told her I had a friend who taught me to see people as flowers. It was hard to describe the whole thing the way it worked, but I said I'd been trying it out, and she showed up as a butterfly, not a flower at all.

I unwound the leashes from around my fingers and spread them across my knees.

"Well a caterpillar certainly does wake up when it becomes a butterfly," she said. "That's good. I like the way your friend thinks."

Emily put the book back on the bench and squeezed my hands. "I know the search you're on is difficult, Zoey, but I'll tell you one thing, and that is that all the people you talk to about your gift are in for insights they'd never get any other way."

I blushed. that was so nice. "Do you really think so?"

"Absolutely. I know you're not very old, but honestly, being with you, well it's amazing how much better I feel." She sat back against the bench and wrapped her arms around herself. She was thinking stuff I couldn't hear, but I could sure feel it in all the quiet.

Suddenly she dropped her arms and turned to face me with a smile that I swear went right around her whole head. She clapped her hands together. "Hey, I just got a great idea I think might work for not only your dad's birthday, but you as well. Want to hear it?"

"I sure do," I felt just as excited as she looked.

"Well I'm a deep sea diver, and normally I'm diving in search of buried treasure. But when I'm diving for fun, swimming in rhythm with the beautiful fish, well that gives me a great deal of peace and quiet beyond anything I can describe. So what I'd like to do is arrange a private diving trip, you and me and your dad for his birthday, my treat."

I wanted to give Emily a hug right then, but as I was getting ready to do it I realized that what she wanted to do wouldn't work. I sagged like I'd been kicked in the stomach.

"What, Zoey?" she asked.

"Dad's birthday is more than a month away and we probably won't be here that long."

"That's not a problem. If you're not here, then let me know where you are, and as long as you're in Florida I can come to wherever you are. How about that?" She dug into her purse and pulled out a card that she handed me.

I read the name of the diving company on the card and *VP Special Projects* under Emily's name. I wasn't sure what that meant, but printed in gold it sure looked important.

I shoved the card in my pocket. "You'd honestly do that for me?"

"After what you've done for me today, you bet I would. And by the way, the phone number on the card is an 800 number so it's free anywhere."

With a quick look at her watch, she dropped her glasses back on her nose and picked up her book. "I'm running late so I'm going to have to go, but tuck the card away someplace safe and we'll be in touch."

She put the book in her purse and the leash on her dog. "C'mon Barney," she said and he leapt to attention. The poodles jumped on the bench and Emily ruffled their fur. "Pretty cute," she said as she hiked her purse strap over her shoulder. "I'm headed to the Keys but I'll probably be back up here in a few weeks. If you're not here, I'll look forward to a call."

I got up, and without even asking I gave her a hug. It didn't seem right to leave her with only a goodbye in case I never saw her again. She gave me a big hug back. Everything about being with Emily had made me feel like I was a grownup, sharing things that only grownups share, like Mom that day with the stuff she normally kept to herself. I hoped the diving trip would happen.

Out of nowhere came Josh, barreling across the park with a sourpuss look on his face. The dogs leapt off the bench and raced to him before I had a chance to attach their leashes.

He scooped them up. "I want to talk to you," he snarled when he got closer.

"What did I do?" I took the poodles from him. They didn't like an angry Josh any more than I did.

"Keep your mouth shut about Zack. Like Dad says, it's none of your business."

"But it's real serious. I heard Zack yelling at Maya, and I'm sure he was stoned too." The dogs wriggled. I put them down and hooked them up. I knew if they weren't leashed they'd take off and run all the way home so they could hide in Mom and Dad's room.

"Well it's none of your business Creep, so shut up about it."

"Does Lauren smoke pot?" Maybe I hoped for a truthful answer, but I knew from the nasty scowl on Josh's face that I wasn't going to get one.

"Look," he said. "I told you, it's none of your business. You keep your attention focused somewhere else. Hear me?" He grabbed hold of my arm. The poodles barked.

I said, "You're scaring the dogs Josh. Let go of me. That hurts."

"You're a damn sissy." He took off. He turned back long enough to say, "It's not a big deal and don't make it one." Right then I wished his firecracker would go off and blow him to smithereens.

"I don't care anyway," I said. He didn't hear me, but the poodles stared at me with their heads cocked and their ears perked. I wasn't sure what they were thinking with that look. I wondered if it was the "I don't care" they didn't believe. Probably. I nestled them in my arms and carried the bundle of love home.

When I got there I found both a big piece of peach cobbler and a note from Mom on the counter, saying they were at the pool, whoever "they" were. I was sure "they" didn't include Josh. I didn't want to swim, but I did want the cobbler, so I ate some and scooped the rest into the "no people food" doggies' bowls that they nosed right into. While they were at it I zipped over to see Angie so I could talk to her about Buddhism.

But the store was a total downer when I got there because it was full of people. Although I felt bummed as I watched them all milling around inside, I actually ended up being kind of glad that Angie was busy. With time to think while I waited for everyone to get out of there, I suddenly got it that throwing new stuff in with everything else I was learning from her would have been too much.

I went over to the pool, and for sure Josh wasn't there, but everyone else was. I flopped on the two-seater chair next to Ty and watched Mom and Dad doing their laps.

"Do you know anything about Buddhism, Ty?" I asked.

"About what?"

"Buddhism."

"No. Should I?"

"A Buddha is a person who wakes up and understands stuff. You already do that naturally, so I bet you'll be a Buddha when you grow up."

"Oh yeah? Is that good?"

"It sure is for me. But right now I like you just the way you are. Do you hide your feelings?"

"Why would I want to do that?"

"Just because that's what everyone does, don't y'think?"

"I think you're messing with your head, Sis. How about you just chill out."

"Angie does that, but she calls chilling out a joyride, that is if chilling out is doing nothing. Is that what it is?"

"I don't think there's any such thing as doing nothing for you, Zo." He got up and pulled me up with him. "C'mon, let's have a swim."

My Time With Mom

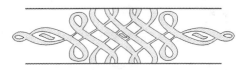

I finally got the letter from Amy I was waiting for, and boy was I glad to finally hear from her. I'd begun to wonder if she'd even been getting my letters. I ripped hers open and practically gobbled it up.

Hi Zo. I just got back from a trip to Long Island with Mom and Dad and I was so glad to get your address finally. It's been awful getting all your letters and not being able to answer them. I talk to them sometimes, like they're you. I know that sounds crazy, but with your picture on the wall and me sitting in front of it, I make up answers to your letters and hope you'll hear them. Why don't you sneak some money from your Mom's purse while she's asleep and find a phone booth to call me. I know it's a fortune, but I want to talk to you instead of your picture.

 Everyone at camp says they miss you too. I read them the parts of your letters that aren't a secret, and I showed them your postcards, and I wish you'd send more so we could see what other places look like. The people you've met sound like fun, especially Angie. When are you going to send the picture you promised to take? Tell your mom to get another camera. Maybe looking at them in your memory is good for you, but it sure doesn't work for me.

What you said about seeing people as flowers, that was sooo neat. With your imagination being the way it is, it was a perfect thing for you to do. I loved Ty being a lily, even though lilies are probably more a girl thing. But honestly, Ty is so sweet that a lily is perfect. I think you and me both being pansies is a great idea. We'll blend together, the way we do anyway.

Your other self was pretty weird, but not too surprising. If I had a guess, I'd bet you have a lot of personalities living inside you, so don't worry about being crazy or anything. I think I have a couple, but mostly they're the same as me. I just think of them as my imagination.

What Angie said about leaving her body was really wild though, but the part about making up your life the way you want it to be, I liked that so much, I told the camp director about it. What she did was turn the whole idea into a play, and we all acted out what we'd like to be. I pretended I was a doctor in the emergency room and some of the kids were my patients. I saved a girl with a ruptured appendix. She didn't like pretending to be a patient but I talked her into it. I don't know whether that's the kinda thing Angie was talking about, but it sure was fun. I felt good being a doctor.

Oh yeah, and I loved what Angie said about Zoey meaning Love. That sure didn't surprise me. You are love, Zo. That's for sure, xoxoxoxAmy.

When the visit with my best friend in the whole world was over I felt awful about the postcards. I just never thought of them because we didn't go into gift stores like we had in Nantucket and Martha's Vineyard, and it rained so hard at the Hyatt campground that I never bothered to go to the gift store. Sure there were postcards in the check-in stores, but not ones of places we visited. Looking at them bummed me out, so I didn't bother.

I wrote Amy back and told her we'd be going to Disney World, so I'd look for more postcards. I said there was no way we were getting a camera, but that Lauren would be taking pictures, so maybe she'd take one of Angie too. After that I brought her up to date on everything else that had happened since my last letter.

I'd just started writing about Emily's diving trip idea when I caught Dad getting ready to leave for the library. I put down my pen and went to ask him when his package was coming so we could go to Disney World.

"I wish I knew, sweetheart. But I'll stop by the post office on my way through town."

"How come you didn't have the package mailed here? Wouldn't it be a whole lot easier to watch for it here than the post office?"

"I guess when I decided I wanted the package I wasn't sure whether we'd still be here. It just seemed easier to work with the post office about forwarding if I needed to. As it turns out I like it here, so you're right, I could have used this address."

"Have you ever done any diving Dad?" Boy, that question fell right out and surprised both of us.

"Where in the world did that come from?"

I had to think fast. "I'm talking about treasure diving. I met a treasure diver over in the park and she dives for stuff that's buried in the ocean. Isn't that neat? I just wondered if you'd ever done any diving, that's all. But it's okay. If you're in a hurry we can talk about it later."

He backed up and flopped on the sofa. "I'm never in too much of a hurry for you Zo. It's just that sometimes you do come out with the darndest things, and I like that about you. So in answer to your question, I've always wanted to dive. Not for treasure but I'd like to get a look at all the beautiful fish. Maybe I'll hire a boat and a diving trainer to give us lessons. It'd be fun. Would you like that?"

"Sure." I tried to sound excited but my crumpled insides sure weren't excited. I could only hope that with everything else Dad had going on in his head he'd forget about a family diving trip, or at least until after his birthday.

"Okay, a diving trip it is," he said. "And in the meantime I'll go by the post office, and if the package is there, then you guys can take off for Disney World." He was out the door.

I went back to my bunk to finish off Amy's letter, and right in the middle of describing how my other self had almost ruined Emily's gift surprise, I realized something awful. And that was that a private diving trip with Emily was not what I wanted for my assignment. Going diving for a day would not be giving Dad peace and quiet for always. The peace and quiet he needed was a whole lot bigger than a day in the ocean looking at pretty fish.

I ripped up the page that had everything about Emily's idea on it, and just ended the letter on the page before, with some hugs and kisses at the bottom.

I was left with a really dumpy mood from realizing Emily's idea wouldn't work. I reached under my mattress and got my bag of notes out to have another look at them and see if there wasn't something in them to get me pumped again.

But as soon as I had them out of the bag, I realized I couldn't take a chance that Mom or the boys would show up. So I stuck them back and took them to the shower room. I locked the door (which was a total no-no) and emptied the bag and spread the scribbles in some kind of order across the long counter of sinks.

The first note I picked up was about Eli, and as I read I couldn't think of a single way to get Dad's creative spirit to express itself. What's more, I figured he'd probably have to have peace and quiet first before he'd even know he had a creative spirit.

I moved on to Ollie and found nothing there other than a big question about whether peace and satisfaction were the same thing. That was too hard to think about so I moved on to Emily, and of course I already knew that her idea wouldn't work, but there was lots of other stuff that she'd said for myself, especially the part about waking up being like understanding something. I loved the idea of Ty being a Buddha some day and then showing me how it worked. It sounded really neat from Emily, and for sure I knew I had a lot of waking up to do if I was ever going to figure out how to get peace and quiet for Dad.

I piled the notes one on top of the other, matching the faces to the words. I saw Maya's huge poppy and Angie's wildflowers and that was fun, but for sure not even close to an idea that was going to fix Dad. And even worse, some people had said I wasn't supposed to fix him, that I was supposed to just be a kid. But how could I be a kid and do kid things if there weren't any kids to do stuff with?

I left the notes on the sink and flopped on the bench in the middle of the room. I wrapped my arms around my head and squeezed my eyes shut.

Suddenly a picture of Amy lit up the blackness in my head. And not only Amy, but all the kids at summer camp. We were leaping hurdles. Not normal hurdles, but wide, going-on-forever hurdles, with about twenty of us together in a long row, leaping over one hurdle after another. The best part was that we were holding hands and the bunch of us were laughing our heads off.

The door handle rattled. "Is there someone in there?"

The voice was loud enough, but behind my covered eyes I went right on hurdling faster than ever.

"Answer me! Who's in there?"

I dropped my hands and my eyes jerked open. In a flash that made me gasp, my friends were gone. I jumped up and stuffed all the notes back in the bag.

"I'm coming," I blubbered, trying to push back a rush of tears that wouldn't stay. I yanked a heap of paper towels from the holder and scrunched them in my eyes. I hurled the tear soaked wad across the room, missing the trash. The tears kept coming. I wiped them away with my fists before I unlocked the door and sped past whoever was standing there. I ran to the trailer hoping no one was home.

No such luck. There was Mom, curled up on the sofa with the poodles. She was attaching the fastener to a string of beads.

I went past her and shoved the paper bag under my mattress. The poodles jumped off the sofa to follow me and I scooped them up. "I'm taking the dogs for a walk." I grabbed their leashes off the table.

Mom held up the necklace. "Before you go, come have a look at this." I looked quickly, but not quickly enough to hide my blotchy face.

"Have you been crying, honey? What's wrong?" She put the necklace on the table by the sofa.

"Nothing's wrong. I want to take…" I started to say, but Mom grabbed my arm and the dogs fell to the floor.

"Wait a minute. I know something's wrong, so talk to me."

I leaned over to leash the poodles but I lost my balance and fell over. They darted off to Mom's room.

Mom slid to the floor and went to put her arms around me and I pulled away. Being that close, with her staring at me, made me scared. The blonde curls I used to twirl in ribbons and play hairdresser on were all gone, and the makeup she used to wear to be pretty, that was gone too. She'd been that way all along, but right then I wanted to grab her hair and makeup from the trash in Baltimore and glue it back on so she'd be my other mother again.

"Speak to me, honey. I can't help if you won't talk to me."

"What do you care?" I got up, and I knew that was mean, but mean seemed to be the only way to keep my tears back. I put the leashes on the table and ran outside.

I didn't get very far. Mom put her hand on my shoulder and whirled me around. "I'm sorry Zoey. Please come back inside."

I went because I didn't know what else to do.

Mom plugged in the kettle in the kitchen. "Let's have a cup of tea. You know, like we used to have sometimes after school."

"I don't want any tea." I started to pick at a hangnail. "Why did you say you were sorry?"

"Don't pick at yourself. You only do that when you're upset." She unplugged the kettle and came to sit beside me.

I shoved my hands under my legs. Although I was upset for a whole bunch of reasons, I just said, "I need you to not be sorry. I need you to be my mother who makes things better, not worse." Maybe that sounded like more mean, but it was true. I wanted so badly for her to make things better. Couldn't she use some of her inspirational book stuff on me? That's what I wanted to say, but I didn't. Her whole body had gone rigid.

She picked up her necklace and started attaching the clasp again. Her fingers moved super fast. I could feel her practicing words inside her head, and after one last wind, she tied the knot. She cut the line with her clippers and put the necklace and clippers back on the table.

Then she turned to me and the practiced words came out real clear, "I said I was sorry because that's how I feel seeing you upset. But more than sorry, I feel responsible. I know I'm supposed to make things better for you and I can't do that if I don't even know what's wrong." She lifted her arm as if she was about to put it around me, but then dropped it in her lap. Her face had that drawn look that goes with being worn out. I knew I was wearing her out and I hated that.

All I heard was, "make things better for you, but I can't do that if I don't even know what's wrong."

"Is that why you say "fine" all the time Mom? Do you use that word when you don't want to talk about stuff. It's weird the way you do that."

The worn-out look sure didn't go away when she said, "I do a lot of things that I'm sure are weird, but right now I'm concerned about you, so please tell me why you were crying."

It was so awful hearing her say that, and all I wanted to do was forget about me and talk about her weird stuff. But I knew she wasn't going to talk about herself, and anyway, mostly I wanted her not to be sorry. I needed the frown to go away so I just said, "There's nothing wrong with me. It's only that I miss Amy and all the kids at camp. That's not your fault. You don't have to be sorry."

And then the frown left. "Of course you miss them. And you've been good about not complaining. But what's important to remember is we're not doing this trip for pleasure. We're doing it so Dad can find a new career idea."

"I know that, but he said we'd be doing fun things, going places and seeing all the stuff in the Big Book. And we're not doing any of it. Did you know all along that there wouldn't be any sightseeing? Was that just more of you keeping things to yourself?" I started ripping a new hangnail, but Mom covered my hand with hers and squeezed tight.

"Please don't do that. Picking at yourself doesn't help anything. I wasn't keeping anything to myself. I had no idea, any more than you, that we wouldn't be having fun sightseeing. I honestly believed we would, and I know Dad did too, but the logistics of traveling and campground living, combined with the job idea search, well it isn't quite as easy as either of us imagined, and I'm sorry about that."

"So are you saying you don't like it?"

"I'm not saying I don't like the trip. But with all the uprooting, I feel like I've been a lousy mother, and that's what I'm sorry about." She took the hand I was picking at and held it in both of hers. "It's difficult to be a mother with everything up in the air like it is. A mother likes to nest, hover over her brood and keep them safe. I don't even know what that means anymore."

She picked up her necklace and stretched it across her lap. "Besides, what I usually am is an artist, a weaver in a studio of other artists. I'm not a craftsy vagabond, and I don't know how to be one of those either." She let go of my hand and scrunched the necklace up.

I took it from her and held it up. "It's beautiful, Mom." I put it over her head and hung it around her neck. It looked really pretty on the white scooped-neck blouse she was wearing. "You should go look at yourself. You're not a craftsy vagabond."

She didn't say anything. She just smiled at me and her eyes got all teary. I didn't get to see the tears spill because she jumped up. "Wait a minute. I've got something I'd like to read you. Maya loaned me a book, and it's helping me try to be a better mother."

A rush of love whizzed through me so fast I had to squeeze my fingers tight to keep from bursting a bunch more tears and ruining everything.

She was back in a minute with the book, and the necklace was still around her neck. She sat beside me, and although she didn't look at me I could see her eyes were dry. She had probably looked in the bedroom mirror and got to feel proud of herself.

"Before you read anything," I said, "please don't think you're a lousy mother. I hate you saying that. You're just not the mother I'm used to, that's all. And I guess nobody's who we're used to, the way we're all heaped together in here."

"I know, and I wish the boys could listen to what I want to read. It'd definitely be good for them as well. The book's called *A Gift From The Sea*. It's a story of mother love, a story of loss."

I gulped right out loud. "I don't want to hear about sadness right now. Can you just read about mother love?" I jammed my hands back under my legs.

"The book is not only about sadness, honey. It's about loss, and what I want to read here is about dealing with loss." She opened to a page marked with a piece of wool.

Whatever that was supposed to mean. All I could think of was Emily, and I felt myself getting freaked out. "What sort of loss are you talking about Mom. Isn't loss always sad? You've got me worried because I don't know what you're talking about."

She sighed as if I was making her crazier than she was making me. She put the book in her lap with her hands clasped on top of it while she closed her eyes and leaned her head against the wall. I didn't say anything, and after a few seconds she opened her eyes. She held the book and turned to face me. "Before I read anything, I'll clarify for you what I know is true for our whole family about loss, and that is we've lost a lot, Zoey. We've lost our home and our neighbors and a familiarity we loved, with friends we counted on, and meaningful activities we took for granted. But the point in doing what Dad's doing is so we'll have a better life, and we'll have a dad who's a real dad, living a life of joy and fulfillment, rather than one of angst and frustration."

With another sigh, this time like she'd just spelled a big word right, she said, "The loss Ms. Lindberg is writing about is a whole lot bigger than any loss I've described for us. But nonetheless, dealing with loss of whatever the level, is all the same. And that's why I want to read about how she dealt with hers."

"Did you cut your hair off to deal with your loss?" Wow! My other self even *thought* stuff before me. That was a whole new idea *I* sure hadn't thought of before.

Mom sighed, running one of her hands over the fuzz on top of her head. "I don't have a good answer for you about why I cut my hair off before I left. But when we went for haircuts, maybe I did do what you're suggesting. All I know is I felt a little crazy that day, and my sense of loss probably had a lot to do with the crazies. I don't know, but that's very insightful, honey. Maybe we should trade places. You be the mom and I'll be your kid. I think I'd make a better child than a mother." She put the book on the sofa beside her and squeezed my hand with both of hers, so tight it hurt.

I felt the squeeze right down to my toes. "Don't say that, Mom. I'd make a lousy mother. I don't feel too insightful, if that means I'm supposed to know stuff."

"You do. You know a whole lot more than you think you do, there's no doubt about that. And applying insight to what you know in order to help you deal with it, that's what Ms. Lindbergh describes here. So let me read what she says, and then we can talk about it. Okay?"

"Okay." I said that, but my insides sure didn't feel okay. I had that crammed feeling I get sometimes when I try to stick more in my head than there's room for.

Mom let go of my hand and picked up the book. She read,

"I want, in fact -- to borrow from the language of the saints -- to live 'in grace' as much of the time as possible. By grace I mean an inner harmony essentially spiritual, which can be translated into outward harmony. I would like to achieve a state of inner spiritual grace from which I could function as I was meant to in the eye of God."

She put the book down, and when she looked at me her eyes were wet. "What do you think?"

"Can you read it again? I only understood some of the words, and I feel scared if it makes you cry."

Mom dug in her pocket and brought out a hanky to wipe her eyes. "These aren't sad tears, they're enlightened tears." She actually smiled.

I didn't know what enlightened tears meant exactly, but Mom's smile made me sure they were good. She started over and read slowly. I paid close attention this time, and there was a lot of what she read that sounded like it fit right in with what I was doing for Dad. "Do you suppose inner harmony is the same as peace?"

"My, now that's insightful. What part of the reading makes you ask that?"

"It just came to me, so I wondered what you thought, that's all. Is Dad reading the book?"

"No, he's not reading the book. What Mrs. Lindberg shares is my goal. Dad's goal is finding a way to make a living, and the best all of us can do to make his job easier is try to provide harmony around him."

At that moment Josh came in. "We got a little togetherness going on here?"

I told him we'd been talking about harmony. "And it's too bad you weren't here 'cause you could sure use some." As soon as those words came out of my mouth I wanted to smack myself. Instead I just asked, "D'you want to read Josh what you just read, Mom?"

"I'm not into harmony," said Josh. "I'm into lunch."

I said, "It's really good, what she read. It'll help you not be so mad about missing football camp."

"Oh yeah? I doubt that, but let's hear it." He flopped on the chair across from us.

Mom picked up the book and read what she'd read me.

"Nice words," said Josh, "but I don't know how they're supposed to fix not going to football camp." He got up and went to the kitchen. "How about lunch? Seems like a good time for baloney sandwich."

I felt like sticking out my tongue, but I didn't. I just said, "Not funny Josh."

Mom got up. "I'll make you a baloney sandwich. I'll make one for all of us."

She did, and after the baloney sandwich, while Mom was doing her best to explain about our family's loss to Josh (and he was actually listening) I said I wanted to run over to the store and get a chocolate bar. That was true, but mostly what I wanted was Angie. Right then I needed another joyride lesson. I wasn't sure Mom and Josh were even listening, so I just took off.

Through the window I could see Angie inside sorting the cigarette display behind the counter. With the jangle of the doorbell, she turned, but there wasn't any star-toothed smile, or any field of wildflowers, only a "Hi, sweetface."

"I know you're working, but can we have another joyride lesson today, Angie?"

She put the carton she was emptying on the counter. "I'm sorry, babycakes. I can't give you much of anything today. My boss was real angry, and he's been hanging around like a hawk to see that I do my job his way."

"Does that mean we won't be able to have a joyride lesson, and that I can't come here and talk to you anymore? Does Monster Man hate me?" I could feel tears building in my eyeballs.

Angie came around the counter and wrapped me in a hug. "Of course he doesn't hate you. But everything's a mess here." She pulled a Kleenex from a box on the counter and handed it to me.

I pushed it in my eyes. "That's terrible! Was it my fault for waiting on the cigarette guy?"

Angie went behind the counter and sat on her stool. She stretched her arms across the glass, weaving her fingers together and popping her hands up and down. "You are so cute. You're about the cutest kid I ever met, and I want you to know that none of this is your fault. Monster Man is the way he is, and I think the best thing we can do about that is take a break, you and me. I've got a job to do, and I need to keep the old guy happy. So give me a couple of days and I'll come up with a plan for how we can get some time together to do more joyride practicing, okay?"

"Okay." I said that, but I sure didn't feel okay. My eyeballs weren't wet anymore, but I stuck the Kleenex in my pocket instead of throwing it in the trash. Before I left I bought two chocolate bars and ate both on my way home.

The Library With Dad

The next day was Saturday and Dad was working at home, but he said he wanted to go to the library to check on something. I was still bummed about no joyride lesson, so to make myself feel better, I decided to go to the library with Dad and look up stuff about angels. Angie's leaving her body made me wonder about angels. In church they called angels heavenly, and for sure Angie was heavenly in my mind, but she only left her body when she wanted, and angels, well I wasn't sure how they got to be heavenly, or even got to be angels for that matter. Anyway, it sure felt like a fun thing to research.

I asked Dad if I could come with him and maybe look around if he wasn't staying for long. Actually, apart from looking up stuff about angels, I secretly hoped that being alone with Dad for that long might finally give me a chance to learn something unique about him.

"Sure," he said. "I just want to get a phone number so I can call to see why my package hasn't arrived. So yeah, you can come."

A few miles into the drive I was trying to think of how to get the knowing him thing started, when all of a sudden my other self barged right in. "Are angels people who leave their bodies, Dad?" I know I was planning on looking up angels at the library, but not right then. I mean my other self had practically taken over my whole life was how it seemed.

"I beg your pardon?" Dad looked over at me when he shouldn't have, missing a car by inches. "Jeezuz! Did you see that? The idiot cut right in front of me."

I pulled a piece of gum from my pocket, yanked off the wrapper and I shoved it in my mouth.

Dad turned on the radio and rock music filled the car. He smacked his hand against the steering wheel and turned it off. "Dammitt, I wish that kid would leave my things alone." Josh had obviously been practicing his driving skills in the campground.

The last time Dad was bombarded with rock station music he made his point very clear. "Turn the damn radio off when you're finished practicing Josh. You shouldn't be driving the car anyway."

Josh stormed out of the trailer.

Mom was there too. "Go easy Sammy. Give the kid a break."

"All I want is the radio off when I get in the car. If he turns it on for some stupid reason, all he has to do is turn if off. Is that too much to ask?"

Mom's reply was a total blur, but back in the car a lot of silence went by before Dad reached his hand across the seat and squeezed my knee. "What were you saying about angels, sweetheart?"

"Never mind, Dad. Can we talk about what you're interested in?"

"Not if you're going to chew gum. I hate that. It reminds me of the idiots at the office who always chewed gum when they were trying to get on my nerves."

I spit the gum into the wrapper and stuck the wad in my pocket. "Sorry."

"You don't have to be sorry. You'd have to do a lot more than chew gum to get on my nerves. Your brother, now he knows how to do that without even chewing gum. I'm the one who's sorry for spouting off. I didn't mean to upset you."

"I'm not upset, I'm just sorry that Josh does stuff that upsets you. I don't want anyone to be upset. I probably hate that more than you hate gum chewing."

"Me too."

"If you didn't have a job, Dad, like stayed at home if you could, what would you do for fun?"

"Boy, that's a good question, sweetheart. I've never thought of it because I've worked all my life, so my focus has been on work. Now, at least I have a chance to work at what I want to do, rather than what I have to do to make a living. Working at something creative, something that'll make a difference in the world. that's what I intend to do for fun. Does that answer your question, sweetheart?"

Honestly, I got goosebumps all over my body. "I guess I was wondering about hobbies or stuff. But what you say is way better than a hobby, isn't it."

"For me, if I find what I'm after, it'll be like a hobby." He reached his hand over and took mine. "And if it's as good as I intend it to be, it'll make a lot of money, so we'll all be happy. Right?"

"Right" I said, "I like you holding my hand, Dad, but I'd rather you drove with both of yours."

"Oh, you're so smart, Zoey. I really like that about you." He put his hand back on the wheel.

The rest of the drive was quiet, both of us in our own heads with everything, I think.

When we got there, Dad pulled up in front of the library and turned off the engine. "Let's go see if they have anything about angels. I don't think you'll have to look too hard though, because you're the best angel I know."

Dad sure knew how to use words to turn himself into a wide open African daisy. I knew I blushed, but he didn't see. He just told me to meet him at the checkout counter after I got what I wanted. He rushed off.

A granny lady with puffy white hair and a pretty pink ruffled blouse sat at the information desk. Her gauzy sleeves fluttered across the desk as she answered questions. I wondered about a flower for her, but my mind was way too busy figuring out angels to make up flowers. After she'd finished helping a couple, I went over to her desk and asked her if she'd show me how to look for angels.

She giggled. "Maybe heaven would be a good start."

The giggle made me want to be playful back. "Is heaven in here?"

She leaned forward and whispered, "Heaven's everywhere. As a matter of fact, you're heaven yourself."

At that point she seemed so perfect for my assignments that I leapt right in. "Do you know what peace is?"

She chuckled. "Land sakes! Angels, heaven, and now peace. You are the inquisitive young thing, aren't you?"

My cheeks burned and I rubbed them. "I guess so. Am I too much trouble?"

"No, no, of course you're not too much trouble. I can see I haven't helped you a bit. Now tell me what it is you're after." She took off her glasses and set them on the desk.

I looked around to make sure no one was waiting. Then I told her I'd come to research angels, but that I suddenly wanted to know whether she had any ideas about peace. I said I wanted to give it to my dad.

She stared at me, but her eyes kept right on twinkling. "Well, now you've definitely got me intrigued. Tell me, what's your name, child? Priscilla? You look like a Priscilla."

"Wouldn't a Priscilla be prissy? I'm not prissy. I'm inquisitive, not prissy."

"I know you're not a prissy girl. I don't know why I suggested Priscilla. My name is Missy, Missy McDougal. And I'm no missy either. I've been married for sixty years."

"Boy, that's a long time." I told her my name was Zoey.

"Everyone around here calls me Grammy. So call me Grammy if you like. And now tell me what this is all about, you wanting to give your daddy peace. I'm not sure what that means exactly. Researching angels sounds a lot easier to me. Are you sure we shouldn't do that?"

"I'm sure. I mean, after living for so long you must know a lot about peace, and right now I'd rather hear about that if it's okay."

"Well of course it's okay. I've lived through a couple of wars, so I know a lot about the kind of peace that follows war, but I'm feeling that's not what you're talking about. Am I right?"

I nodded my head real hard. "I'm talking about the kind of peace that goes with peace and quiet. I want to give that to my dad for his birthday. The only problem is I'm not sure how to do that. So I'm asking people what peace means to them, hoping maybe I'll hear something I can turn into a gift"

"My oh my. That is not exactly the kind of question a volunteer at the library is asked to answer." And with one of those cute granny chuckles, she added, "I surely have lived a long time, you're right about that, Zoey. So I should know a good deal about peace, and I'm sure I do. But what instantly comes to mind happened just last week when I got to have probably the best peace of my entire life."

She sat back on her chair with a wide grin that carved a thousand tiny lines all over her face. She crossed her arms as if she was satisfied with herself, the same way Ollie had with his big fish. "I'd like to tell you about it," she said. "But you look like you're in a bit of a rush. Do you have time to sit a minute or two?"

I looked around and there was no sign of Dad, so I sat on the empty chair across the desk from Grammy. "I think I've got time. But are you sure you shouldn't be doing something else?"

"I'm a volunteer, so I can do whatever I like, and what I'd like to do is help you with your precious gift."

"That'd be really nice."

She uncrossed her arms and clasped her hands on the desk. "Well, what I'm referring to happened last Monday, in the early morning when my darling son called to tell me that he'd retired from active duty on the police force. Forty years on the streets with terrible violence and many murders, those years filled my days and nights with tremendous worry.

Then, on that blissful day, just like that, my worries lifted. Our boy gave his daddy and me such a gift of peace that we spent the whole day sitting in quiet at the foot of our garden, our hearts overflowing with gratitude." Grammy bent her elbows and pressed her palms together. "Talking about it, well I feel a surge of gratitude in here right now." She patted her heart.

I could almost feel what Grammy was feeling, the way her eyes watered and her smile looked so sweet. But at the same time, what she said had me worried. I clasped my hands in my lap real tight when I said, "For Dad to get the kind of peace you're talking about, I'd have to do something really big for him, like your son did for you, something huge to take his worries away. And I don't even know what most of his worries are, Grammy. So do you think that means I can't give him peace and quiet?"

Grammy slid her chair back and opened the desk drawer. She took out a folded sheet of paper. "I'd like to share something with you, Zoey, something that might be of more help than my story of peace and quiet." She closed the drawer and slid her chair back. "I'm afraid it's not another gift idea. However, maybe I can offer you some advice for your own worry about your dad's worries. Would you like that?"

"I don't know. I think I'd rather hear another peace and quiet idea."

"Well we'll share this first, and as long as your daddy doesn't come along, or nobody interrupts us, we can talk about other peace and quiet ideas after we've talked about this." Grammy unfolded the paper and said she'd brought it to share with one of the ladies that worked there. "It's called *The Serenity Prayer,* and I honestly feel that sharing it with you is important right now. She picked up her skinny half glasses, perched them on the end of her nose and read,

God grant me the serenity to accept the things I cannot change, courage to change the things I can, and wisdom to know the difference.

Grammy took her glasses off and handed me the sheet. "Here. I'd like you to read the prayer to yourself. I'm not sure that only listening to it is reaching your precious heart."

I read the prayer and it reached my heart all right, but my heart didn't like it much. "I'm not trying to change Dad, Grammy. I just want to give him what he says he wants, that's all."

With another eye-crinkling smile Grammy reached across the desk, and squeezed my hand. "The paper has nothing to do with your daddy's gift. It only has to do with an old lady's nosy view of the situation. And that is, I honestly feel you're asking a lot of yourself to want to get rid of your daddy's worries for him. I believe it's his job to do that for himself. And for yourself, accepting his need for peace and quiet as being his, not yours, would be an enormous burden released from your young shoulders." Grammy let go of my hand and clasped hers again.

I read the prayer over once more, and then I put it down and asked her if it was hard to know the difference between what you can and can't change. "When I want to do something, I have a hard time not doing it. I don't ask God for anything, Grammy. I wouldn't know how." I handed her back the prayer so I could hide my hands in my lap and pick at my fingers.

Grammy folded the paper and slipped it back in her drawer. "You stick with the angels, child. God and the angels, they talk to each other."

Right then Grammy's eyes looked past me. "Oh, oh! I guess we're not going to be able to continue our precious talk. I think your father is on his way over here. He looks like a man on a mission."

I turned, and she was right. "He's always on a mission, and I know I can't change that." I signaled to let Dad know I was coming. I asked, "Can I come back and talk to you again?"

"That's hard to say, Zoey, because I don't have a schedule, so I only come when I'm needed, and I never know when that will be. I'm awfully glad I was here today though, because this has indeed been a treat for me."

"It has been for me too, and I'm sure glad you were here." I got up.

"Now, away you go, precious child. And know that the angels you came here looking for are not on the library shelves. They're running right along with you."

"Will they show me themselves?" I asked, partly teasing and partly serious.

"They won't have to. You'll feel them." She blew me a kiss so I blew one back.

When I caught up with Dad he told me he got the number and made the call, that the package was on its way and he should have it any time. "Did you learn anything about angels, sweetheart?"

"I didn't get a chance to look because I got busy talking to the information lady. She was really nice. Do you worry about stuff Dad? Is that why you want peace and quiet?"

"I beg your pardon? What does me worrying have to do with the angels?"

"I just wondered if that's why you want peace and quiet so much, to keep you from worrying."

"Worrying? Peace and quiet? What were you and that lady talking about?"

"She told me about her son who used to be a policeman and how much she worried about him."

"And what's that got to do with peace and quiet, or angels?"

"Nothing." I felt myself falling right into my own trap. I caught myself with, "It's a long story and it doesn't matter. I should've looked up angels. Can we do that now?"

"Not now, sweetheart. Anyway, if you do research on angels, you'll probably take the magic away."

"Do you think angels and people who leave their body have anything to do with each other?"

Dad stopped dead in his tracks and stared at me. "That is the craziest thing I've ever heard. First of all, people don't leave their bodies, and secondly, angels don't have anything to do with people. So what are you talking about?"

"People do leave their bodies. Angie over at the store, she leaves her body. She told me how she does it too."

"Why should I be surprised to hear that? Your mom says you've been spending too much time over there, and if that's what you talk about, no wonder Mom says she's crazy."

He reached for my hand as we headed out the door, but I shoved it in my pocket. "Angie's not crazy. She's a nice lady. She takes care of her almost blind granny and works hard at the store. You're not being fair."

"Well maybe it's time we considered settling down so you can go to school when it starts. Would you like to live in Florida?"

Obviously Dad hadn't heard a word I'd said about Angie, and for sure the angel conversation was over. "I'd like the diving trip you promised and I'd like to see Disney World, but those are the only things I'd like about living here. When are we going to have the diving trip anyway?"

"Funny you mentioned that. I've been thinking about it a lot. The other day I noticed a store about a block from here where they arrange trips. Why don't we go over now and check it out?"

I couldn't believe my ears. "That's a great idea Dad." We practically raced down the block. We didn't bother to take the car.

Then came the lousy part. The store had a big sign on the door. AWAY FOR A MONTH. The window was filled with diving gear on mannequins in a made-up underwater scene. I couldn't believe the owner would leave the store closed for a whole month.

Dad groaned. "I'm sorry. The sign wasn't there the other day, so it must be new." He took my hand. "But how about we stop at the post office on the way home. Maybe if we're lucky, the package will have arrived, and then your mom can take you guys to Disney World tomorrow. How would that be?"

"Really?" I let go of his hand jumped up and down, the way Amy and I used to when good things happened.

Dad laughed. "Yeah, really."

We got the car and stopped at the post office. Sure enough the package was there. I could hardly wait to share the Disney World news with everyone.

When we got home, Mom, Maya, Josh, Lauren, Jesse and the poodles were sitting at our picnic table, the poodles wrapped in Jesse's arms. Ty was roasting hot dogs on the barbecue.

"Did you get lunch?" asked Mom.

"Hot dogs would be great," I said. "We were too busy for lunch. Dad got his package at the post office, so that means we can go to Disney World tomorrow."

"Far out," said Josh. "Disney World, here we come." He put his arm around Lauren. "You want to come with us?"

"Disney World can wait," said Mom. "I've got even better news." With a huge smile, she threw her arms around Dad's neck. "Maya has made us an offer we can't refuse."

Dad untangled himself. "Oh yeah? What might that be?"

"She's offered to take care of the kids so you and I can have a break and get away by ourselves."

"Hey, I like it."

"But Dad," I groaned. "You said…"

Maya jumped in. "Okay, so I'll make a different deal. I went to Disney World on a teacher's conference right after The Magic Kingdom opened, so it'd be great if you'd take Jess and Lauren with you tomorrow, Meg. And when you get back, you and Sam can take off for as long as a whole week if you want, and I'll look after the kids. How's that sound?"

"A whole week for just one day, that doesn't sound exactly fair," said Mom.

"It's not about a time amount Meg, it's about getting what we both need. I need a day alone with Zack and you need a week away with Sammy. Simple."

Boy, that sure was the teacher part of Maya, the way she made everything sound so good for everybody.

Mom didn't say anything, but Dad did.

"Actually, that's perfect. Tomorrow I'll get the work I just got in the mail handled, and then I'll be free to take off the next day. How's that, Meg?"

Mom smiled really big. "Sounds good to me. Thanks, Maya."

Dad's grin went practically right around his head. "So you guys take off first thing in the morning. You'll need the whole day to get in all the rides. Right, Jesse?

With a mouthful of hotdog, Jesse nodded his head extra hard.

Ty handed me a hot dog, plastered in mustard and ketchup. "This is yours Sis. I'm practicing cooking for when we're alone."

Ty cooking sounded like fun, but being left alone with Josh sure didn't.

I decided not to think about that. Instead I let my thoughts soar with the idea of spending a whole day at the biggest playground in the world. Well maybe not the whole world, but the biggest one I knew about. I wished we could've left right away and stayed the night in a hotel, but I knew staying overnight in a hotel was way too expensive, so I didn't bring it up.

That afternoon my soaring mood got flattened real fast. I was in the trailer reading my book in my bunk when outside I heard Mom and Maya talking at the picnic table. Dad and Ty had gone off somewhere in the car, and Mom probably thought I'd gone too, so it would never have occurred to her that I was in the trailer.

I got off my bunk and hid behind the curtain and peeked out to see Mom with the poodles and Maya sitting across from them. I sat back, but I couldn't help eavesdropping through the open window. I knew if I was ever going to learn anything about anybody, this was my chance.

The first words I heard were Mom's. "I don't feel good about leaving you with the kids, Maya. I know you offered, but honestly…"

Maya cut Mom off. "There's no discussion. You and Sammy need to get away. Your haircut was a clear sign that things aren't exactly mellow around here. I don't want to go prying, but are you okay girlfriend?"

"Don't you worry about me. You've got a lot more going on that's out of balance than I have. You and Zack need to get away yourselves. Maybe we can do a better tradeoff than only one day for you. When we get back, I'll get Sammy to bring home enough work so that you can take the car and we'll stay here with the kids. How's that sound?"

"It sounds great, although I think Zack's past getting away. But I do think having tomorrow alone will be a good chance to do some talking. Honestly Meg, I felt hopeful with the thought of a new start for Zack, but I think he needs some real help, more than travelling can give him. Converting the bus was fun, ripping out the old, putting in the new, was great. We had a lot of laughs and I thought the old Zack, my guy, was back, but I don't know now. All I know is that he's a mess, a depressed wreck."

I pulled my knees up to my chest to keep from running outside to give Maya a hug, and Mom too for that matter. Other than something happening to Zack from being in the war, I had no idea what was wrong with him, but knowing he was sick was a whole lot better than thinking he was mean. I didn't want to eavesdrop anymore, so I went back to my bunk and imagined Amy lying beside me, the two of us sharing stuff the way we used to.

But pretending didn't make Amy real, so I grabbed my pen and paper and started to scribble what I'd say if she was there, like confess that I'd just eavesdropped. I knew she'd want to hear that Zack wasn't a mean guy.

Writing a letter to Amy worked a lot better to help me than reading the one she wrote. Reading hers was fun, but writing was kind of like the feeling I get when I want to throw up, but can't, and then I finally do, and there's this huge feeling of relief. That's how I felt after writing about the hard stuff at my place.

But then, honestly I think my other self took over, because words raced out of the end of my pen so fast I could hardly keep up with them. I mean there was all the stuff about Emily and Buddhism and the promised diving trip, and Dad and the serenity prayer from Grammy at the library, and then Disney World going to happen, well there were just so many different feelings that came with all that stuff that there was no way I would've been able to describe them by myself. Reading it back was amazing, because everything was there and described perfectly. The thing was so thick I had a hard time getting it in an envelope.

The next morning everyone bubbled over as we piled in the car, ready to take off for our day at Disney World.

Dad took the poodle basket out and stuck pillows in its place to make room for the overflow of bodies. I hugged him tight before I climbed in with the pillows. I chose to sit back there because it looked so comfy.

On the way we had loads of fun playing riddle games and telling corny jokes. We laughed and sang songs and acted much sillier than we did when we were just our family.

The rides at The Magic Kingdom were super fun. We rode the biggest roller coaster twice, screaming and flailing our arms around like monkeys out of control. It was hilarious. I tossed balls for lots of stuffed animals, but didn't win a single one, only a stupid plastic doll that I gave to a little girl. We stuffed ourselves with hot dogs, hamburgers and cotton candy, without ever sitting at a table. Lauren took two rolls of pictures, one for her family and one for Amy, leaving a few extras on the film for a picture of Angie. And for sure I bought lots of postcards to send home.

Mom became one of us, giggling her way through probably her best day on the trip. For sure it was my most fun day, and I bet Josh's and Lauren's and Ty's and Jesse's too. We all fell asleep in the car on the way home while Mom drank bottles of Coke to keep herself awake.

By the time we got home it was close to midnight. I gave my sleeping dad a kiss. Maybe he wouldn't know the kiss was thanks for the trip but I wanted to give him one anyway. The poodles were snuggled next to him and they didn't make a peep.

But they sure made lots of peeps in the morning when they saw Mom and Dad packing up their suitcase. I wrapped them in a bundle and held them to my chest to let them know I wasn't going anywhere.

As Dad loaded the car, the happy that was all over both Mom and Dad sure wasn't pretending. Even though Mom's hair wasn't long enough to be daffodil petals, I saw them anyway, intertwined with Dad's open African daisy. I shivered.

Mom hugged me and the poodles, probably thinking shivers meant I was scared, "It's okay, honey. We'll only be gone a week, and think of all the freedom you'll have without parents to boss you around."

"Tell Josh not to pick on me." I gave him my best glare.

"All you have to do is pay attention," he said, "and nobody'll pick on you."

I wanted to blot out the huge firecracker that took the place of my brother right then, but blotting out didn't work. I sure hoped his firecracker wouldn't explode while Mom and Dad were away.

"It'll be fun, Sis," said Ty. "We'll play lots of games."

"And we'll be back before you know it," said Mom. "Remember, you've got Maya next door if you need her."

I wanted to add that Angie was there too, but of course I didn't. After thinking that, I could hardly wait to get back to the store to see if she had a joyride plan made. She said a couple of days and it'd been more than that already.

Mom and Dad drove away and I handed Ty the poodles. I told him I needed something at the store. I took off with my heart pounding like crazy.

It slowed down real fast when I saw both Angie and another lady behind the counter. Angie looked like she was teaching her stuff, and that's exactly what she was doing. She told me she was leaving the store to do something for her granny, and that she was still trying to put together her plan, but hadn't gotten it figured out yet. She looked in a hurry but said she'd see me later.

In the meantime, all I could hope was that someone else would show up to take my mind off the joyride lesson, because I sure didn't want to turn into a nuisance for Angie.

On Our Own

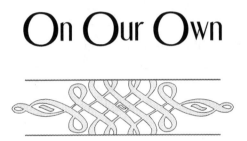

Well somebody else did show up, and that was Zack. He didn't exactly show up. He'd been there all along, but with Mom and Dad around I knew there'd be no way I could get to talk to him by myself. Whether I could talk to him about my assignment or not I wasn't sure, but I was sure that he was the perfect distraction from the no joyride lesson.

Even though I'd heard Maya say he was sick, I couldn't help but wonder if maybe part of why he was sick was that he was lonely. I knew about being lonely. I'd had lots of times when I felt that way myself. Anyway, I wanted to know if he needed a friend.

I was trying to figure out how to do that, when all of a sudden I didn't need to figure out anything. The campground owner came and invited all of us to a celebration of the expansion he'd just finished. A huge barbecue pit at the opposite end of the campground was where he was holding the party, and he said he'd have hot dogs and hamburgers for everyone, including the dogs. We hadn't been to any parties and everyone, except Zack, wanted to go. Of course I wanted to go too, but

I also wanted to use the everybody gone chance to go see Zack. I told Maya I had some clothes over in the dryer and I wanted to get them out when they finished so they wouldn't wrinkle. I hated fibbing, but I needed an excuse that made sense.

She said, "Just make sure you're not too long. I don't want you missing anything."

"Don't worry. I don't want to miss anything either."

They all left and everything got super quiet, except for the racket inside my head. All the reasons why I shouldn't go bombarded my brain, especially how Mom and Dad would freak at me bursting in on a druggie guy.

I didn't let my thoughts stay there though. Instead I pictured him all better, talking and maybe even laughing with all of us. I got myself pumped and headed over to the bus, feeling hopeful instead of either scared or guilty.

Through the bus windows I didn't see Zack, so I lifted my hand and knocked on the door.

"What d'you want?"

My mind went blank, and I didn't have an answer.

"I said, what d'you want?"

"It's Zoey from next door. I cut my finger and I need a bandage." Boy, that was for sure one of my other self's outbursts. There was no way I could've made up anything that good.

The door opened. "Show me."

I held up my finger that I'd wrapped in my other hand. "I can't. I'm holding the blood in."

"You can't hold blood in, smarty pants. You're making that up, so tell me what it is you want."

We stood, just looking at each other, and although I had no idea what he was thinking, I was thinking calling me smarty pants wasn't mean or scary. He didn't even look scary. He looked sad, with dark circles around his eyes. He didn't have the headband on and his hair hung down the sides of his face.

I unwrapped my finger. "I made that up because I wanted to see if you were okay. You only come outside when you go to the shower room."

"And why do you care about whether I'm okay or not?"

"I don't know. I guess I want to know what you're like. I mean Maya, Lauren and Jesse are great and I want to know if you're great too. Are you?"

That brought a smile to his face. "Nobody's called me great for a long time."

"Does that mean you'll let me talk to you so I can find out?"

"If I was great, I guess I'd have to say yes, wouldn't I?"

"Will you come out? There's nobody around. They're all at the party and I'm supposed to be there too. Why did you call me smarty pants?"

"That's what you are, coming up with that cockamamie story to get my attention."

"I didn't plan that. My inside self made it up."

"Of course it did. I've got a feeling that made up things happen a lot for you."

"So will you come out or something?"

"I like the "or something" part. The or something is that you ought to go along and forget talking to me. I'm not much for talking."

"Why?"

"Well there's a lot of reasons, and I don't think you want to hear any of them."

"But I do. I like Maya a lot and I want to like you too, but I can't unless you talk to me."

Zack stepped out of the bus, closed the door and looked around before he sat down on the picnic bench. He was holding a skinny cigarette with a squished end, and he was wearing jeans and a tie-dyed sleeveless t-shirt. His feet were bare and his toenails and fingernails were clipped short and neat. I guess I didn't expect that. His hair was long, but it was cut straight and looked clean, even shiny. I imagined that

Maya was the one who kept him neat like that, the way she did with herself and Jesse. I figured Lauren did it for herself.

Zack put the cigarette on the table and tucked his hair behind his ears. "What do I have to say to make you like me, smarty pants?" He picked up the cigarette, lit it and took a deep puff that he held in before he turned away and blew the smoke out.

He blew it away from me, but I could smell it and it sure didn't smell like the cigarettes Dad used to smoke. I didn't bother asking, I just figured it was pot, although I was kinda surprised that he'd smoke it in front of me. I always thought it was something you did secretly, but I guess I was wrong because he sure didn't look guilty or anything. I kept all those thoughts to myself. I just said, "I guess you can tell me why you stay inside all the time."

"That's a long story. Why don't you tell me why you've got all this curiosity going on?"

That was the perfect chance to talk about my assignment, but with him sitting there taking drags and holding them in, with his heel bouncing up and down a mile a minute before he blew them out, all I could think was that he needed one of Angie's joyrides.

"Do you ever meditate?" I asked.

"What? Why would I want to do that?"

"I don't know. That was another one of my other self questions. What I wanted to say is that my dad's having a hard time on this trip with all of us being stuffed together in the trailer. So I've been talking to people about what I can do to make him happier, and that's what I came to ask you."

Zack actually laughed out loud, running his fingers through his hair and shaking it out so it fell back down around his face. "Don't expect to hear about happy from me." He took another drag and put the cigarette on the table while he tucked the loose hair behind his ears.

Once he'd let out the smoke, his foot started pumping again. "As for your old man, you're right about no happy there. I've seen him in the shower room and he's a stone wall. I know I'm no Santa Claus myself, but your father's a real hardass." He picked up the cigarette, took another drag and held it in before he blew it out, just like he had before.

"That's not fair. You don't even know him."

"I don't need to know him to know he's one lucky sonofabitch."

Zack's words, and the look in his eyes scared me, but not enough to shut me up. "What's that mean?"

"I don't want to talk about what it means. Just know the guy's a lucky sonofabitch. And let's leave it at that."

"I can't. He doesn't seem lucky when he's always hollering all he wants is peace and quiet. What's lucky about that?"

"That's all anyone wants, smarty pants. He's lucky 'cause he's a normal guy, doing what he wants t'do, making things happen for all of you, and getting on with life. And that's all I have t'say about him. So have you had enough now? Do you want to go to your party before you're missed?" He took two more quick drags before he leaned over and buried the tiny butt in the sand.

"I'll go to the party, but before I do I want to say that my best friend and me, we talk about stuff when we're not happy, and sometimes we get turned around by talking."

Zack bolted to his feet. "Drop it!" he practically shouted. "We're not talking about happy anymore. Okay?" With that, he headed into the bus. "I'm getting another smoke."

I wasn't sure he was coming out again, and I wasn't sure I wanted him to either. I'd made him mad and all I could think of was the fight when he'd yelled at Maya. The same scary feeling I'd had then shot through me like a lightning bolt.

I jumped up and was leaving when Zack called, "Wait a minute."

I stopped and turned around.

He was in the doorway. "I can get mean if people push me, and I was getting mean there. I don't want to do that with you, so you're right to go while you're ahead. But before you do, I want to say you're one helluva kid."

"I don't know about that, but thanks. I only wanted to be your friend if you needed one."

He sat on the bus steps and took another one of those long drags. Even though I wasn't real close, I could see his eyes were watery. Whether it was held in smoke, or held back tears, I wasn't sure, and I didn't want to find out, so I didn't go any closer.

He blew out the smoke and sagged his shoulders. "I'd make a lousy friend, smarty pants, but thanks for the offer."

"Can I come see you again?"

"I'd rather you didn't. The crazies don't like company. Today, your cockamamie story got my attention, but don't count on it happening again."

He smiled when he said that and I sure didn't see any crazies in his smile. I was glad I got the smile before I left. It took any scared feelings I had away, including the black widow spider I saw him as when he was yelling at Maya.

I'd never met anyone like Zack, or talked with someone like him, but I hoped I'd helped him feel a little bit special. Maybe having a kid care about you wasn't a big deal for a grown guy, but it was for me, so I'd like it to have been for him too.

I went to the party. I didn't say anything about talking to Zack. Every time I had an urge to talk about him I got over it by jamming more chocolate cake in my mouth.

Because Zack and I hadn't talked at all about my assignment, I wandered around the party trying to find someone else to talk to, but that sure didn't work. With all the people packed together and the racket going on, there was no way I could even begin to pick anyone out. What was weird, one more time, was that there just weren't any kids my age.

At least Ty had Jesse, and sure he was younger than Ty, but he was fun on the beach, and playing games and making Legos stuff. All any of that did was make me miss Amy, and want the joyride lesson even more, probably as much for myself as Dad.

The next morning I went to the store with my fingers crossed, hoping Angie would be back and she'd be alone.

She was there all right, and she was alone, but she sure didn't look like she was ready to teach me anything. She was all dressed up like she was going somewhere special. She had on a black skirt, fancy black sandals and a black-and-white striped blouse. Her hair was combed flat and her makeup was all toned down.

She smiled when she saw me. "Hi, babycakes."

From way down inside I smiled too. "Wow!" I said. "You look pretty. You going somewhere?"

"I am. Me and Granny, we're going to the doctor. She likes me to look like a lady when I take her out, even though she can't see me very well. She knows from when she could see me that ladylike clothes aren't exactly my style. So now she feels the clothes I'm wearing, checking how long the skirt is, all of it." She stroked her blouse. "She likes silk."

"Is she okay?"

"Blood pressure's a little high, but she's good."

"Is that same lady coming to look after the store?"

"Yup. She's the fill-in around here. Quite a change, huh? I think Monster Man's had enough shockers with me around. He's probably training her in case I get totally out of hand." She laughed, and it was so good to see her star tooth again. "I've missed you. What y'been doing?"

I told her that Mom and Dad were away, and that we'd been to Disney World, but I didn't want to take time away from what I was there for, so in case the other lady showed up, I said, "I haven't been doing anything that's all that good. But I have been making up good stuff just the way you told me to. And it's neat how you can make stuff up and have it feel real. Do you think we'll be able to have the peace and quiet kind of joyride lesson soon? I really want it."

"I know you do. Let me get Granny settled down and then the three of us can get together and I'll teach both you and Granny."

The lady came in and Angie hopped off her stool. "I guess I'm outa here," she said. "But c'mon back in a few days, sweetface, and we'll see what I've come up with. Okay?"

"Okay," I said, but a few days seemed way too long.

The only thing that made the days I had to wait okay was that Maya offered to teach us how to tie-dye t-shirts. I was pretty excited, because all along I'd been hoping she'd do that, but I hadn't wanted to be pushy enough to ask, what with the bead stringing and everything.

When she was in town buying groceries she picked up a bunch of white cotton t-shirts and some boxes of dye and a package of rubber bands. She brought everything over to our place, along with a big metal pot and some sets of tongs. Ty, Jesse and I wasted no time getting right into it. Josh and Lauren couldn't have cared less, because surfing and each other was all they cared about.

Maya had an old sheet that she ripped up so we could practice with all the elastics and stuff. Seeing how the whole thing made pretty designs was fun, and once we'd practiced enough to get good at it, we all made two shirts each, and Maya made a big one that she said was for Dad. We all laughed because it was obvious Dad and tie-dyed t-shirts didn't exactly match.

"Well I'll just add it to Zack's pile. And incidentally, Zack wants to go to the movies this afternoon. *Batman* is playing in Jacksonville. Are you two up for that? He thinks it'd be fun for Jesse, and Jesse thinks it would be too. Right, Jess?"

"Yeah, I'm excited. D'you guys want to come with us?"

Being invited to go anywhere in the bus was a huge surprise. I knew it was my chance to see inside, but I didn't want to badly enough to have to sit through *Batman*. "Thanks, but no thanks," I said. "I hate bats. I mean why would anyone want to watch someone pretending to be a bat flying all over the screen."

"You're crazy, Sis. The movie's great, but I've already seen it twice, so thanks." said Ty. "I think I'll stay here and maybe catch some fish."

"Then I guess it'll be me and my guys," said Maya. "Lauren and Josh aren't going, and that's probably good because I'd rather know you're well taken care of."

"Ha," I said. "You think Josh takes care of me? That's a joke."

"Well Lauren, she's the caretaker of the age, having practically raised Jesse. Anyway, enough about that. I told them and I'll tell you too. There'll be no going in the water."

"Fishing doesn't count for going in the water, right?" said Ty.

"I'm talking about swimming, and that's what I told Josh and Lauren. So be good."

Ty laughed. "Like how else would we be? We're model kids, haven't you noticed?"

Maya laughed too. "Actually, I have."

Maya and Jesse took off and Ty went to check out the surf. I decided maybe that'd be a good time to go see if Angie had come up with something.

Buy then suddenly my eyes about popped out of my head as I watched a new assignment chance happening right across from our campsite. An Airstream trailer, smaller than ours had come in, and two old ladies climbed out of the Cadillac that pulled it. They looked exactly alike, wearing pink pedal pushers and white sleeveless shirts, tied in knots at their waists. I figured they had to be twins. They wore white ankle socks turned down over bright pink sneakers. Pretty modern for old ladies is what I thought, and if I could get to talk to them I'd have two for the price of one.

I was waiting for them to get settled enough for me to go over there when Ty came back. "The surf's perfect, Sis. Do you want to try casting in the troughs like Ollie, and maybe catch some flounder."

"But if we want to catch flounder we have to use shrimp, and I don't have any money. Do you?"

"Josh has the money and I don't know where he is. He and Lauren went off somewhere. Forget Ollie and shrimp. I'll get the sand flea trap."

I was planning to go see Angie, but fishing alone with Ty was always fun, especially because he did all the yucky stuff for me if I caught anything.

When we got to the beach, Ty was right and the surf was perfect. I dug up a bunch of sand fleas while Ty set up the rods and loaded the hooks.

He handed me my rod and he ran into the surf with his. He tossed out his line and scurried backwards. I copied him to make sure I was standing beside him.

With our lines out there and nothing happening on them we talked for a long time about everybody in the family and how different the whole trip was from the way Dad had described it before we ever left Baltimore.

"He's talking about not going anywhere anymore Ty, like settling down somewhere in Florida. Has he said anything about that to you?"

"No, but I'm ready. I like Florida. The beach is nice and I like how everything's so blue, so light and airy, y'know?"

"No I don't know because I'm not ready. But I'm pretending I am. When you pretend stuff it sometimes happens."

"Honestly Sis, you say the darndest things sometimes. What's that supposed to mean?"

I was about to answer, when WHAMMO, my line jerked with a bite, a big one.

"Wowee! I got one Ty!" I yanked the rod in the air and jerked it from one side to the other like Ollie had. I began reeling in my first decent fish ever, and boy was it heavy. "I think it's huge," I hollered.

"Hey, great! Want any help?"

"No, I got it." I could barely turn the handle it was so heavy. "I didn't do any planning and it's huge."

"You didn't do any what?"

I let out a big sigh. "Never mind." I brought the fish to shore, and it was no flounder, it was a catfish. We all knew that Florida catfish were bottom feeders and lousy for eating.

"Bummer," said Ty.

I dropped my rod in the holder and grabbed the fish with my bare hands to get Ty to pull out the hook, and before I realized how stupid that was, I got stabbed by one of the spikes sticking out of the side of the fish's head. I screamed.

A couple down the beach came running. While the fish thrashed around on the sand, the man examined the wound. "Ow, baby!" You better get on home real fast and put peroxide on that sucker. It's gonna be sore. You got what you need at home? We got some peroxide in our box."

"That's okay," said Ty. "We're staying in the campground. We've got a first aid kit, and I know there's peroxide." The lady took a wad of paper towels from our tackle box and wrapped my hand while the man dug in our box and brought out pliers. He held the fish in my towel, pulled out the hook and flung the fish in the ocean. "I hope that sucker swims a way off. I don't want him on my line. You okay?"

"I think so." But I wasn't sure, because my hand stung like crazy. But it didn't sting crazy enough to take my mind off the nice people. I mean a couple would probably be really good for my assignment.

"Well get on home," said the man. "We'll be down here for awhile if you need help."

"Are you staying in the campground?" I asked, hopefully.

"Wish we were, but no," said the lady. "We just dropped by to catch a fish, and I'm glad we did because that was quite a scare for you. Does it hurt?"

"It stings, that's all, but thanks for the help."

"You're welcome," she said. "Take care."

They took off and so did my heart. I sure would've liked to talk to them but I knew I had to get home.

I got Ty to dump all the fleas in the wet sand so they could squiggle to safety, and then we collected our stuff and ran back to the trailer. We dropped everything on the ground and rushed inside.

The poodles bolting to greet us weren't enough distraction to keep us from seeing Josh and Lauren in Mom and Dad's bed. Josh jumped up and grabbed the sheets while Lauren hid behind him.

"Don't you say a word to Mom and Dad or I'll kill you," he said. "I swear I will." Jacques and Jolie barked and Lauren started to cry. "Get out of here. Just get out."

Ty scooped up the poodles and we bolted through the door. "They've been smoking pot, Sis. It smells like it does in the bus. That is so stupid."

"Well I'm sure not going back in. I don't ever want to see Josh again."

Ty was hooking the poodles to their ropes when the door flew open. Josh and Lauren leapt out and darted across the campground toward the beach.

"C'mon," said Ty. "We can get the peroxide now."

Ty cleaned the wound and wrapped it with a roll of gauze. "You're such a good brother Ty. Thanks."

He cut the gauze and taped it. "I think I'll make us a steak tonight. It's better than fish anyway. What d'you think Sis?"

"Goody is what I think."

Right then, out the window I saw the old ladies across from us, driving the Cadillac into their parking spot. I hadn't even noticed they were gone, but for sure I was glad they weren't around for the mess at our place. I wanted to go talk to them like I'd wanted to before, but my hand hurt too much so I took an aspirin and stretched out on my bunk. I guess I fell asleep because I didn't hear the bus pull in, but I did hear Maya's voice when it woke me.

"You guys up for burgers?" she called through the screen door.

Ty was in the kitchen. "No, but thanks. I'm going to make a steak in celebration of Zoey not dying from the catfish stab."

I jumped off the bunk and held up my bandaged hand.

Maya yanked open the screen door and charged in. She dropped the McDonald's bag on the counter and peeked inside my bandage. "It looks sore all right, but I don't think you're going to die, Zo."

"Did you guys have fun?"

"We did, yeah. Zack and Jesse loved the movie so that was good. Me, I liked the popcorn. And talking about eating, how about we heat up the burgers and toss them into the mix to share when you're ready."

"We want to eat by ourselves if that's okay," said Ty. He showed Maya the two cobs of corn. "We've only got these and one baked potato. The steak's small and Josh would grab it for himself."

"That's not very nice," said Maya. "So where are Josh and Lauren anyway?"

"Probably at the rec center," said Ty. "We haven't seen them."

Boy, that about threw me for a dozen loops. Lies coming out of Ty didn't match up with his lily self at all. I'd never heard a lie out of Ty in my whole life, and I hated that he was so good at it. I badly wanted my other self to come flying out and spill the whole story so Maya could do something about it. But that didn't happen. I just sat there saying nothing with my hand in the air.

"I'll get Jesse and take the burgers to the rec center for the rest of us," said Maya. "Zack already had his share on the way home."

After Maya had gone I could hardly wait to get at Ty for saying what he did. "You never lie Ty. I hated that."

"Yeah, well I hate what they did. It was stupid, and I hope Josh gets into a lot of trouble."

"He won't unless we tell, and I'm not telling, are you? I mean we'd be dead if we did."

Ty shrugged his shoulders. "So be it. I'm going out to light the barbecue. Do you want to bring the chess board?"

"No, I don't want to play chess. I think I'll go over and talk to the ladies over there." I pointed out the window. Right then they looked even better for talking to than they had before. One of them was sitting on a chair holding a skein of wool between her hands, and the other one was winding the wool onto a ball. "Look what they're doing Ty. Granny and me, we did that last summer."

Ty looked out the window. "If that's what floats your boat Sis, go for it."

"I'd rather talk to them about knitting than worry about Josh. Let me know when you're ready for dinner. Just holler and I'll come back."

"Yeah. I'll holler all right."

"Are you okay? You don't look okay."

"Just go. I'm glad someone's got something fun to do. I'll let you know if I need any help."

I ran over with my hand in the air. Without saying hi or anything, I told them I'd done that same wool thing with my granny. The words fell out so fast that the ladies put the wool down and stared at me like I was a babbling idiot. "Watching you made me think of her," I said. "I hope I'm not bothering you. I'm Zoey from over there," I said, pointing to our trailer.

"Of course you're not bothering us, Zoey. I'm Hazel and my sister is Harriett." She didn't tell me a last name. "A grandmother is a lovely thing. We don't have any grandchildren, but I still remember my own grandmother. What on earth have you done to your hand?"

"It's just a stab from a catfish spike. It's okay, but it feels better if I hold it up."

"That makes sense. I'm sure it's sore. Would you like something to drink? We have some fruit punch in the fridge. Would you like that?"

"No thanks, I'm not thirsty. Are you twins?"

"We are," said Harriett. "We're from Nebraska on vacation from our dairy farm."

They looked like they barely weighed a hundred pounds between them. I laughed to myself as I imagined either one of them sitting under a cow, yanking udders. I asked them if they milked cows.

"Got big boys for that," said Hazel. "Our sons, they run the farm and we pay the bills." She chuckled. "We're good at handling money. We bought ourselves this Airstream. Not as big as yours, but sure nice for a couple of old gals, don't you think?"

"Sure is. Nebraska's a long way from here isn't it?"

"That's the good part about traveling. You get to see the country, and that's what we're doing. Have you come a long way, and seen a lot of interesting places, Zoey?"

I told her we'd come from Baltimore but I didn't say anything about Dad quitting his job, only that he'd been busy researching new ideas so we hadn't had much time for sightseeing.

Right in the middle of their description of Sea World, my other self did her thing, "Do you get peace from being twins?"

"Peace?" Harriett's eyebrows darted up her forehead like everyone else's seemed to when I asked my question. "Well, Zoey," she said. "We certainly didn't get much peace at Sea World, but why do you ask such a question?"

"I'm sorry. It just came out because I'm doing something for Dad and I'd really like to know."

"What sort of something is that?"

"Is it okay if I don't say? I'd just like to know what you think if that's okay. I don't have time for the whole story."

"Well I'm not sure how to answer that, dear," said Harriett. She got up and handed Hazel the ball of wool. She moved another skein of the feathery wool off a stool and put it on an empty metal table. She patted the seat. "We can't talk about such a subject unless you set yourself down. I think your hand needs a rest. Would you do that?"

"Sure. I'd like to." I hoped Ty wasn't going to call me any minute. Harriett went back to her chair. "What do you think, Hazel?"

Hazel tapped her upper lip with her finger. She said, "I don't know about getting peace from being twins, Zoey. But I do definitely get comfort from the connection I have with my darling Harriett."

"I'll agree with that," said Harriett, blowing a kiss at her sister.

Hazel blew one back. "See? Can you feel that connection, Zoey?" She chuckled again.

I did, and I nodded real hard.

"But I don't only connect with my sister, I connect with everything. It's a lovely way to live my life." She pointed at the pot of geraniums on her picnic table. "My flowers, I talk to them. I study their leaves, their blossoms, and I feel connected with them when I do that."

Hazel became that geranium. I wasn't *thinking* about people flowers, but she just became one. I couldn't help but wonder if that was going to happen with everyone forever. It sure was distracting. I made myself stop wondering and just listened. I didn't want to miss anything.

"And I don't only connect with my flowers, Zoey, but with everything around me. I connect with the trees, the rocks, the birds, the little bugs that scurry here and there. I don't let anything pass me by without taking the time to feel a connection. Just the way I do here with you."

She smiled right through her geranium, that same smile Grammy had when she talked about her son at the library. "A calm comes over me when I connect, and although I've never thought about what I get from that calm, I guess I definitely do get peace." She rearranged the wool on her knee as if she was looking for words to add. I could actually feel Hazel's connection with the wool. It was pretty cute. "Does that answer your question, Zoey?"

Harriett popped forward in her chair. "I'd like to add a little something of my own to my sister's wonderful description, if I may. Would that be all right, dear?"

"It'd be really nice. I'd like that a lot."

"Well, the peace Hazel gets from connection, I believe that comes from being content. My darling sister and myself, we're very content, which allows us the calm required to connect with things the way Hazel has described. We're seventy-five next month, so we've had many years to develop contentment."

Hazel interrupted very fast. "Now wait a minute, old girl. I have to disagree with you if you don't mind. I don't believe for a minute that old is something you have to be to be content. For me, the big secret to being content is accepting yourself, and you can surely do that at any age."

I didn't have the foggiest idea whether Dad accepted himself. "Is that the same as liking yourself? Or is that harder, 'cause it sounds harder."

"First of all, Zoey," said Hazel. "You have to know who you are in order to find out what you need to accept. Although you seem very wise for your young age, I'm afraid we're making your very simple question quite complicated. I think it would have been much simpler for us just to have told you that, yes indeed, we do get peace from being twins."

"Maybe it would've been simpler, but then I would've missed how you get it. I mean that's really important. And what you've just said about accepting yourself is neat, because I spend a lot of time trying to figure myself out and it's really hard. So I guess my big question is whether it would even be possible to get Dad your kind of peace when I have no idea whether he knows, or even likes or accepts himself. How does all that work anyway?"

"Well," said Hazel. "Of course I don't know anything about your daddy, so I can't really help you with that. But in answer to *how* it works, well it works in as many different ways as there are different people in the world. It's a personal internal quest. And, I might add, unfortunately most people don't have any idea who they truly are. They're far too busy finding distractions outside themselves to take the time to connect with their internal guide."

"I have another self inside me who speaks up sometimes. Do you think she might be my internal guide?"

"I bet you that's exactly who she is, Zoey," said Hazel. "You're a very mature young lady. I'm sure you have a lively internal guide."

Right then Ty whistled so loud it's a wonder an alarm didn't go off in the campground. That was one of Ty's unique talents, but so far it hadn't had a chance to show up on the trip.

"I guess my brother needs me, so I better go," I hopped up. "He's making a steak for us. Mom and Dad went away for a few days and he's gotten really good at cooking."

"That's lovely," said Harriett. "I wish we weren't leaving in the morning. It'd be a real pleasure to meet the rest of your family, especially your father."

With that came another loud whistle.

Hazel gasped. "My, oh my. Your brother about scared the wits right out of me. I think he wants you over there pretty badly."

"I guess he does, doesn't he. But thanks a lot. You told me some good things to think about."

"We hope so. Don't we Hazel?"

"We certainly do, and we wish you all the luck in the promising life your little mind has ahead for you. Now run along before another whistle permanently scares the wits out of both of us." They laughed and I did too.

I didn't think I'd been gone long enough for dinner to be ready, and I was right. Ty only wanted me home for company. I sort of liked being wanted for company so I didn't complain, even though I would've liked to hear a lot more from the twins.

While everything was cooking we played Chess and I got to feel connection with my brother, like *really* feel it, and boy was that neat. Even though he was studying his next move I asked, "Do you like yourself Ty?"

"I don't know. What're you talking about?" He made the move and then got up to turn the steak, the potato and the corn over. He had them all wrapped in tinfoil. "It's your move Sis, and you better make it a good one because you're in trouble."

I moved, but I honestly wasn't concentrating. "Do you think Dad likes himself?"

Ty sat back down. "I have no idea. Do you want to play chess, or talk drivel. If you want to play, you've got to pay attention."

"Sorry." We played some more, but honestly no matter how hard I tried I couldn't pay attention.

"Let's forget the chess, Sis. The dinner's ready, anyway. The plates are here, so why don't you get the butter and sour cream. Maybe while we're eating you can tell me what went on over there with the old ladies that got you talking about liking yourself."

"They just said some things that made me wonder. That's all."

"Well, I don't know anything about me or Dad liking ourselves. But I do know, even though you messed up the chess game, I like *you*. Isn't that enough? Now go get the stuff, and bring some salt."

I wanted a serious answer, but I should've known I wouldn't get one. Ty probably never took even a minute to think about anything so stupid.

Granny's Gone

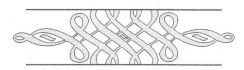

Seeing as the connection thing was so messed up with Josh not even speaking to us or anything, I decided I'd do what I'd promised myself before Ty and I went fishing, and that was to go see Angie. Sure, I wanted a joyride lesson, but more than that right then I wanted to talk to her about Josh, because Angie and I had a real connection. I pumped myself with hope and headed over to the store.

Well the pump flattened real fast when I saw through the window that Angie wasn't alone. And worse than that, she was with of all people, Monster Man.

I didn't even go in. I just turned around and slumped my way back to the trailer.

Ty wasn't there, but the poodles were, so I decided to put on their leashes and take them for a walk on the beach. If I couldn't talk to Angie, I figured I could at least try working on having good thoughts to make stuff better, because I really needed to find a way to fix the mess at our place.

Well it wasn't long before I got it loud and clear that fixing the mess meant fixing Josh, who was the mess, and none of even my best thoughts could come close to doing that. I plunked myself down on the sand, sat the poodles in my lap and told them how hard everything was, looking for at least some sympathy from somewhere.

Honestly, their little heads twitched this way and that, their eyes sparkled and their little ears perked with every word. I knew they were listening, and even understanding everything I said, because both of them smothered my face with sloppy kisses. Maybe they didn't solve my problem, but I sure felt their love.

When we got back to the trailer, Ty was there. The poodles bee-lined it right past him to Mom and Dad's room.

"Wow, what's with them, and you too, Sis? You look awful, and I guess that's how they feel. So what's wrong? I just made some macaroni and cheese. Would that help?"

"I hate the way everything's so terrible around here, Ty. How come you're acting normal. I mean, nothing's normal."

"So what's normal anyway?"

"Normal is everyone getting along, that's what's normal."

Ty started stirring his macaroni. "Well, y'know what, Sis? The only thing that isn't normal is you worrying about Josh. I'll tell you something, and that is that Josh isn't spending even a second worrying about you, so why waste your time and energy worrying about him. You need to mind your own business, Sis. Just do your worrying about yourself if you have to worry, and leave Josh out of it." He put the spoon down. "Have some macaroni. It's ready, and it's my specialty."

I wanted to hug my brother right then. "Macaroni's not your only specialty, Ty. Minding your own business is your big specialty, so thanks for reminding me."

"Hey, anytime."

We dug into the macaroni and cheese, and boy was that good.

The only trouble was that 'good' didn't work when it came to all of us together. I mean if Josh showed up, he didn't talk, and for that matter nobody talked. He'd just find whatever he came for, get what he wanted to eat, and disappear with it. He had to come home to sleep, but he always made sure it was after we went to bed, and he was gone before we even woke up, always with his surfboard.

The worst part was that if I was supposed to be practicing minding my own business, that meant I couldn't talk about the Josh mess when Maya and I were stringing beads. Having all that stuff trapped inside wouldn't even let me feel connected to her. So when we were beading, which was a lot, I hardly said anything at all. I did get pretty good at making lots of necklaces though, and that seemed to at least make Maya happy, or that's what she said anyway.

But I guess she was pretending happy, because the day before Mom and Dad came home she showed up at our door. Josh and I were in the trailer, but we weren't talking or anything. I mean it was like a huge block of ice in there. I'd just brought home the laundry and he was looking for something in it.

Ty and Jesse had been planning to make a sandwich, but when Josh showed up they picked up the poodles and took off.

"What's going on over here?" asked Maya through the screen. "I saw Ty and Jesse bolt out the door with the poodles. I don't know what that was about, but I'm here because I want to talk do you. Can I come in?"

"Have at it," said Josh, in his best surly voice while he poked through the laundry.

I pushed the door open for Maya. I didn't say anything but I could hardly wait to hear what she had to say.

She stepped in and the door clicked shut behind her. "Am I interrupting something?" she asked, looking from one of us to the other.

"Do you want to sort laundry?" Josh asked.

"I'm not here for fun, Josh. I'm here because I'm worried. First of all, like we planned, I haven't cooked for you half enough, and I want to know why I've had this feeling for the past several days that you haven't even wanted me cooking for all of us, or eating together at all for that matter."

"Who cares," said Josh. "What's it matter who's been cooking, or how and where we've been eating. It's just food for Pete's sake."

"Well I'd certainly say something's not right. Did you and Lauren have a fight? She's sulking, and you're not exactly chummy. So what's going on?"

"I'm okay, and I don't know about Lauren." He pulled one of his bathing suits out of the pile and went in the bathroom. He came out in seconds with the bathing suit on. He brushed past us. "I'm going surfing."

"Wait a minute," said Maya. "I want to talk to you." He slid out the door with nothing but "Later."

Maya stared after him, and then looked back at a stunned me. "Any ideas Zo?"

"Not really," I said, trying hard to mind my own business.

"Well I guess it's obvious that things aren't exactly right with Josh and Lauren. But, now what about you? Don't think I haven't noticed how quiet you've been when we're beading. I've wanted to say something, but honestly up until now I haven't known what to say."

Maya plunked herself on the sofa with the laundry. She reached for my hand that I didn't give her. "Please tell me what's gong on, Zoey, because this is definitely not the way it's supposed to be."

Maybe I didn't take her hand, but I did sit beside her with the laundry between us. "Nothing is the way it's supposed to be," I said, remembering Eli's comment and seeing how it really worked for the first time.

"And exactly what does that mean?"

"Nothing."

"Now you even look upset. You're acting like you did on the beach that day. So this time, instead of taking off, tell me what's wrong."

"Nothing's wrong with me. It's just Josh. Everything's wrong with him, and that ruins everything for me. I've even tried to see a nice flower for him to make him different, but all I ever see is a firecracker, and I bet you anything one day it'll go off."

Maya actually laughed. "I hope not. That's taking my flower idea to a whole new level. You've got quite an imagination, young lady."

"I wish I didn't. I hate everything being like it is."

Maya moved the laundry to the other side of her and shifted over. She put her arm around me. "Well, your folks are coming home tomorrow, so how about I make a special casserole for tonight and you and me and Jesse and Ty, we'll have it, and Lauren and Josh, well that'll be up to them. I'll ask Zack if he wants to join us. He seems to be in a better mood since the movies. So, what d'you think?"

"I'd like that. It'd be great." I especially liked the part about Zack joining us. "Ty's a decent cook, but you're better."

Maya got up, took my hand and pulled me up with her. She gave me a hug, a real connection hug that sure made all my rattled insides calm down. I gave her a huge one back.

"Boy, I like your kind of hugs," she said. "Why don't you forget the laundry for now and come to the store with me. That way if I can't get what I'm planning, then we can choose something else, something you like."

"Sure, that'd be good. You're great, Maya. I wish you were my teacher. You're really good with kids, aren't you""

"I don't know about that. With some I am, and some I'm not, but with you Zo, it's easy to be good." She squeezed my hand. "C'mon, let's go."

We were just out the door when I got a great idea. "Would you do me a favor while we're there?"

"Of course. Like what?"

"I want a picture of Angie. Lauren left room on the Disney World film and she said she'd take one, but this would be a perfect time if you don't mind. I've tried to describe Angie in my letters but there aren't any words to describe her that I know of."

"I can imagine. I'd have a hard time finding words myself. As long as Angie doesn't mind, sure I can do that. I'll grab the camera."

When we got to the store, Angie was a total shockeroo. She was alone, which was good, but she was dressed in total black, with black lipstick and black nail polish. Her face was covered in white makeup. That sure didn't make for taking pictures.

Maya took one look and stuffed her camera in her purse. She headed over to the food shelves.

I guess I was gawking, because Angie said, "It's okay, sweetface. I'm in mourning. My granny died."

Maya called, "I found the right kind of noodles, so do you like lasagna Zo?"

"I love it," I called back, but my heart was about to burst right through my chest. I did everything I could to bring back Angie's wildflowers, but they wouldn't come. "I'm really sorry, Angie. That's awful."

"Don't be sorry, babycakes. It was time. Maybe not for me, but for Granny it was time. The only hard part is that I guess you two won't get to meet."

Maya brought a box of noodles and cans of sauce over to the counter. "I thought Halloween was in October," she said. "What's with the costume?"

I about fell through the floor. "It's not a costume, Maya. Angie's granny died. She's in mourning."

Maya slumped her shoulders way into her chest. "Oh my god, I'm so sorry. I know how it feels to lose a granny. I've lost two, actually, and neither of them was easy."

"Thanks," said Angie. She got up and took Maya's money. She rang up the box and cans and put them in a paper bag.

"Can I do anything to help you Angie?" I asked.

"Sure you can. You can have an extra helping of lasagna for me. It's my favorite." She smiled when she said that.

"I like that gold star in your tooth," said Maya. "I've never seen one of those. You must have a pretty creative dentist."

"I come from LA. Everything's creative out there if you have the bucks to pay for it."

"A good investment. It looks great." Maya picked up her bag and turned to leave. "You coming Zo?"

I didn't want to go but I didn't know how not to, so I told Angie goodbye and she just smiled, a sad smile.

When we got outside, Maya said, "That was some outfit. It didn't seem like something we'd want to photo. She's got a lot of nerve to dress like that while she's working."

"Angie's got a lot of nerve, period. She's really neat, and I like her."

"Your mom doesn't seem to think all that much of her, and I haven't paid her any attention. I get what I need and that's about all I do in the store. Can we maybe take a picture later?"

"I don't think so. I think I'm just going to keep describing her and Amy can see what she likes. I don't want to make a big deal of taking Angie's picture, especially since she's probably sad now that her granny's dead. The two of them played old-timey music and danced her wheelchair around their apartment when she was alive. Angie'll miss that."

"Maybe I ought to get to know her if she's that special to you, Zo. I guess I've been influenced by your mom's concern."

"Mom and Dad are freaky about her and I hate that. Would you mind if I went back? I want to find out what happened. We used to talk about her granny a lot, and I was even supposed to meet her. Would it be okay?"

"Sure. I've got work to do anyway. I'm going to make you a meal you won't forget, and maybe I'll make some extra for Angie. Will you tell her?"

"Yeah. That'd be nice."

I went back, and when Angie saw me she gave me a much bigger smile. "Well that was fast."

"Maya wanted me to tell you that she's going to make you some lasagna."

"Hey, that'd be nice."

"Is it okay to talk about your granny? You're really going to miss her. I know you are."

"You're right about that. I will miss her, but life goes on." Angie reached over the counter and tapped my nose. "And you're still here."

"Is it okay to talk about what happened?"

"Not much happened, sweetface. A couple of nights ago we had a good laugh listening to an old George Burns show on the radio. We kissed goodnight, went to bed and in the morning she was lying there quiet as a mouse, with a sweet smile on her face. I'd have to say she died in her sleep and that's what she was ready to do. Granny pretty much always did what she was ready to do." Angie looked down at herself. "In Granny's day people wore black when their loved ones died. That was respectful. They're not as rigid about that anymore, but I am."

"Are you sure it's okay that I'm here?"

"Having you here is better than okay." She came around the counter and put her hands on my cheeks. "You, little ray of light, are exactly what I need today. You remind me that my granny's life goes right on living through you." She gave me a hug and I was quick to give her one back. "I'm sorry you never met Granny," she said. "Your spirit and hers, they're intertwined, and I can feel that right now, standing here with you."

"That's really nice. I wish I could've met her."

"Yeah, I do too. But we missed that chance, and now I want to talk about you. Granny's moved on, and you're still here, and I can see something is on your mind. So whatever it is, let's have it."

"How can you tell that? How can you see stuff in me?"

"Easy. It's called mental telepathy, and reading how people are feeling is easy for me, especially when they're an open book like you are. You don't hide yourself too well."

"That's awful. I wish I did."

"No you don't. You're perfect, exactly the way you are. So let's hear what's on your mind."

"It's just that something happened, but are you sure you can talk about me when you're in mourning? And what about Monster Man?"

"We're not worrying about him. He's out of town." She went around the counter and sat. She patted the seat of the other stool that was still in the same place as before. "Sit down and tell me what's going on."

The second I sat, all the caring in Angie's eyes got words tumbling out of my mouth so fast I could hardly keep up with them. "Things are bad at my trailer, Angie. Ty and me came back from fishing and we found my brother and his girlfriend doing IT in Mom and Dad's bed. They were probably stoned too. The trailer smelled like pot, and now everything's a mess and nobody's talking about it, or not talking about anything for that matter. It's awful. I've been trying to have good thoughts all the time, but it's really hard."

"Hey, hey! Simmer down." Angie got up and grabbed a can of Coke out of the cooler. She popped it open and took a sip. She offered me one but I didn't want it.

"So you don't want a drink, but do you want to tell me how you know your brother was doing IT, as you put it? Maybe they were only fooling around. Maybe you let your imagination run away with you." She crossed her arms over her black tank top with *LIFE IS LOVE* printed across it in white this time. She said, "I've met your brother, and he's a decent kid. He's got a good head on his shoulders and he wouldn't do anything stupid."

"He sure doesn't seem to have a good head to me. He's real mean. He says he'll kill Ty and me if we tell."

"Well I wouldn't bother telling, and I wouldn't bother worrying. I'd get on with living your own little life and make sure you be true to *your* self, and that means you don't muck around in other people's business." She picked up the Coke again and handed it to me. "Here, wash away the nasties you've got going on in there."

I took a sip this time but swallowing it didn't do a thing, so I gave it back to her. All I could think was that I had to tell Mom and Dad so they'd make sure Josh didn't do it again.

When I told Angie that, she jumped off her stool. "Now wait a minute! You go telling on your brother and you don't gain anything, other than you get your brother pissed off." She squished her eyebrows together, making the white makeup on her forehead crack, but she didn't seem to care. She sat again. "I'll tell you a secret. Your brother will go on doing whatever he does, but the only difference is he'll have a mother who stays up nights worrying about him, if she doesn't do that already." She brushed her forehead with her fingers. The white flakes spilled onto her black top and she just flicked them off, as if none of the makeup mess mattered.

But it did to me. "You're messing up your face Angie. Is that okay?"

She reached over and stroked my cheek. "I can take care of my messed-up makeup, but I can't take care of the mess-up you'll cause at your place if you don't stay true to yourself." She took a last sip of Coke and dropped the empty can in the trashcan beside her.

"I've been practicing minding my own business, Angie, but being true to myself, I feel like have to tell Mom and Dad. I think they'd want to know."

"Well, maybe they would, and maybe they wouldn't. But honestly, it truly isn't your business to go telling on your brother."

Angie shifted around, and I knew I was making her crazy just like I'd made Mom that time we talked.

She got off her stool. "Let me go straighten up the forehead and I'll be right back."

I watched her go into the bathroom, but she didn't walk with the same bounce as she usually had. I wanted to start a new hangnail or get some gum to chew or do something to stop my insides from doing their own bouncing all over the place.

Angie came back with her makeup perfect again. She sat down. "Now, that's handled, and I think maybe this is a perfect time for the joyride lesson. Would you like to give that a try now that we don't need to worry about Monster Man showing up?"

"Are you sure? I mean, would it be good for you to have a joyride too?"

"I think it would be perfect for both of us, so let's do it."

Right at that moment, a black car pulled up in front of the store and Angie jumped off her stool, practically toppling the thing over. When I saw Monster Man, I practically toppled my stool too.

"Oh my God!" said Angie. "He wasn't supposed to be back until tomorrow. He's not going to dig the way I look, I can tell you that."

"Does he know about your granny?"

"He doesn't know nothin' about nothin'. He won't care about Granny. He'll only care that I look like I do."

"Can you leave your body? Is it to late to do that? Can I do anything? What can I do?" I knew I was babbling but I couldn't help it.

"The only thing you can do is get your little fanny outa here before the so-called shit hits the fan. I'm telling you, whatever goes on when he sees me isn't going to be pretty." She tapped my behind. "Now go!"

I left fast, whizzing right past Monster Man without looking at him. I couldn't stop my mind from wondering whether I'd ever get a joyride lesson with everything being so messed up for Angie.

When I got home, I found Ty putting together a mess of hamburger with all the leftovers from the fridge, like canned peas and corn and potatoes and onions. The concoction floated in stewed tomatoes.

"Maya's making lasagna," I said. "Didn't she tell you?"

"She told me, and when she saw what I was doing she said we could have the lasagna tomorrow for Mom and Dad's coming home celebration. Anyway I felt like getting inventive. A little early for supper, but do you want to try it?"

"Sure."

Ty spooned out a bunch of his concoction into a couple of bowls and we took them outside along with our books. We'd gotten into reading while we were eating, instead of playing games.

I liked Ty's concoction a lot and I told him I did, but reading wasn't working because my head was still stuck on what Angie said. "Are you true to yourself Ty?" I asked.

"What?"

"Angie, over at the store, says the most important thing in life is to be true to yourself, and I'm wondering exactly how to do that. She said minding your own business was a big part of it. And seeing as you're so good at that, I just thought I'd ask. But I'll read if you want me to."

"To tell you the truth, I have no idea what you're talking about. And I don't know anything about Angie other than Mom and Dad thinks she's strange. She seems nice enough, but what's being true to yourself got to do with her."

"Nothing."

"Okay, so now you're pissed."

"No I'm not. I just wanted to know what being true to yourself means, and if you were true to yourself, that's all. But forget it. Let's just read."

"No, I won't forget it Sis. Sure I'm true to myself, and being true to myself only means I figure out how to live in a way that feels right, and works, that's all. It's simple."

"Oh, is that all. I can do that." I couldn't, but I pretended because I sort of did, but only sort of, and it sure didn't seem simple to me. "Thanks. I'm going to read now." I picked up my book, but my head didn't stop spinning.

"Good. You do that." Ty picked up his book too. He was on the last of his three books. I'd never gotten into even the first one again after the mess next door. Even looking at that box of books brought back such a bad memory, but Ty liked them so much I promised myself I'd read them one day, all of them, by myself, when Zack and Maya weren't living next door.

After the really good concoction, and obviously enough reading for Ty, he said, "I'm going over to the rec center. D'you want to come?"

"Nope. Josh is probably there and I'm not up for being with him."

"I won't be with him. I'm going to take the poodles. Everyone loves them, and besides I want to watch TV."

"Fine." Mom's word sure came in handy sometimes. "You go. I'll clean up here."

One of the deals on the trip was that whoever cooked the meal didn't have to wash the dishes. So I washed them, wishing there was something to do other than eat, wash dishes, read or watch TV. I pictured my old back yard and all my friends running around playing "Kick The Can" while we laughed our heads off. That memory sure didn't make for good feelings, but then I changed to Angie's way of pretending stuff, and suddenly I saw all of us for real, and just pretended myself into a better mood.

Maya called through the door, "Zo, are you in there?"

I went to the door. "I'm here."

Will you take this lasagna to Angie before it gets cold? I'd take it myself, but Zack needs me." She was standing there with a casserole.

I opened the door and took it from her. "Sure. Angie'll love it. Thanks."

I hurried it over, but so much for having it before it got cold, because four people were waiting to check in. Angie's white makeup was gone, so Monster Man must've made her wash it off. She didn't say anything about that, she just took the casserole from me and put it under the counter. "Tell Maya thanks." She winked, but no hint of see you later or anything so I just went home.

I almost fell over when I got there and found Josh in the trailer. He was leaning against the kitchen counter eating something in a bowl that was probably Ty's concoction.

Without saying anything he turned and rinsed out the bowl and put it on the counter.

I needed not to see him because I had no idea what to say or how to say it, so I went back to Mom and Dad's room. That was one of those times my other self needed to show up, but I could tell from my knotted stomach that I wasn't getting any help.

"Can we talk, Zoey?" Josh called from the kitchen. He never used my name. I was always Creep.

"I s…suppose." I got off the bed and found Josh sitting on the sofa. I didn't want to get too comfortable in case he got mean, so I didn't sit.

There was a lot of quiet while he studied his tangled fingers in his lap. He looked at me for only a second and then back at his fingers. "I'm sorry about the other day. I'm sorry for what I was doing in there."

He poked his head toward Mom and Dad's room. "I shouldn't have done that."

A rush of blood flooded my cheeks. My brother had never apologized for a single thing in his whole life.

"They're leaving," he said. "They're leaving as soon as Mom and Dad get back. Maya's pretending Zack has to go back to work, but I know he's sick. You were right, he's stoned all the time."

I stared at my brother and I knew my eyes were the size of golf balls. Josh telling me stuff like that, and apologizing, was way past amazing.

"Were you and Lauren stoned?" Boy, was that ever my other self! I thought for sure I'd be slammed.

But that didn't happen. All Josh said was, "Lauren had some pot, and well…" He looked right at me. "You're not going to tell are you? Ty promised he wouldn't."

After so much time working on minding my own business, and especially after talking to Angie, I knew I wouldn't tell. But it was more than any of that. I felt like I'd hit a homer with Josh, him telling me private stuff and not being mean. "I won't tell," I said. "You and Lauren don't seem close anymore anyway."

"We're not. It was stupid what we did, and now we don't know what to say to each…"

A tap on the door stopped Josh mid-sentence. "Josh? Are you there?" It was Lauren.

"Yeah, I'm here." Before I knew it he was out the door. No goodbye or anything. But I didn't care. I'd just seen something that Eli would say was unique about my brother. He had feelings, and maybe he even cared about me if he shared that stuff.

I pulled out Amy's notepaper and although I didn't write about what had happened with Josh and Lauren, I did tell her that Josh had talked to me like I was human for the first time ever. Some day I'd give her the details, but putting them on paper was way too hard. I wrote about everything else, including our trip to Disney World and the pictures Lauren took, but I didn't bother saying they weren't developed yet.

After that, I went on to write about the twins because I knew Amy would like the stuff about connection. We had a big one, and we never talked about it, but I knew we got something that other people didn't have. I finished off the letter by telling her to get busy and write me back, and then I filled the rest of the notepaper with bunches of hugs and kisses that made me miss her so much I would have burst into tears if Ty hadn't showed up right then.

"Hey, there's a great movie on TV tonight," he said. "It's called *Rear Window,* and everyone over there says it's supposed to be really spooky, lots of suspense. D'you want to see it? Why do you look so sad, Sis?"

"I just wrote Amy and that always makes me sad, but a movie would be great. I'll mail the letter at the same time. I stuck it in an envelope and stamped it. "Did you really come to get me, and where are the poodles?"

"Of course I did, and the poodles are over there with Maya, Jesse, and some other people. I knew you'd want to see it. It won't be on for about an hour but we can play some pool first. Have you seen Josh? He was over there but he left."

Boy did that question ever make sadness go away fast. I could hardly wait to tell Ty about seeing Josh. I knew he'd faint when he heard, so I made him sit down. Then I went right through the whole thing beginning to end, practically jumping out of my skin I was so excited.

"Hey, that's great," said Ty. "I guess he isn't going to kill us now, not that I cared anyway. I'm glad he said he was sorry though. He sure never told me that."

He probably will, because I think he really meant it." I got up. "So let's go to the movies." I wanted to take my brother's hand, but I didn't.

The movie hadn't started so Ty and I played pool, taking turns with other people. I was hoping Josh would be there so Ty could see how different he was. But he wasn't there, and neither was Lauren.

While I waited for my turn to play, I started talking to a couple and before long I got to find out that I was right about why I hadn't met any kids. They said their kids were at camp and that hanging out with their parents was about the last thing they wanted to do. They laughed when they said that, but I sure didn't. They wanted to know if we were having fun. Well thank goodness I didn't have to say anything about that because it was my turn at the pool table.

Finally the movie came on and it was really good, full of suspense and a lot of scary stuff, especially at the end. The movie credits started and people were getting up to leave just as a scream came from the beach. It was Lauren's voice yelling "Mom!" over and over again.

I grabbed the leashed poodles from Maya and she raced out the door. We all flew outside where people charged from their campsites to the beach. Josh was hauling someone out of the water. My mind totally freaked when I saw it was Zack. Josh had let go of him and he was crouched over, spewing out buckets of water. Maya put her arms around him and Josh came over and told us to go back to the trailer.

Ty put his arm around a totally freaked Jesse just as Angie showed up.

"I hear you performed a rescue, Josh, and I agree that it's time to leave them alone. But Lauren, when you get a chance, will you tell your mom the lasagna was great."

"Sure I will," said Lauren.

"We're all proud of you Josh," said Angie. "I gotta get back and open the store, but you're a hero, big guy."

"I don't know about that, but thanks Angie."

"See you later, sweetface," she said to me as she squeezed my hand before she took off.

"Wow! Sweetface! I like that," said Ty, taking my hand that was still holding onto the totally confused leashed poodles. I let go of the leashes and Ty swept them up. They licked his face like crazy and the minute he opened the trailer door and put them down, they flew past everyone and into Mom and Dad's room where they were under the pillows in seconds.

Lauren and Jesse clung to each other on the sofa with Josh wrapped around both of them. I would've clung to all of them if there'd been room.

I sat in the chair across from them and Ty perched on the arm of my chair. "What happened, Josh," he asked. "What was Zack doing?"

Josh got up and flopped on the sofa. "Who knows?" He reached over and squeezed Lauren's hand. "But whatever he was doing wasn't good."

Through the door came Maya. She ran right over to Josh and threw her arms around him. "You saved him Josh. He's back in the bus and he's safe because of you." She kissed Josh's face all over before she went to Lauren with the kisses. "Thank God you were down there. Whatever would've happened if you hadn't been?"

"We thought he was taking a swim," said Josh. "I guess he didn't see Lauren and me, or maybe he wasn't looking. Anyway, he headed into the water and started swimming and kept on swimming straight out. When his arms started flailing around I took off after him."

"Yeah," said Lauren. "And I freaked. Honestly I thought they were both goners."

"Can I go see Daddy now?" asked Jesse.

"Of course you can," said Maya. "I bet there's nothing he'd like more."

"Me too," said Lauren. She ruffled Josh's wet curls. "I'll see you later."

I pulled Ty off the arm of the chair so he was jammed in beside me. He put his arm around my shoulders. Ty didn't need words to do the right thing.

After they left, Josh told us the whole story about Zack being in the Vietnam war and how he got poisoned by Agent Orange, stuff that army helicopters sprayed on the bushes to kill them so there'd be nowhere for the enemy to hide. And what was even worse was that a whole lot more soldiers than just Zack got poisoned by the spray.

I hated that anybody had to have an enemy. All I could hope was that Zack would get the help he needed when he got home.

Sounds Like It's Over

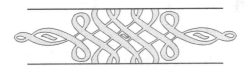

Mom and Dad came back the next afternoon. We were supposed to have the lasagna that Maya had made, all of us together, including Zack. But with the awful thing that happened, Maya decided to freeze it for another time. Zack apparently was okay but not exactly in the mood for doing a big meal together. Though Maya told me I could cook it for Mom and Dad, I wanted to wait and have it with the bunch of us before Maya and Zack left. Besides I really wanted to make my own homecoming dinner. We had a chicken in the freezer so I thawed it, and even though it was still partly frozen when I started cooking it, it came out great.

I was just finishing up the dinner when the car pulled in. I opened the trailer door and held it open with my foot while I presented a platter of toasty brown chicken, surrounded by a pile of potatoes, carrots and onions all mixed together. My grin squeezed my ears.

Seeing Mom pop out of the car felt like I bet people feel when they've been rescued. Maybe I wasn't being rescued, but I sure felt lucky to have parents.

The poodles darted between my legs, flying like spitballs straight into Mom's arms, totally knocking her off balance. "Well that's about the best homecoming I've ever had." She laughed as she smothered the dogs with kisses.

"I guess they outdid my surprise," I said. I went out and put the platter on the picnic table. "Where's Dad?"

"He's over in the phone booth doing some business, and I couldn't wait. She leaned over and sniffed the platter. "It looks and smells wonderful. You're a star."

She attached the poodles to their ropes and gave me a big hug that I clung to for dear life. "I really missed you Mom. You can't go away ever again while we're on this trip."

Mom stood back and stared at me. "Why? What're you saying, honey? Didn't you have fun?"

"I'm not saying anything other than don't go away again." Then to get off that subject real quick I pointed to the platter. "It's your welcome home present. D'you really like it?"

"Absolutely. I love it. Did Maya help?"

"Nobody helped. I did it all by myself."

"Maya must've helped with something. I like your t-shirt."

"She did help with that. I have an extra one if you want."

"Not exactly my style, but thanks. How is Maya? Did you wear her out completely."

I laughed. "Nope. We didn't wear her out at all. But it's a mess over there, Mom. They're leaving. Zack tried to drown himself last night and Josh saved him." Right then I would've smacked my nosy other self if I'd known where she was.

"He what?" Mom flopped onto the bench. "He tried to drown himself? You're kidding! And Josh saved him?"

"It was awful, but he's okay. I hope Maya won't hate me for telling you. Maybe you ought to go over there because the dinner's spoiled now anyway." I sunk onto the bench.

"Don't say that. The dinner's not spoiled." She put her arm around me. "What Zack did isn't all that surprising. He's a troubled guy and has been for a long time. Thank heaven Josh was there to save him. I'll see Maya later and I'm sure she'll tell me all about how the whole thing happened. But right now, let's not let anything get in the way of enjoying what you've done. Where are the boys?"

"They're next door. Should I go get them?"

"No. Look, here comes Dad," she said, pointing up the street.

He drove into the campsite and the poodles yipped their welcome on the end of their ropes. He flung open the car door and swept them up, "Me, too," he laughed through all the kisses.

With a huge grin, Mom picked up the platter. "Look at Zoey's homecoming present, Sammy."

Dad put the poodles down and closed the car door. He pulled me into one of his best hugs ever. "We missed you, baby girl. That's one heluva gift. Sorry for the language, but it looks delicious."

A leftover glow of their time away lit up the whole campsite, probably the whole campground.

The boys came home at that point and Ty was carrying a box of puzzles and games. Josh was carrying nothing but a dumpy look on his face.

Ty dropped his box on the table and gave Mom and Dad hugs. "Welcome home. We missed you guys a lot. And nice going Sis. The dinner looks great."

Josh went in the trailer without saying a word.

"Hello to you too, son," said Dad. "What's with him?"

"They're leaving, Dad," I said. "They're going back home."

"Oh, I get it. So, I guess that means no more Lauren."

Ty picked up his box and came in with me to get the dinner plates and stuff. He put the box on his bunk. Josh was behind his closed curtain. "C'mon Josh. Don't ruin the homecoming."

"I don't care about the homecoming."

"Of course you don't, because you don't care about anything but yourself."

We got what we needed and went back outside.

"So, no Josh?" asked Dad.

"Doesn't look like it," said Ty.

"I'm losing Maya," said Mom, "and you don't see me sulking."

"Enough about all that," said Dad. "Let's get into this incredible meal while it's still hot."

We all sat, and Dad picked up the carving knife but he didn't carve. He said, "I hate to delay eating, but it appears we could do with some good news around here." He put the knife on the platter.

Boy, did that perk up the table. "Good news? What good news Dad?"

"Yeah, Dad," said Ty. "What's going on?"

Dad went to the door. "Hey Josh," he called. "Come out here. I've got something you need to hear. I think you'll be impressed."

Josh grumbled words I couldn't make out.

Dad said even louder, "How about riding the best waves in Florida? Would you like that?"

In a flash Josh was at the door. "What?"

"Yeah," said Dad. "We're heading down to Sebastian Inlet tomorrow."

Josh practically went airborne. "You're kidding! Sebastian Inlet's the surfing capital of the east coast."

"I knew you'd be impressed. C'mon out and let's get into the chicken. Your sister scored."

Josh came out, and he actually gave Mom a kiss and Dad one of those guy smacks. "That's really cool, Dad. I dig it."

Dad carved off the drumstick and tossed it onto Josh's plate. "The cool part is we'll finally have a place we can settle, spread out, get into the work I need to do."

"What d'you mean?" I asked. "What about the diving trip you promised?"

"We can't hang around for the diving trip. We'll do all the diving we want when we get settled. Besides school's already started and you guys need to get registered."

"Rats," I said under my breath.

"What's that mean, sweetheart," asked Dad. "I heard you." He didn't look at me, he just sliced through the rest of the chicken and served it up.

"It's good news Zo, because the research has paid off. Dr. Osborne, the owner of the cabin we'll be renting, he's a minister and runs a church in his own house on the property. He also has a workshop and he's offered to let me use it to work on my ideas. He and his wife are great. You'll love them."

I didn't care about loving them. "I'm glad for you Dad. I just like it here, that's all."

"Well you're going to like it there better, believe me, Zoey. Right Meg?"

Mom was serving veggies with a big grin like Dad's on her face. "It's amazing, kids," she said. "The place is right on the ocean, the people who own it are amazing too. Your dad's right. You're going to love it, all of you."

Both of them looked happier than I'd seen them in ages. I wanted to look like that too, but my insides squished together. Sure, I knew it'd all be over, but I'd hoped it'd all be over in Baltimore, not Florida, and that I'd have Amy back in my life. I wrapped my arms around myself real tight to keep from spitting out all my bad thoughts. I had a slew of them, like what about my assignment? And what about Angie and my joyride lesson?

Mom and Dad didn't stop swooning over wherever, and finally when Mom took a look at my untouched food, she said, "You're not eating anything, honey. Are you okay?"

I got up. "The chicken needs that barbecue sauce they're giving away at the store." I slid off the bench. "I'll go get some samples." I didn't want the sauce. I wanted Angie.

"Hurry back," said Mom. "Your dinner'll get cold.

At the store Angie looked like a whole new person. She was wearing a bright red mini-dress. Her nails were bright red too, and so was her lipstick, along with some new spikes in her hair. She almost looked on fire.

When she saw me her face lit up like she *was* on fire. "Well, hi. I was hoping you'd show up so I could return this." She reached under the counter and brought up Maya's dish, all washed. She handed it to me. "Did everything get handled last night? That was a real scare."

"I know. I think Zack's all right but I haven't seen him. I came to get some of the barbecue sauce samples. You sure look pretty."

"Do I? That's nice. Thanks, babycakes." She pushed the box across the counter. "Help yourself. It's really good."

I took a handful of packs, lifted the dish cover and dropped them in. I held the bowl against my chest. Angie reached across the counter and put her hand over mine. The frown on her face said something not good was coming. My heart skipped about a dozen beats.

"I'm glad you showed up, sweetface. If you'd waited 'til tomorrow I would've been gone. I got fired and I'm outa here."

"You're kidding! Monster Man fired you?"

"He called me a freak, but that's okay. I needed out anyway. I've got to fly Granny's body to LA, and I'll be back in a few weeks to sell her things and close up the apartment. So maybe we can meet then and get our joyride lesson in. How would that be?"

I dropped the bowl on the counter, and out burst a bucketful of tears.

Angie darted around the counter and pulled me into a hug. "It's okay. I'll be back. We can have our lesson. Don't cry. Please don't cry."

I grabbed some Kleenex out of the box on the counter and stuffed them in my eyes. "We can't have any more joyride lessons Angie. We're leaving. The trip's all over and I can't talk about it since everyone's waiting for the sauce." I crumpled the soggy Kleenex and picked up the dish.

"How about you come back after supper and tell me about it, and we'll get the joyride lesson in. If Monster Man shows up, we'll tell him to shove it."

"But there's always customers after supper. And besides it's too late for a lesson. It's all over, the whole thing. Dad doesn't need a joyride. He doesn't even need peace and quiet anymore. He's all happy about some new idea he's got, and my assignment's a waste of time."

Angie grabbed my shoulders. "Now that's a pile of crock. Your assignment is definitely not a waste of time. It might be over for your old man, but let me tell you something, babycakes. It was your assignment that gave you to me and me to you. And that, as far as I'm concerned is one huge gift for both of us. Now pull your little self out of the dumps and think about how lucky we are to have each other. Did you tell your folks about your name?"

"I didn't yet. They'd want to know who told me that and I wasn't ready to hear anything not nice about you. They think you're scary Angie, and I hate that." I shoved the Kleenex back in my eyes. The tears gushed and I had to get more. "How can you say we have each other when we don't, or we won't once everything's over."

Angie hugged me. "Please don't cry. I'm going to be with you any time I want." She stood back and patted her heart. "You're right in here, so I won't need your body in front of me any more than I need Granny's body to know that she's still with me. You both have a special place in my heart that's yours, and that means I'll be able to feel you with me any time I want. I'm sorry your folks think I'm scary, but I'm sure glad that didn't rub off on you."

"Me too. I don't know what I'll ever do when you're gone. I mean can you really feel people in your heart? How do you do that, Angie, because I need to feel you in my heart. That's really neat." My tears stopped as I waited to hear how.

"It's like I told you, sweetface. Whatever you make up is what you get. So just like Maya telling you to make up flowers for people, and you saw them as those flowers, you can make up that I'm in your heart and you'll feel me there, as well as in the wildflowers that are all over the place. I'll even plant pansies in my garden behind the house in LA so I can see you every day. How's that?"

"That's awesome, Angie. You're amazing."

Angie took the soggy Kleenex out of my hand and tossed it in the trash. "So, no more tears?"

"I don't feel like crying anymore. You fixed all that."

"No, you fixed it. *Zoey is Love*, remember?" Angie picked up one of her receipt books, ripped off a page, turned it over and scribbled her name and address on it. "This is my folks P.O. box in L.A. They've had the same one for forty years and they'll probably have it for forty more. So whenever you get settled somewhere, send me a card with your address, and when you're sixteen I'll even send you a plane ticket and you can come visit."

"That'll be great, it really will. I can hardly wait." Just thinking about something that fun yanked me out of the hole I'd made for myself. Angie was not only a field of wildflowers, but she was for sure the funnest person in the world.

She handed me the receipt and I stuck it in my pocket. "Seeing as I have your address can we write letters Angie?"

"Absolutely we can. I'll just need to know where you are, so you write first."

"I can hardly wait. Thanks." We had one last very big goodbye hug before I picked up Maya's dish and left, wishing I could be sixteen a lot sooner than almost five years.

When I got home all the plates were empty and Mom ran in to get mine out of the oven. She didn't ask what took me so long because the whole bunch of them were all wound up in Dad's big story. I didn't need to explain why I had Maya's dish, since nobody noticed any of that. I stuffed my face with chicken and veggies without any sauce.

I guess my other self got tired of all the blabbing because she burst out with, "Did you guys know that Zoey means Life?"

Everybody shut up and stared at me.

"Who told you that bull?" asked Josh.

"Angie did. And it's not bull. It's Greek. Angie's Greek."

"That's perfect because it sure sounds greek to me."

"It's not funny Josh. It's really nice, just like Angie, and I'm proud of it."

"That's wonderful," said Mom. "Considering where it came from, I guess I'd have to question the validity. I think that lady's capable of making up more than the meaning of your name."

"Don't say that. Angie's the best person I've ever met. It was stupid of you guys not to get to know her."

"Hey, hey," said Dad. "Wherever the meaning came from, I love it. You're full of life Zo, so it sounds perfect to me."

"Yeah Sis. That's neat," said Ty. He put his arm around my shoulder. "Can I get extra life if I tie myself to you? Boy, that'd give my name real meaning. I could go for that."

That was the perfect time to tell my white lily brother about *Life is Love*, but there was no way I was going to say anything else about Angie.

"You're a real lifer, bro," said Josh. "The only thing missing is a prison to put you in."

With that, everyone laughed, but I didn't.

The next day might have meant no more Angie, but it also meant no more bus people. We'd be moving on and so would they, us to Sebastian Inlet, and them home. I gave Maya back her dish along with a big thanks from Angie.

As it turned out saying goodbye to her wasn't half as hard as I'd expected it to be. I made it easier by thinking good thoughts about all the things she taught me, like making beaded necklaces and tie-dying t-shirts and turning people into flowers. Everything left perfect memory pictures for me to look at whenever I wanted, including one of her big red poppy with the purple center, planted right in the middle of my heart.

Mom interrupted our goodbye when she pulled the car up beside us and pushed open the passenger door. She and Maya were going into Jacksonville to not only return Ty's library books that he'd finally finished, but to a restaurant for a goodbye lunch. Before she left, I told

Maya I'd get Mom to plant poppies in our garden when we got one and asked her to plant pansies in hers. She laughed. "I'll do it." She gave me a tight hug.

Right then, for some reason I wondered what kind of a flower my other self would be. What I decided was probably a cactus because a cactus had both prickles and a flower. For sure, whoever she was she'd have both those things.

Mom and Maya drove away just as Ty came out of the trailer carrying a plate of sandwiches that he put on our picnic table. He was biting into one of them when I asked him if he had an inside self.

He practically choked. "An inside self? What's that supposed to mean?"

"It's just that I have this inside self who comes out with things sometimes, and I wondered if you had one of those."

"My thoughts don't come out unless I say them. You're nuts Sis. Go get the iced tea that's on the counter? I need a drink."

"I'm serious. I really do have another self."

"Sure you do. Just go get the tea. Here comes Jesse. Hey buddy," he called. "Get over here and have a sandwich."

I went and got the tea. Jesse came over and I couldn't help but notice the crumpled look on his face. He picked up a sandwich, but he didn't eat it, he threw it at Ty. The poodles scrambled to recover the parts, sand and all.

"Hey wait a minute," said Ty. "What's that all about? That's not very nice."

"I hate you," said Jesse. "You won't be my friend anymore."

"Who says I won't be your friend anymore?"

"Daddy says you're leaving and I'll never see you again."

"That's true, but I'll still be your friend. I'll be a memory friend. Sometimes they're the best kind."

I didn't think Ty had ever actually talked to Angie, but that sure sounded awfully close to having a friend in your heart.

"That's stupid," said Jesse. "There's no such thing."

"It's called pretend. So now pretend you're hungry and have a sandwich." He handed Jesse another one.

Jesse didn't say anything, but he did take a bite of the sandwich.

Right then Lauren and Josh showed up. They were freaky about their goodbyes. I could tell, by the way they were pretending not to care, that they cared a lot. They didn't say much, just munched away on the sandwiches, probably so they wouldn't have to talk.

What zapped my mind away from thinking about them was Zack coming out of the bus. Nobody looked surprised, but I could feel my eyes bugging out of their sockets as he headed our way.

"Hi, Dad," said Lauren. "Do you want a sandwich?"

"That'd be good. Thanks." He sat down on the bench beside Jesse and put his arm around him. "You okay, kid?"

Jesse nodded hard.

"We got it straightened out," said Ty. "I told him we'd be memory friends. I think he's okay with that." He nudged Jesse who actually smiled. It was absolutely unreal to be sitting there with the bunch of them acting like this happened every day.

I passed Zack a glass of tea and he thanked me, but he didn't drink it. He lifted the glass and held it toward me. "This one's for you, smarty pants. It's been good to know you, so I felt like coming over to say goodbye." He actually smiled. I didn't say anything, but for sure I blushed. I took a big gulp of tea.

"That was nice, Dad," said Lauren.

"And that's not all." Zack pointed his glass at Ty. "I want to drink to you too, kid. You've been good for my boy and I'm grateful for that."

"Thanks Zack," said Ty. "It's been fun."

And maybe it had been fun for Ty. For sure he'd been in the bus playing games with Jesse, and no doubt knew Zack better than any of the rest of us. I wondered right then why I'd never thought to ask him. But then I remembered his thing about minding your own business, so he probably wouldn't have told me anything anyway.

Thanking Ty wasn't the end of it for Zack. He pointed the glass at Josh. "And thanks for taking care of me the other night, man. I owe you one for that. Besides you've been good for my girl. So thanks for that too. You're all right, the whole bunch of you. Maybe next time things'll be different."

With that, he drank the whole glass of tea in one gulp.

I couldn't remember Josh ever being lost for words, but right then he was. He stuffed his face with another sandwich after he'd already had two.

"Why'd you call my sister smarty pants?" asked Ty.

"No big deal. It's a compliment." Zack tucked the hair hanging in his face behind his ears and smiled at me. I wondered if almost drowning had maybe changed him.

Dad was working on unhooking all our campground attachments. He seemed busy enough to not be paying any attention to what we were doing. But for some reason he dropped the cords he was working with on the sand and took off down the beach.

"What's with him?" asked Josh.

"Who knows," said Ty.

"Is it because I threw the sandwich?" asked Jesse with his face all screwed up. "Did I make him mad?"

"Heck no," said Ty. "He's got a head full of business going on and I think it was probably the racket."

Zack got up. "It was probably me. I'm outa here." He picked up a sandwich and headed for to the bus.

I called, "Bye," and he waved the sandwich over his head without looking back at me.

Josh and Lauren got up. "We'll be back," said Josh. The two of them went toward the beach.

"So how come it's been good knowing you, Sis," asked Ty. "Did we miss something? Have you ever even talked to the guy?"

"I talked to him when you were at the picnic. He came out and everything. He was nice. I liked him."

"Wow. I guess he must've liked you too. But that's no surprise, because what's not to like." He took the plate and the glasses in the trailer.

He came out with the dog leashes, untied the dogs and hooked them up. "Let's take a walk so you can tell me about the other person who lives inside you. I bet she's pretty nice too."

"I don't want to talk about her anymore. We'll just take the poodles for a walk and we won't talk. I have a lot of figuring out to do about what just happened."

"We can talk about how nice it was of Zack to show up and say all those things. He's an all right guy. It'll be good for him to go home and get some help for whatever's wrong."

We went for the no-talking walk and when we got home Mom was back, and so was Dad. Actually, everyone for that matter. Dad was at the table, finishing up the sandwiches, and the bus was gone.

Mom said Maya was going to get some groceries, but my guess was that she made that up just so she and probably Lauren and Jesse too, and maybe even Zack, wouldn't have to watch us drive off. It sure made it easier for me.

Josh was leaning against the side of the trailer, staring at the empty space the bus had left.

"Are you missing Lauren already?" I asked.

"What's that to you, Creep." He shoved his hands in his pockets, not even looking at me.

"Jeez. Sorry."

"Yeah, I'm sorry too. But sorry doesn't make up for the fact I'll probably never see her again."

"You can see her in your heart. That's what Angie says."

He looked over at me like I'd just lost my marbles. "Maybe that crap works for you. What works for me is she's gone, and that's that."

"Y'mean you won't even write her?"

"What for? It's over, kaput. Let's get in the car." Ty, the poodles and Mom were already there.

Dad was climbing in. "C'mon, you two. We're leaving."

Off To Sebastian Inlet

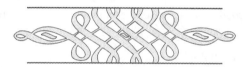

On the way out of the campground, to stop feeling sorry for Josh I decided to bring up something good, and that was Zack coming over to our place. I wasn't sure Mom knew.

"We had lunch with Zack, Mom. I mean he came and ate at our table and thanked us for being good to Jesse and Lauren. Can you believe that?"

Mom whipped around in her seat. "Really? No, I can't believe it. I hope someone tells Maya, because that would mean a great deal to her."

"He seemed really sincere too," said Ty, "especially when he thanked Josh for saving his life."

"No big deal," said Josh. "He probably would've made it back to shore on his own."

"It was a big deal," said Dad. "Take some pride in it."

"Yeah. Okay," said Josh. "But talking about big deals and pride, why don't you tell us about what you're planning, Dad, the big deal that'll make *you* proud and *us* rich?"

"I don't know about rich, But I do know I'm planning on coming up with something that's productive and will make me a lot prouder than creating fancy words to sell toilet paper."

Josh laughed. "What's more productive than selling toilet paper? Who doesn't need that?"

"Look, Josh, this is no joke. Twenty-five years of selling products I don't care about is enough for me. I want to develop something that matters. Something fun for a change."

"Then let's hear it. Fun seems like what the whole family ought to be in on."

"The whole family will be in on it when I've got it figured out. A rule in business is that you don't talk about your plans while they're being formulated."

"Does that mean you're in the dark too, Mom?"

"I know the rule, Josh," said Mom. "I use it myself when I'm planning a new weaving project. I know that whatever Dad's working on is more important than having to talk about it. I respect his privacy and I'm looking forward to when he wants to share." She reached up and gave Dad a kiss on the cheek.

"Thanks Meg," said Dad.

"The whole thing's stupid," muttered Josh.

"I'm glad it's going to be fun Dad," I said. "I'd like you to have fun."

"Thanks Zo," he said. "Me too. But let me finish by saying that possibilities are what I'm into at this stage. Variables. That's what all the research has provided, variables. You'll see soon enough. It's a big world out there, with lots going on. Making something that's new, and adds to the quality of life, well that takes a lot of research and development. Not idle chit chat, or at least not yet."

Right then a picture popped into my head. There was Dad headed to home plate. I squeezed the bag of assignment notes between my feet and my legs tingled. I wanted to bounce up and down and yell out loud what was happening, but I couldn't. All I could do was grab the pencil and some paper I kept in the bag for note scribbling and write out what was in my head before it bubbled out of my mouth. I only had my knee to write on, and that wasn't working.

Josh poked me in the arm with his elbow. "What're you doing?"

"I'm writing Amy."

"You can't write on your knee."

"I can do whatever I want."

Ty reached across Josh and handed me a bunch of his comic books. "Here, write on these."

I didn't take them. "Thanks, but I don't want to write anymore." I put the paper and pencil back in the bag.

"Let's play magnetic chess, bro," said Josh. "I feel like some fun."

"Whatever you play, keep it down," said Dad. "I've got a lot of things to work out in my head before we get to the Osbornes'."

"We'll make it checkers then," said Ty. "Chess is never quiet with Josh."

"Good idea," said Josh. He pulled the magnetic board from under Dad's seat.

I tucked the pillow between my head and the window and closed my eyes. Before long I drifted off to sleep and must've slept a real long time, because before I knew it Josh was nudging me with, "Hey Creep, wake up. We're here."

I peered out the window, blinking my eyes into focus. There was a white cabin with green shutters and a red door. The cabin was cute enough, but tiny. There didn't look to be enough room for one bedroom, let alone three. "Are there any bedrooms in there Dad?

"There's only one and your mom and I will have it. You and your brothers will stay in the trailer."

"I think I'll get a tent," said Josh. "I've had enough trailer."

I opened the car door and the dogs leapt over the seat and out the door, racing down the long driveway towards a man and a lady who swooped them up.

"I guess the pooches know how to win over the landlord," the man said when they got to us. They introduced themselves. They were the minister and his wife, Dr. and Mrs. Osborne, that Dad had talked about. I hadn't paid a lot of attention to who they were, but I had heard Dad say something about a church in their house. I couldn't wait to see how a house got turned into a church.

You could hardly see the house through the flowering bushes and palm trees that were all over the place. There was a lot of water behind the house that turned out to be the Intracoastal Waterway, where big boats come in from the ocean. It was also called the Indian River because that's what it was, a not very wide, but deep river. The whole property went all the way from the Waterway to the highway, and across the highway was the ocean. The highway right there wasn't very wide. I figured that from our cabin at the edge of the property, I could probably whip a Frisbee over the highway and it'd land on the beach. Pretty neat is what I thought.

The minister wasn't a bit like our stuffy minister back home who wore a stiff white collar and black suit. Dr. Osborne had on a blue shirt and jeans. His wife had on purple slacks and a blouse that looked like a rose garden. Her pink-rimmed glasses and white fluffy curls reminded me of angels. I tried to imagine a flower, but nothing came. Turning people into flowers sure helped me understand about letting people be the way they were, but the whole thing got complicated when people became other things in my imagination. I decided absolutely not to do that anymore.

Dr. Osborne told us that they were about to take a walk. "But now that you're here, let's go in the cabin and have some fruit punch. We've been anticipating your arrival."

The Osbornes carried the poodles inside and put them down. They had the whole place sniffed out in seconds and were quick to hop on the sofa and watch all of us. The cabin might not have been very big, but it did have a decent bedroom with a double bed and a dresser and a real closet. Mom and Dad could hang up all their clothes if they wanted to. There was also a bathroom with a shower, and a kitchen with a regular stove, fridge, and lots of cupboards.

The main room had a big old table in front of the window with six chairs around it. Against the opposite wall was the comfy looking sofa the poodles had snagged, with tables and lamps at either end. A coffee table and two stuffed armchairs were everything else.

Barely inside the cabin, Josh zoomed in on the chocolate-chip cookies that were on the table. Four cookies were gone in seconds. "These are great," he said, gobbling them up, "and I like the air conditioning in here. Can I set up a tent?"

Mrs. Osborne said thanks about the cookies, but only chuckled at the question because Dr. Osborne began telling us about how everything worked, especially all the wiring if we wanted power in the trailer.

"So I won't need a tent. We can have air in the trailer, Dr. Osborne?" asked Josh, with a big smile.

"You can have air in the trailer, lights and everything else."

"Wow, that's cool. Thanks."

"Our pleasure."

There wasn't a lot of space in the cabin, so putting the two places together felt like we'd just won the jackpot.

"Now, would you folks like to have a tour of the property?" asked Mrs. Osborne.

"You've given us a lovely welcome," said Mom. "But can we wait a while for the tour? It's been a long day and I think I'd like to get settled first."

I'm sure Mom's head was spinning, just like mine. Taking in any more right then was just too much. Mrs. Osborne poured the rest of the punch in our glasses and agreed that getting settled was a good idea.

"I'll be in the workshop when you're ready, Sam," said Dr. Osborne. "We'll need to do some space organizing. There's a lot of heavy equipment we'll need to move around."

"I can help," said Ty.

"Sounds good," said Dad. "How about after supper. Would that be okay?"

"Perfect," said Dr. Osborne.

I wasn't interested in the workshop. I wanted to hear about the church. "How do you make a house into a church?"

The minister laughed. "Anywhere is a church, my child. All you need for a church is a belief in God. It's a place for people to get together to worship."

"How's the surfing, Dr. Osborne?" asked Josh.

"The surfing is good." Dr. Osborne started warning Josh about the dangers of surfing near Sebastian inlet that was only about a half mile away.

"Now James," said Mrs. Osborne, "I think we'd better be on our way. Don't scare the poor boy."

"You're right, Hazel"

She put her empty glasses and plate, along with the empty pitcher, on the tray, and after a lot more thanks for the super welcome, they left smiling.

As soon as they'd gone, Dad took over explaining how the whole living thing would work for us. The plan was that he'd park the trailer on the other side of the driveway and run a power cord between the cabin and the trailer. Like he'd already told us, my brothers and I would stay in the trailer and he and Mom would take over the cabin.

"Dibbs on the big bedroom so I can have privacy," I announced.

"What do you need privacy for? What've you got to hide, eh, eh?" said Josh, poking my arm with his finger.

I whapped him with one of the pillows from the sofa. "Mom, make him stop."

"Enough!" said Mom, a lot louder than she needed to.

Dad put his arm around her. "It's okay, babe," he said. "It's been a long day, and of course Zoey can have the bedroom."

"Thanks Dad," I said. Ty hadn't said a word the whole time.

Josh punched his fist against the wall and I hoped it hurt. It sure hurt the doggies when any of us got mad and made a racket like that. They were cuddled together on the sofa and I knew they were missing having Mom and Dad's bedroom to run to. I picked them up and took them to the new bed, and before I even had a chance to puff the pillows, they were under them.

Josh headed to the trailer and came out minutes later in his bathing suit with his surfboard.

Dad burst out the door and yelled, "You're not going surfing now! There's work to do."

With the board under his arm, Josh whirled around and bolted back into the trailer.

Dad, whose face was close to purple, yelled again, "Get out here Josh! I'm going to park the trailer and I need you to get the bikes down so I can unload the storage."

I peered out the door. "C…can I help?" I offered.

"Help your mother with supper," said Dad. Mom was in the kitchen checking out the cupboards.

Josh came out of the trailer, yanked his bike from the bike rack, hopped on it and wheeled out to the road.

"Get back here. Now!" yelled Dad, super loud this time. Josh kept going.

"I can get the bikes Dad," I called, rushing out. Ty dropped the bag of charcoal he had in his hand and ran to help me.

"Hold it," said Dad. "I'll get the trailer parked and you two can unload the bikes when I'm done."

He got in the car and revved the engine, backing the whole thing up and pulling onto the patch of grass that Dr. Osborne told us to use. In a whole lot of quiet Ty and I took down the bikes and dropped the stands. Dad set up the cords to make electricity in the trailer work and then he unloaded the storage while Mom and I got the salad stuff from the trailer fridge. Ty fired up the barbecue to make hot dogs.

While Mom and I were in the trailer I got this urge to tell her about the seashell. I took it off my shelf to show her. "Aunt Alyssa gave me this when we left home. It's supposed to bring luck and happiness near water. Do you suppose it's working. Are you happy?"

Mom put the salad bowl she was carrying down and gave me a hug. "Of course I'm happy, because you make me happy, Zo. I feel very lucky to have you in my life, but I'm not sure that has much to do with a seashell. Alyssa showed me the shell and I thought it was sweet. I've never been all that superstitious but I have to admit the message is pretty apt. I like it."

I hugged Mom back and squeezed my shell at the same time. I sure felt happy right then and probably lucky too. I was finally going to have my own bedroom, even if it was only in a trailer.

I put the shell on the table beside my new bed in Mom and Dad's room and went to help her take the other stuff over to the cabin.

After the salad and hot dogs that we ate in a lot of silence, Ty and Dad took off to set up the workshop.

"Aren't you worried about Josh, Mom?" I asked. "Where do you suppose he'd go on his bike? Is there a neighborhood around here, or somewhere other than the highway?"

"There are lots of side streets that your dad and I explored when we were here before, so it's safe enough. We can't worry about your brother. He's going to do what he's going to do because that's who he is. So let's go stretch out on the new bed and see how it feels."

"Do you think we're going to be here forever?" That just fell out and even I wasn't ready for it.

"Hardly forever," said Mom. "Only time will tell how long. I'm going to get the sheets out of the trailer and make up the bed in here. Do you want to stretch out with me?"

"No. I don't want to stretch out. I want to go look around the place."

"Fine. You do what you like, but I want to go and snuggle with the poodles. I think they need some company." She went over to the trailer just as the front door burst open and in came Josh.

I wanted to smack him. "That wasn't funny Josh. Dad wanted your help."

"If Dad wants help he needs to find a better way to ask for it." He wolfed down one of the three hot dogs that Mom had left on the counter for him. He didn't even bother heating it, he just scarfed it down in seconds and said, "I'm going surfing."

"You can't go surfing if you just ate.

"I didn't eat. One hot dog's only a snack. I'll have the other ones later."

The beach sounded more interesting than looking around by myself so I asked if I could go with him.

"Sure. But you better get your bathing suit if you're planning on swimming." He already had on his bathing suit. "I'll get my surfboard."

We went in the trailer just as Mom came out.

"Where've you been, Josh?" she asked, probably more calmly than she felt.

"Just checking the neighborhood out. We're going to the beach. Wanna come?"

She had all the sheets bundled in her arms so I asked her if she wanted any help with the bed.

"No. I think I'll revel in the quiet for a while. You go to the beach, but keep an eye on your sister Josh."

"Always." Josh went in and grabbed his board and headed out. "Move it Creep. I'll see you over there."

When I got to the beach the waves were big and Josh was already in the ocean with other kids. So much for keeping an eye on me. He did at least wave.

Probably because it was suppertime, there was hardly anyone on the beach. I had pretty much decided to go back and look around after all when I noticed a guy sitting by himself up by the dunes. He wasn't just sitting there, he had his feet up over the tops of his legs, his hands on his knees with the palms turned upside down. He didn't have on a bathing suit. He had on cutoff jeans and a sleeveless t-shirt. He looked like he was probably in his twenties.

Out of the blue I thought about the connection thing and began wondering if I could make a connection with him that might even turn into talking about peace. For sure Dad still needed it.

Seeing as I'd decided not to swim, and I could do the tour later, I spread out my towel and sat in the sand a few feet away from him. With his thick hair dangling over his face I couldn't tell whether his eyes were closed. He didn't seem to notice I was there so they probably were. I shifted my towel around to see if I could get his attention, but that didn't work so I decided to try staring at him. I'd heard if you stared long enough at someone, they'd look at you. That didn't work either.

What did work wasn't my doing. It was a surfer who whooped so loud over a big wave that the guy popped his head up on his own.

"Hi." He looked over at me as he tucked his hair behind his ears. "I didn't see you sitting there."

I told him I hadn't been there for long. "The way you're sitting looks awfully uncomfortable." I tried to pull my feet up like his but I couldn't get them over my thighs.

The guy laughed as he watched my effort. He pulled one of his legs up and stuck it behind his head. Then the other one. He had both of them wrapped around his neck at the same time. "How about this?"

I figured he must be triple-jointed and I told him he should be in the circus.

"Mind over matter," he said. He stretched his legs out in front of him, grabbed his feet and pulled his head to his knees before he sat up. "People limit themselves by thinking they can't do things when they oughta go the other way, like know they can do anything they make up their minds t'do, y'know?"

"My brother told Mom he'd watch me at the beach, and as soon as he got here he ran into the waves. He didn't even wait to see what I wanted to do. I'd like to smack him. Do you think I could do that?"

The guy laughed. "That's not exactly what I'm talking about. Brothers are like that. I treat my sister like crap sometimes." He crossed his legs normally, the same way I had mine.

I felt real comfortable sitting there with him when he did that. I asked him what he was thinking before with his feet up over his legs and his eyes closed.

"I wasn't thinking. That's what I was doing, not thinking. I just got fired, so I'm working on emptying my mind of all the leftover junk from work."

"Oh that's too bad. I'm sorry you got fired."

"Don't be sorry. Now for the first time in ages I've got time to myself."

"My dad quit his job and I bet he wishes he had time to himself. But it's not working that way." I told the guy about how we were traveling around while Dad was thinking up another job idea. "Sometimes I bet he wishes he'd gone off by himself to think of a new thing to do."

"Maybe he wishes that and maybe he doesn't. He made a choice to do what he's doing with his time. My choice is to use the time to get my head on straight."

"Is that what you're doing now, getting your head on straight?"

"Well yeah, I guess you could call it that, if you call doing yoga getting your head on straight."

"I don't know anything about yoga, but I have a friend who meditates. She closes her eyes and sits quiet like you were doing, but she doesn't pull her feet up on her legs the way you had yours. She does leave her body though. Do you leave yours?"

He laughed. "Not exactly. If anything I get into mine more. I integrate with everything around me, if you understand integrate." He smoothed out a mound of sand in front of him and looked at me. "Do you?"

"No, I don't think so." I pictured the twins when he said that so I asked him if integrating with things was the same as connecting.

"Sort of, but it's more than that. It's like becoming part of, joining with, y'know? It's like you join with the forces of nature where there's all this energy. That's what I was doing before you came along. The no-thinking thing I was doing is part of joining with the forces of nature."

"What do you mean by the forces of nature?"

"Right here and now, I mean the ocean. Look out there. Maybe all you see is a body of water, but if you listen you can feel that it's nothing but energy." He stretched his arms out behind him, leaned back and stared out at the waves. "If you close your eyes you can actually become the rhythm of the waves."

I didn't close my eyes because I was watching Josh who had just caught a wave. "That's my brother, the guy that's closest to us, who just caught a wave. All that energy in the wave that's sending the board to shore, is that the energy you're talking about? I never thought of that as energy. But boy, I guess it is, isn't it?"

"That rhythm and energy is power, and for the most part people don't tap into it."

"I met a guy who taps into the ocean and pulls out fish because he plans it that way. How do fish swim around in all that energy?"

"Fish are naturally tuned to the energy, and sometimes energy is quiet. It doesn't have to be tumultuous, it only has to be what you connect with that makes you feel like you're part of something much bigger than yourself. What's your name anyway?"

"My name's Zoey. What's yours?" He told me he was Mike.

He reminded me of Eli and how he'd said his unique self was more than the guy who rode around on a motorcycle. I didn't know anything about Mike, but for sure the way he was talking was unique. Right then I felt so connected to Mike and the ocean and the waves and the sky and the beach, everything filling me up so full I thought I'd burst. I wanted to reach out my arms and pull all of it in and package it up for Dad's gift.

"Do you get peace when you connect with the rhythm of the waves?" I asked.

"Sure I do. I get lotsa peace when I tune into the source. It's like tuning the radio. Until you tune the radio, you get static. You gotta fine tune your life to get peace."

"That's weird. I never thought of radio static like that. Sometimes it's really hard to get rid of, isn't it."

"What is this with you, all this curiosity? You're like a buzzing bee whizzing around. Have you chosen me as a landing pad?"

"Have I? I guess I don't know, but maybe I have. I'm trying to figure out stuff for my dad, and what you said about no thinking got me thinking."

"Yeah, I noticed. So what're you thinking right now?"

"I was wondering how I could make Dad think like you do. The energy at my place isn't like being here with you. I want some of this for my dad, and my brother too."

"I assume you've got lotsa static going on at your place." Mike scooped up a pile of sand and let it sift through his fingers. "All these tiny grains of sand, watch how they work together to make a perfect stream. Don't you wish people would do that, work together to make a perfect stream? There's no static there."

"I'm only eleven, but I wish that a lot."

"Where d'you live, anyway?"

I pointed across the road. "My mom and dad and my two brothers, and two dogs, we live in a trailer over there. We're parked on the driveway of a minister's house that's also a church."

"Wow, that's quite a mix."

Suddenly a whistle sounded off. One of Ty's kind of whistles, but not quite as loud, but loud enough that I looked, and Josh was beckoning like crazy. "I guess that means I gotta go doesn't it."

"Looks that way, but it's been fun. You're quite a kid, Zoey. Lots going on inside, and that's good."

"I don't know about good. I just know I want peace for Dad, that's all. Will you be down here again so maybe we can talk more?"

"Nope. I'm headed to Miami in the morning, but the best way to help your dad get peace is to tell him to tune the radio in his head, y'know, get rid of the static. I don't know what's going on with him, but living in a trailer with a bunch of people on a minister's driveway while he's trying to come up with a new career idea, well I get static in my head even thinking about that, so I wish all of you luck." Mike laughed, but honestly I didn't think that was funny. It sort of hurt.

There was another whistle, louder than before. "Or maybe from the looks of your brother," said Mike, "he oughta be the one t'do the tuning. There's lotsa static going on with him. I can feel it from here."

"Yeah, me too, but the only way to get rid of Josh's static is to turn him off." I got up.

"Turning him off, y'got that right. Tuning life's no easy feat for any of us, and tuning your family, well that's right up there, big time. I know. I've got a family and the static's through the roof. Give yourself a break Zoey. Have fun."

"Thanks, I'm sure trying."

When I got to Josh I asked him why the hurry. He said he was starved, that one hot dog wasn't enough. I could've said a whole lot more about that, but I knew it'd just bring more static.

At home I peeked in Mom's room and she'd fallen asleep with the book on her chest and the poodles nestled next to her. I closed the door.

"I'm going to go look around," I whispered. "D'you want to come?" Josh was into the leftover cold hot dogs.

"You go," he said, without whispering. "I need to wax my board. I don't like the way it's handling."

I didn't tell him I thought his board handled great, and that I'd watched him and he was good. I didn't feel like he deserved a compliment after everything he'd done wrong, like not whispering, running off on Dad, and ignoring me at the beach.

I set out to look around the property and the first thing I came to was the workshop.

Dad showed up in the doorway. "Before this gets out of bounds with secret plans unfolding Zo, come take a look at the great space Dr. Osborne has given me."

I went in and the minister wasn't there anymore but everything was pretty well organized, with all of his equipment on one side, and a big empty worktable on the other that I figured was for Dad. There were all sorts of tools and stuff hanging neatly on the walls, and Ty was on a ladder shifting boxes on the shelf above the worktable.

"Where's your mom?" asked Dad. "You both should wander around, get a look at the property. It's pretty impressive."

"She's stretched out in the cabin so I'm doing that by myself. Maybe you can show her later."

"Good idea."

I took off, but I hardly got anywhere before I decided I'd wait and do the tour with both of them, because I had this real urge to write Amy.

I ran back to the trailer yanked out some paper and started scribbling.

Dear Amy,

I needed to write and let you know we've moved again, and this time you'll be able to write and keep writing because I think we'll be here a real long time. We've rented a little cabin in Melbourne Beach that's across the highway from the ocean and on a really big property that has the Indian River behind it. The owners are letting us park our trailer beside the cabin so we can spread out. It's pretty neat. The property belongs to a minister and he runs a church in his house, and has a workshop that he's loaning Dad to make this new thing he won't talk about. The address is on the top of this letter, so get writing.

I was glad to hear that you don't think I'm going crazy because my other self keeps saying stuff that doesn't sound like what I think of as me. It's kinda fun really. I'm hoping she'll help me with a final assignment idea because I haven't come up with one. But I did meet and talk to this really neat guy on the beach today. His name was Mike and he talked about tuning into the forces of nature to get peace. To try it out, I want you to go outside the next time it's windy and feel the wind on your face, see if you can tap into the power of that wind and know you're part of that power. I did that with the power of the energy in the waves, and honestly, it was amazing the feeling that came over me. I bet that sure felt like peace. I wanted to package everything Mike had told me and turn it into Dad's gift.

By the way it was really hard to leave the bus people behind, especially for Mom and Josh. Josh sulks a lot, but I'm sure he'll get over it, and Mom, she and Maya said they'd write a lot of letters now that we're pretty well settled. And saying goodbye to Angie was awful for me, but she said she feels people in her heart and that she'd feel me forever. We promised to write each other and she said she'd send me a ticket to LA when I turned sixteen. Save your money for the next five years so you can come with me.

I don't think I told you about sneaking over to the bus to see Zack when everyone was at a picnic. I liked him. He wasn't mean or anything, and he smokes pot all the time because he's sick from something awful that happened to him in the war. He actually tried to drown himself but Josh saved him. At least Josh is good for something.

Anyway, enough for now. I'm sure we're going to be here for a long time, so write down the address at the top of the letter and I'll look forward to hearing from you. Love ya loadsxxxZo

Settling In

Living at the Osbornes was so different from what I'd been used to in Baltimore that it took a lot of time to get it figured out. Meeting new kids and getting picked up by a school bus felt strange after a whole lifetime of the same kids, and a walk to school that was only four blocks away. What was good though was that the classes were a lot smaller than my old ones and the teachers seemed to know the kids, like know all the different stuff about them.

The hardest part about the changes was making friends for myself. If I made one I'd have to have her over to my place. All I had that was mine was my bedroom in the trailer and it was too small to hang out in. That's what my friends and me used to do. We'd either hang out in rec rooms if we had one, or hang out in our bedrooms.

And on top of that, there was no neighborhood place to go, like no shopping center or stores or movie theaters or anything. Of course there was the beach, and I went there a lot. But seeing as no kids my age were on the bus, none were on the beach either.

What I decided to do was go out for sports so I could stay for practices and games after school and get to know kids that way. I'd always been better than most kids at any sport, so I made myself popular really fast.

But I hadn't found a way to be popular after school. I had to make excuses when I was invited to someone's house, because that meant I'd have to be polite and have them back to my trailer. Anyway, if I did get invited, mostly I couldn't go because Mom had to pick me up after whatever practice or game was going on. There weren't any public buses on the beach, only school ones.

Ty and Josh's high school was on the mainland, and big, but only half as big as the one in Baltimore. It was full of a lot of surfers, so Josh had a bunch of surfing buddies who were on his bus. He'd didn't bring any of them home, but he did hang out with them at the beach all the time. I was surprised that he didn't go out for football seeing as he was so good at it, but maybe he didn't want any reminders of his old life. Josh and I didn't talk about that kind of stuff, and seeing as I was getting good at minding my own business I kept all my thoughts about him to myself.

The high school had a great science lab that Ty got right into. He made a couple of friends on his bus and he'd bring them home and they'd concoct crazy test-tube experiments that they'd blow up in the kitchen sink in the cabin when Mom and Dad weren't around. Dad was always in the workshop, and Mom wasn't around since she was into quilt-making with Mrs. Osborne at her house, along with a lot of other ladies who made quilts for hospital and church projects. Mom seemed happy being almost as busy as she used to be with her weaving friends.

The poodles were the happiest of all, hanging out with the Osbornes, who spoiled them rotten with doggie biscuits and lots of ball-tossing on the huge lawn. Mrs. Osborne trimmed their hair with electric clippers which was pretty cute since it had gotten really scruffy.

On Sundays we'd go to the church service in the Osbornes' living room, where all the furniture was moved to the side so they could set up about fifty chairs that were almost always full. There was no organ, only music played on a piano by a guy who wore jean shorts. Dr. Osborne had built his own pulpit that stayed in the living room all the time. I liked going to church there, and Mom and Ty did too, but Josh and Dad didn't. The Osbornes didn't seem to care who in my family went and who didn't. I always hoped maybe I'd meet kids at church, but so far that hadn't happened.

Finally I got another letter from Amy. She told me she'd been away again, this time for two weeks on a trip with her aunt to San Francisco. She said she had all the letters from me piled up when she got home and the best part of the letters was all the stuff about my other self. She said something so neat. She said I had to have part of me that was outspoken because for sure the one everyone knew was far too nice. She said most people weren't as polite as me and she was glad to know I had an inside part that said stuff that needed to be said. She said she really agreed with the twins about my other self probably being my inner guide. She admitted she wasn't real sure what that meant, but liked that someone had my best interests at heart, seeing as she wasn't around. That was nice. And she really liked what the twins said about connection. She said she could even feel our connection when she wrote, and that she'd start saving her money so go see Angie with me when we both turned sixteen.

After that, her letters came regularly. I'd read them over and over to feel better. Mostly she'd tell me about all the things she was doing, and I'd tell her about all the things I wasn't doing (trying to be funny). That's how I'd keep from getting into the dumps about my shortage of friends. I worked hard at having good thoughts.

One day I was sitting on the lawn brushing the poodles when Mom came panting her way back from a run on the beach. "Hey Zo, I just saw a couple of girls your age on the beach who I've never seen before. Get yourself down there. You might be lucky and find a new friend."

I hadn't told Mom about not wanting anyone over because of my dumb bedroom. I'd only said that I hadn't met anyone I liked well enough to bring home. It was no secret that I hung out with Amy's letters. "So am I supposed to just go barge in on them?"

"We'll take the poodles for a walk and you can check them out."
Mom grabbed my hand and pulled me up. "C'mon, get on your suit."

"Jeez, it's not that exciting."

"It might be. It's definitely worth a try."

"Fine," I said to myself.

When we got to the beach there they were just like Mom had said, two kids that looked about my age. One was sitting on a blanket, leaning against a backrest reading, and the other one was lying beside her. There were bunches of people running around with Frisbees and dogs and swimming and sitting around and stuff, but kids my age, well this was for sure a first. My heart started to race. I knew I wanted a friend, but I didn't realize how much until that very moment.

Being with Mom wasn't exactly the way to meet new kids, and I guess Mom knew that because she said she'd go on the dog walk by herself and catch me on her way back. She laughed when she promised not to let the girls know I had a mother.

I didn't have a blanket like they did, but I did have a towel, and I had on my bikini which was good. That's what they were wearing.

When the girl who was sitting saw me coming she stuck the book she was reading in her bag. She didn't smile like I hoped she would. She just sort of stared at me from behind dark glasses, so I couldn't see her eyes. She had blonde curls that were so thick she'd have to have trouble getting a brush through them.

The girl lying beside her didn't look at me because her eyes were closed. She had reddish-brown, skinny pigtails. The sitting girl was probably closer to Ty's age than mine.

When I got there, I said "Hi."

The sitting one pushed her sunglasses up on her head and said "Hi" back. Still no smile or anything. I wondered if she was mad about putting the book away. The other one, well she didn't open her eyes, or even move a muscle.

The whole thing felt uncomfortable, with me standing there, and them acting like they could care less. I made myself ask if they lived close by, but honestly I wanted to throw up. Then I remembered everything I'd learned, and made myself think good thoughts about having a new friend. That at least made wanting to throw up go away.

"We live over there," said the sitting girl, pointing across the highway. It looked like she was pointing at the Osbornes' house. I told her that was where we lived.

She jiggled her finger somewhere else. "We live past the Osbornes' place. Sorry, I pointed wrong. I know the Osbornes because we go to their church."

My legs felt about twelve feet long with her sitting there looking at my knees while she talked. I asked her if I could sit. She gave a weak smile when she told me to go ahead. I laid out my towel and plunked myself down.

"We're sisters," she said. "She's deaf and probably doesn't know you're here." She poked her sister, who opened her eyes long enough to give me a smile before she closed them again. "It's hard for her when new people show up. It's easier to pretend they're not here. My name's Cindy and hers is Becky."

I hated that Becky was deaf, but I sure liked not being ignored on purpose. "I'm Zoey. Has your sister always been deaf?"

"Yeah. Her eardrums were messed up when she was born. She uses sign language and reads lips. She's a great kid. Not hearing doesn't affect that."

"That's amazing. I bet it's hard to be deaf."

"I'm sure it is." She picked up her lotion and rubbed a handful on her arms. "Want some?" She handed me the lotion and the top and I rubbed it on myself. I put the top on and laid it on her blanket. She said she hadn't been to the Osbornes' church for over a year, since their Dad had to take the family to England for his job. "We got back the other day and it sure feels good. England's gloomy compared to Florida."

"How old is your sister?"

"She's eleven."

"I'm eleven too. How old are you?"

"I'm thirteen."

"You're probably going to be on my brother's bus when you go back to school, and Becky will be on mine. There aren't any kids my age down here, so it'll be nice to have company."

"My sister won't be on your bus. Mom drives her to a special school for the deaf."

"Where's that?"

"It's over the bridge on the mainland, but she's the only deaf kid on the beach, so there's no bus for her school."

"That's too bad. Do you like the church?"

"Yeah, I like it a lot." She picked up the lotion and checked the top was tight before she dropped it in her bag.

"It's weird going to a church in a house, don't y'think? I mean, it's fun. But it's sure different."

"I don't think it's weird. I like the way people get up and talk about things they do with the Lord, experiences they have that they share."

Now that got my attention. "How can they do stuff with the Lord? Isn't the Lord Jesus? He's not here."

Her mouth twitched like she wanted to laugh. But she didn't. She just said, "I don't mean hang out with the Lord. I only mean they talk about things they're guided to do by the Holy Spirit."

Nobody had talked about that and nobody had gotten up either, or not since we'd been going, so I shook my head. "Do you get peace in church at the Osbornes' house?"

Cindy stared at me. "I don't know. It depends on what's going on. Why do you want to know that?"

I didn't have an answer. I hadn't intended to ask the question but it just came out and it didn't take long to figure out from where. There I was, trying to make this new friend and my other self had moved right in. I hadn't planned on getting into my assignment, but obviously she had. Maybe I was supposed to hear something helpful. I had no idea what, so I just went ahead and said, "I'm doing an assignment on peace and I wondered what it was like for you if you got it there."

"What kind of assignment are you talking about?"

"I'm trying to find out what peace is so I can give it to my dad for his birthday."

Cindy didn't only twitch her mouth like before, but she actually laughed out loud. "Peace can't be a present. Presents come in boxes with paper and ribbons. Why don't you give your father a real present like maybe a new bathing suit. We gave our dad a bathing suit and he loves it. It's the color of the ocean and has dolphins on it."

I shot to my feet before I could do a thing about waiting for my other self to fix things, or have my own good thoughts, or anything else. I told her I had to go.

"Hey don't get frazzled," she said. "It's only an idea."

"Yeah thanks, but I don't have any money." I leaned across Cindy and tapped Becky's leg. She lifted her head and looked at me.

I mouthed, "Bye, Becky." She lifted her arm with a sort of wave and she smiled. I told Cindy "See ya," but I didn't care if I ever saw her again. Somebody who made fun of my idea wasn't who I wanted for a new friend.

Mom and the poodles were a little way down the beach so I caught up with them. I couldn't wait to tell Mom I didn't want Cindy as my friend, that she was snooty and older than me anyway. I told her the girl my age was deaf and I hadn't talked to her at all.

"Maybe a deaf friend would be better than a paper friend," Mom said, pretending to laugh, but I sure didn't laugh back. I knew she was trying to be helpful and that sure wasn't the way.

"Forget it, Mom," I said. "Amy's not a paper friend. She's a forever friend in my heart. I don't need anyone else."

Life At The Osbornes'

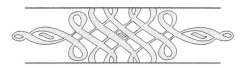

Mom got lots of letters from Maya and she always sent love to me. Mom shared some of them and I was glad to hear that Zack was getting help for whatever Agent Orange had done to him. She said the kids were doing fine and Lauren had a new boyfriend. I didn't write Maya myself. I couldn't write about my assignment, and I couldn't write about new flower people since I wasn't doing that anymore. I did wonder if she'd planted a pansy garden, but I couldn't get Mom to ask her, seeing as all that stuff was still part of my secret. I promised myself I'd write Maya after Dad's birthday.

I could hardly wait until we had our own place so I could plant both poppies and wildflowers. I always sent Maya heaps of love when Mom wrote. Maya also wrote that the bunch of them would drive down over Christmas when the kids were out of school. When Josh heard that, he practically went airborne. We didn't bother to tell him Lauren had a new boyfriend.

I did write Angie though. I told her I felt like Dad was working on some big secret that was making him more excited than I'd ever seen him. I said I knew he probably didn't need peace and quiet anymore but I wanted to give it to him anyway, just for fun. My only problem was that I still hadn't figured out how to do that. Angie wrote back that she knew something would come to me at the right time and not to worry about it because *Zoey is Love* would make it happen. She said she had planted a whole bed of pansies for me and I got chills when I read that.

Finally the big day came for Dad to show off whatever he'd been working on so secretly. How we got to find out about that was a huge surprise. It was a regular Sunday, or sort of regular. The big difference was that Mom didn't wear her normal clothes. She was all done up in white shorts, a white sporty shirt, and brand new white sneakers and white socks. "What's the deal?" I asked. "You look like a gym teacher."

"You'll see," she said. "Don't ask questions."

I should've figured right then that Dad's surprise was part of what was going on, but I didn't. I just got my own self ready in normal clothes and so did Ty. Josh, well the waves were big, so he was in the ocean where he practically lived.

Anyway off to church we went. Everything was the same as usual, that is until Dr. Osborne looked over at Mom and announced he had some news to share at the end of the service. From that moment on, what he said was a blur because I was almost positive the announcement had something to do with Dad. My mind wound itself in so many tangles that trying to listen to Dr. Osborne's sermon just made my head ache. I squirmed on my seat until Mom reached over and grabbed my hand. The squeeze didn't loosen the tangles, but it sure let me know I was right about Dad.

When the service was over, Dr. Osborne asked everyone to go to the garden. Normally I'd be helpful in the kitchen with refreshments, but this time I charged out the back door.

Well there was Dad all done up like Mom in a white shirt and white Bermuda shorts with white socks and gym shoes. He had all these things in his arms, like a school playground ball, a wooden bat, a hollow pipe with a sharpened end on it, and a small plastic ball with holes in it.

The congregation all gathered around Dr. Osborne as he clapped his hands and announced, "Today is a special day for us, my friends. Hazel and I are privileged to tell you that our little church has finally found the recreation director we've been wanting for so long."

There were lots of whoops and lots of claps, and then silence while everyone stared at Dad whose chest puffed like Popeye the Sailor Man.

Dr. Osborne's smile was super wide when he said, "Sam Warrington is about to introduce to us his new game. It's called, "Toppleball," and Sam is not likely to brag, so I want you all to know this is the first new playground game in the United States in over fifty years." Everyone clapped and whooped even louder than before.

I looked at Mom. She tilted her head, raised her eyebrows, and smiled, all at the same time. I looked at Ty and he stuck his thumbs in the air. Right then Josh showed up with a t-shirt over his bathing suit and his face doing that usual gawky thing it did when he had no idea what was going on.

Dad put the bat and the playground ball on the ground. He shoved the pointed end of the pole into the ground and set the ball with holes in it on top of the pole.

"The object of the game is to topple the whiffle ball," he said as he tapped the pole and the ball fell off, dangling at the end of a piece of rope.

He picked up both the playground ball and the bat (that looked like a shortened canoe paddle) and went on to describe how twenty fielders would form a circle around the plastic pole that would be guarded by a batter who'd whack balls thrown at the post by the fielders. Every time the batter whacked a ball over the heads of the fielders, he would run to the edge of the circle and back, counting runs until one of the returned balls got past him, hitting the post and toppling the whiffle ball. Dad zipped all over the place demonstrating everything, and everybody clapped when he was finished.

To start the thing rolling, Dad took his place at bat and about twenty people offered themselves as fielders as the rest watched, waiting their turn. Ty flung the first ball and Dad whacked it, sending it over the heads of the fielders and into the neighbor's yard. He ran to the edge of the circle and back, getting about twelve runs before the fielder got the ball, heaved it over Dad's head and hit the post. Everybody cheered like crazy. That guy got to be next up to bat and new fielders replaced the old ones so that everyone got to play.

Right away I felt so happy for Dad as I realized he'd found what Angie had talked about, the amazing part being that it wasn't just a new business idea, it was a REAL BALL GAME, where you swung at a ball, hit it and got homers. And boy did Dad get homers. I could hardly wait to write and tell Angie.

We all played like crazy, everyone yelling and screaming in a way that was hardly churchlike, but for sure fun for Dad, the big inventor who I knew felt all the love and trust in the world from the praise he was getting.

We were so busy having fun, I didn't have even a second to think about how the game was the big invention that was supposed to make us rich. But all of a sudden I got this whammo flash in my head, showing me that the game *was* the big invention that was supposed to get us a house where I could have my canopy bed and my stuffed bears and all my things, and where my friends could come over and hang out.

Well, now everything I'd hoped for was gone. We'd probably never have a house and we'd be stuck in a trailer forever. There was absolutely no way a game could buy anything, let alone a house. I felt scared and mad. I wanted to run in the Osbornes' house and call Amy, or at least get away from Mom and Dad before I burst into tears.

"Would you pass the lemonade and cookies that are on the table, Zoey?" asked Mrs. Osborne, appearing out of nowhere with this big smile on her face. "Isn't this an exciting day we're having? That was truly quite a surprise, and I can't believe your father kept it a secret so well. James and I are thrilled, and it's a wonderful day for our church. I think the congregation could do with some refreshment, don't you?"

I guess I'd heard everything Mrs. Osborne was saying, but honestly I felt like I was part of a play and everyone around me, they were all the actors playing these parts that were full of happy stuff that I sure didn't feel a part of. Mrs. Osborne fit into the play perfectly with her pretty dress covered in yellow roses and daisies. The little poodles were snuggled in her arms with tiny yellow bows in the fur over their eyes.

"I'm sure they're thirsty," I said. "I'll get the tray." I tried to smile, but it sure didn't feel real.

I guess it looked normal enough because Mrs. Osborne just said, "Thank you, dear."

My knees wobbled as I picked up the tray, so I stiffened my legs and forced them to move, going from one person to the next as they all swooned over Dad and his game. When the tray was almost empty Mrs. Osborne came up to me again and asked me to take a drink to the lady who was sitting on the dock by herself.

"Her name is Helen Sanders and I think she needs a lift that I know you could give her Zoey. And I'm sure she'd be grateful for a little refreshment as well. Would you mind?"

I was hardly into giving anyone a lift, but it was my chance to get away so I wouldn't have to listen to everyone swooning over Dad. I told Mrs. Osborne I'd be happy to do that. I gave her the tray and I took a cup and headed off.

I'd never actually met the lady, but she came to church a lot and I always noticed the pretty dresses she wore.

She seemed friendly when I handed her the cup.

"Oh my, that's very sweet of you." She took a long drink. "I was very thirsty. Thank you so much."

Being away from everyone sure helped lift my dumpy mood. Mrs. Sanders looked like an angel in her pretty pink dress. She had on pink high-heeled shoes with a purse to match. She even wore a straw hat and lacy white gloves. I hadn't seen her that dressed up before.

She finished the lemonade and put the cup on the dock beside her chair. "I didn't know we'd be playing games today, or I might have been more sporty with my attire."

"I didn't know either."

"I beg your pardon? You didn't know?"

"Nope. It was a big surprise for everyone."

She scrunched her eyebrows together. "You don't seem very happy about it, Zoey."

"I hate surprises. Especially ones like that."

She reached over and slid the other chair closer to hers. "My name is Helen Sanders, and I know you're Zoey from Dr. Osborne's introduction when you first arrived. I'm sorry that you didn't like the surprise, but I would love to have you join me and tell me about this journey you're on in that Airstream. Your father's a very adventuresome man. It's truly an accomplishment to invent the first playground game after so many years. Quite amazing, I'd say." She put her empty glass on the dock beside her.

Mrs. Sanders sure didn't look like she needed a lift, and I sure didn't want to hear anything else about how smart my father was. But suddenly this huge wave of guilt swept over me. I mean there he was up on the lawn making everyone happy with his big invention, and here I was being this spoiled kid, thinking awful thoughts about the whole thing. I wanted to jump in the water by the dock and sink to the bottom.

"I know you don't like surprises," said Mrs. Sanders. "But I guess I don't understand what you hated about this surprise when it was so exciting, Zoey. Can you help me with that?"

"It's just that Dad's been keeping it a secret from us, saying he was going to do something new that'd never been done before, and I wanted the something to be big enough to buy us a house. I don't think a game will do that and I guess I hate the surprise because I feel cheated."

There. Now the truth was out and for sure that honesty came from my other self because I didn't have the nerve to say I felt cheated. I wished there was some way to trade places with my two selves, take the wimpy one inside and bring the bold one out.

Mrs. Sanders asked, "Did you hear what Dr. Osborne said about hate in his sermon this morning, the part about how the opposite of love is not hate, but fear? Do you remember that?"

I didn't want to admit I hadn't listened, but I pretty well had to. So I told her that I was too busy to listen because I was thinking about Dr. Osborne's promise for after the service. I said I was sure it was going to be about Dad.

"And you were right, weren't you. The surprise was about your dad, but it's too bad you didn't hear the sermon. It addressed exactly what you're talking about when you say you hated the surprise."

"Was it really? Can you tell me what he said?"

"Well I'm no preacher, but I can try to repeat his words, not as a sermon, but in how the message applies to my own life. Would you like that?"

"Sure, if you think it would help me feel better about the whole thing."

"I do. So let me try." She clasped her hands in her lap. "For some time I have had a great deal of hate in my heart for my alcoholic husband, who I used to love dearly, before the drinking changed him." She put her finger over her upper lip, the way I'd seen people do when they were telling a secret. She sort of half closed her eyes, no tears or anything, but like she was thinking hard about how to say what she wanted me to hear.

She put her gloved hand back in her other one and turned to me. "But after hearing Dr. Osborne talk about how the opposite of love is not hate, but fear, I realized that it is not hate I feel for my husband, but fear of the disease that's destroying him."

She looked at her clasped hands for a couple of seconds before she said, "And I was just sitting here contemplating the freedom in that awareness when you came along. Understanding fear of the disease, that is much easier to handle than hating the man I have loved for fifteen years."

I couldn't help wondering what that had to do with Dad, but I didn't say anything. I could tell she was still thinking, like picking the right words.

"And now, Zoey, if I can be so bold I'd like to take the application one step further and suggest that perhaps the hate you're feeling for the surprise of your dad's new game is not hate at all, but rather fear that you're not going to have the house you want." She sighed and the thinking look turned into a smile. "Do you think that's a possibility?"

Right then Dad called me. I sure wasn't ready to go, but I waved to let him know I'd heard him. "That sounds really selfish Mrs. Sanders, doesn't it? I mean the game is good and Dad is so happy. Am I terrible?"

"Of course you're not terrible. You're just a normal girl who wants a regular house and there's nothing selfish about it. Besides, my guess is that a regular house for your family is right at the top of your father's list of priorities. And Toppleball, well it's just the beginning for all of you."

"Do you really think so?"

"I certainly do. But unfortunately I won't be here for your dad's progress. One of the reasons I'm so dressed up today is that after church I'm leaving to head north with my husband to visit his aging parents for a few months, and although I haven't been looking forward to that, now, with this new awareness, maybe I am. I think we can use the time to discuss what I've learned."

"Boy, that's great. I sure wish I'd listened to the sermon, but you sure did a good job of talking about how it works."

Mrs. Sanders reached for my hand that I let her have. "I can see the confusion in your eyes, Zoey. What I've told you might not feel like a gift right now, but believe me, if you can transfer the feeling of hate into the understanding of fear, that's enough for now."

"I'll sure try Mrs. Sanders, and thank you. I guess I have to go, but I love your lacy gloves. I've never seen that kind before."

She let go of my hand and held her hands up sort of proudly. "They're new. I feel that gloves go with dressing up, and it's nice to dress up when I'm in God's presence. I think He likes it, and I think the lacy ones will work perfectly for hot weather."

I wanted to tell her about *Life is Love* because that's what she felt like. But I didn't have time. She stood up and insisted on a hug goodbye before I ran back to Dad who was calling me again.

The little poodles spotted me and wriggled out of Mrs. Osborne's arms. They came flying across the lawn like I'd been a magnet for them. I scooped them up and crushed them against my chest with kisses that messed up their little yellow bows.

When I got to Dad, it wasn't the game he wanted me for, it was a favor. He pointed across the lawn. "That girl over there under the tree, her name is Becky and she's deaf. I thought maybe you could mouth the instructions to her and then she could play the game with everybody. Dr. Osborne says she's good at lip reading."

My first thought was, What about Cindy? Why wasn't she teaching her sister? Then I realized Cindy wasn't there. "Okay, I guess I can." But before I did that I made sure to tell Dad his game was great. "It's really fun and everyone loves it, don't they."

"They do seem to, don't they sweetheart. I'm excited." He ruffled the poodles' curls. "I don't know how excited these guys are though. All the commotion has them pretty freaked."

I got up onto my tippy-toes, teetering with the doggies in my arms in an attempt to kiss Dad on the cheek, but he was too tall, so me and the poodles just banged into him and he caught us. "Sorry, Dad. It was supposed to be a cheek kiss, but you're too tall." I laughed.

He did too. He leaned over and kissed the very confused poodles before he gave me his cheek. "I can always do with a kiss from you, sweetheart." He stood up. "Now scoot." He blushed, which I'd never seen him do before. I darted off.

The poodles and I plopped down beside Becky. I let go of the dogs and they sniffed her all over. She giggled.

"I think they like you," I mouthed. "Their names are Jolie and Jacques."

"They're cute," she mouthed as she petted them.

I gathered the doggies together and nestled them in my lap. I mouthed, "Do you want to learn how to play the game?"

It didn't take Becky more than a second to shake her head and mouth, "I just want to watch." She smiled with a bigger smile than she'd given me on the beach. I felt a whole lot more welcome with her than I had with her sister. Part of me wanted to ask where her sister was, but the bigger part didn't care.

"I just want to watch too," I mouthed. Actually it was fun watching everyone running around tripping over each other and laughing like crazy. I knew there'd be lots of time for playing later.

We watched for a while, but then we began to mouth simple sentences back and forth about the church and the Osbornes and living there. Lip reading was fun, and although I would've liked to have told Becky about my assignment, I knew it'd be far too many words to make with my lips. I had a feeling she was going to be my friend anyway, so there'd be lots of neat stuff we could do that wouldn't have to include my assignment.

I mouthed, "Do you have a lot of friends?"

"Some," she mouthed.

I mouthed, "I'd like to be your friend."

"Me too." She had a big smile when she mouthed that.

Everything that happened that day was so much fun I felt my head swelling. Always when my head got that full I had to write Amy to let everything out. So I got out the notepaper and started by telling her about Mrs. Sander's description of Dr. Osborne's sermon, about how the opposite of love wasn't hate, but fear. While I was writing that, it was weird how suddenly I got that maybe I didn't hate my brother, that maybe I was just scared of him, and then I sort of got it how it wasn't him I was scared of, but the way he acted, just like Mrs. Sanders had described. I could even see how he acted that way because he was scared about not being able to play football.

When I'd finished describing all those thoughts to Amy, whose head for sure would be spinning, everything began to make a lot of sense about how fear was making me think I hated both the game and Josh. I sure wished Amy was there to talk about all that stuff because I knew she'd have a lot to say.

I didn't go into any of the feeling cheated stuff, but instead I made sure to tell her about how much fun the game was to play, and how I met Becky and how we'd been lip-reading while the game was going on. I wasn't sure I'd even told Amy about Becky and Cindy, so in case I hadn't, I did a rerun of how we'd met on the beach. I said that even though Becky was deaf, she'd probably get to be the friend I needed. With a bunch of extra hugs and kisses I made sure Amy knew *she* was still my best friend. I signed the letter and sealed the envelope, wondering when I'd get to see Becky again.

Well that happened the following Sunday. We sat next to each other in church, and after that in the garden, where we actually played the game this time. I wanted to see her out of church too, so after the game playing was over I asked her for her phone number. She laughed because she couldn't talk on the phone and of course I blushed. But she did mouth words to ask me to ride my bike over to her house after school the next day, and that's exactly what I did.

We lived close enough that it wasn't long before we were riding our bikes back and forth all the time. She began teaching me sign language, and I helped her to get better at reading lips. She even told me she thought the trailer was fun to hang out in. We played checkers and scrabble and cards and chess, and we even went to the beach with Cindy and Ty. They started hanging out together a lot, and after getting to know Cindy myself, she wasn't a snob at all.

It sure felt good to have a real friend. But what didn't feel good was the birthday was coming up and I didn't have my assignment figured out.

The boys, Mom, Dad and the poodles were all at the beach, so I pulled the bag of notes out from under my mattress to go through them one more time. Like always they were a jumbled mess, but what stood out was Emily's white card. I remembered her diving promise in the park that day, so I jumped off the bed with the card in my hand. Maybe I'd already decided diving with her alone wasn't what my assignment was all about, but maybe I could get her to take all of us out, the bunch of us for a family birthday gift.

Dad had never gotten around to planning the diving trip he promised, but at least I knew he wanted to go diving, so the idea was perfect. What was even better was I wouldn't have to worry about giving him the peace and quiet he didn't seem to need anymore. A day diving with Emily would be a great birthday present from all of us.

I zipped over to the cabin. Emily had said her phone number was free anywhere, so I knew it wouldn't cost money to call her.

I dialed the number and the woman who answered said that Emily was in the Bahamas for a month. "Shoot!" I said out loud.

"You okay?" Mrs. Osborne was standing in the doorway.

"Not really. Mom's at the beach. Did you want something?"

"I just made a pitcher of lemonade and I thought someone over here might like some. How about you?"

"Gee, thanks. The phone call didn't work so that'd be great." I hung up the receiver.

"The phone call didn't work? I'm sorry."

"That's okay. Lemonade would sure make it better though. I'd like that."

She reached for my hand. "Then let's get some. Holding her hand felt so perfect right then that I held it all the way across the lawn and into her screened porch at the back of the house.

Dr. Osborne was sitting with an open bible in his hands. "Well, hello there Zoey. What a nice surprise. Are you going to join us?"

"Your wife was probably looking for Mom, but she found me and I'd sure like to if that's okay."

"I'd say it's more than okay. I'd say you're a lot more than a substitute for your mother."

The porch was quite big, but the padded wicker chairs, matching table, and colored, braided carpet made it cozy. I sat in the chair next to Dr. Osborne and Mrs. Osborne sat across from us.

"It's hard to get my whole family together for anything, Dr. Osborne."

He put his bible and his glasses on the table beside him. "Well Zoey, we certainly managed to do that with the presentation of your daddy's new game, didn't we. We've been praying a long time for a recreation director, and now that we have one we feel truly blessed. Your father is indeed a very inventive man."

"I know he is, and it's going to be his birthday in a couple of weeks."

"Wonderful. We'll celebrate at church. Will it hopefully be on a Sunday?"

"No, it's on a Wednesday, but that's good because he'd be embarrassed if you did that."

"No he wouldn't. I imagine he'd love the fuss."

Suddenly I remembered I'd left my jumbled pile of notes on my bed and I didn't want anyone coming back from the beach and nosing through them. "Can we talk about that in a minute? I forgot something."

"Of course," Mrs. Osborne said. "We'll see if we can't think of something else for your daddy. We wouldn't want to embarrass him."

I ran to the trailer and stuffed the notes in the bag and put it under my mattress.

When I got back and was hardly sitting down, Dr. Osborne said, "If you don't think a fuss at church is a good idea, we wondered if the family might have another plan that we could participate in?"

"I don't know about everyone else, seeing as nobody's said anything. I sort of have a plan of my own, but I'm not sure it's going to work anymore."

"Well, would you like to tell us about it? One of our jobs here is to help people make their plans work."

"If I tell you, will you promise not to laugh? It's probably not the kind of plan church people usually want help with."

"I doubt that we'll laugh, unless it's funny. Then it'd be good to laugh, wouldn't it Hazel?"

"Indeed it would." Mrs. Osborne smiled with a big, perfect church lady smile as she lifted her glass and sipped the lemonade.

I pretty much gulped mine before I said, "I want to give Dad peace and quiet for his birthday."

Dr. Osborne scrunched his bushy eyebrows together, and Mrs. Osborne smiled, but no big smile this time, just one that didn't say what she was thinking. For sure neither of them laughed.

My cheeks got hot. I finished my lemonade, and Mrs. Osborne refilled my glass as well as the empty one Dr. Osborne had put on the table.

He sat back in his chair and crossed his arms over his chest. "My, oh my, Zoey. That is definitely some plan, and certainly not one to laugh at. However, I guess I can't imagine what your father would do with peace and quiet. He's a wild man. I've never seen anyone as excited about anything as he is about Toppleball."

Maybe I'd expected Dr. Osborne to laugh, but I sure didn't expect another assignment put-down. My eyes flooded.

Mrs. Osborne handed me some Kleenex from the box on the table. "Here now Zoey. Don't you listen to what James says about your father. You have a beautiful plan, and I think a little peace and quiet for anyone would be lovely."

I wiped my eyes. "Do you think so?" I looked at the minister. "Is she right Dr. Osborne?"

"I'm sorry. I'm afraid my words didn't come out quite the way I'd like them to have. What I meant to say is I can't imagine making peace and quiet a gift. I'd be very interested to hear how you came up with such an idea."

"It was just that while we were traveling around, Dad kept hollering all he wanted was peace and quiet. I hated watching him be so frustrated with all the commotion, so I decided I was going to find a way to give it to him. I figured the quiet part was easy since he got lots of that in the libraries doing research. I've talked to lots of people about peace and made a lot of notes, but I haven't learned how to turn the notes into a gift. And now, like you said, Dad doesn't need it anymore anyway." My heart kinda sunk into my stomach when I heard myself say that, but at least I wasn't crying.

Dr. Osborne rested his hands in his lap and linked his fingers together. "I wouldn't give up on your thoughtful plan quite yet, Zoey. Can we explore it a little further?"

"Sure. I'd like not to give it up. I mean it seemed like a neat idea when I thought of it."

"Well you definitely have my curiosity peeked, because to be perfectly honest I don't have peace figured out yet either." He grinned when he said that, the grin that I'd seen in church when he talked about not being sure about what he'd said. I liked the way it made him a real person to not know everything. Mrs. Osborne didn't add anything, but she sure looked like she was paying attention.

Dr. Osborne's grin turned into a wide smile. "However, I would very much like to share something with you, my child, and that is, I do find enormous peace when I visit God."

Of course I thought of Angie, but there way no way I could picture Dr. Osborne leaving his body. I said, "I guess I don't understand what visiting God means."

"Visiting God only means that I pray to be given peace when there's turmoil in my life. As a minister, I have many parishioners who long for peace in the midst of great turmoil. When I don't have resolutions for their problems, I ask these precious people to pray with me. Together we offer our hearts to God, and in the silence, a space opens for God's peace to enter, 'a peace that passeth all understanding'. Now those are not my words, my child. They're from The Good Book." He reached over and patted his bible.

"Wow! You sure make God sound like more than just an old man up in heaven with a white beard and flashing blue eyes. That's what I learned about him in Sunday School."

Dr. Osborne laughed. "I know, and for a lot of people God has a cheery face with a long white beard. I guess if a picture is necessary, a cheery face is a nice one. However, for me God doesn't have a face. God is a divine presence. Jesus came to earth as a glorification of that presence, and he did indeed have a face. Many of the people in my congregation have a personal relationship with Jesus, and that's what they like to talk about when they witness during some of my services."

Mrs. Osborne squeezed her husband's hand. "What you say is lovely, James. However, I think you're getting away from Zoey's search for her daddy's gift. Sam is definitely not a church-going man."

"Is it rude that he doesn't go to church, Dr. Osborne, especially when you're so nice to let him use your workshop all the time?"

Dr. Osborne laughed. "Of course not. Your father's contribution to our church is a lot bigger than sitting on a chair in my living room. I don't know how he feels about God, but I do know that God loves him, and has definitely endowed him with many gifts."

"Does God do that, endow gifts? Back in Baltimore, at my church we were told if we wanted something, we should pray to God in heaven. But I've never done that. It seems weird to talk to a place in the sky."

"Well, in our church you don't have to talk to the sky. You can talk to God right here, or over at your trailer, or down at the beach, or wherever you like. He's always with you, in or out of our church."

Dr. Osborne leaned toward me and whispered, "Don't tell your dad, but He's in the workshop as well."

Right then I wanted to talk to him about his sermon on love and hate, but honestly I was totally drained and overflowing all at the same time. "I think I'd better go and write down everything you've said, Dr. Osborne. I don't want to forget any of it."

"My suggestion is that you talk to God about your plan. It's too lovely an idea to let slip away."

"How do I know he can hear me?"

"I can't answer that for you, Zoey. God works in mysterious ways, and for each of us it's different. My heart is attuned to God's desires, so if decisions I make feel right in my heart, then I know that God's guiding me."

"You make it sound so easy. Does that work for you too, Mrs. Osborne?"

"It does, dear. But you must remember that we've been talking to God for many years. I wish somebody had shared His presence with me when I was your age. It brings great joy and satisfaction to our lives."

"Well thanks for sharing it with me now. I'll try talking to God and see what happens." I drained my glass and put it on the table before I got up to go. "And thanks for the lemonade too. I'm sure glad I got you guys all to myself."

"Our pleasure," said Mrs. Osborne. "Remember that we're always here for you Zoey."

"My exact thoughts," said Dr. Osborne. He smiled at me, reached over and picked up his bible, perching his glasses back on his nose.

The Birthday's Here

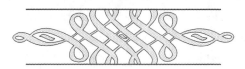

When I got back to the trailer I closed the door to my bedroom and pulled out a sheet of notepaper. I just had to describe being at the Osbornes' house, and tell Amy everything they said, especially the part about talking to God, because I knew Amy had the same idea about God as I'd always had. Everything came out so easily that when I read it back to myself I actually felt like maybe God had helped me write it. I tucked the letter under my pillow and planned to read it over lots before I sent it to Amy.

I decided that if God had helped me write the letter, maybe God could help me figure out what to do about my assignment without having to get the bag of notes out again. I bowed my head and closed my eyes, and even put my palms together against my chest like Dr. Osborne had.

I didn't say anything, but in the next few seconds a picture of Dad and me on the beach in the early morning, with the sun coming up shone so bright inside my head that my eyes sprung open. The glow was so real that I knew God was telling me that going to the beach was what I had to do. I'd trust that when we got there, the important stuff I'd learned from doing my assignment would come out on its own. I sure liked *feeling* God for the first time ever.

"Zoey, are you in there?"

That was Josh. "Yeah, why?"

"Ty and I got a gift for Dad's birthday. Want to come in on it with us?" That was a surprise. Maybe there was more going on with the birthday than I knew about.

I opened the door. "Maybe." I said that, because a normal gift might be a good idea. "What is it? I don't have any money though."

"Money doesn't matter." Josh had this big grin that sure was unusual for him. "I won the betting pool for catching the most waves last week and I'm loaded. Besides lately you've been really nice for some reason, so how about I pay your part. Ty did some weeding for Dr. Osborne so he' got his own cash. We thought our idea would be a great gift from all of us, that is if you haven't already got one."

"Mom too?"

"No. It's just us. I don't know what Mom's doing. Are you in?"

Ty was up front in the trailer with a bag that had wrapping paper sticking out the top. He had a grin on his face that said he was holding a prize. He reached into the bag and pulled out something red.

"Ta Da!" he said, dropping the bag and holding the present by the waistband.

I couldn't believe what I was seeing. It was a bathing suit, not with dolphins on it, but whales, and not blue like Cindy had described, but red. "Where did you get it anyway?"

"It was Cindy's idea. I've seen her father in his and it looks great, so I know Dad'll love this one. And let's face it, we all know he needs a new bathing suit. I chose red for the fire in his belly these days."

The trip to the beach seemed to be my final idea, so maybe a new bathing suit to replace the old yellow one would be a great addition to whatever God came up with on the beach.

"C'mon, Zo," said Josh. "Dad needs a new bathing suit to go with his new mood. He's a real blast these days."

"Yeah, a real blast! Okay, I'll do it And thanks for paying. I couldn't do it otherwise."

"Well like I said, you've been so nice lately. Why is that anyway? What's the big deal?"

"No big deal. I just like you Josh. Is that okay?"

"Better than okay. Thanks." He almost looked embarrassed, if that was possible for Josh.

Ty shoved the suit back in the bag and tossed it to me. "All you have to do is wrap it, Sis."

"Does Mom have something planned for Dad? It's weird the way nobody's talked about the birthday, don't y'think?"

"Who knows," said Josh. "Dad doesn't need anything anyway. His best present was all the fuss everyone made over his game. The bathing suit's just a bonus."

A few days before the birthday Ty asked Mom if she wanted him to make a cake for Dad. I knew Ty was getting to be a great cook but I wasn't too sure about him as a baker.

"Go for it Ty," said Josh. "Four layers of chocolate."

"That'd be lovely," said Mom, "and I'll take Dad to the beach after breakfast and you can make the cake while we're gone. I've already got the mix and icing, so if you make it, we'll have the Osbornes over for cake and ice cream. I've wrapped the World Future's book I got for him, and I'll say it's from all of us if you want. Or maybe you can make the cake your present. And how about you give him another surfing lesson, Josh?"

My stomach curdled over Mom's beach idea, but I pretended a laugh over Dad surfing. The one lesson he'd had was all it took to let us all know that Dad was no surfer.

"Don't worry, Mom," said Ty. "We've got the gift thing handled. Cindy's mom bought us a bathing suit. She's the big shopper, so we told her what we wanted and she got it for us. Josh paid for Zoey with his surfing-betting money, and I used the garden-weeding money I got from Dr. Osborne. So we're all set. I'll show it to you. You'll love it." He ran over to the trailer and came back with the bag and a huge grin.

Mom took it out of the bag and held it up. "Exactly what your dad needs, a bathing suit with real splash. I've got some wrapping paper if you need it."

I told her we had some, and asked her if we should call and remind Aunt Alyssa because she always had a party for Dad.

"She'll remember, and I'm sure she'll call Dad herself. Maybe by next year we'll have our own house, and then Alyssa and Amy can come stay with us, and we'll have a real party."

"Do you think so? I mean, will a game let us have our own house?" Boy, was that a surprise from my other self. I hadn't said a word out loud about that to anyone but Mrs. Sanders, and I could hardly wait for Mom's answer.

"Maybe not one game, Zoey, but your father has plans that go way beyond just one game. How long it'll take to have our own house, I'm no fortune teller so I can't say, but it'll happen, I'm sure."

"This is cool right here," said Josh. "We're on the ocean. You can't beat that."

Josh saying that flipped my mind over to the beach and my peace gift. "Can we give Dad his bathing suit the night before the birthday?"

Josh freaked. "What're you talking about? Why would you want to do that for Pete's sake? The birthday's on the birthday, not the day before."

For sure that was one time when I quickly practiced Grammy's prayer about knowing what you could and couldn't change. "Forget it," I said, even though I sure didn't mean it.

"Good idea," said Josh. "I've forgotten already."

Well, as if that wasn't a bad enough start to my birthday idea, the worst part came the night before the birthday when I asked Dad if he'd like to go and watch the sunrise with me for part of his birthday present in the morning. I didn't know whether Mom had said anything about taking him, but if she had, this was a great way to find out.

"Why in the world would I want to get up at dawn, Zo? Me and your mom sleeping in and then having breakfast in bed, that's my idea of a birthday morning."

There were lots of times on the trip when my whole body froze, but this time I felt like a total block of ice. I couldn't think of a single thing to say, and for sure Grammy's prayer wouldn't help because I absolutely HAD TO change Dad's mind.

Dad was sitting on the sofa having a cup of coffee. He picked up his newspaper. "Is it okay for me to read now?" His puzzled look dug big grooves between his eyes.

Mom didn't look puzzled at all. "I think going to the beach for sunrise would be a great idea, Sammy. Maybe we could all go." I was at the table with Mom who was having an extra piece of pie.

With those words, suddenly the block of ice melted and out of me burst the biggest flood of tears I'd ever felt, or even knew I could make.

Mom dropped her pie fork. Dad tossed his newspaper on the sofa and rushed over. He sat on the edge of the chair next to me and pulled me into a hug. "What's going on Zo? Is this about the sunrise? What's wrong?"

I managed to babble that I really wanted him to come to the beach alone with me, and then babbled for him not to ask why.

He hugged me. "Of course I'll come. If you promise not to cry anymore, of course I'll come."

"Can't we all go Zo?" asked Mom. "That'd be fun."

All I could do was shake my head and out came more tears.

Mom handed me her paper napkin. "Why, honey? I don't understand why you're crying."

I jumped up and tried to get out of there, but Dad grabbed my arm. "What's happening sweetheart? Talk to us."

"It's just something I need to do with you, Dad," I garbled through the tears. I stuck the napkin in my eyes.

"Well, whatever it is, we'll make it work, won't we Meg." He moved onto the chair next to Mom and squeezed her hand. "How about you stay in bed and I'll come back after sunrise and join you. Then after a while, you can make me breakfast and we'll have our regular breakfast in bed. How's that, babe?"

I couldn't see Dad's face, but when he said "after awhile" I was sure he winked, because Mom's confused expression turned into a smile. He said, "That way I'll get what *I* want and I guess Zoey will get what *she* wants, which seems to be me to herself, for whatever reason." He looked back at me. "Right, sweetheart?"

I felt all the tears drying up, so I crumpled the soggy napkin and squeezed it in my hand. "Thanks Dad," I said. "That is what I want. Do you mind Mom?"

"I guess I don't have any choice, do I?" She sort of half laughed.

We all got quiet for a few seconds, and then Mom's half-laugh turned into a really nice smile. "I don't know what this is about, Zo, but it sounds very sweet, so of course I don't mind. Now give me the tear-soaked napkin and I'll toss it in the trash."

I handed her the napkin, but then I had to get out of there.

Without saying anything I got up and ran back to the trailer and practically ripped a piece of notepaper out of Amy's box. I cried like crazy the whole time I wrote about how much I missed her, and how scared I was about the next day.

Just like all the other times I'd written, I felt so much better that I didn't need to cry anymore. All I had to do was go to sleep so the morning would come soon. I ran back to the cabin and hugged Mom and Dad goodnight so they'd see I was okay. "I'm going to bed now, and you'd better too Dad. Sunrise comes early."

They both hugged me and that was a good feeling to take to bed with me.

The next morning when the sky started to get light, I got up and put on my bathing suit. I yanked a brush through my tangled hair and stuck an elastic around it in a ponytail before I grabbed a towel and ran over to the cabin. I knocked on the bedroom door and opened it a sliver. "Happy birthday," I whispered. I closed the door and in minutes Dad showed up in his bathing suit. Even though it was still the old one I was too excited to care. He grabbed a towel from the bathroom and took my hand. "C'mon sweetheart, let's go."

When we got to the beach the peeking sun was sending huge yellow rays into the sky. I took Dad's hand and led him down the beach, close to the water where the sand was dry enough to sit. We sat on our towels that were touching at the edges.

At that moment it was sooooo beautiful the way the yellow began to turn orange as the sun inched its way out of the ocean. It began flooding the sky a reddy-gold as we sat there watching, with only the sound of waves lapping in perfect rhythm the way Mike had described. I didn't know even close to enough words to describe how I felt sitting there with my dad in all that glow. All I could hope was that God or my other self would show up and sort out everything I was supposed to say.

"Do you want me to do something?" Dad asked. "Is there a plan? You're being awfully quiet."

"Uh…not yet."

I wasn't getting any messages, so all I could think to do was cross my legs and pull my feet up over my thighs and hope that maybe a yoga pose would turn up with some help. I could sit like that easily since I'd been practicing doing it a whole lot. So I asked Dad to try doing it too. He yanked and pulled and laughed all at the same time. Laughing sure wasn't part of my plan, so I just told him to sit with his legs crossed and asked him if he'd like to meditate, even though I wasn't sure how to do that myself.

"Meditate. You want me to meditate? That's what hippies do. I'm no hippie."

Angie's advice to Josh about deep breaths to keep from losing it sure came in handy right then. I took a bunch of them before I said as calmly as I could "You don't have to be a hippie, you only have to close your eyes and be quiet."

"But if we close our eyes, we'll miss the gorgeous sunrise. Isn't that the point of being here?"

Maybe the sun was rising up, but my heart was sinking right down into the worst pit it had ever been in. I had no idea what to do next. I tried to remember other stuff from my notes, and the only thing that came to my mind was that we were there because God had told me taking Dad to the beach was what I should do. So I figured maybe I was supposed to talk about some of Mike's stuff.

"There's more to the point than just watching the sunrise, Dad. I met a guy on the beach the other day and he was meditating. He wasn't a hippie or anything. He told me that when he was meditating with his eyes closed, he felt the energy of the ocean inside, like the rhythm of the waves, and he actually became the rhythm. He talked about joining with the forces of nature to feel something bigger than himself." I closed my eyes and thanked God for making all those words come out just the way Mike had said them.

"I don't get it Zo," said Dad. "That's pretty far out talk from my little girl so early in the morning. Isn't looking at the beautiful sunrise enough? I have to say I feel very blessed sitting here with you right now."

"I feel blessed too, I honestly do Dad. But what I want is more than us feeling blessed, or watching the sunrise. I had a plan…but I guess it, well, I don't know. Will Toppleball make enough money for us?"

Well for sure that was exactly what I should've expected from my outspoken other self, and I could've smacked her. Absolutely the last thing I wanted to do was talk about business. I felt like I'd gotten myself caught in one of those wringers on an old-fashioned washing machine, squashed so tight I could barely breathe.

Dad glowed like an over-lit Christmas tree. "Of course it will. Like Dr. Osborne said, Toppleball is the first new playground game in the country in over fifty years, and that's a big deal. It'll be huge. We'll sell it to every school and recreation department in the country. And that's only the beginning. I've already got another game on the drawing board, maybe even better than Toppleball."

All Dad's joy leapt from him over to me and I felt myself spring right through the ringer. "Honestly? The whole country? Wow!"

Dad reached his arm around me and slid close. "Maybe the world, sweetheart, because with some time and a lot of effort, before you know it I'll be just as successful as I was before, only this time it will be for us rather than some corporation out there."

I didn't get to say anything, because real fast he shifted around and faced me head on. "But, what's all this really about anyway? I'm confused as to why you wanted me all to yourself, with no Mom, no brothers, only me."

"I don't know. The angels told me to do it." I wanted to say God had told me, but I figured Dad at least knew I liked angels. For sure I had no idea what it was all about, or where the birthday gift was going.

"Well good for the angels. It's wonderful." Dad gave my cheek another kiss and popped to his feet. "Now the sun's shining on us, it's done its thing, so how about a swim?"

Part of me wanted to go with him, but another part didn't think I was finished. Which part was who, and which one was right or wrong had me so baffled I didn't do anything. I just sat there. After all, I'd hardly talked about a single thing I was supposedly there to talk about, so in case something else showed up, I thought I'd better wait. I told him to go ahead. "I don't want to swim quite yet. "D'you mind?"

"I don't mind, but am I doing what you want me to do?"

"Yeah. You're perfect. I'd like to sit here and watch you swim. It's your birthday."

"Okay. If that's what you want." Dad ran in the water and dove through the surf.

I watched as he played in the waves. He threw his arms around beckoning for me to come and play with him. "C'mon in. It's great," he called.

"GO FOR IT BABYCAKES" Angie's voice echoed in my ears, and an overwhelming sense of joy yanked me right off the sand, lifted me up and propelled me into the water. I looked up at the sky to see if there was a rainbow with Angie sitting on it, but in all that blue sky of course there wasn't.

But I sure felt her as I watched my happy Dad having a joyride, maybe not the peace and quiet kind, but the kind I knew Angie wanted for him. It was like I was the one getting the gift, not the other way around. We dove in and out of the surf laughing our heads off. Finally we'd worn ourselves out and only had enough energy left to paddle back to shore.

Maybe nothing had happened like I'd expected. But something was sure going right. All the happy I felt from both of us as we headed home had my feet barely touching the ground. I clasped the hand Dad had over my shoulder, and stretched my other arm around him as we headed back to the cabin.

We opened the door and a blare of voices came at us with, "SURPRISE!" And there, right in front of us was not only Mom and my brothers, but my best friend in the whole world and Aunt Alyssa.

Amy came flying across the room and hugged me so tight I lost my balance. Dad and his sister were doing the same, with the whole place bubbling over like crazy. The table was covered in plates full of pancakes and sausages, as well as wrapped presents.

Mom told us that she'd planned for Aunt Alyssa and Amy to fly in from Baltimore and stay at a hotel by the airport. So when Dad and I took off for the beach, she called the hotel and let Aunt Alyssa know she'd be over to pick them up. Ty stayed home and put together the big breakfast of pancakes and sausages, and Josh even made coffee and toast. For the first time ever, I was sure glad Mom was so good at keeping secrets because this one was perfect.

Dad and I put on some dry clothes, and we all got into the breakfast feast that was totally delicious. After lots of praise for Ty's cooking, with every scrap gone, Aunt Alyssa piled the plates and took them to the kitchen so Dad could get into his presents.

Mom put the little pile in front of him and he opened her World Future's book first. It was a big hit. For sure that made Mom happy.

Next he took the card off our present and read the mushy words I'd written inside. He blew kisses to me and my brothers, and then he unwrapped the bathing suit and held it up with a big grin on his face.

"Good choice. Thanks, kids," he said as he got up and pranced around the room like the model he wasn't. We all had a good laugh at that.

He sat down again and Aunt Alyssa handed him the present that she said was from both herself and Amy. Amy grinned wide. The present was wrapped in silver paper with a huge purple ribbon and bow.

"Quite a presentation," said Dad. He grinned back at Amy as he undid the ribbon and removed the paper. A white box appeared. Dad lifted the lid to see what looked to me like one of those handmade diaries I'd seen in stores. The cloth cover was light purple and the words were sewn on the cloth in dark purple. Dad sat next to me, so I leaned over to see what the words said, and right away my face burned hot as I read *Peace & Quiet For Dad*.

Aunt Alyssa reached across the table and covered my hand. "Are you okay Zo? Amy shared your letters with me and I felt compelled to have them pressed flat and bound. I hope that's okay."

Dad put his arm around me as he turned the pages. "You wrote what's in here sweetheart? It looks beautiful. I don't know what it's about but I like how it looks." He reached over and squeezed his sister's hand. "You did some job with this Alyssa. It's beautiful. Thanks."

I whacked Amy who was on the other side of me. "Those were private Amy. You knew that."

"Hey, c'mon Zo, don't be mad at me. I thought it was a good thing. I knew you were having a hard time and I wanted to help, but I didn't know how, so I called your aunt and told her what you were doing and she jumped right in with the idea. We both thought you'd love it."

"Good going, you guys." said Josh. "Does that mean no more yelling, Dad? Hey, that beats the bathing suit." He stuck his arm out to grab the gift. "Can I read what's in there?"

Dad held onto it. "Not before me Josh."

I grabbed the gift and ran from the cabin across the driveway and into the trailer. I slammed the bedroom door and threw myself and the letters on the bed.

A minute later I heard a knock on my door. "Zo, please let me in." It was Amy.

I rolled off the bed and opened the door. I burst into tears. "This isn't what I wanted, Amy," I wailed, picking up the gift. "These are *our* letters!"

Amy reached her arms around me. "I'm sorry it's not what you wanted, but I know it's what your dad would want." She took the letters from me. "He'd want to know about everything in here. His own sister said he'd understand what you were trying to do if he read the letters, and that's why she had them bound. She even copied all of them so I'd have them myself forever. The idea seemed perfect to me, especially since you never told me anything great you'd come up with."

"But what about all the complaining I did about Dad, all the things I don't think he'd want to read?"

"Your aunt thought those things would be good for him to read. She said it'd be good for him to have a look at how he is sometimes. But mostly the letters are about the people and what they told you."

"You don't think Dad'll be mad at some of that stuff about him?"

"It doesn't matter. When he reads what everyone said about peace, there's no way he could be mad." Amy took my arm. "C'mon, don't ruin your dad's birthday. There's no peace for anyone if you're upset. If he reads it out loud and you don't like listening, you can choose to leave your body, float up there with the angels. After all, life is love, isn't it, and Zoey is too, remember?"

"I guess I forgot to remember, and I suppose that was mean, running out like I did."

"I think so, but we're not going back until you sit down and tell me what you ended up doing about the assignment."

We both sat on the end of the bed while I told her the whole story of the beautiful sunrise and all the stuff about how I couldn't get Dad to do what I'd learned from Mike, or from anyone else for that matter. "It was crazy. We ended up talking about Dad's plans for Toppleball, and the other new games he's going to invent and sell all over the world."

"You're kidding. What about all the stuff you learned about peace? You didn't tell him any of that?"

"It just wasn't coming out of me like I hoped it would. And you're going to laugh like crazy when I tell you it was my other self that got us talking about business. Then Dad got so excited it was too late to be serious."

"That's a bummer, so now that makes your letters even more important, Zo, because everything he'll read will be from when it happened."

"I know now, but I sure didn't know that at the beach, and I felt bad that I didn't say anything I thought I was supposed to say. But, y'know what Amy?"

"Like what?"

"As it turned out the real birthday gift wasn't about me giving Dad peace and quiet, it was about you guys showing up. Did you see how happy he was?"

"Yeah I did, and at least he'll get to read all the stuff you learned about in the letters, so I'm glad about that. Maybe you ought to reread the letters yourself so what you learned stays new. Forgetting everything you thought you needed to say was weird, but what your Dad's doing, and going to do, that's awesome. You'll have to show us the game, tell us more." Amy got up and pulled me up with her. "But if me and your auntAlyssa coming is supposed to be the big deal birthday gift, we better get back or all the happy your Dad's feeling will be gone."

"Talking about happy, let me show you something before we go." I went to the night table and picked up the seashell. "Aunt Alyssa gave me this. It means 'luck and happiness around water'. I'd like to take it over and tell her thanks, because it brought me both those things a lot of times, and now, especially with you guys coming and everything."

"I knew your aunt was giving it to you. But I didn't want to talk about it then with you going away, and I don't want to talk about it now that you're not coming back. Do you have to take it over there?"

"I'm sorry. I'll just thank her when you're not around." I put the shell back on the table.

"What about the eagle's head? I'd love to see it, and I know everyone else would too. Where is it?"

It was still in my private drawer. "Yeah, I guess I can show it off now, can't I. Dad sure loved it." I got it and handed it to her.

She twirled it around just like I had. "Boy that Eli was really something. Let's take it with us. I know you're Dad saw it but it's too beautiful to hide"

"Good idea. Let's do it. You sure know how to be a best friend, Amy, and all the miles between us will never change that. Agreed?" I stuck out my hand and we locked little fingers.

"Agreed," she said. The tight tug turned into a tight hug for both of us.

I picked up the letters, and when we walked into the cabin, everyone clapped, which was pretty cute. There were lots of oohs and ahs over the eagle's head that Josh wanted to snag, but I wouldn't let him. I just told a shortened version of how I got the carving and how I wanted it for my own as a reminder of Eli. I figured everyone would get to read about the creative spirit if they read the letters and it looked to me like that for sure was going to happen. I mean they were out there in plain view for anyone and everyone. Somehow instead of being mad, I felt kind of proud.

I wanted to get into the chocolate cake in the middle of the table that the Osbornes had brought over. It had a bunch of colored candles on it and a circle of little red hearts with the big words , *We Love You Sam* right in the middle of the circle. Dad not only got back my letters, but a chorus of Happy Birthday that actually made his eyes dribble. He held the letters to his chest.

After having cake and ice cream, Dad said he wanted to go sit on the Osbornes' dock so he could read the letters in private. Nobody said anything about him taking off, although Josh tried to get a look again. I got Josh's attention real fast when I asked him to show everyone how good he was at surfing. Well that was all it took to get us into our bathing suits and off to the beach.

When we got home, Dad was still gone. While everyone was changing into their clothes, I flung a towel over my wet bathing suit and snuck off to peek around the corner of the Osbornes' house to see if Dad was on the dock. He was, and he was sitting on the same chair Mrs. Sanders had sat in. I couldn't see the expression on his face, but I watched as he read and then put the letters to his chest for a bit before he kept on reading. I wanted to be with him, but I was too embarrassed. I tried to remember the order of the letters, wondering where he might be, and who he might be reading about.

I felt a hand on my shoulder and I turned around. It was Mom. "Go to him, honey. I don't know what's in the letters but I think he'd like to have you there."

My heart literally flew around my chest. "I'm scared Mom. What if he doesn't like them?"

"It doesn't look that way to me. He looks pretty touched from where I stand."

"Do you think so?"

"I do. Now go on and get down there." She gave me a hug.

That's all it took. "Okay."

Dad had his back to me, so he didn't see me coming. I snuck up behind him and wrapped my arms around his neck. "Happy birthday Dad."

He spun around, leapt up and threw his arms around me. "Thank you, baby. Thank you so much." When he stood back, he didn't have just wet eyes, he had real tears coming out.

"Wow! I'm sorry if it makes you cry." I handed him my towel.

"It's a good cry, sweetheart." He wiped the tears away with the towel and then wrapped it around my neck. "I need to cry over being such a horse's ass. I'm sorry. I wasn't much fun, was I."

"Sure you were. Do you like reading what everyone said about peace? Pretty neat, huh?"

"The whole idea is what's neat. Wanting to give me something that special is a way beyond being neat. Honestly, well it's hard to put into words how touched I am." He sat back down.

I pulled over the other chair and sat next to him. I loved my dad so much right then. "I'm glad you like it Dad," I said.

"That Eli guy, I liked what he said about the creative spirit. I think I've been using it without even knowing I was. I'd say my game is pretty unique, wouldn't you?"

"I sure would. Have you read about Angie yet?"

"I have, and I certainly had her pegged all wrong. I liked her description of life being a ball game. Wouldn't she be surprised if she could see I've found a new ball game that comes with a regular bat and ball? That's wild, isn't it?"

"I've already written her about that, but I haven't heard back. If you'd gotten to know her you would've liked her a lot. I know you would."

"Well mostly I'm sorry about how much time I spent doing research. I neglected you guys and I'm very sorry for that."

"Don't be sorry. You got what you needed and that's what the trip was for, right?"

"That's what you'd say, sweetheart. You're great to have cared about your old dad, and I love you for that. How about I finish reading now and we can talk more when I'm finished."

"I think they're missing you. We probably should go back to the cabin, don't y'think?"

"There you go. I'm doing it again, aren't I, thinking only of myself. You're right. I've got lots of lessons to learn from you, Zo." He held the letters to his chest. "I'll take my time with the reading, probably several times over. There's a whole lot in here that's going to make me a better dad, maybe even a better person."

On the way back to the cabin I told Dad I thought we ought to play Toppleball. He liked the idea and so did everyone else. Our circle wasn't very big, but it was big enough to have a good time and get us all sweating enough that everyone put their bathing suits back on and headed to the beach.

We had so much fun there, throwing balls for the poodles and collecting shells. I got to tell Aunt Alyssa how much I loved hers while Amy was doing something else. I told her a little bit about how it had worked, and she liked that.

As soon as we got home we got dressed to go and have a drink with the Osbornes. But what we found when we got there was not just drinks, but a total fried chicken, potato salad and coleslaw feast that they'd put together on their back lawn. I'd wondered why they hadn't come swimming with us, but of course that was exactly what I should've expected. They were just so good at thinking about everyone over themselves.

The whole day was super fun, not just for Dad, but for everyone.

The only hard part of the whole thing was that Amy and Aunt Alyssa being there didn't last forever. Three days was all we got before they had to go home. While they were there, the Osbornes invited them to stay in their house. Aunt Alyssa was sure happy about that, but Amy and I didn't want any time away from each other, so she shared my big bed with me.

Dad surprised us one day by taking the bunch of us deep sea fishing. The whole thing was great, that is until Dad, Josh and then Ty all caught a fish, one right after the other. Watching them work at bringing their big fishes into the boat was fun, but not the rest of it, like banging them over the head, and then digging out their guts.

Well fortunately, Mom, Amy and me got to miss that because a school of dolphins showed up as the perfect distraction. We sat up on the front of the boat, away from the fishing part, and watched the dolphins do their thing, with Amy taking pictures like crazy. By the time the dolphins were finished leaping around and swooping up and down, and then chasing each other, the nasty part of the fish-catching was over and the captain was finishing up getting our fish ready to take home.

Mom had brought along a scrumptious picnic lunch that even the captain (who got to have it with us), swooned over. The whole day was amazing, including the dinner that Aunt Alyssa made out of such a big catch. The Osbornes, with the little poodles clutched to their chests, came to have the dinner with us. To be honest, the pooches looked so cozy, I wondered if we were ever going to get them back.

Another night, all of us went to Becky's house for a barbecue. Becky and Amy liked each other a lot, and I got to see how much Becky's lip reading had improved from our practicing. Although we didn't get to spend much time with Becky, it was great to have Amy like her, because I sure did.

One thing Amy insisted on, while she was busy taking pictures of Becky, was that she take the roll of film from Disney World (that we'd never had developed) home with her. She wanted to see what the bus people and Angie looked like.

When the party was over and we were all home getting ready for bed, Amy took the roll of pictures out of her pocket and put it on the dresser with her other stuff.

I begged her to promise not to get mad at me when she found out there was no picture of Angie, and before she had a chance to say anything, I told her the whole Granny dying story and Angie's weird mourning costume that we couldn't photo. Tears grew behind my eyeballs just thinking about it, but they didn't fall out.

Amy didn't get mad at all. She gave me a hug and said it was okay, that we'd see Angie in person in five years anyway.

I thanked her for being the best friend ever and hugged her back even tighter.

We got our jammies on and climbed into bed, Right then it seemed like the perfect time to show Amy the letter about the Osbornes that I'd never mailed. I knew that after meeting them she'd really want to read it. I got it out of the night table drawer and handed it to her.

She liked it so much, particularly the part about God. She liked how the Osbornes made God so real. I thought maybe she'd think I was nuts, getting God to help me with my assignment, but she didn't, she just said she'd start talking to God too, and we could compare notes in other letters.

She made me promise to give the letter to Dad. I said I would, but as soon as I got those words out I told her I'd changed my mind, that I wanted to keep it for myself, since Dad never went to church.

She agreed that Dad and Dr. Osborne were playground buddies, not church buddies, and she said I should give her the letter, that it was for her in the first place. I couldn't argue with that, so while she went to sleep, I spent a half hour copying it. That way we'd both have the letter forever.

I knew I should go to sleep, but I didn't want to waste a single moment of what was our last day together. So I woke Amy and gave her the copied letter and told her we had to talk for the rest of the night.

We tried, but honestly we'd already talked ourselves purple, so finally we just gave in to all that was left to do. Together we held hands, bowed our heads and thanked God for the perfect time we'd had. After that it was easy to go to sleep.

In the morning, after lots of hugs from my brothers and the Osbornes, Aunt Alyssa, and Amy, with me hanging on to her, climbed into the car with Mom.

Dad drove us to the airport and saying goodbye, and then watching them walk through the door to the plane, was awful. Even though I tried to think all the good thoughts in the world, nothing could stop the flood of tears that spilled all over the airport floor.

It took me a lot of days to get over being sad, but what finally worked was watching my letters turn into a big hit with the family. I may have hated the idea of Amy and Aunt Alyssa turning them into a gift for Dad, but somehow watching everyone reading them made me really happy.

Pretty much the favorite person was Angie. Dad said that when he got past the gold star and nutty hairdo, he chose her because she was fun, and he was so glad he was finally getting to be a fun dad instead of a workaholic.

I guess the best fun for me about the assignment was meeting all those people and hearing what peace and quiet was to them. The craziest thing was that Angie had said it when I first asked her what peace and quiet meant. "It's just a phrase people throw around like Frisbees," was what she said. I didn't get it at the time, and maybe I would have if I'd been using my head, but I wasn't using my head, I was using my heart to get Dad something he really seemed to need, like a thing. Weird.

Well, that was then and this is now, and Dad is way past needing anything. Sure, he wants to buy us a house, and the way things are moving I think that's going to happen pretty fast. I don't let myself picture my new bedroom yet though, because I don't want to ruin the fun Becky and I are having in the trailer by picturing something else.

Dad rented an old warehouse, bought a whole bunch of game parts and hired guys to put them together, pack them up and ship the games out. The only hard part was finding some kind of machine to make the bats that he had hand-carved in the beginning, but like everything else, Dad made it happen..

After he had all that done, he made an amazing brochure using all his good selling words. Then everyone in the family stuffed them in envelopes to send out to all the schools and rec departments in the country.

What's sort of sad is that we still don't have our doggies back home. They've fallen in love with their big, woolly bed at the Osbornes', along with all the spoiling, which is sure fun for them. But after all, they are ours, and I for one really miss snuggling with them in my bed at night. I think one of the reasons they stay at the Osbornes' for the night is then they don't have to decide who to sleep with at our place. And honestly, the way they care so much about everything, I think it's just 'cause they don't want to hurt our feelings by making a choice. We do at least get to play with them all we want during the day.

The fun part of all this is that they're going to get their own poodles when we finally move into our own house. That way we"ll get to see the new ones when we come to church, and maybe even bring our poodles over to play sometimes.

Anyway, now that Dad has made his dream come true, the dream that I want to make come true is figuring out my other self. I'm turning twelve in just over a month, and I'd really like to get me and her together as a birthday present for both of us.

Angie would say she's the love part of me, like in Zoey is Love. And the twins, well they said she's probably my internal guide, and for sure Eli would say the whole weird double self thing is pretty unique. His eagle head carving, that sits on the table beside my bed, is a constant reminder of how special being unique is.

I know Angie said she makes up her life the way she wants it to be, which is so neat. My other self does that, like she comes out with stuff I wouldn't have the nerve to say. And Angie says she only makes up stuff that's true to herself, and that's what my other self does too. She comes out with stuff that's true all right.

That is so crazy. I mean there's only one me. I remember Amy saying she was glad I had another self because the one I showed was too nice. I thought that was a compliment, but now I'm not sure. Being nice maybe isn't like being true to myself. I think my other self knows that, and maybe I've been scared to own her because I haven't wanted to be outspoken like she is sometimes.

The really stupid part of all this is that what both of us are saying is what everyone is hearing, like nobody else even knows there's two of me, which I guess means there's not.

Well, after a month of working with my notes to help me figure this stuff out, I finally got it that all my words are just mine, my very own, and that all I'm doing is saying what's true to myself, however freaky the words may sound. And wow, is that ever freeing.

I guess Ty has noticed the new me, because just this morning he said, "Did you get a hold of some of Zack's pot, Sis? You seem a lot happier."

"Sorry, no pot. It's just that my other self, the one I told you about, well she doesn't feel like someone else anymore. Y'know? Like, maybe I'm just one me after all. What d'you think?"

"I think when it comes to you, Sis, the more selves you got, the better for all of us. So bring 'em on and we'll put a hundred candles on your cake next week."

Author's Note

Although Gathering Peace is a work of fiction, my husband did indeed quit work at 40, sell our house and move me, our three children and, not two, but three, poodles into a 32-ft Airstream. His purpose and goal were definitely the same as in the book, but the places visited, the friends made, and young Zoey's search for the meaning of peace and quiet, as well as the characters she interviews, were definitely fictionalized.

However, what wasn't fictionalized was the invention of Toppleball that, after forty years, is still being played in schools around the country, as witnessed on the Toppleball website, which I only recently discovered.

The fictionalized personalities of the family, particularly Zoey, are pretty close to real life, as are the varied distresses and delights accompanying the family on their journey.